DAUGHTER OF DARKNESS

DAUGHTER OF DARKNESS

TERRY BROOKS

THORNDIKE PRESS
A part of Gale, a Cengage Company

**LIBRARY OF CONGRESS CIP DATA ON FILE.
CATALOGUING IN PUBLICATION FOR THIS BOOK
IS AVAILABLE FROM THE LIBRARY OF CONGRESS.**

ISBN-13: 979-8-8857-8553-2 (hardcover alk. paper)

Published in 2023 by arrangement with Del Rey, an imprint of Random House, a division of Penguin Random House LLC.

Printed in Mexico
Print Number: 1   Print Year: 2023

For the Kids
Jill, Amanda, Alex, and Hunter
and
In memory always of Lisa

ONE

The Goblins come for us in the early-morning hours, the heavy cloud cover blocking both moon and stars, rendering them all but invisible. The ertl warns us, its piercing chirp waking us instantly. Harrow and I, lying next to each other in bed, roll out and stand silently facing each other.

Goblins, again. At first it was a surprise; now it is business as usual. You would think we would be done with Goblin intrusions. We thought we had sent the last of them packing almost two years ago — just before the Human invasion led by my father. The invasion that my mother put an end to. Yet here they are, returned once more. Five times in two months.

It was frightening in my early days in Viridian Deep; now it is mostly an annoyance. We don't even know what they are trying to do or what they want. It was me they wanted in the old days. They came for me

7

twice then — sent once by my mother and once by my father. But that is the distant past. My birth parents are both dead, and there were no Goblin threats after.

Until now, when suddenly they've started up again.

But why? What is the point of coming after us now? Who is responsible for these most recent intrusions?

The front door creaks slightly as it opens — something Harrow engineered to give us warning after the first two nighttime visits. The ertl is a further safeguard, and a more reliable one. You can sleep through the creaking of a door, but you cannot sleep through the chirp of an ertl.

The ertl is a forest bird, but it can be domesticated and trained to perform simple functions. This, as it happens, is one of Harrow's specialties. It took him less than two weeks to turn the ertl into an early warning system, and it has paid off. We now keep the bird caged in the house each night, and three times has it alerted us to these Goblin attacks — including tonight's. Goblins have been enemies of the Sylvans since forever, and Harrow and I know them well.

Though perhaps I know them better, for I did spend five years in a Goblin prison.

We creep over to our closed bedroom door

and stand waiting patiently. We have trained rigorously for moments like these. We know without any communication what we need to do. The front door closes and soft, cautious footsteps approach our hiding place. They must believe we are sleeping. You would think they might have learned better by now.

I look over at Harrow. His deep-green skin is striped with shadows, and the tiny leaves that grow in his hair are rumpled as if knocked about by a strong wind. *Rats' nest.* I mouth the words so he can read them on my lips, remembering the term from my time in the Goblin prison. He touches his hair in response and then points to my head. I reach up to find my leafy locks as tousled as his. The momentary look he gives me is one of irritation. His patience with these invasions is at an end. I nod my understanding. Another day, another infestation of Goblins.

We considered moving to a different residence to discourage these incursions, but this has been my home since the first day Harrow found me in the wastelands — an almost twenty-year-old girl who had managed to survive for twelve days with almost no food or water. It was Harrow who first told me of the existence of the Fae and suggested that I might be one of them — even though I did not look it. It was Harrow who later took me back to the Human world and the city of Harbor's End to find out the truth — a truth so horrendous that it nearly destroyed any hopes we harbored for a life together.

But love endures. We loved each other then and we do so now, and we remain committed to the promise we made when we partnered: that this would never change.

Still, so much of my past remains a mystery, so much of who I was before my time in the prisons a dark vacancy in my mind. No amount of effort to discover the truth has uncovered my past; the long stretch between what little I remember of my childhood and my incarceration is a deep empty hole in my life. I have promised myself I will find all that is missing from my memory, but to date I have discovered so little.

And that will not change today.

I focus on Harrow as the footsteps stop at our doorway, and he smiles in quick reassurance. We have been here before. We have survived worse.

The door bursts open, practically ripped from its hinges, and the Goblins surge in. The foremost pair carry nets with which to snare and bind us so we cannot use our weapons, should we have one or two close at hand. Five times they have come at us this way, and they *still* don't get it. Regular weapons are unnecessary. We have our *inish* and we carry that inside us — always at the ready, always just a second's thought away from surfacing. In this case it doesn't take even that long, since we already hold it at our fingertips.

The two that follow the net bearers wield blades and axes. They are so certain of themselves, these Goblin intruders, that they exercise little caution. They look neither left nor right, but straight toward the empty bed before they realize the truth. And by then it is too late. Harrow and I have used our *inish* to propel the rear goblins violently ahead into their companions, so that all four are knocked off balance. By that time Harrow and I are out the bedroom door behind them and charging down the hallway. The front door stands open, and we rush through into the open air.

Here, atop the second level of the tree lane on which our cottage sits — not much more than fifty feet from Ancrow's house where Ronden now lives with her sisters Ramey and Char — we turn to fight.

It is a deliberate choice, made shortly after

the last bunch of Goblins tried to catch us off guard. Why wreck our bedroom when we can deal with the matter outside? Plus, there is more space to maneuver out here, with less chance of being cornered by cottage walls. Not to mention the possibility of someone from the nearby houses coming to our aid. Not that we can't handle four Goblins easily enough, but with hand-to-hand combat, there is always the risk of something going wrong.

Not that it seems likely to now. The furious Goblins burst back out through the front door and come for us, a disorganized melee armed with nets and blades, but they never get close. Using a combined web of *inish* we have practiced assembling and casting, Harrow and I scoop the Goblins up and throw them screaming off the elevated walkway. They continue to scream as they tumble away. It is almost a hundred feet to the ground below. When they land, the screams stop.

Maybe I should care about the damage I've inflicted — maybe I should feel remorse or regret — but I don't. I am sick and tired of being hunted, and of the Goblins, both.

But when I turn to Harrow, I find his attention fixed on something else, and I regret my earlier confidence.

Not a dozen feet away stands an armored giant.

This is no exaggeration. The giant is eight feet tall and broad across the shoulders and chest, with huge arms and tree-trunk legs. It is encased in metal — and I'm not talking just armor plating. No, what covers this beast is more on the order of a second skin — a formfitting, flexible coating that I can tell would shimmer and reflect in the light. I have never seen anything like it. If this being has a face, I cannot tell. A helmet encases its head, hiding its features entirely. Black light flickers from behind an opaque faceplate, as if something liquid is contained within.

Strangely, it carries no weapons. Its arms hang loose; its hands are empty. There are no blades strapped to its body. But its size alone is intimidating, so I suppose that makes some sense. What does something this large need with weapons?

Harrow and I exchange a look. The giant has squared off with him, meaning Harrow is the one it thinks the more dangerous. Little does it know. If we have to fight, I will change its mind quickly enough.

We wait for its attack, but it just stands there. Where did it come from? I don't remember seeing it when we rushed from

13

the cottage. Is it allied with the Goblins? I think it must be, yet it seems not to know what it should do next.

I watch its head move slightly as its gaze travels from Harrow to me, and now I can sense it looking at me more closely. As it does, something odd happens. Almost as if it is startled, it takes a step back. I read all this from one small movement, and yet I am certain I am not mistaken.

"What do we do now?" I ask Harrow quietly.

He shakes his head, then takes a step away from me. As he does, the giant moves with him — a clear indication it will not allow us to get past. Well, at least we know one reason it is standing there. I take a step in the other direction, but the giant doesn't respond. It has indeed chosen to focus on Harrow rather than me. I should be grateful — and I am. But I am also oddly irritated to be seen as less of a threat.

A burst of activity from Ancrow's house catches our attention. The front door flies open and Char appears, rushing to the rescue once more. Her thick mane of leafy hair is flying out behind her as she pelts toward us with a stout cudgel in hand. I admire my little sister's pluck, but despair at her lack of caution. Once before, when I first came to Viridian Deep, she charged to my rescue in a foolish display of bravado and love. That time I was able to save her. This time I don't know if I will be.

When she sees the giant, she skids to a stop at once, the cudgel lowering as she realizes what confronts us. Then, "You get away!" she shouts, raising the cudgel once more, demonstrating her determination to take action. "Get away right now!"

Where in the world, I wonder, are Ronden and Ramey? How are they managing to sleep through all this? As I glance about, I wonder the same about all the residents bedded down in the darkened homes surrounding the square. No one has appeared. Are they all such sound sleepers? Or do they simply think it unwise to interfere?

"Char," Harrow says in his calm, measured way, "go back inside, please. Let us handle this."

The giant seems content to let that happen. It has barely glanced at Char since her emergence and doesn't bother to do so now as she slowly backs away toward her house. I glance again at the other houses for some indication of help but find nothing. It seems that Harrow and I will need to manage this threat alone.

If there even is a threat. Thus far, the giant hasn't approached us; it just seems intent on blocking our path. I take a moment to consider why. The elevated tree lane continues to wind through the old growth toward the west end of the city, past a scattering of houses that sit mostly to one side.

One of which is Ancrow's, into which Char has just disappeared.

Suddenly I realize what is happening.

"Char!" I scream, and rush forward.

Harrow is a step behind me, and it is he that the giant continues to evaluate, ignoring me completely. My *inish* is already gathered, so I send every bit of power I can summon hammering into the giant, but the creature barely reacts, as if my strike were no more than a bothersome breeze. I scream at Harrow to run, to find help, but he ignores me and advances on the giant. When the two collide, the sound is audible. Harrow gives his best, but the giant is too much for him, breaking his grip and shoving him aside. Then it comes for me. For something this huge, it is amazingly quick. It is on me before I can reach Ancrow's house, its huge arms drawing me into its grasp. But Ronden's lessons on overpowering a stronger foe have stayed with me and I use my *inish* to spray the planking in a wide slick that takes the giant's feet out from under it the moment it touches me. It topples and skids away in a thrashing heap — though it does not follow the first Goblins off the tree lane.

Still, this gives me enough time to reach Ancrow's house and rush inside. Ronden lies unconscious in the hallway and Ramey pounds on the closet door from inside. Goblins have hold of Char and are hauling her toward the doorway in which I stand. I am debating how to stop them when huge hands grab me from behind and lift me off the floor. The giant has me, and the Goblins rush past us with Char in their grip. I see the fear in her eyes.

Then all three are out the door and gone.

I try to use my *inish* to break free, but the giant has been paying attention. One hand holds both of mine locked together while the other covers my mouth. It looks into my eyes, studying me. No, not just studying me. Identifying me.

This creature *knows* me!

I stare back. "Who are you?" I snap.

But the giant simply sets me aside — almost gently — and goes out the door after the Goblins, swiftly disappearing over the side of the tree lane. I scramble up and rush after it, almost colliding with Harrow as he arrives in the door. Without speaking he points to where the giant leapt off the pathway, and we charge over to look down. We catch just a glimpse of it disappearing into the darkness, accelerating so quickly it is gone almost instantly.

"Char!" I scream and start in the direction I think the Goblins have taken. Harrow starts to follow, but I shout over my shoulder, "No! Go back! Ronden needs you! Don't worry about me!"

He hesitates, but then turns around and I tear down the nearest stairs after Char's captors. The giant must have been with them; there is no other explanation for its behavior. It will follow them, so I must go after it. I do this without stopping to consider what I am risking. How can I not? This is Char we are talking about. Char, for whom I would do anything.

Once at ground level, I turn into the darkness where the giant disappeared. It is so quick; I am not sure I can catch it. But if it is with the Goblins, it will have to slow down. Goblins are strong but slow moving. What I will do once I catch them remains to be seen, but I will have to come up with something — especially if the giant is with them.

As I run, I remember how the creature looked at me as if it knew me. But I have never encountered anything like it — or at least, not that I recall. Which might be the crux of the issue. Though I have learned a lot about myself in the past two years, I still don't recall more than fragments of my past before I entered the Goblin prison. Still, it doesn't look to be Fae and it is certainly not Human. I can think of no one and nothing I have encountered that might fit the description.

Yet it seems to know me. It doesn't make sense.

I push on through the network of buildings and shops that is Viridian Deep, farther into darkness until no artificial lights are visible and the only illumination that guides me comes from the moon and stars, now revealed as the cloud cover lifts. I have not yet caught sight of those I track, but my instincts — which I have come to trust implicitly — tell me they are not far ahead. I skirt a series of small ponds and head toward a broad stretch of heavily wooded hills. There are Goblin settlements north of where the Sylvan territory ends, but all of them are miles off, and I doubt that Char's kidnappers intend to travel all night. More likely, they will stop to rest a little farther on — perhaps no more than another few miles.

It grows more isolated and lonelier, and I

find myself wishing Harrow had accompanied me after all. But I couldn't let him leave an unconscious Ronden behind, with Ramey locked in a closet.

I reflect briefly on my family, and how close we have all become. We were kindred spirits from the start — even before we knew we were related by blood or adoption. Ronden and I are half sisters and the only blood children of Ancrow, while the younger girls are adopted — and Harrow, too, although he didn't know it until my arrival turned his world upside down. But even in the midst of that chaos, Harrow was my rock, and the girls were my champions. When Ancrow died, we bonded even more tightly. Ronden moved home to stay with Ramey and Char while Harrow and I, now partnered, remained in the cottage down the lane.

But still, there was one thing that kept me separated from them, and that was my physical appearance — for I looked completely Human. Or I did, until right after Harrow and I pledged at Promise Falls. Then my hair, sleek and dark, began to take on a greenish tint, little leaves blossomed among the strands, and my feeling of alienation lessened. Since then, I have begun to assume further Sylvan characteristics. Now my skin is changing from Human olive to Sylvan pine. My hair has begun to sprout more of those soft tiny leaves that always make me want to run my fingers through Harrow's locks, and the undersides of my arms and the insides of my legs have exhibited a steady growth of short fringe from shoulders to wrists and thighs to feet.

I am not entirely altered; further change will take more time. Or maybe I am already as Sylvan as my body will allow — whether that be from my half-Human heritage, or because of whatever my adoptive father's medicines might have messed with, in his efforts to keep me looking Human and safe in a world hostile to the Fae.

One day, I tell myself, I will know. One day I will know everything.

I have reached the boundary of the city, and I pause to see if there is any indication of where to go next, but I have lost the trail. I stand rooted in place as the darkness looms ahead, trying to figure out what to do next. I should go back. I should find Harrow and return in daylight to track the Goblins and the giant when I can see evidence of their passing. But I dislike the idea of giving up.

Just a little farther, I think. Char is depending on me. I will walk another mile and then turn back and begin again when the night fades.

I set out once more, searching out anything that will confirm I am on the right track. I work my way deeper into the trees, catching a glimpse of an owl as it flies past and listening to the distant sounds of night birds hunting. But I can see no traces of the Goblin trail. Either I have missed a sign or I have misinterpreted what my instincts told me earlier. I have to give up for tonight. I have to turn back.

Yet when I attempt to do so, I find myself face-to-face with the giant.

It blocks my way like a wall, staring down at me. My heart is in my throat. How did it manage to get so close without me knowing?

I consider running but know I won't make it past the first two steps. And as I hesitate, the giant picks me up like a toy and holds me in front of its concealed face.

Again, I am being studied, examined in a way that suggests familiarity. Its head cocks one way and then the other, and it moves me close to its faceplate. I cannot see inside, but I can feel its eyes on me.

A deep rumbling rises up from within. "Auris?"

I stare in shock. It *does* recognize me. It

22

knows me.

"Auris?" it asks again.

And suddenly, I know that voice. Something about it . . . Something is familiar . . .

But it can't be.

"Malik?"

Two

The shock is profound. His voice is not the
same, yet the inflection and the tone both
attest to the same truth. Malik is alive.

"Malik?" I say again. "Is it really you?"

The giant shifts me in its grip, just enough
to confirm what I already know. "It's me."

"But I thought you were dead!"

"As I thought you were."

"No. I was just roughed up and knocked
unconscious when I was thrown from the
ATV. But you were inside, with the others,
when it crashed."

"And they died — everyone but me and
Khoury. We ran. Got split up. She was
caught first; I could hear it happening. They
took her back. Is she dead?"

"She is. She was shot."

"At least it was quick. What happened to
you? Why do you look like one of the Fae
now? You've got greenish skin and leaves in
your hair!"

"I am a Forest Sylvan — or at least half Sylvan. It's a long story. What about you? You look different, too. How did you get to be so big? And why do you look like a robot?"

His laugh is deep and unpleasant. "Yes, my new look. An example of what technology and a twisted imagination can create. Is anyone with you?"

"Can you put me down so we can talk?"

Malik shakes his massive head. "Can't do that, Auris."

Vintage Malik. Straight to the point. He never used more words than he had to when we were imprisoned together, and his tone of voice says that he means what he is saying. "Can't or won't?"

"Does it make a difference? I let you go once already, when I realized who you might be. I hoped you wouldn't follow. But you disappointed me."

He let me go deliberately. What is going on?
"If you let me go once, why won't you let me go again now?"

"If I do, will you turn back and stop following me?"

I consider lying. Decide not to. "I can't. That little girl? That's my sister, and I want her back."

"We all want something we can't have."

25

I can hear the regret in his voice, but I am not sure if it is directed toward me or him or both. "Will you take me to her?" I ask.

He makes a snorting sound. "The Goblins took her to get to you. They couldn't find another way. I didn't know who you were or maybe I could have stopped them."

"Would it have made a difference? Are we still friends?"

"Difference? Probably not. Friends? Always."

"Then help me get her back to her family."

He sighs inside his helmet, an odd wheezing sound. A shrug. "I can't do as much as you think."

Again, regret is evident in his words. I frown at him. "I would think you could do almost anything you wanted."

"I could say the same about you. You've got that Fae magic, don't you? That way you hit me, trying to get past? I felt that. Where does your magic come from? You didn't have it in the prison. How did they make you like them?"

"I was always like them," I answer. "If you put me down, I will tell you everything. And you can tell me everything, too. We owe it to each other. We're all that's left of our friends, and I have so many questions. How

26

did you get so big? I mean, you were always big, but not . . . like this." I pause. "Can you take that helmet off and show me your face? I want to see what you look like now."

His laugh is harsh. "No, you don't. No time anyway; I have to catch up to the others. But I'll take you with me. At least, you can be with your sister."

"Goblin prisoners, the both of us? Sounds delightful. Are we to be hung and dismembered?"

Malik's posture changes — a suggestion of discomfort. "The Goblins won't touch you. They want you for someone else — for my creator." His voice changes as he says this. Whoever did this to him is someone he hates. "But Chorech — that's the Goblin leader — was clear: No one is to hurt you or your sister. I promise, Auris. I won't let anything happen."

"And is that a promise you'll be able to keep?"

He doesn't answer. "I need your promise that you won't use your magic. Not for anything. Not in the littlest way. And I need you to promise you won't run off. You wouldn't get far anyway."

I nod my agreement. "I've seen how fast you are. I promise not to use magic or to try to run. You know my word is good."

27

"I do, or I wouldn't have bothered asking for it."

He sets me down carefully, surveys me for a moment, then nods. It seems he knows about my *inish* and how it works. Nevertheless, I will not do anything to endanger Char.

Our pact made, we start walking, with Malik leading the way and me following. Whatever else happens, I have to get Char back before I can think about freeing myself. I cannot bear for anything to happen to her, no matter what happens to me as a result.

We thread our way through the woods, two silent figures in a dark and shadowy world. Malik is easy to follow. Anything that big is hard to miss under any circumstances, and impossible to lose sight of when it is right in front of you. The faint light from the moon and stars does not penetrate this heavy forest save in small glimmers and narrow spears. If we are following a path, I cannot tell where it lies. I assume Malik has the ability to see better than I do.

"My friends will come after me, you know," I say at one point.

"Better if they don't. I can maybe protect you. Not them, though. Is one your mate, your partner?"

"Yes. His name is Harrow. We have been

28

partnered for two years now. He saved me when I fled the ATV wreckage and crossed the wastelands."

"You crossed the wastelands? Such determination. Guess that's why Tommy liked you so much. I was always jealous. I loved Tommy, but he liked you more than he liked me. Not that it matters now. Not that anything from back then matters now."

"I suppose."

Malik is quiet again, his bulk a shadow on the path ahead. "We aren't the same anymore, you and I," he says finally.

"No, I guess not."

"I never saw it coming. Always thought I would get free. But even when I did, I really didn't. Get free, I mean. I'm still in a prison." He leaves this enigmatic remark hanging. "So you were always part Fae? Did I hear that right? You look like one — well, a bit like one. Not entirely."

"I was born to a Fae mother and a Human father. I looked Human when I was born and before I came here. But then I began to change — mostly after I partnered with Harrow."

Malik is silent. Then he says, "Doesn't make sense. They must have done something to you, like they did to me. Why would partnering change you?"

29

"I wondered that, too — for a long time. But in a way I think it did. I was always Fae; I just never looked like one until I was free of the Goblin prison and living in Viridian Deep. My Fae mother gave me away to Humans as a baby, and the man who took me in and became my father was a scientist. He used various drugs to keep me looking Human so I would be safe from those in the Ministry, who sought to experiment on the Fae. Every time I started to show evidence of a change, they medicated me."

I pause. "But thinking back on it, I wonder how I survived five years in a Goblin prison without ever changing back to Fae? Then I had no help from Father — no medicines, nothing to keep me from reverting. I have been told — and I've come to believe it might be true — that I have a Changeling element to my magic, one that may alter how I appear. I was a Human living in the Human world, and now I am Fae living in the Fae world. I think my body adapts to my surroundings; it helps me survive. Maybe it's my *inish* that alters my physical appearance. Do you know the word — *inish*?"

He nods. "I've heard about it. Your soul, in Human language."

"Well, mine is very strong. So strong, I

think it has altered my appearance."

"On its own? With no input from you?"

"Maybe not consciously. But subconsciously? That probably had a huge influence."

"That makes some sense. I wouldn't think drugs alone would ever be enough to turn someone from Human to Fae. Or the opposite. Funny, though. I had drugs used on me, too. But then I was rebuilt after I was recaptured. I was trying to find my way back home. They caught up with me near the border. I killed four of them before they bound me. They broke both my legs to bring me down. I thought they would kill me, but they didn't. They took me to a Ministry medical center, where some doctor decided to use me in an experiment instead."

He stops talking, and we walk for a time in silence. "An experiment," I say finally. "My real father wanted to experiment on me as well, back inside the prisons. Maybe it was the same man who experimented on you. Do you remember his name? Was it Allensby?"

"I never knew his name, but he was way too young to be your father; he didn't seem much older than me. But I thought some other man was your father . . ."

31

I sigh. "Allensby was my real father. The other was an adoptive father. It's another long story."

"Tell me."

"I thought we had to catch up to your friends . . ."

"They are not my friends," he snaps. "Anyway, they left me behind to capture you if you followed. I'm supposed to make my own way back to the camp, so we have as much time as we want. Tell me your story."

I do. I tell him all of it. I begin with the circumstances surrounding my birth and carry forward to the present. I tell him how I lost almost all my memories and still have only a few from before my time in the prisons. I tell him about my birth parents and my adoptive parents. I tell him how I discovered the truth about myself — about my parents and my birthright and my belief in what I was meant to be. He listens silently and does not interrupt. I wonder what he is thinking.

When I finish, he suggests we sit for a while before continuing. I am grateful for the chance to rest. I was woken in the middle of the night, fought a battle, chased a giant, and now find myself a prisoner of my own making. It's enough to exhaust anyone.

He guides me out of the trees and up a hillside to where we can sit and look back at the black canopy of the forest we have just passed through.

"Your story is better than mine," he says quietly. "You escaped and found a life for yourself. I escaped but found a life I don't much want, even though it allows me to survive."

I hear the sadness and resignation in his words, and I turn to look at him. "Tell me what happened after the crash. I told you mine; now tell me yours."

He doesn't respond right away. He just sits there facing me silently. Then he gives a brief nod. "All right. I'll tell you everything."

He takes a moment to collect his thoughts, his eyes shifting away from me and looking off into the distance.

"The night we escaped from the prison? I thought we would make it. I really did. Tommy was so smart, and all of us were so careful. But it went wrong so fast. After Tommy was killed, it seemed like we lost whatever chance we had. JoJo wasn't the driver Tommy was. You were up with the spitfire, doing some damage to those Goblin

ATVs, though; that was something. But it wasn't enough.

"When we got hit with a rocket and crashed, I never did see what happened to you. One minute you were there and the next you were gone. I was knocked around, but not hurt much — just scratched up and bruised. I was holding Tommy after he died, and I think his body cushioned the impact of the crash. But JoJo was dead at the wheel, and Breck and Barris were just pulped. I crawled free with Khoury and Wince, but Wince was hurt so bad we had to leave him.

"Khoury was in a bad way as well. She was dizzy and disoriented and not able to find her way. There was blood leaking from her head, and I think her vision was a problem. We tried to disappear into the wastelands. We were pretty far away when the Goblins arrived at the crash site. We could just see them against the light from the flames once the ATV started burning. They milled around, probably counting bodies, and then they came after us. They didn't have the Ronks, though, so that helped. Khoury was crying, and I could tell she was losing it. We made it as far as a stretch of swamp. By then she was walking better, but the Goblins searching for us were getting closer.

"I found some heavy brush, and we crawled into it. There were thorns everywhere, so we got cut up pretty badly, but the Goblins didn't find us. When they were far enough away, I dragged Khoury free and we started out again, but then she panicked and started screaming. I don't know why, and I couldn't quiet her down. I didn't know what to do at that point, because the Goblins were coming back. Then she bolted right back the way she had come and they had her, so I just kept going by myself.

"I hated myself for leaving everyone — you included, even though I was pretty sure you hadn't survived the crash. But I had to save myself. I still don't feel too good about that, so maybe that's why things turned out like they did — a sort of punishment. Things like that happen, don't they?"

I give him a wan smile. "You did the best you could. We all did."

He grunts. "Anyway, I walked for days after that. Didn't know where I was going; I just kept moving. The sun told me I was heading west and north, but I couldn't be sure. I didn't have anything to eat or drink. I found some water that was all right, and then some roots. Pretty nasty stuff, but it kept me going.

"Guess I thought I would make it, but I

kept getting turned around, and after almost four weeks of wandering I was finished. That's when the Goblins found me again. An entire patrol. There was maybe a dozen. I still managed to kill four of them before they captured me, but then they broke my legs using iron bars. Thought I was a dead man, but I guess they had orders not to kill me. Instead, they took me to a place called Harbor's End, to some Ministry medical center. There I was strapped down and fed intravenously for days. I didn't know what was going to happen, but I found out later that the Ministry was performing experiments on its own people to see if they could be physically enhanced for combat. The way I had fought back against those Goblins made them think I was a suitable candidate."

He gives a deep, weary sigh. "So I was given over to these Ministry people — these doctors and scientists and whoever. For weeks I was there in that bed. Sleeping mostly. Then this one doctor comes to see me. Young guy, with the strangest eyes. When he looked at you, it was like he saw you only as an interesting specimen, a potential waiting to be revealed. He had some other doctors with him, but he seemed to be in charge. They all stood around me and talked about my bones and muscles and stuff. They talked about me like butchers talk about a piece of meat. I told them to get out, but I didn't have any way to enforce that. The head doctor finally said if I didn't quiet down and let him do his work, he would give me back to the Goblins. He told me I was practically dead when they found me and might still die if they didn't rebuild my body. He said that once they did this, I would be much better off.

"I asked him if they could just patch me up and let me go, but he shook his head. I found out later that they would have put me down before they let me go. What they were doing was a secret — one they intended to keep. I was sick and tired of everything and more than a little afraid of what would happen if I didn't become strong again, as strength was really all I ever had going for me. So after a night of thinking it over, I agreed."

His laugh is sour. "Dumbest thing I've ever done."

He stops talking and looks at me. "We should get moving again. No tricks, Auris. Promise to stay close?"

I give him a nod. I don't intend to abandon Char, so giving my word is not an issue. At least, not until I have her back again.

We set out again, walking through the slowly lightening darkness — two old friends reunited only to find themselves both profoundly changed. I mull over what he has told me so far. It is clear that he has been rebuilt much more radically than he was expecting. He looks to be completely altered in every way save behavior and voice. Of course, I am guessing about his face, which he has kept hidden, but I have to believe he is appalled by it. They succeeded in making him bigger, faster, and stronger, yes — but they made him decidedly less Human, too.

Yet I sense something of the humanity that defined the old Malik, still buried inside him. There is that familiar kindness and concern for others. There is that calm he always exuded, even under the worst circumstances. There is his steady self-confidence.

As we walk, he resumes his story.

"Once I agreed to the doctor's demands, I was taken to another wing of the building. I was put in a room filled with medical stuff — instruments and machines and supplies. I was scared, but I was too weak to do anything about it, and in too much pain from my legs. They removed the straps but put a guard on me. When his shift ended, someone else replaced him. I was never alone.

"Right away they began giving me pills and injections. Growth and healing medicines, they told me. They checked me twice every day. I didn't know what they were looking for, but I began having serious pain in my joints and my bones — first in my hands and feet, then my arms and legs. They gave me different stuff for the pain — or that's what they told me anyway. I think they were lying. It was helping, but I think it was doing something else, too.

"This went on for days before they began operating on me. The lead doctor told me my bones were weak from the beatings and lack of food and mal . . . malnur . . . rish-something or other. He said I'd need something called composition extenders, and that an operation was required to install them. I said no, but he injected me anyway, put me under, and opened me up. He did my arms and legs first, then did something to my spine and ribs. I was in constant pain — sometimes unbearable — so I was shoveled full of more drugs to help me survive. Because that was all I was trying to do by that point: survive.

"Being awake was agony but being asleep was worse. I had constant nightmares in

39

which I was tortured by monsters. I woke up thrashing and in pain, but they just injected me with more medicines and put me back to sleep. This went on for what seemed like forever. I kept begging them to stop, even to kill me. I was half out of my mind.

"Then, one morning, I woke up and nothing was hurting. I don't know how much time had passed — maybe a year, maybe more. The young doctor came in, all happy and smiling. Everything was fine, he said. The operations had all worked. I was on the mend and would be able to begin training before I knew it."

Malik shakes his head. " 'Training?' I asked. 'What does that mean? Training for what?' "

I don't say it, but I can see it coming.

"I was unstrapped for the first time since I got there and given an exercise regime to carry out under the doctor's supervision. It wasn't so bad — at first. I was just tired a lot. But then it got worse — just as everything else had. My muscles were screaming at me to stop, and my joints were on fire. So they gave me more drugs and injections and worked me harder. They wouldn't let me stop — even when I said I couldn't keep going."

"That must have been scary," I venture.

"Try inhuman. They started using electric prods. You know, the way they do with cattle? If I slowed, they shocked me. If I complained or asked to rest, they shocked me. The lead doctor was the worst. He seemed to enjoy it. He had a handheld model that he carried with him everywhere. I don't know how I survived it — though I'd noticed by then that I wasn't the same anymore. For one thing, I was much bigger, and I was lifting over a thousand pounds easily. I was never given a mirror, but I could see how big and muscular the rest of my body was becoming. When they had me do sprints, I could tell I was fast. Really fast."

He looks away again, but not as if trying to remember — more like trying to forget.

"I didn't feel like myself anymore. Nothing about my new body felt right. I was strong, fast, and incredibly tough, but I wasn't me. It felt like I was locked inside someone else, and nothing of what I was belonged to me.

"After what must have been another six months, I told the doctor I wanted to stop. I thanked him for what he had done, but said I didn't want to be here anymore. He just smiled. 'You don't understand,' he said.

41

'You can't leave. Most of what you are now is thanks to the Ministry. We did it to save you, to make you strong again. To make you better. But there's a price for such help. You belong to us now. You see, one of the things we changed is how your nerves register pain. Without our aid, you would be in unbearable agony every single day. As long as you are with us and taking the medicines we give you every other day, that pain is masked. But if you try to run, and no longer have access to the drugs, you will be in increasing pain on the third day, in constant pain on the fourth, and in agony on the fifth — pain so bad you will wish for death as a reprieve. So you can see why it is in your best interests to remain compliant."

A weary pause. "That's what he told me, and I knew the medication he was talking about; I had to swallow it every other day at the same time."

"Was he telling the truth?"

"That's what I needed to find out as well. So I escaped."

"And?"

His voice is grim. "He was wrong about one thing. They rebuilt me stronger than they knew. I made it eight days before the pain was too great and I had to come crawling back. Then I was under their control again."

"Were there others who underwent the same procedure?" I ask. "Did you have anyone to talk to, to train with?"

He shakes his head. "I was the only one. But by then I wasn't letting them do anything more to me. They tried, but I wouldn't let them get close. I killed two of them. I would have killed them all if I could have. All that kept me going was my determination to escape again — this time with the medication. Even if I died trying, I was getting out of there. So I was just waiting for my chance. Then one day I found it."

He smiles at the memory. "Usually there were three guards when they gave me the medicine, but one day there was just one.

"The doctor always took the medicine he needed from a supply that was stored in a metal-wrapped glass container. That was so it wouldn't break if it was dropped, I guess. That day, I let the doctor give me the dose, then threw him into the guard, snatched up the glass container, and was out the door."

He laughs. "Just like that, I was free again, and I found my way here, to the Fae homeland."

"How did you even manage to get into Viridian Deep?" I ask. "No Humans are

43

permitted here. The magic keeps them out."

He shrugs. "Maybe I am no longer Human enough to be affected by the magic. Maybe I am mostly machine."

I ponder his assessment. Possible, I think. And terrible.

"So how did you end up with the Goblins?"

"Because I failed yet again. Even stretching it out, taking it once every three days, the medicine only lasted so long. And besides, it turned out they had a tracker on me anyway. I managed about three months of freedom before the medicine ran out and they sent Chorech in with more medicine to gather me up and chain me again." He shrugs. "So here I am."

He gives another deep sigh. "I hate those doctors, all right, but I hated myself, too. Hated what I knew I would look like to others, what they would think. They had turned me into a monster, but inside I was still me."

His voice is so sad that for a moment I think he is going to cry. But instead he merely shakes his head in disgust.

"So what can I do about it, Auris? Not much. Not then, not now, not ever."

He stops talking abruptly, and I want to cry myself. His story is both terrible and familiar. We are so much alike, in so many ways. We are both half one thing and half another, both remade over the past two years. Both object lessons in how dramatically your life can change without your consent. I look neither all Human nor all Fae. He looks neither all Human nor all monster. We are each some of both until we experience yet another transformation. *If* we experience another transformation.

I can only imagine what he must be feeling about the Ministry doctors. He was once a perfectly normal Human boy, but he is now a freakish giant with a massive body and a face he feels he cannot show even to me. I know enough of Allensby to remember how blind he was to everything but his own desire to gain mastery over Viridian Deep and the Fae magic. His obsession with this cost him his life, and my mother's life, and almost mine as well.

No doubt the doctor who changed Malik was cut from this same cloth.

And now Malik's creator, for whatever reason, has set his sights on me. I can't imagine I will fare any better at his hands than I did at Allensby's; the thought that his goons now have Char is enough to make me sick. I can't imagine they will use her only as bait; the lure of having a full-blooded Fae will be too much for them to

45

resist, if they are anything like Allensby. I have to reach her fast, and if Malik cannot help me free her, and I am going to have to find a way to do that on my own.

THREE

The moon is down, and far to the east the sky is just beginning to show a faint hint of dawn's appearance. I glance over at Malik as we walk. I am awed by how huge he is — how much bigger than he used to be, and he was big then. The details of his story are horrific, and I have so many questions.

I hadn't wanted to interrupt him while he was relating his ordeal, but there is so much I still want to know.

"Three hours," he announces. "Then we'll be at the camp and you can see your sister."

I wonder then about Harrow and my other two sisters. Are they all still back in the city waiting for me? I suspect Harrow and Ronden will have come looking for me by now. I badly wish they could rescue me, but at the same time I hope they don't. Should they appear — whether I am alone with Malik or captive in the Goblin camp — the fight will be fierce and either one of them

47

could be injured or killed. I would rather take my chances on my own, once I have Char with me again. I might not have my weapons or my *inish* staff, but I do have my wits and my magic to protect us. Malik will take me to Char, but after that all bets are off.

As we keep walking, I search for the right way to reopen the conversation. I don't want him to think I am pushing, but at the same time I feel an urgent need to know more. Once we reach the Goblins, he will hold my life in his hands, and I need to get a sense of what he will do to help me. And, more to the point, what he will do to help Char.

We are in hilly country by now, with the dark shadows of mountains visible against the skyline to the east. The walking has turned to climbing, and the air is cooling, despite the rising sun. I wish I had warmer clothing, and then worry about Char in her thin nightgown. It makes me furious to think that Malik helped the Goblins take her — even if he didn't know about me and didn't realize she was my sister. There isn't any excuse for what he is doing, but I'm sure the Goblins have some sort of hold over him — probably to do with the medication he needs. The Malik I knew would never have cooperated with them otherwise.

Although, I remind myself, he is no longer the Malik I knew.

"When we get to where we are going," I say quietly, "to this camp and to the Goblins, are you going to help me?"

"I am going to help your sister. If I can."

"But not me?"

"No."

"Will you tell me why?"

"No."

"Can't or won't?"

"Does it matter?"

"One is an absolute, the other is a choice. If this is a choice, I want you to tell me why you are making it."

He stops where he is and turns to face me. "You haven't changed, have you? Still as determined and rigid as ever. But listen. This was your choice, to come with me. You demanded that I take you to your sister. You could have fought me when there were only two of us and not an entire camp full of Goblins. Soon there will be too many for you to fight and they will take you back to the Human world and my creator while Char will be released. That's the best I can promise you. Now walk."

I go silent again. It is clear that Malik has decided to keep hiding the reason he can't

49

or won't do more than he has already promised, but I suppose that if he swears to see Char released, then my journey here will have been worth it. Though the prospect of returning to the Human world and their medical experiments is truly terrifying.

I already know I would rather die. And probably will, once I have done what I can for my sister.

We travel deeper into foothills that front the northeast section of the Skyscrape Mountains. This is country into which I have never traveled and with which I am unfamiliar. I know the Goblins claim this region of Viridian, and I know as well that the other Fae have decided they are welcome to it. The landscape is devoid of almost everything but scrub and hardy conifers. Huge boulders released in centuries-old avalanches are scattered here and there in odd formations. The countryside dips and rises such that, once inside its boundaries, it becomes almost impossible to see anything beyond the mountain peaks and your immediate surroundings. And everywhere you go, you have the feeling that something untoward awaits around the next rock formation or dense stretch of forest. I expect at every moment that something is going to jump out at me.

So it comes as less of a surprise than it might have when Goblins step into view so suddenly they might have materialized. I stop where I am as Malik walks up to them. Goblins are big creatures, but Malik is head and shoulders taller. I try to listen to what they are saying, but while my *inish* allows me to understand any language now that my Fae side has begun to surface, their voices are low and I am reluctant to get any closer.

After a moment, the Goblins turn and walk away. Malik beckons to me, and we follow silently. There is so much more I want to ask him, but I know he won't answer in our present situation, so I have to be patient. But now that we have found the Goblins, I am suddenly on edge — worried for both Char and myself.

Our walk is a short one. We round a huge boulder and suddenly are standing in a Goblin camp with at least a dozen of them turning to stare. The look on their faces is not reassuring. I try to be stoic as their eyes drift over me, try to stay expressionless and calm. It is not easy. These huge creatures are the enemies of the Forest Sylvans, and they have no reason to be kind or generous toward me. But showing fear will not help.

"Auris!" I hear Char cry out.

It takes me only a moment to find her. They have tethered her to a heavy stake driven into the ground at the back of the camp, with a leather cord fastened about her neck. She looks a bit rumpled and clearly worn out, but I am not surprised to find she seems more angry than frightened. Whatever else she is, my little sister is tough.

"Can I go to her?" I ask Malik.

He shakes his head. "Wait for Chorech."

A moment later, a truly unpleasant-looking Goblin with gnarled features criss-crossed with scars comes over and addresses Malik like he owns him. He speaks quickly and without any deference, gloating about how his plan to acquire me has finally worked, and berating Malik for failing to secure me. (Though I sense he is secretly delighted by his assumption that I am simply too cowed by Malik's size to resist.) Malik gestures toward Char and says that, now that they have me, it would be a good time to let my sister go. After all, wasn't this the plan?

This evokes all sorts of angry rumblings and scrunched-up faces. Apparently, as I had feared, this is the plan no longer.

Seconds later, Chorech confirms this, saying, "And why should we part with a second prize? The Humans will pay extra for another. Besides, our target killed a lot of us, so why should we do her any favors?"

It's true, I've killed my share, but they have always been the aggressors, not me. I'd have been content to leave them alone for the rest of my days. They are the ones who keep coming after me repeatedly. Besides, it annoys me that Chorech is talking across me as if I am not there.

"Do you expect me to apologize?" I snap.

He ignores me and stomps away. I am thinking about summoning my *inish*, fighting my way to Char, freeing her, then making a stand on my own while she escapes. She is no longer the little girl she was when I arrived here. She is ten years old — still quite young in the world of the Fae, but surprisingly mature. (And I won't even bother getting into Ramey's level of maturity at fourteen, because she might as well be my age at this point in her life!) But perhaps this is simply what growing up with an emotionally unavailable Ancrow will do to you.

I look over at Char and give her a brief wave and a nod to keep her quiet. I hate seeing her tethered like an animal, but I know it could be worse. These Goblins are dangerous — quick to anger, slow to understand, and hard to bring to heel. They are barbaric by both nature and culture, and they have been so for centuries. Or so Harrow told me early on. He also explained that while they are mostly slow-witted and disinterested in what the other Fae consider important, they are fiercely loyal to one another. Some of them, I imagine, lost friends or kindred at my hands. So perhaps their hostility is not unwarranted.

In the wake of Chorech's departure, several Goblins advance on me. Immediately I brace to defend myself, but Malik is quick to move close, facing me with his back to the approaching Goblins.

"Let them take you," he whispers. "Don't resist. They think you are helpless without your weapons or staff. Don't give them reason to think otherwise. Patience." And he steps aside.

I go perfectly still and do not stop the Goblins from binding my wrists and looping a cord around my neck. It is hard to let them put their hands on me. It was hard in the prison, too; I have not forgotten. But I forced myself to endure it then and I do so now, because something in the way Malik spoke that last word suggests that his insistence on doing nothing might not be as final as it seems. I have to believe he will try to help me. I have to.

The Goblins take me over to Char, fasten the loose end of my tether to the stake, then move away again. My sister and I look at each other, and in spite of the obvious danger and our seeming helplessness, Char smiles.

"Someone's in for a surprise when you finally decide to do something," she whispers. "They don't know about you, do they?"

I smile back. Brave little girl. "Not everything."

"You came to get me, Auris. I knew you would."

She knows I am letting this happen — that I am allowing it in order to get close to her. She thinks that I am waiting for the right moment to free us both. I hope she is right, but I am not entirely sure yet.

"How did that giant capture you?" she presses.

"He didn't, exactly."

I explain how we are friends — that he was one of the prisoners who escaped with me, only to be taken prisoner once more. I tell her the rest of the story as well — in particular, how he came to be what he is. Or at least tell her what I suspect.

"He's still the old Malik inside," I say, wondering even as I do if it is true. "He got me this far. Now we just have to find a way to escape, though I can't be sure yet what that way is. Malik told me that you were initially taken just as bait for me, so I could be returned to the Human scientists; that they always intended to release you." I cannot bear to tell her that they seem to be changing their minds. So instead I say, "We just have to make sure they keep their word."

"Humans, again? Those same doctors and scientists, like the ones who did those horrible things to Mother and you?" She grimaces. "Do they want you back again?"

Even the words are enough to cause me to shudder. "For whatever reason, I think they do." I look around at the Goblins, who are otherwise engaged and don't bother to look back. "Malik seems to think so anyway."

"If Malik is your friend, why isn't he helping you?"

"Because they have some sort of control over him."

"The medicine he needs to stay free from pain?"

I nod. "Apparently."

Her face crinkles in sudden sympathy. "Poor Malik. The pain must be awful, for him to avoid it this way."

I feel a surge of gratitude, in the midst of all this horror, for Char's generous heart. If anything happens to this little girl, I will kill those responsible myself.

We sit quietly for a bit after that, watching the Goblins going about their business. Malik said earlier that no harm would come to me, that I am to be taken back to the Human world untouched.

But I don't intend to let that happen.

An hour passes. Two. Why aren't we moving? This clearly isn't their home, and they have found and captured what they came for — me — so what are they doing stalled out in this camp?

"I'm scared," Char says softly at one point.

I give her a look. "That can't be true. I've never seen you afraid of anything."

"Well, I am. There are so many Goblins and only two of us."

"Maybe so. But we're a lot faster and smarter."

"I'm sorry, Auris. I should have stayed in my room instead of rushing out. I was trying to scare them off."

I picture it, and I can't help smiling. Tiny Char, confronting a clutch of giant Goblins. "Well, next time you'll know better."

"If there is a next time . . ."

"Oh, come on!" I lean in and give her a

57

nudge with my shoulder. "Do you really think we won't get away?"

She stares, then shakes her head. "I think we will. Are Ronden and Ramey all right? And Harrow?"

"I think so."

"Are they coming after us?"

I wonder. "Don't you think I'm enough?"

She bites her lip. "I hope so."

Eventually, Malik wanders over, seemingly for no reason other than to look at us. When he has done that for a few moments, he kneels down to test the knots that secure us in place.

"Don't look at me. Listen. They've been in communication with my creator, and they are taking you both back to his lab at Harbor's End. It seems my creator wanted you for an experiment, but now plans to use your sister, too. Char will not be released."

"Will you help us?" I ask once more.

"I can't. They have my medicine. If I help you, they will destroy what is left and . . . I can't go through that again. So, no."

His response was what I expected, but still I try again. "Malik . . ."

"Shut up!" he hisses. "Just listen."

He rises and reaches over to move Char closer to us. Char is wide-eyed with fear,

58

but her face is laced with anger. "Don't touch me!"

Malik barely gives her a glance. "We'll leave for the coast shortly. A Goblin warship is hidden up north, waiting to take you back across the Roughlin to Harbor's End. If you get on the ship, you won't be coming back. But there are passes and cliff trails and ravines to navigate before then. You will have your chance to make an escape. If you are quick enough, it seems unlikely either the Goblins or I could do much about it — especially since we don't fully realize the extent of your magic."

He pauses in his pretense of testing the knots and rises. "Am I clear?"

I nod. "Thank you."

"See you again sometime, Auris," he says softly, and turns and walks away.

FOUR

Char and I are released from our tether as the Goblins prepare to break camp for the coast, but we are then roped together by a six-foot length of cord tied to our necks while our hands are bound before us. We are given room to move as we travel, but not much freedom. The bindings don't bother me; I can break them using *inish* in seconds. But they are an annoyance and an unpleasant reminder of how we can expect to be treated.

I have already vowed I will not return to the prison. But now I have some small reason to believe that Char and I have an ally in Malik. He clearly has a plan for getting us free, and we must keep watch for the opportunity. We understand what this means and are resolved to make the best of it. Malik has said he cannot help us, but he has either changed his mind or found a way to help without implicating himself. I am appalled that he is chained to these Goblins by the medicine he needs to stay pain-free, and I cannot imagine what suffering it must unleash to be without it. What must it be like to live with that sort of threat hanging over you every day? Even so, he has shown me nothing but kindness. You can have no better friend than that.

So escape we will — whatever we must do to make it happen. I wonder again if Harrow and Ronden are coming to rescue us. I worry that something bad will happen to them if they do, and it will be because of my insistence on coming after Char alone. I do not think my choice was wrong; saving Char is important. But by leaving Harrow behind as I did, I put him in an impossible situation. He loves me too much not to come after me, so if anything happens to him, I will be forced to shoulder just as much guilt as I would have if something bad happened to Char.

But there is nothing I can do about it.

We begin walking east in the early afternoon, and to my surprise it is Malik who takes the lead. I find it hard to believe he is more capable than any of the Goblins, but as I study him while we travel, I notice how quickly and easily he chooses our path and come to understand it is one he knows well.

61

Clearly, this path is one he has taken before, and I wonder how he spent his three months in Fae country before the medicine ran out and they sent the Goblins after him. It seems exploration was a large part of it. Our journey proceeds smoothly, but by the time we have reached a campsite for the evening, I have seen no signs of an opportunity to break free. So now I worry that Malik might not be able to make good on his assurance, no matter how much he might want to help.

As sunset arrives, we pause for the night in the shelter of a small canyon. Our campsite is open to the sky but bounded by the walls of the canyon. It is a well-protected location, I think. The Goblins can defend it easily.

We are shunted off to one side and tethered once more. We are given a little food and ale. At one point, as we are eating, Malik passes by and without slowing says, "Stay alert."

Then he moves on. Char and I look at each other, our shared glance signaling that we have both heard his admonition. It can only mean one thing. Something is going to happen — and soon.

While we wait to see what it is, I tell my sister a little more about Malik and our time together in the Goblin prison. I tell her of his strength and courage, of his many kindnesses, of his affection for Tommy. I loved Tommy, too, in my own naïve way, and he did as much as anyone to keep me sane while we were caged. But Malik was the backbone of our small group with his strength and loyalty and decency.

"Once, after the guards had beaten me for some violation or other — I can't remember what — he held me in his arms while I cried and never said a word. I knew he was there, protecting me, and that was enough. He always seemed to know when a few words or a simple gesture was required to get you through a rough patch."

"I see that in him," Char whispers back, nodding. "You were lucky to have him."

"I wish I had him back the way he was." I cannot help voicing the feeling that has been with me from the moment I realized who he was. "I hate what has been done to him by his own people. They could have chosen to heal him properly, yet they betrayed him and made him into what he is now, a tool in their hands. It is such a violation."

"Like they did with Mother. Like they tried to do with you."

She knows the stories by now. Over the past two years, Ronden and I have told her the truth about Ancrow, so she understands

63

not only what happened to her mother when I was conceived but also why she died as she did. Secrets are destructive; the truth, even when hard to hear and harder to bear, is better. Char listened, learned, considered, and eventually found a form of grace.

She once asked me, some months after it was all over: *But wasn't it also Mother's poor choices and bad behavior that brought us all together?*

She has always been like that — more understanding, kind, and accepting than we probably deserve. At the same time, she has also been our fiercest defender — though sometimes too impulsive and protective where family is concerned. Char is a complicated young girl, but I think she brings out the best qualities in all those who love her.

Right now, it is Malik's presence that reassures me most. Though what waits for me if I am delivered to the Ministry labs is beyond terrifying, I am certain that Malik will not let this happen. His calmness and steadiness persuade me to be patient, and to believe Char and I will get our chance to escape. I trust him, and I know he will find a way to rescue us.

Our meager dinner finished, Char and I are lying on our backs looking up at the stars through rifts in the clouds when the shadow passes overhead, sailing out of the cloud cover and then quickly disappearing back into it again. The Goblins, busy with their own suppers, seem oblivious. "What was that?" Char asks at once.

I am trying to decide. It was hard to judge its size, but it was considerable. It had arms and legs, but also broad wings. A new kind of Fae, I think immediately. Perhaps an animal — a nighttime predator searching for food. I can't be sure from that one brief glimpse. It is about an hour past sunset, and the skies are dark.

"I don't know," I answer belatedly.

As we sit up and wait for it to reappear, a huge figure slips past us, silent as the night shadows, and a voice whispers, "Get rid of your bonds."

Malik. Something is about to happen.

Using my *inish,* I cause first my bonds and then Char's to fall away. We sit where we are, wrists together as if still tied, waiting for something more to happen. A glimpse of movement in the sky above us draws our attention, and the winged shadow passes over once more. I scan the camp swiftly. Everyone is otherwise occupied save for the guard on watch at the head of the camp, who stands so still he might be made of stone, until . . .

Suddenly he topples over and does not rise.

Seconds later winged shadows descend on the camp and throw it into chaos, yanking several Goblins howling and screaming into the air. Dropping our pretense at being bound, Char and I are already on our feet and racing for the opening leading out of the canyon, toward the concealment of the trees beyond. I risk a quick look back as I run. The camp is in chaos as the Goblins snatch up weapons to fight back against their aerial foes. They do not look our way. Their eyes are drawn to the sky where their ensnared companions continue to cry out in rage and fear.

Until their captors drop them from several hundred feet in the air and they fall to their deaths.

More shadows swoop in, and more Goblins are taken. That is enough for Chorech and those who remain; they bolt for the shelter of the rocks where their predators cannot reach them without landing. As Char and I reach the concealment of the trees, not one Goblin has noticed we are gone. In the madness of the moment, their sole concern is with staying alive. What becomes of us — for the moment at least — does not matter.

I see Malik only once as he moves with the others, staying in their midst. He is too big, I think, for these winged creatures to lift, so he is somewhat better protected than the Goblins. Whatever the case, he does not look our way and in seconds has ducked into hiding.

Char and I move swiftly. It will not take the Goblins long to realize we are missing and come looking for us. We hasten down the slopes to the forest, deep into the trees, heading away from the Goblin camp — though before long that cover runs out, and we emerge instead onto a rocky slope with little cover. We need to get to the bottom as quickly as possible and from there to a much larger stretch of forest beyond. We are miles from home and hours from safety, but we have one advantage. While I have never traveled here before, I know the direction I need to go and the general nature of the terrain. If need be, I can read the stars and the moon to find additional help. I have no doubt we can find our way home. If we are lucky, we will run into Harrow and Ronden searching for us.

But I also know we can't count on that. It will be up to Char and me to make a successful escape, but at least we are free and together. If the Goblins come after us, let's just see how they like my *inish.*

We run, and then we run some more. We cannot go as fast as we might like because, even with the moon and stars to help light the way, the ground is rugged and our path forward uncertain. We both go down several times during our flight but scramble up quickly, uninjured save for bumps and bruises. There is still no sign of pursuit, and no Goblins giving chase. I wonder if they will send Malik again — not necessarily tonight, but on another night when I think myself safe.

Then I wonder where and how Harrow and I will live once I am home again. I wish he were here with me. I wish we were together again. I wish . . . I wish . . .

I don't hear them. I don't see them. I don't sense them.

I don't know they are there until clawed feet clamp on my shoulders with an iron grip and I cry out in shock. Beside me, Char screams, ensnared in a similar fashion. We are lifted into the air, struggling futilely. It happens so swiftly we are a hundred feet off the ground before I can think to bring my *inish* to bear, and by then it is too late. Anything I do might cause our winged captors to drop us, and I can't risk Char's life or my own so foolishly.

I close my eyes to try to shut out what is happening as we are carried away into the night.

I close my eyes to try to shut out what is happening as we are carried away into the night.

FIVE

We fly a short way into the mountains, over the highest peaks and past sheer cliffs and craggy rifts. Char and I hang helplessly in the claws of our abductors, unable to do anything more than hope for the best. At first, I worry that we will be disposed of in the same manner as those Goblins they snatched earlier, but eventually, with the Skyscrape Mountains all around us, it becomes apparent that we have been taken for another reason. If our deaths had been the motive for grabbing us, they could have managed that in the first five minutes.

I consider more than once how this latest abduction might have come about and end up each time deciding that Malik must have known it was going to happen. Perhaps he arranged for us to deliberately trespass in enemy country, knowing we would be snatched away, or perhaps somehow Malik managed to get word to these winged creatures of our coming and arranged a rescue. Different scenarios likely with very different outcomes. Char and I have to hope for the best.

I wonder what will happen next. I glance over at Char every now and then, and one or twice she glances back, but we do not try to speak to each other. The wind howls with such ferocity that we could not be heard unless we were right next to each other and shouting as loudly as we could. Just when I think things can't get any worse, it begins to rain. It is freezing at this height and we end up shivering hard enough that I worry we might cause the winged creatures to lose their grip and drop us by mistake.

But this doesn't happen, and we are left to suffer through the bone-chilling cold as best we can. I consider trying to take a closer look at whatever it is that has ahold of me, but it feels that doing so would accomplish little. It is better to wait until we are on the ground again. I look over at Char's carrier. Its body is similar to my own, if more elongated. It is lean through the torso, arms, and legs. Its head is hooded, its face hidden. Its wings are huge leathery protrusions that extend from the shoulder blades, the skin stretched tightly over a structural web of interconnected bones. I don't know what these creatures are called and cannot remember having heard any mention of them before now. I wonder if Char knows something, but there is no way to ask her.

My mood is dark and my hopes fading. We are deep enough into the mountains now that I cannot imagine finding an easy way out — even assuming we got the chance to try. I am already cold and sodden and miserable, and I know Char is the same. No one knows where we are or how to find us. We have left no trail to follow, so no one will come to save us. We will have to rely on ourselves — or at least on me, as I am the one with *inish* strong enough to attempt an escape. It makes no difference what holds us captive — Goblins or these winged creatures. In the end, I will have to fight.

Before long, our captors begin to descend toward a craggy cliffside dotted with caves and broad defiles, with protruding ledges on which large bonfires burn. As we draw nearer, I can see other creatures like those who abducted us emerging to watch us descend through the pouring rain. They slouch about — some on two legs, some on four; some huge, some small — but all with the same general build and proportions as our own save the wings. Well, that and their heads, for each creature bears a large beak and a triangular hawkish skull, with horned protrusions that suggest a predatory disposition. I stare back at them, trying to find something familiar in their birdlike features. As we fly lower still, I can make out a broad defile opening onto a wide, flat ledge that spans a gorge.

Our speed diminishes and we descend to a ledge thousands of feet above the valley below. We are set down carefully, our abductors' claws releasing their grip on Char first and then me, so that we are left standing not six feet away from each other. I glance over my shoulder and see the two who carried us here backing away, great wings folding in against their bodies until it almost looks like they are simply wearing cloaks.

I glance at Char and she at me. *Wait,* I mouth silently. *Patience.* She nods in response, her face wearing that familiar look of determination as she brushes back stray locks of her tangled green hair. She might have been frightened while we were flying, but she has locked down her fear and will stand her ground. We are ringed on all sides by the winged creatures — a mass gathering of the inhabitants of this cliffside community — and all of them are studying us intently, a few making audible but unintelligible sounds amid a steady clacking of beaks.

I grow weary of waiting. I am cold and wet and tired; I want this to end. But no one steps forward to act as spokesman. I begin to wonder if anyone will when the crowd parts and an aged, stooped figure, hooded and cloaked, appears to confront us.

For a moment he says nothing and just stares at us silently. (I am assuming at this point that this is a male, but I cannot be sure.) Then he pulls back his hood and reveals his face. Fringes of black hair encircle the crown of his head and frame his gaunt features, much of it shot through with gray. His face is seamed and bony, and his nose and mouth are formed of a single hard proboscis, with nostrils little more than tiny air holes in his beak. My immediate impression is that he is very old.

"Your small companion looks to be Sylvan, but you look to be more a hybrid," he says. There is an odd avian quality to his voice. "What are you?"

"I am in transition," I tell him. "I am becoming Sylvan. I was born to a Sylvan mother and a Human father."

A muttering arises from those gathered,

and it has a dark tone. The old man frowns. "Interspecies marriage is forbidden."

"It had nothing to do with marriage. My mother had no choice in the matter."

We stare at each other, and then he nods. "Do the Goblins think to breed you?"

I shudder; this was the very thing I escaped their prison to avoid. "They would sell me to the same Humans who took my mother," I tell him.

"And the giant? What is he to you?"

Malik. I sense I need to be careful. I shrug. "He serves the Goblins."

"Do you know why you are here?"

I shake my head.

"It is because the Goblins trespassed on forbidden ground — on Aerkling ground. It is our practice to kill such offenders and seize their prisoners."

And do what with those prisoners? But I manage to hold my tongue.

"We didn't know we were trespassing," I say instead. *But Malik did. That was his plan all along — to rely on the Aerklings to rescue us.*

"Why did they take you prisoner? And your companion?"

"My sister," I answer, indicating Char. "They took her as bait, so that I would

75

come after her. When I did, they took me, too."

"That was foolish of you."

Hard to argue. "I love my sister. I would do anything for her."

"So why do the Humans want you?"

I provide him with an abbreviated version of how both Goblins and Humans have tried repeatedly to capture me since I found my way home to Viridian Deep. When I mention my mother's name, the oldster holds up his hand to silence me. "Wait. You are Ancrow's daughter?"

I startle. He knows of my mother? "I am."

"I am told she is dead. Is this true?"

"She died defending Viridian Deep against a Human invasion led by my biological father. That was two years ago. You knew her?"

He nods. "She has been a friend to the Aerklings for many years. We fought together in the Ghoul Wars; we stood with her at Rampellion in the final battle. She was invincible that day. I have a hard time believing she is really gone. But . . . what do the Humans hope to gain by having the Goblins deliver you to them like merchandise?"

I hesitate. Where to begin? "They believe I can provide them with a way into Viridian

Deep. And that, because of my mixed parentage, I can teach them how to use Fae magic. Or that they can extract it from me; I'm not sure which."

The muttering and clacking of beaks resumes, but all I can think about is how cold I feel. The old Aerkling seems to sense this and calls over his shoulder, gesturing. Blankets are brought and thrown over our shoulders.

As the disgruntled sounds continue, the Aerkling who has been speaking to us glances at his fellows and launches into a short angry speech about politeness and respect for old allies that quiets them down, although a few make gestures that are hard to see as anything other than signs of contempt. One Aerkling, whose eyes glitter with such brilliance I have to look away, stomps off.

The winged oldster turns back. "It is too late to return you to your Sylvan home today, so you will stay the night with us, then you will be flown back in the morning. No harm will come to you."

"Thank you," I tell him. "The sooner you can get us back, the better. Search parties will already be out looking for us."

His face does not change expression. "Understood. Orphren!"

77

A small Aerkling with a more feminine appearance separates from the crowd and
comes over. "Take them to shelter," the old
Aerkling says. "Give them more blankets
and food." He looks back at me. "Sleep now.
We will talk more in the morning."

"This way," Orphren says in Sylvan, beck-
oning.

Char and I follow as she leads us from the
cliffside through the gathered and dissatis-
fied crowd. I wish I understood more about
what was happening, but this is not the time.

Even so, the sounds track me like warn-
ings, and I believe we are not yet out of
danger. I glance at Char and see a hint of
worry on her young features, but there is no
help for it. We are deep inside the Skyscrape,
thousands of feet up on a mountainside,
among a species of Fae we know virtually
nothing about and at whose mercy we have
been placed.

In the world of the Fae — as in all other
worlds — sometimes you have to put your
misgivings aside and simply hope for the
best. And I am too tired to fret about it
further.

Orphren leads us to an enclave in the
mountainside that wends back into the rock
face. Here we find pallets and blankets on
which to rest. With a final look of reassur-

78

ance over to Char, I roll into my bedding. I am exhausted by the night's events, and I instantly fall asleep.

My sleep is brief.

I am woken by Orphren less than an hour later. She shakes me gently and, when I open my eyes, puts a finger to her lips. I climb to my feet and wake Char. The Aerkling girl beckons, and together we follow her to the opening of our stone shelter, where we peer out into the night. There are fires burning everywhere, and from where those biggest and brightest burn, a voice roars out forcefully, transcending the voices of the other Aerklings. I can't make out the words at this distance, but there is no mistaking their tone, angry and full of hate.

Orphren turns to me and whispers, "That is Tonklot. He is leader of the dissenters seeking to remove my grandfather as leader of this Winglish. Your coming has given him an excuse. Too many heed his cries for change. Too many have fallen under his sway. Some, he has destroyed by stealing their minds. He is a powerful figure in our tribe, and the balance of power has been uncertain since his coming. My grandfather must eventually fight him for the right to lead. But if he loses, Tonklot will claim leadership and throw you and your sister from the cliffs. My grandfather thought he could postpone this confrontation for tonight, but he thinks so no longer. You must flee now."

"Can we do nothing to stop this from happening?" I ask.

She shakes her head. "This is an Aerkling matter and others are not allowed to intercede. My grandfather has friends who remain faithful to him, but many of the inhabitants of the Winglish listen to Tonklot. Please, you need to go. Perhaps then my grandfather can persuade the clan to allow him to remain leader. Two of the Aerklings still loyal to my grandfather are waiting to carry you out of the mountains, but you must leave now. The crowd grows restless."

"This is your grandfather's wish?" I press her.

Her eyes meet mine, and I see desperation there. "He values the friendship he had with your mother. He would be shamed if he allowed anything to happen to her daughter. Please."

"Then we'll go," I say at once.

She hands us hooded cloaks, which are clearly meant to help conceal who we are. I do not know how we will avoid detection with so many of our captors so close, but

80

Orphren seems confident. We slip into the cloaks and pull up the hoods, then follow her to our shelter's opening and peer out. Several huge bonfires burn at the center of the broad ledge, masked by heavy mist and filled with shouting, spectral forms. A solitary figure stands on a rocky slab, addressing the assembled crowd. The sound of his voice is oddly compelling, and I feel myself drawn to it. I want to hear what he is saying, to find the meaning and purpose of his words. It is an unsettling response to his hate-filled voice, both nightmarish and terrifying.

I force myself to cease listening. It is not easy.

Sentries stand not ten feet away from our shelter, clearly placed there in order to keep us from escaping. "Do not pay them any attention," Orphren says to me. "They will choose not to see you."

Then she steps into view and we follow, our heads lowered into shadow, our movements mimicking her own. We crouch as we slide along the walls of the cliff face, aware of how exposed we are. But the sentries do not look our way and in seconds we are moving through deep shadow as Orphren leads us back from the edge of the cliff and those gathered to hear Tonklot. The backside of the defile narrows but allows for passage to the far side of the stone bridge that spans the void below us. We walk for several minutes, and I glance back to where Char follows, afraid I might lose her, but I needn't worry. She is right behind me.

Suddenly figures appear before us, and I see Orphren freeze as they step into view, blocking our way. When she takes a step back, I respond instinctively to the obvious danger. I have used my *inish* sparingly before, but I put it to use quickly. I sweep up the figures before me and lock them in place, unconscious statues. It is a new skill that Ronden has been teaching me, and I have learned it well. I would not risk using it on a larger crowd; it would drain me too fast. But it is very effective on a small number. Those in front of us no longer know what is happening, and that will not change anytime soon, if no one comes to wake them.

Orphren looks back at me in shock, not certain what I have done, then hastily moves ahead. Char and I follow silently. We are safe for the moment, but I must hope those I've frozen just stumbled on us by chance and were not sent specifically to bring us back. I have to hope they were only sentries guarding any rear entry into the Aerkling settlement, guards that had no chance to figure out who we were. If they recognized us, Orphren is in danger. But there is no help for it now.

At the backside of the bridge we find two more figures waiting. But Orphren does not hesitate to approach them, so I know they are here to convey us to safety. There is still a chance for escape.

"Dotris and Panaskan will carry you out," Orphren says, turning to face us. "They will fly you back to your own country and leave you there to make your way home."

Rain is sheeting down once more, leaving Char and I sodden and cold again, and I think I want nothing more in the whole world than what the Aerkling girl is promising.

"Thank you," I say, moving to embrace her. "Thank your grandfather, too. I hope he will be safe."

Her birdlike face peers up at me. "He has lived a long time and has survived what others have not. This Tonklot is just one more obstacle. I know he hopes to see you again."

Char hugs her as well, and whispers something I cannot hear, which causes Orphren to tighten her embrace. Then the Aerkling girl steps back and our bearers catch us up and wing away into the night.

I will come back here one day, I think, as we lift skyward. I will thank the old man and his people for their kindness. The Winglish recedes into the darkness and the blur of my sudden tears, and the glow of the bonfires dims.

My instincts tell me this is not the end of the story, and my instincts are seldom wrong.

SIX

As dawn lights the sky, Char and I are lowered back to earth by the Aerklings about a mile north of Viridian Deep and left to walk in. I am so happy to see our journey come to an end — not least of all because I am tired of being hauled around like a sack of potatoes where the drawstrings feel as if they could come loose at any moment and let you spill out all over the place. But also because I am just tired. This is my second night in a row with little to no sleep.

Still, Char and I thank both our carriers at length for helping us escape, asking them to watch over Orphren and her grandfather. I know almost nothing about their family or their situation beyond the few things that were revealed during our short stay. But it is enough to know that they welcomed us as friends and honored their relationship with our mother. I wish we could do something to help them, but there is no way to intervene in the affairs of another group of Fae without sparking further antagonism. We must trust to fate and time, and both of us promise as we walk home that we will go back one day.

Harrow and some others had indeed been searching for us yesterday and were on the verge of starting out again when Char and I stumble through the front door of Ancrow's home, so exhausted we are in danger of collapse. Uncharacteristic of the calm, steady girl who seldom displays emotion of any sort, Ramey flies to meet us, her delighted cries loud enough to summon Harrow from next door. (Though poor Ronden, we soon learn, has been sent to the healing center for the concussion and the rather severe banging-up she received at the hands of the Goblins the other night.)

Both reach us in record time, and once again we are all hugs and tears and smiles that leave no chance for explanations.

Harrow and Ramey press us for information, but it is soon clear we are both too tired. Harrow quickly recognizes this and dispatches both of us to our beds. Ramey takes charge of Char, while Harrow sweeps me up in his arms and carts me off to our cottage. He runs a hot bath, lowers me in, and the water not only washes away the dirt and grime but also seems to dispel a bit of the pain I carry from having left Malik, Orphren, and her grandfather behind.

I sink into the warm water and delight in the soft touch of my life partner's hands, and slowly my world re-forms. I have brought my sister home and found Malik again — though I cannot help wondering if I will ever see him again. Yet just as with Orphren and her grandfather, I feel in my heart that fate will reunite us.

Harrow finishes cleaning me up, helps me slip on a nightgown, and carries me to bed, crawling in beside me. I revel in the feeling of his arms cradling me, of the warmth of his body and the certain knowledge that we were meant to find each other, until sleep finally takes me and everything else disappears.

When I wake again, it is late afternoon on the following day and Harrow is gone. As I later learn, he has called off the search and alerted everyone that Char and I are both safe, for word of Char's abduction and my pursuit has spread throughout the city. Because most know by now of my involvement with Ancrow and the subsequent destruction of the invading Human army — not to mention my slow transformation into a Sylvan — I am already a bit of a local celebrity. But this adds fresh interest and new concerns.

My time in Viridian Deep has been bumpy, to say the least. There were many who wanted nothing to do with a Human, no matter how unfortunate my story. That I was half Sylvan made no difference as long as I looked fully Human. And though my eventual change won some over, there are others who will always regard me as a freak. But I have long since accepted this. Sweet young Presence and Yul, my next-door neighbors, fuss over me constantly — offering everything from surprise dinners to garden parties — and I am not one to turn such attentions down. A few houses away is Bluklan, a widower with a smile that could charm a mountain tiger, and a joking word for everyone. Even irritable old Cranny Bee is never anything but kind beneath her harsh exterior. I am lucky to have them all, and they are but a handful of the Fae who have gone out of their way to be my friends.

But I am still a one-of-a-kind oddity, and therefore a subject of speculation by all. At least most of the Fae are respectful and pleasant, and I believe that once I appear fully Sylvan, most of the interest in me will wane.

Harrow returns by the time I am washed and dressed, and he tells me we are going to see Ronden at the healing center with our sisters. Harrow considers them his sisters, too — though only Ronden and I are blood-related. Harrow, Ramey, and Char were all adopted. But though we consider ourselves family, I still can't think of Harrow as a brother, because to me he is not. Instead, we fell in love as strangers, and now we are partnered for life. The beating heart of our relationship is grounded in our commitment to each other, to share our lives for however long we have. And possibly — though we have not really discussed it — to bring children into the world. I hope we can. I want his children badly. I want to be a mother. I want a life that I once thought lost to me.

Tonight dinner is prepared by an insistent Ronden who has commandeered a guest room reserved for family parties in order to demonstrate to one and all that she is perfectly heathy. At first, she appears so — although she still bears more than a few marks and bruises from her struggle with the Goblins. But when I observe her more closely, I see her wince at the bright lights and frown at loud noises, so I know she still has more healing to do. We sit at the guest room where it adjoins the kitchen as savory smells waft past, and Char and I relate everything that happened to us after Char was taken, pausing now and then so our family can ask questions.

But it is Ronden who asks the one question that matters.

"Won't the Goblins — and maybe even your friend Malik — come after you again?"

I have wondered about that. Malik would not participate willingly, even if the Goblins were to risk coming for me yet again. But he may not have a choice, given that Chorech still holds his medicine. I can only expect so much from my old friend when his very existence is at stake, and I cannot ask for his life in exchange for my own.

"We need to find a way to keep them from reaching any of us again," Harrow says after a few moments of silent thought. "We can't spend our lives waiting for further abduction attempts."

"Do we need to move?" Ramey asks.

"I don't want to move!" Char announces with such insistence that I can see trying to countermand her would be difficult. She has already lost her mother, and she does not like the idea of any more changes. Besides, she is only ten years old. For all her recently acquired maturity, she is still a child.

"It seems to me," Ronden says as we look at one another, "that what we really need to know is who is behind these attempts at getting Auris back to the Human world. We know the Goblins are after her, but it now appears they are doing so at Malik's creator's bidding. Did you meet another scientist while you were in Human custody?"

"Not anyone of his description," I answer. "Malik said he was young; not much older than us."

"Could it be one of the scientists who worked with Allensby?" Ramey asks. "Or one of the ones who took your parents in an effort to get at you?"

"Or whoever had you put in the prison?" Ronden adds.

I don't have the answers to these questions because I don't have the memories that would provide them. But suddenly I wonder if a visit to the Seers might give me what I need. When I first arrived at Viridian Deep, I allowed the sisters to probe my mind for forgotten memories that would yield clues to my past. They were successful in opening a few doors, but definitely not all of them. What if I could unlock more memories — specifically around the night I

91

escaped my home when the Ministry came and took my parents? Might these memories reveal some small bit of information about the young scientist who wants to bring me back to the Human world?

It certainly wouldn't hurt, so I resolve to look into it. But I also just as quickly decide not to discuss it with my sisters. Better to mention it to Harrow when we are alone. This unlocking of past memories is a minefield, and I don't want anyone else involved until after I have uncovered what was hidden. Harrow is my life partner and the only one I trust with all my secrets.

So we let the matter slide after agreeing that Harrow will find and capture another ertl, and train it to serve as an early warning system for Ronden and the girls. At least then we will both have a reliable way of knowing about the Goblins in advance. It works well enough for Harrow and me, and it should work for the resourceful Ronden. Moving is pointless; it would only postpone the attacks, not prevent them.

The following morning, Harrow and I go to visit the Seers. Learning more about my past has long been something I have wanted to pursue, but this is the first time I have had an urgent need to do so. If there is a way we can discover the identity of the scientist behind the Goblin efforts to abduct me, then I mean to make use of it.

It has always troubled me that I was there when my parents were taken by Ministry soldiers, yet not able to remember what happened between then and finding myself in the Goblin prison with Malik and the others. This is the biggest black hole in my life — one I am desperate to shed some light on — though most of my childhood is a void as well. The few memories I have of my adoptive parents are good ones, so I would like to regain a few more. Maybe this is my chance to find them.

Harrow and I travel along the tree lanes of our elevated neighborhood to a set of winding stairs that take us to the ground, where we can begin the short journey through the city to its western boundaries. I know my way now, for I have spent almost two years investigating the streets, byways, and paths of the city, and finding new surprises at every turn. The sisters — Benith, Maven, and Dreena — live in their oddly shaped, fairy-tale cottage some distance away from the city. It is not that they don't seek or desire the companionship of their fellow Sylvans, but more that living apart serves them better in their chosen profession. Or perhaps the word *chosen* is a bit misleading, since a Fae is either born a Seer or not. This isn't a craft that can be learned; it can only be mastered.

The sisters are strange in both habits and personality — probably beyond what their gifts for exploring the memories of others require — but I would argue that this is true of us all. We are all, in some ways, odd in the eyes of others. So I try not to judge, because I know I am not a particularly reliable judge of myself. But even if I find the sisters odd, I also find them to be three lovable elderly ladies, and spending time with them is always a joy.

Admittedly, it is actually Harrow who is their favorite. I think they see in him someone they remember from their past, enjoying his handsome, strong features and his warm way of teasing and sharing. How can I begrudge their love for him? It is why I love him as well, and it pleases me to know that his charms do not go unrecognized by those whose opinions I value.

We walk up the lane toward the house, and even before we reach the front door Benith is rushing out to meet us. Surprisingly, she bypasses Harrow, comes directly up to me, and enfolds me in her warm embrace.

"Thank the Fates that watch over us you are safely returned, Auris," she whispers. "I did fear the worst. Even while telling myself that you are more than capable of looking after yourself, I did worry."

I hug her back and thank her for her concerns and tell her I am happy to be home again. She gives me a final hug, then she is off to embrace Harrow. Once finished, she leads us up the walkway where Maven and Dreena are waiting, and we begin the greeting process all over again.

Fiery Dreena is abrupt and condemning. "You were foolish to risk yourself like that, Auris. You need to banish your impulsive behaviors and embrace whatever common sense you can muster! But at least you're back. And still capable enough, it appears. This handsome heartbreaker standing next to you is evidence of that! Good thing, too. Otherwise I would be forced to take him for myself."

"You look none the worse for what you've been through," Maven adds pointedly. "Welcome home, young lady."

Once inside, Benith retires to prepare tea and arrange a plate of scones she has baked. I am pretty sure she bakes something every day so she will always be prepared should visitors appear. After she brings it out,

Dreena orders me to relate everything that happened and be sure to leave nothing out.

I do, and the sisters listen intently until I am finished.

"What was done to your friend is unconscionable," Benith says at once. "Those Humans who pretend to work in the cause of science are abominations. Nature has made us the way she intended, and we are exactly the way we were meant to be. To pretend you know better and have the right to alter what She has created is an astounding display of arrogance and foolishness."

"Is there some way he can be changed back?" Dreena wonders. "Perhaps an imaginative use of your *inish*?"

She is looking at me as she asks this, and I want to roll my eyes. "I think he is mostly concerned with trying to stay pain-free. Apparently there is a medicine he requires that he will descend into agony without, and the Goblins have control over it . . . and hence over him."

"We will try to find a way to help him," Dreena announces as she reaches for another maple-sugar scone. "His efforts to save you deserve some sort of reward. We will give it some thought, won't we, sisters? Any friend of yours, young lady, is a friend of ours. Now, have you rested up sufficiently to consider a new adventure? That *is* why you are here, isn't it?"

It is, of course — although I am a bit put off by the way she seems to dismiss the possibility I have come simply to let them know I am well.

"What happened has raised fresh questions about her past," Harrow says. "We now know the Goblins are pursuing her for the express purpose of bringing her back to the Human world and giving her over to the Ministry and another of its scientists. But why now, after two years? And who is it that wants her back so badly?"

"Who indeed?" muses Dreena.

"Does she think this is a memory she has locked away with all the others?" Maven asks.

"She must think it possible," Benith declares.

I am irritated by the four of them talking about me as if I am not there. "What *I* wonder is what happened to me after my parents were taken," I interject. "I have no memory of anything until I found myself inside the Goblin prison. I have no idea how I got there, or where I was before. I want to see if I can discover something about that."

"That might be possible," Dreena says slowly, giving it some thought. "But it won't be easy."

I give her a look. "What part of my life has ever been easy? But I have fought through worse before. Mostly I think of myself as incredibly fortunate."

"Well, you are that," Dreena agrees. "What do you think, Maven?"

The smallest sister has a twinkle in her eye as she looks at me. "I think that, while you might be changing on the outside, you will never change on the inside. Are you sure you want this?"

"I am."

"And again, it might not give you what you seek. Are you open to that?"

"I think so. After all I have had to come to terms with up until now, can it be any worse?"

"Oh dear," Benith interjects at once. "Never ask that particular question."

The way she says it makes it plain she is not joking.

So after drinking the tea and consuming the scones, I move over to the couch to sit between Benith and Dreena, while Maven kneels in front of me. Even Harrow comes to stand close, wanting to provide additional support. The sisters give me a cup of special tea to consume, which I do, and then I sit

98

back and close my eyes. Benith is already humming softly — a warm song without words, but the sound is mesmerizing, and the tone and cadence and loveliness all combine to provide a sense of peace and calm.

But doubt and fear tug at me as well. I remember the last time I recovered a memory, and it was not pleasant. The process is demanding, and the results are unpredictable. It is one thing to uncover lost memories, but another to do it accurately. Even the sisters, skilled as they have proven, are not always able to reveal what is hidden. Sometimes they miss things or skip about; sometimes they fail entirely. A kind of inescapable certainty takes hold of me, warning that it will not be any different this time and to prepare myself for what I am about to see.

Though, of course, there is no good way to prepare for such a thing. Instead, you must tighten down your expectation and hopes. You must let go of everything and harden yourself against a barrage of hard truths and sharp-edged pain.

How do I do this?

By staying strong of will and steady of mind.

The Seers continue their mesmerizing

99

song, and I slide clear of place and time and — eventually — of myself.

A banging on our front door breaks my concentration as I listen to my parents discussing what to do with me. Then bodies slam against the door, the wood frame cracks, and the lock that secures it snaps as a flood of Ministry soldiers charge inside.

Sensing the danger, I have already rushed up the stairwell to the second floor of our home, into the security of my bedroom. I caught only a glimpse from the stairs, but that is enough to tell me who threatened us. My father's worst fears have been realized. In this moment I remember the words he spoke to me months ago when he sat me down to warn that this day might come.

A single word resurfaces at once.

Drift.

Then what my father told me unspools itself in full.

"I don't want to alarm you, Auris, but I do want you to be prepared. I am running a great risk with the work I am doing, and the man who hired me is not happy with me because of that. So far, he has left me alone, but this may not always be the case. If a day comes when you feel yourself threatened because of my research — whether your mother and I

100

are with you or not — seek sanctuary with your appointed mentor. He has been your teacher as much as I have, and he will see you clear of any danger that threatens. Go to him and stay with him until you know it to be safe again. When we can — if we can — we will come for you. In the meantime, do not be deceived by anything others might tell you."

I must do what he told me and make my escape. I do not want to leave my mother and father behind, but I lack the ability to save them from so many soldiers. Two or three, perhaps. But there are more than that — too many for one almost-fifteen-year-old — so I must flee instead.

I throw open the window to our backyard and catapult through to the sandpit below where I sometimes train. I roll as I land, and am back on my feet immediately. I can hear my father's angry shouts and my mother's panicked screams, and the pounding of feet charging through the house as the intruders spread out. They have not thought to secure the back — a natural reaction to the mistaken belief they are dealing with a scientist, a housewife, and a kid.

I am about to prove them wrong.

Two bounds to the fence wall and a third that takes me to the top, and I am flipping all the way over to land on the other side.

Once I am over, no one can catch me.
At least, not on that day.

The memory fades, and I wake. My eyes
find Harrow first, because he is the one I
always look for. I can tell he knows what I
am going to say before the words leave my
mouth.

"I remember now. He was my teacher, my
mentor. But as for his name . . ." I shake
my head. "Gone."

They crowd closer, the Seers and Harrow,
full of love and reassurance.

"There, there," Benith whispers as she
embraces me. "Let it all settle, Auris. Do
not rush yourself. We are all here with you."

Her words are soothing, and her warmth
a gift, as I feel a chill run through me. Why
is his name lost to me? Why have I forgotten him so completely? I know he was
important once — a huge part of my life.
How have I managed to forget all the details
yet retain the certainty of it being true?

Yet I have done just that. I remember the
feeling, and nothing else.

"It's been so long," I whisper back.

I trail off, embarrassed, uncertain of what
to say or do. I can't remember anything.

Maven has risen and brought over a reviv-
ing cup of tea, and I accept it gratefully. I

have so much to explain, but where do I begin? At the beginning, of course. But what if you can't remember the beginning?

Suddenly I panic. This is all too fast. I have to get out of here. I have to have time to think about this. I have to find a way to discover more of what I have forgotten. But not here and not now.

I set down the tea and rise, fighting an almost overwhelming impulse to flee. Harrow is next to me instantly, holding out a hand. "Auris?"

I squeeze his hand as I address the sisters. "I need time alone to think about this. I need to try to retrieve more memories of this person, my mentor — though not with help from you. I need to do this on my own. If that fails, I will come back again. But for now . . ."

I take a deep, steadying breath and give them a reassuring smile. It takes everything I have to do this. "Please take me home, Harrow," I beg.

The three old ladies offer reassurances of understanding, and Harrow and I proffer apologies and expressions of gratitude as we depart, but my legs feel as unsteady as if I were on a ship at sea.

I cling to Harrow as he leads me down the walkway and onto the familiar old road.

My mind is flooded with names and faces, but none of them are right.

I am almost home again before I remember, and then I speak the name aloud, almost shouting it.

"Drifter! He called himself Drifter!"

Harrow sees my smile and hugs me close.

SEVEN

Harrow takes me back to our cottage, saying nothing, just holding me against him as we walk down the pathways and up the tree lanes while I struggle to remember more about Drifter. Harrow is what he always is in these situations: patient and kind and supportive. I know he wants to ask me why this name has shaken me so, but I cannot tell him anything when I remember so little. The whole memory is so close now with just the sound of his name that I can almost reach out and touch it. Yet like many forgotten things, it remains maddeningly elusive, no matter how hard I try to access it. Instead, I must wait for it to come find me.

Which, after I sleep for a time in our cottage with Harrow's arms about me while my mind wanders where it will through snatches of dreams, it does. I wake sufficiently to realize what is happening as another portion of my forgotten life returns,

105

albeit fragmented, with scattered memories of Drifter appearing and falling into place like the pieces of a puzzle, each hinting at the wider picture that still refuses to emerge, but I can almost reconstruct from what I am given.

I do not move for a long time, just lie quietly as I give the memories space and time to settle back into my brain. I drift in and out of wakefulness, aware of what is happening, wanting to give it the chance it needs to solidify.

Until, finally, I roll over on the bed to face my love and look into those depthless eyes. "I remember some of it now."

He nods, but he does not speak. He waits on me.

"He was my teacher," I say. "My teacher in the skills of self-defense and weapons usage, when I was only still very young."

My voice is scratchy, but I push on. "He was the one who taught me everything about hand-to-hand combat. You once remarked how someone must have taught me how to defend myself, and someone did. Drifter. He was my mentor. He came into my life when I was nearly thirteen and my father was beginning to fear for my safety."

I feel as if I am meandering in my explanation, but I am still trying to piece it together from fragments. And I wonder anew at how I could ever have forgotten something that was once so important. Have I subconsciously kept it hidden from myself over the years? Has someone or something arranged for it to be hidden? If so, who or what?

I don't have the answers yet, but I lean forward and kiss Harrow on the nose. Then I tell him what I have recalled.

My father introduces me to Drifter two days before I turn thirteen. He brings this stranger home unannounced, and after greeting him with a warm hug, my mother looks once at me and disappears. My father then introduces the stranger and tells me I am to be his student, and that these will be my most important lessons yet.

I give my father a stubborn look. I don't want this man to be my teacher. I'm busy enough with my homeschooling. Why do I need this man to teach me further? What lessons will he give me?

My father looks stern as he bends close. "Drifter," he says very quietly, "will teach you how to stay alive."

Then he exits the room, leaving us alone. Drifter and I look at each other appraisingly — he more directly at me than I at him. At not quite thirteen years of age, I am not all that confident about myself. But I have learned how to maintain my calm in uncertain situations, and so I do. Drifter is short, wiry, and compact. Dark skin, darker hair, and a body that seems so tightly coiled it is a miracle that skin and clothing alone can contain it. This is an odd assessment, but my already developing instincts tell me this man is much more than he seems.

"Are you ready to begin your first lesson?" he asks.

I nod. "Yes, Drifter."

"No, Auris," he says at once. "You will call me Master until you earn the right to use my given name. Because, for now, I am the master and you are the student. Come with me."

We leave the house, and he leads the way to a nearby park. I notice for the first time that he uses a walking stick for balance. Perhaps he has an affliction that requires it, but I cannot detect one. I think that maybe I have been too quick to follow him into the unknown, but my father has made it plain that this man is my teacher and I should do my best to master whatever sort of lessons he provides. But how will he help me to stay alive?

Once at the park, Drifter walks to an empty bench set off by itself near a stand of spruce, props his staff against the wooden backing, and sits down. When he beckons me, I sit down beside him. His face remains stern, although I see something deeper in his eyes; I just can't put a word to it yet.

"We will just talk for today," he tells me. "We will begin our lessons in earnest in a few days. I am charged with teaching you to survive on your own, should something happen to your parents. The world is dangerous, and the people who live in it are largely responsible for this. But I will show you how to prepare."

He pauses, obviously waiting for me to say something. I clear my throat. "Father hasn't said anything about me being in danger. Has something changed?"

"Only that you are now old enough to learn how to defend yourself and your parents, should the need arise. Before, you were a child. Now you are a young lady on the way to being a young woman. And I intend to see to it that you become strong enough to stand up to whatever threatens. I want you to know what to do in every dangerous situation. I want you to become confident in your ability to stand strong. I want you to master the use of every weapon with which I am familiar — and a few with which I am not. Lastly, I want you to become as capable physically as you will be mentally. Your father and mother have taught you traditional lessons. I will teach you *what they cannot."*

I stare at him. "What if I don't want this? I don't have to, do I?"

"I think you do. If you refuse, you will be disappointing your father in ways you cannot yet understand. I don't think you want that, do you?"

I shake my head. Of course I don't. But I don't see how whatever Drifter teaches me will change anything. I don't much like weapons and don't much care to learn to use them. I am all for a good hike or an occasional race or climb, but I do not think fighting will ever become one of my skills.

"This is what we will do, Auris. Every day, without exception, unless you are ill, we will engage in a series of exercises to strengthen your body and improve your agility and speed. That is all we will concentrate on for several months. After that, we will start adding in combat training that involves self-defense techniques and attack skills. These will be punishing, but you will come to love them. When you have mastered that, you will begin to train with weapons."

He pauses. "We will start meeting for a couple of hours every day, then increase the times of your sessions as you progress. The rest of the day will be reserved for your other studies. One day a week, you will rest. You will not train unless I am there to supervise you. It is dangerous for you to train alone, and above all I do not want you harmed."

He pauses again, perhaps seeing the uncertainty and concern in my eyes. I learn on this day — the very first time we meet — that I will never be able to hide anything from him.

"Your training — and your time with me as your teacher — will last two years. After that, you will be ready to train on your own."

I stare hard. Two years is a lifetime. Two years is too long. Two months is too long. My child's voice squeaks with dismay as I say, "I don't see how —"

"No!" He cuts me off as surely as if he had used a knife. "You don't. Not yet. First lesson: Do not ever say no to me. You are not allowed to use that word. Or the words can't or don't." He gets to his feet. "Stand up."

I all but leap to obey. The command in his voice — the feeling that disobedience is an invitation to something awful — is unmistakable. I stand before him, close to tears but fuming as well. This isn't how I am used to being treated.

He reaches over to retrieve his staff and hands it to me. "Take it," he orders.

I do so and stand there holding it limply. What is he going to do now?

"Take the staff firmly in both hands and try

111

to hit me with it. Do not hold back. Swing it at me as hard as you can."

I stare at him in disbelief. He wants me to hit him? Conceivably to hurt him? I don't think I can do this.

"Hit me," he says again. "What's wrong with you? Should I hit you instead? Maybe so. Maybe that is what it will take." His voice lowers, suddenly taunting. "Little wilting flower. Timid little toad."

The words burn; they make me feel weak and foolish, and I don't have to put up with this. I swing the staff as hard as I can at him, but my blow never lands. He catches the staff with his hand in midair and snatches it away from me.

He hands it back. "Try again. Hit me anywhere but try not to let me see what you are planning before you do it. You gave away your last attempt with your eyes. Try harder to fool me."

I am determined this time. I make him wait a moment, shifting the staff around a bit, looking here and there, then I abruptly swing at his head, my attempt swift and sharp. I have him . . .

But of course I don't. Again, he is too quick for me and catches the staff before it touches him. Again, he wrenches it away.

He steps close. "By the time we are finished

with your lessons, Auris, you will be able to do this to me."

Then he turns and walks away. "I will come back for you on the day your family celebrates your birthday," he calls over his shoulder.

Standing there as he disappears, I realize what I saw in his eyes earlier. He was taking my measure.

Drifter is as good as his promise. He returns on my birthday and instructs me to come with him. It is midday on a beautiful sunny day, and my father has gone to work — though not before instructing me how to dress for my first lesson, in loose clothing and lightweight sneakers.

I am not looking forward to whatever is coming, and Drifter is quick to read this in my voice and posture. He tells me we will begin slowly and work our way into the lessons at a pace I can handle. He reminds me of the importance of dedication and commitment. And that knowledge and experience will ultimately banish both fear and ignorance.

I nod agreeably, and at the same time wonder if he is right.

Much of what happens that day — and presumably on most of those that follow — remains unclear. I remember it in general, but not so much the specifics. It may be in large *part because so much of it is repetitious. Once begun, the lessons take on a familiarity and thus a sense of sameness that makes it difficult to pick out the differences.*

Some things, however, do leap out. I remember being tired all the time at first. I would work as hard as I could at my lessons — both mental and physical — then collapse exhausted at night to sleep the sleep of the dead, rise again, and repeat. Until one day I woke rested and strong, and never looked back.

I remember thinking I would never master certain skills, especially those involving weapons. But in the beginning, I spent my days simply learning to run and dodge and leap and bound for what seemed like an eternity. I could feel myself getting stronger and tougher, but it was slow going. It still took a long time to be able to run five miles without pausing or to pull myself up into a tree or run up a wall or somersault over any obstacle, but these I could build myself up to mastering.

When we begin working with weapons, though — with blades and bows and arrows and throwing stars and javelins and various other blades (knives; I remember knives with a mix of hatred from the cuts and joy from my eventual success at learning to avoid them) — I think mostly of how long it takes before I can do what Drifter demands of me. There are always targets and it takes hours and days and months to hit them more than once in every fifty tries. I am not strong enough. I am not accurate enough. I am not quick enough. I am a thirteen-year-old girl and nothing I do is good enough.

Yet I persevere, because one thing I have never been is a quitter. Drifter urges me on. My father praises my efforts. My mother comforts and soothes me when I come home so beat up I just want to go straight to bed.

And near the end of my thirteenth year of life, spilling over into my fourteenth, I begin to get better. And not slowly, but all at once. It is as if someone has pushed a button. Apparently my body is finally ready and willing. I find my center; I become steady and smooth and strong. I discover the importance of breathing and how to make it serve me. I see things differently than I did when I was younger and less focused. I am able to block the pain and the stress and the sense of failure that has plagued me. I begin to feel pride in who and what I am. I begin to see myself as both strong and skilled.

In my fourteenth year, Drifter introduces me to Human weapons — to the weapons intended to maim or kill more quickly and efficiently. By now, I am all in. Spitfires are my *favorite; I am very good with these. But Drifter simply shrugs when I mention this. "Remember," he tells me, "weapons are nothing more than tools. Never grow too fond of them or come to rely on them too much. You are what matters. You make the choice to use a weapon or not, and your choices will always matter more than the weapon itself, for weapons have a tendency to steal away compassion, empathy, and any consideration of what you are doing. Life is never to be taken lightly — yours or others' — and your mind and your heart are what will enable you to survive without losing too much of yourself."*

And so it goes, for almost two long years.

Drifter never varies in his treatment of me. He is scant at handing out praise but also at offering criticism. He tells me early on that neither much matters. All that matters is success or failure — and the latter must never be allowed to distract me when I am trying to defend myself. The mantra he champions eventually becomes mine as well. And while he maintains that calm, steady demeanor where praise and criticism are always kept closely guarded, I remember that as our time together winds down, he begins to smile more.

One day he comes to me and says we are finished. I remember staring at him in disbelief. He must be mistaken. Our work together has become a part of my life — so integral to who and what I have become that I cannot imagine it ending. Nor do I long to be separated from him as I once did. He has become as important to me as my parents, and I will be bereft if he chooses to walk away. I believe he will do this, you see. I know him well enough to understand that he has his life, and it is his to do with as he chooses. He has taught me what he knows and watched me grow and benefit from his lessons to a point where there is nothing more he can teach me. My training is done.

I am three months shy of my fifteenth birthday, and I am feeling strong and confident. So I tell him I understand. I tell him I am ready.

But I have no idea what is coming for me.

"Which is what, Auris?" Harrow asks as I pause in my recitation.

I shake my head. "I don't know exactly. That part of the memory . . . Well, I don't seem to recall it. I think it must have had something to do with how I ended up in the Goblin prison."

"We can go back to the Seers," he suggests. "You've gotten this far; maybe you can retrieve the rest."

But I am weary from the effort and do not care to venture further today. The probing of my memories, the efforts to push me to remember what has been lost for more than seven years, is draining both emotionally and physically. If I am to try to recover it, I need to rest up first. I sense there is more to be revealed, but the past few days of struggling to find Char and escaping both the Goblins and the Aerklings has taken a lot out of me. I need to back off for at least another day.

"Can we maybe just go out and walk around for a bit?" I ask instead.

We rise and depart the cottage. We walk back down the tree lanes and then the road beyond and don't say a word to each other. We walk through the city, meandering without any destination in mind, and then suddenly he takes my hand and steers me in a different direction. We walk only a short distance before I realize he is guiding me toward Promise Falls and its amazing Gardens of Life. I smile over at him in gratitude, for what he recognizes I need: a calm place in which to think things over while I allow my emotional shock to fade. His intuition about how this latest memory has affected me is emblematic of how deeply we are connected.

Once at the gardens, we walk the pathways for a time and neither of us speaks. I let the smells and sights of this marvelous place wash over me. How can anything be so lovely and so new every time you come into it? And how can you be anything but grateful for the way in which it can soothe and heal both mind and body? It is a gift that exists nowhere else in the world, and I feel so connected to it that it is almost scary. It is as if this is where I was really born, as if this is the core of who I really am.

Friends and acquaintances come over to greet me and wish me well. Most have heard at least a little of what has befallen me over the past few days, and they want to be certain I am recovered. I smile and laugh and joke with them, because they are people I care about and wish to keep close. So much of my life has been empty of any relationships save those I shared with my fellow prisoners in the Goblin compound, and I sense that my childhood was isolated as well, limited mostly to my adoptive parents and Drifter. But over the past two years I have regained my ability to trust in friendships and the warmth of familiarity with other people, and I do not take any of it lightly.

But Harrow presses on, and soon we are sitting across from Promise Falls, staring over the verdant sweeps of grasses drifting down to the lake and across from there to the silvery sparkle of the falls. I am at peace here. I am able to let go of everything and just breathe in the beauty that surrounds me. I am able to let it work its magic.

After a time, I say, "I feel so much more complete for having my memory of Drifter restored. I cannot understand how it was lost for so long. It makes me wonder how much else I have lost."

Harrow squeezes my hand. "I would feel the same way, if it were me. I would want it all back — everything I had lost — even without knowing what that might reveal. I would not feel complete otherwise."

I give him a quick smile. I am so lucky to have him in my life. He sees things so clearly. Those vaunted instincts with which we are both gifted bind us in so many ways, but none are more important than how well we see what we each need from the other. It is a connection that I had never thought to find with anyone, and it defines the nature of our relationship in ways nothing else can.

"I think I have to know the rest of what happened to me if I am to be whole again," I tell him quietly. "I think you are right; I may have to go back to the Seers and ask them to help me one final time."

He gives me a gentle nudge. "You say that

as if you are seeking something you think I might discourage."

"I suppose I want your support."

"When have you not had it?"

I nod. "It's the reassurance that I still have it that matters, I suppose."

"And I think you shouldn't limit this visit to 'one final time,' either," he continues. "None of us know how long this process might take. You suffered a great trauma when you lost your parents and were imprisoned like a criminal, and then lost all your friends while trying to escape. Anyone would require healing after all that. You should not ever apologize for that, or limit what you may need to fully recover."

I stare at him, amazed. Oh Fates of Fae and *inish,* how I love him!

I lean into him. "What it requires of me right now," I say quietly, "is you. Can we go home now? I need to have you all to myself, to hold me for a while."

His arms come around me, pulling me close. "You've had me since the first day we met."

I smile inwardly. "That's some pretty thick syrup you're pouring, Watcher," I tease.

"Want a little more? You are the best thing that has ever happened to me."

Now I am kissing him. Between kisses, I

say, "A little proof wouldn't hurt."

We stare at each other a moment longer, and that's all it takes for me to fall into his amazing eyes the same way I've been doing since we met.

He smiles. "I think we can manage that."

We leave the bench and Promise Falls, arms about each other, walk home and hold each other close for the rest of the day.

EIGHT

Two more days pass, and my life becomes tranquil once more. No further attacks come, despite my fears, and I am given the time I need to rest and recover.

My sisters Ramey and Char are there to help, but they need me as well. They need the reassurance that family comes first, and that new journeys away will not end for Harrow, Ronden, or myself as they did for Ancrow. Losing a mother is a terrible experience for anyone, and more so for the young. It was bad enough for me at nineteen, but worse for them, as Ancrow was always there. She raised them herself, becoming their rock and their certainty, their safe haven against the world. So her loss was titanic. The pain of having someone so integral stripped away in an instant does not fade quickly. Even two years later, they still miss her badly.

I miss her, too, but our relationship was

123

so much different. We found each other after years of separation, and with a firm conviction that our mother/daughter reunion was impossible — though our reasons for this were vastly different. She was afraid even to think I could be the daughter she had given up, while I was unaware of her very existence — and both of us were fighting time and circumstance and a raft of warring emotions about what it meant to be brought back together so dramatically. I did not trust or much like my mother once I found her, and a full understanding of what she had been through and what she meant to me was slow in coming. Distrust, dislike, and dismay combined to keep her at arm's length in the short time we were given.

But this is not Char's or Ramey's reality. For them, Ancrow was always a mother, and they still remember her almost entirely in those terms. They know what she did to me; they understand how wrong and cruel it was. But while they can sympathize with me and feel my pain, they have their own very different memories of how it feels to lose a mother.

So I remain committed to being their older sister and caregiver in the same way Ronden does, and my time with them is precious. And though other wants and needs press in, demanding my time, I have learned how to keep such intrusions at bay.

As well, there is my time with Harrow — still so new and so precious. I have found my center, my love; I have good reason to feel happy. But I also cannot simply accept this as settled and think it will always be there, because neither may be true. My bond with Harrow is a gift I cannot take lightly or with some blind expectation that it does not need nurturing. It does. It needs warding; it needs protecting. But my time with him is both healing and reassuring. He gives me strength of spirit and a new sense of emotional stability. I am not entirely over my sojourn in the Goblin prison, and I likely never will be. It is a raw wound on both my soul and my heart, and seeing Malik again has opened it anew. For years I had so little — my former life stripped away and forgotten, and my present life a living hell. But I came through it while my friends did not, and that sort of knowledge works on you like sandpaper on skin. You endure it in whatever way you can, and you live with the knowledge that the memories will never entirely fade.

So while I spend time with my family doing not much of anything in particular in the days since Char's abduction, I think often of Malik and wonder if I will ever see him again. To have found him alive when I was so certain he was dead remains a stunning reality I still have trouble reconciling. But as my intuition has told me, I don't think Malik and I are quite done with each other, for which I am glad.

As for the rest . . . Finding Drifter to see if he can tell me anything about my past that might be important in understanding my present — perhaps helping me to discover the name of the enemy who stalks me — can wait. So can asking the Seers to help uncover more memories of my past. Finding a way to help Malik and free him from his bondage — or even his dependence on the medicine that keeps him agony-free — feels more pressing, but at the same time more distant still. Most of what Malik requires I am likely unable to provide, and most of what I want for him is probably a dream that cannot come to pass. Lastly, finding a path forward for myself that does not involve Goblins coming for me in the middle of the night might not be a goal I can achieve. I am Ancrow's daughter, after all, and the circumstances surrounding my return to Viridian Deep and the extent of the *inish* I possess seem to have brought danger and enemies both — just as they did for my mother.

So I prevaricate or delay or resist — or whatever you choose to call it — and embrace my excuses to stay with my family, my friends, my city, and my life as I wish it to be, and I do not leave on any further expeditions.

Until, three days on, the unthinkable happens.

I have gone fishing with Harrow and the younger girls. Ronden, to her profound annoyance, is still under observation at the healing center, so she is not with us. But the rest of us travel southeast to Sparla Springs Lake, a two-mile walk to some of the best freshwater fishing in all of Viridian Deep. I have been recently introduced to this particular form of recreation — although, from the way I took to it, I think I might have done this in my early life. But either way, I am quickly entranced. I find it a wonderful way of passing time — more relaxing than I had expected it to be, and just challenging enough to keep things interesting.

The day is gray with an overcast sky, but warm and pleasant enough otherwise, and it is our plan to fish until late in the afternoon before walking home again with our catch. That we will have caught something

127

is a given. Harrow and the two younger girls are already seasoned practitioners, and assured enough to guarantee we will not go home empty-handed. So my purpose is mostly to spend a day in a lovely place with those I care about most.

It has been a week since the last attack, and no further bands of Goblins have come for me. In addition to our own ertl, Harrow has procured and begun training another for Ronden and the younger girls. I am beginning to relax again, and so I give myself over to the pleasures of our outing, laughing and smiling and loosening my vigilance.

So when the Aerklings appear, I am caught off guard completely.

They materialize without warning, more than a dozen of them surrounding us — dark and winged and looming like wraiths. They have Harrow and me encircled, so that we have no place to flee save into the lake. We hold fishing poles instead of our *inish* staffs, which are lying close but just out of easy reach. Ramey and Char sit between us but are busy examining their catch and have not yet seen what threatens.

Yet is this a threat, or simply a visit? I am assuming the former, because in the moment this is how it feels to me. I search the

Aerkling faces, but I cannot tell which is their leader or read their expressions — though the set of their bodies and the look in their eyes is not reassuring. They do not hold weapons, but they wear blades strapped about their waists. Nothing about this suggests a mere visit, so I wonder why they are here.

I risk a quick glance at Harrow, who is aware of them, too, and together we rise. I lean over and quietly tell my sisters not to panic. I know them well enough — seasoned little warriors that they are — to believe they are equal to what is coming.

How wrong I am.

A few further moments pass, with all of us frozen in place, then I reach down for my staff and take it in hand. Harrow does the same. Better that they see we are neither cowed nor helpless. If required, we will defend ourselves, for we possess the means to do so. There are too many of them to expect we can prevail — yet we have done so before, and against greater odds.

The difference this time is that we have two young sisters to protect, as well as ourselves.

Another Aerkling steps from the shadows of the trees and makes his way forward. He slouches and stumbles as he comes — as if hindered somehow — his gait odd and its movements strangely skewed in a way that is noticeable even beneath his folded wings. Yet in his eyes I can detect a clear hint of what appears to be dislike or even open antagonism. He bears no weapons, but he demonstrates no fear, either. As the light fully reveals his face, I recognize the rebel I saw trying to persuade the Aerklings to overthrow their old leader on the night Char and I escaped from the Winglish. His manner suggests he is the leader of this band, and it is to him we will need to speak.

"Close enough," Harrow says as the Aerkling comes to within a dozen feet. "What is it you want?"

The Aerkling halts obediently. "To talk."

It is not what he says that gives me pause. It is how he says it. It is what he might be thinking, and of that I cannot be certain.

"And merely talking requires so many of you?" Harrow asks, the iron in his voice unmistakable.

A shrug. "These are dangerous times. It is best to be careful."

Harrow nods. "I am called Harrow." He waits for me to speak, but I say nothing. I am taking the speaker's measure, my eyes fixed on his. There is something extremely troubling about him — a darkness born from his very presence, one that almost seems more like a memory. Yet I do not know this creature. Harrow speaks for me. "This is Auris." He gestures toward me and then further. "And these are our sisters Ramey and Char."

"I recognize Char," the Aerkling says. "And Auris." His eyes shift to meet mine, holding my gaze fast for long moments. "So many years since I've seen you last. Look at how you've grown. A young woman of capable means. It is a joy to find you so well." He gives me a small bow. "As it happens, it is to you that I wish to speak."

I have no memory of ever meeting this Aerkling face-to-face — no recollection of ever seeing him before that night at the Winglish. How can he speak of me as if I should? But his eyes and voice have a strange effect on me — a deep calming sensation, one that reassures me all is well. His voice is astonishingly beautiful, and I wonder why I ever thought I was in danger. My hand loosens around my *inish* staff.

"My name is Tonklot," he says — the same name I recall Orphren saying in referring to the Aerkling who was threatening her grandfather. "I am not sure you ever knew that, Auris. Currently, I am the newly chosen leader of the Aerkling people."

131

"What of the old leader?" I ask, then finding myself wondering why it matters.

He smiles, his strange eyes making me feel so warm and welcome. "He is gone from this life. His time has passed, and a new age begins. Much will change for all of us who live atop the cliffs and fly the skies above."

"And what has this to do with me?" I ask.

"Much. We knew each other once, long ago. I merely . . . seek to renew that connection."

His gaze shifts to Harrow, and I feel suddenly bereft. "And you are her partner, are you not? You mean so much to her — so strong and assured, so skilled and talented. Harrow, isn't it? We must be good friends, you and me. And you and I, also, Auris."

Something feels off — but then his gaze shifts again and I find myself basking in his regard. I am barely aware of it when he gestures, but I let my *inish* staff fall from my fingers and see Harrow drop his as well.

"Auris," I hear Ramey whisper urgently — a clear indication that she sees something is wrong — but what can she possibly have to fear?

"Ah, little ones," Tonklot whispers, his gaze falling on them. "Do not be frightened. All will be well. No harm will come to you. Children are precious, no matter who they

132

are. Do you not feel safe with me?"

His gaze fixes on each in turn, and I hear murmured sounds of agreement, but I am having trouble concentrating on much of anything but the soothing sound of Tonklot's voice and the warm feeling of his eyes as they meet mine once again. I stand there unable to move, to even think. Did he really say those words or am I imagining it? Does it even matter? I wish only to hear him speak more, to look deeper into his eyes. I wish only to be made captive to his wonderful presence, to this sense of peace and comfort that he offers, to the sanctuary I now realize he can provide.

"Lay down, Harrow, Ramey, Char," Tonklot says, addressing each of them in turn, making a sweeping gesture to indicate the ground. "On your back, please, arms and legs extended, eyes closed. Your heart will be warmed and you will be assured of my good intentions. Do this now."

Harrow and the girls do, lowering themselves, stretching out as bidden, their faces calm and their features settled. It is then — only then — that I sense something is wrong, and I take a step forward to intervene. But Tonklot turns to me instantly, fixing me with those marvelous eyes and humming softly in a way that makes me understand that no danger can come from this.

He speaks then to his companions. "Help me keep Harrow and the children where they are while I do my work. Hold them fast. And Auris as well."

Even though I hear the words clearly, I know what he is saying. *Help keep her safe, my friends. And Harrow and the children, too. Let them all feel the light shining through them and the feeling of peace and comfort enveloping them. Do not let them feel abandoned.*

I smile as I feel the Aerklings close about me and gently tighten their hands about my arms and body so that I cannot move, and know that others do the same to Harrow, Ramey, and Char. I should be aware that this is wrong; I should be terrified by what is happening. But I feel only a deep sense of calm and well-being. And so we are all willingly made prisoners.

Tonklot walks right up to me and touches my face. "I was so surprised to see you in the Aerkling village, so shocked to discover you were even alive. I would have spoken to you then, but the Aerklings would not have allowed it. And then you were gone again. But I have found you, haven't I? So why don't we see how much you have changed, eh? For you have changed, haven't you? You are not as you were before. Do you remember that time?"

His strange eyes study me as he says this, and I can feel him — or some part of him — working to get inside me. Into my mind and my thoughts. I feel him there, probing for something, and oddly it is a familiar feeling. I know I have experienced something like this before . . . but how?

Still, his touch is persuasive, so I want to let him in, to let him discover what he seeks, because how could it be wrong?

There is a gentle tugging sensation within me, as if he seeks to pull something free — something that will not yield to him. He frowns, and his taloned hands press into me. Now I can feel an intrusion that extends much deeper — as if his efforts have penetrated skin and bone and blood and found the very essence of me — to places not even Harrow has been.

My body reacts instinctively and violently to this violation, even though I feel no stress or danger. What I do feel is an unmistakable refusal to yield, so powerful it jolts through me and into him with such force that he winces and abruptly withdraws.

I expect to see disappointment on his face, but instead it looks almost like anger. "Hssssssst! The *inish* that protects you is still

135

strong — too strong. I thought it might be less of a barrier by now. I thought my own abilities substantially improved, more than capable of overpowering your own. Damn you, girl!" He pauses for a moment, as if considering; then a crafty expression crosses his face. "But perhaps a different approach is required. A locked door simply requires the proper key." He gestures to his Aerkling companions. "Hold her fast, my brethren. Take hold of the children, too."

He backs away from me as the Aerklings close about, and for the first time I feel different emotions emanating from beneath his calm expression.

Frustration. Rage.

Tonklot turns abruptly to where Harrow lies on the ground. "Hold the man down for me. He will become the bargaining tool I need."

And with his gaze turned away from me, the fear floods back, the sharp sense of danger. I use every ounce of strength I possess in an attempt to break free of those who hold me, but my hands and arms are held firm, and a hand clamps over my mouth.

Tonklot kneels atop Harrow, bending close, his strange features transforming. His beaked mouth dissolves and reshapes into a wide circle as it fastens over and tightens down atop Harrow's mouth and nose. In seconds he has begun to inhale, so that it appears he is sucking out Harrow's breath. Harrow just lies there at first, letting it happen. But soon he begins to struggle violently, his body jerking and his legs thrashing. He is trying to resist, but he cannot. He is held fast as Tonklot does his work, and eventually he quits moving entirely and lies still.

But Tonklot continues his strange behavior, and beneath him Harrow seems to diminish.

I fight harder to break free, but to no avail. And so I am rendered completely helpless as my love, my life, my everything, is defiled in front of me. I can't even understand yet what is happening to him; I can only see him thrash and fail and diminish by turns.

Until his ordeal ends and he lies there on the ground with his mouth wide and his eyes fixed and his body so still I know he must be dead.

Tonklot rises and turns to me, his face reforming into its beaked shape, his warm gaze upon me once more. But this time I turn away at once and stare down at my feet. I am crying openly, though still held fast, still helpless. I can hear my sisters crying, too, Char's sobs so heartrending I do not think she will ever stop. I am furious, bereft, devastated — and one thing more. I am ashamed. I let this happen. I allowed myself to be persuaded not to intervene. I gave myself up to this creature that now stands before me.

"You must listen carefully now, Auris," he says to me, and the kindness that was there before is gone, replaced by a grating certainty that makes me cringe. "Once upon a time, long ago, I tried to do to you that which I have done to Harrow. I tried to steal you from yourself and make you mine, just as I have made your partner mine. But you were blessed then as you are now, more deeply protected than he is. I could not do to you what I have done to him. You were able to resist me then as you do now, but he cannot."

He bends close, his face gone harsh and unfeeling, his eyes like iron coals heated with fire.

"Harrow is lost to you. He is mine now, and he will remain mine for as long as I wish it. Should I choose to do so, I could claim your sisters as well. Do you want that to happen? Should I take your sisters, too?"

I shake my head slowly without looking up. A hand is still fastened over my mouth so that I cannot answer, but it doesn't matter. He doesn't require an answer. He already knows what it would be.

"You managed to flee the Winglish with your youngest sister, and there is a price for such behavior. The old man who allowed it has already paid. That very night, we removed his wings and threw him over the cliff edge. But I think you will prove more useful to us alive. So I will spare your sisters. But to earn my mercy, you must do something for me in return."

I nod, desperate to keep Char and Ramey from harm. And Harrow? The truth is a burning in my heart. Harrow is gone.

"You think him lost, don't you?" Tonklot whispers as he bends close to my ear. "But he is not. Not yet. You can have him back again, as he was, if you do as I say. Are you listening? Because I am only going to say it once."

I nod again, filled with fresh desperation. But at the same time, I know he lies. Harrow is dead. He is not coming back to me.

Tonklot bends so close his beaked mouth is right up against my ear. "I want you to bring me a Dragon by the next full moon. It is a new moon now and it is on the rise, so time is short. Bring me a Dragon before your time expires. You may think this impossible, but I know better. You can find a way. Bring a Dragon to me. Do it however you can. Do it, and Harrow will be yours again."

Then a cloth soaked in chemicals covers my nose and mouth, and everything goes black.

NINE

I am woken by a firm shaking of my shoulder and the ragged sound of Ramey's voice in my ear. "Wake up, Auris, for Fate's sake! We need you!"

I blink and my eyes open to the light. I immediately shut them again. I have a splitting headache, and the wailing I am hearing in the background is not helping to ease the pain. For a moment, I wonder where I am and who is so unhappy.

Then I remember Harrow and sit up fast. Blinding pain engulfs me; my head feels like it might explode. I fight it off and squint against the light's unexpected brilliance to find Ramey staring at me from about five inches away, her tearstained face rigid with determination. "Are you okay?" she asks me quickly.

Instantly I am overwhelmed with a tidal wave of suffocating horror. Harrow is dead. Tonklot killed him. *God, no, don't let this be*

141

true! Make it a bad dream. Make it go away!

But it isn't a bad dream, and it won't go away.

Not ever.

I look past Ramey to see Harrow's unmoving form. Char kneels beside him, crying loudly, her hands cradling his head in her lap. The Aerkling leader did something to him — covered Harrow's mouth with his own and sucked the life out of him. I cannot think of any better way to put it. It was terrifying to watch and is now impossible to forget. He ripped Harrow's life away and left behind an empty shell. Harrow is dead, and I did nothing to stop it.

All this flashes in my mind as I struggle to come to grips with it.

Is it even true? Is Harrow really dead?

I scramble up and lurch over, dazed and weak, to collapse beside Char. I reach down to find Harrow's pulse. Nothing. I lean down to hear his heart. Again, nothing. Char has stopped wailing, reduced to hiccupping sobs, and watches me through tears and heartache, a shadow of hope reflected on her young face. I hold myself close to his mouth to find a hint of breath. Still, nothing.

"He can't be dead," I whisper, tears streaming down my cheeks, my heart broken in a million pieces.

Ramey has come over to join me and lowers herself next to me. She puts her arm around me to draw my attention. "He isn't, Auris."

I look over, confused. "What do you mean?"

"Harrow isn't dead. He's catatonic. He has been stripped of the ability to act voluntarily, but he is alive."

Char is watching closely. "She told me the same thing. But she's wrong, isn't she?"

"I'm not wrong," Ramey insists. "His pulse and heartbeat and breathing are slowed to almost nothing, but if you wait a few moments and listen carefully, you can hear his heart and feel his pulse. Go on, Auris. Please. Give it a try."

Though feeling swamped by the hopelessness, I do as she says. I wait patiently but find nothing to confirm what she has told me. Until . . .

Suddenly I feel something. A pulse, so tiny it almost isn't there. A heartbeat, too, faint and momentary.

Ramey is right. Harrow is alive, if only barely. I don't know what has been done to him, but life remains. Tonklot claims to have taken him, and in some sense he has. Harrow, as we know him, is no longer present,

143

and what remains is a shell. But Tonklot has also claimed he can restore him to what he was, so maybe we can as well. I have to cling to what small hope that possibility offers.

I pull myself together. No more tears. No more feeling sorry for myself. Only helping Harrow matters now. We have to get him home and under care.

"Char," I say at once, "go into the woods. Cut some sturdy poles so we can make a stretcher. We will use blankets and cords to finish it and take Harrow home to the healing center."

Char dashes off, a knife and hatchet in hand. I know that she is devastated by what has happened to her brother; giving her something to do will help take her mind off her fear.

I turn to Ramey. "I thought Harrow was gone. I really did. I stood there and watched it happen, and I couldn't make myself do anything to stop it. And when it was over, I was sure he was dead. You were wise not to panic, Ramey, when I was in danger of doing so. I am so proud of you for being so strong."

She blushes — which is rare — shaking her head in denial. "I am not all that strong. I wanted to save him, I watched it happen, too. I couldn't move either. None of us could. There was something about that man's eyes. And his voice. I think we were mesmerized."

"That much is certainly true," I agree, "but I think magic might have been involved as well. I don't know enough about Aerklings to know whether or not that's even possible, but at least some must have those powers, since Tonklot clearly possessed them."

Ramey nods, and I stand. "Let's see what we have that we can use to make a stretcher. If I know Char, she won't be long finding those poles. Harrow is too heavy to carry, so we'll have to drag him back as best we can."

Ramey and I find our packs and pull free waterproof cloaks and some wrapping for our supplies and fishing gear, then tear it all apart and sew it back together again in patchwork fashion to make the hammock. Long before we are finished, Char returns dragging two sturdy poles she has fashioned and joins us in our work. Our efforts to build the stretcher give us something to do to stop thinking about Harrow's condition, but all of us glance over at him regularly. He hangs between life and death. I recall Tonklot's final words and know he needs Harrow to remain alive until the full moon if I am expected to do what he has commanded — never mind that I have no idea how he expects me to find a Dragon for him, or even why he thinks I might be able to do so. I didn't think Dragons even *existed* anymore!

Then there is the odd fact that he seemed to know me from somewhere, had spoken of us meeting before. Could this be another event lost in the void of my pre-prison days with the rest of my memories?

So many mysteries, and none with an easy answer.

When the stretcher is completed — an effort of no more than half an hour — we bring it over to where Harrow lies motionless and lift him into place. He is much heavier than I thought he would be, and even the three of us working together struggle to fit him in place without causing any damage. Once that is done, we take hold of the poles at one end — me on the right, my sisters on the left — and start dragging him back home.

I glance back momentarily at the campsite. We are leaving everything else behind save some food and water, hoping we might come back for it. Will it still be there when we do? Do we even care? What we are taking with us is all that really matters.

The trek seems much longer returning than it was coming. The effort of dragging the stretcher with Harrow tied in place is arduous, and the trail we follow seems much rougher. I know it isn't — that it's the same trail we arrived by — but that doesn't change how it feels. Nor am I sure what we should do once we are home again, save take Harrow to the healing center. But will they be able to do anything for him? Is there anything that *can* be done for someone in his condition?

Halfway back, we stop to rest for a few minutes, as the girls are much more tired than I am. They are young and strong enough for their ages, but nowhere near as fit as I am. Yet I cannot haul Harrow by myself, so I will have to hope they can find a way to continue.

It is late afternoon before the city comes into sight, and by then all three of us are near exhaustion. We stop to rest again, and I battle a wave of despair, lack of hope, and desperation. I must save Harrow, and I really have no idea how to begin, or if it can even be done.

Char, Ramey, and I sit with Harrow, placing ourselves close enough to observe any changes that might come over him while we finish the last of the food and water we brought with us. I stroke my life partner's cheeks and brow, finding them cool and dry, and take some comfort from that. I check again for a heartbeat and pulse and find them both. Harrow doesn't seem to have changed as much as I feared since his catatonia first took effect. Perhaps Tonklot told the truth about his condition, and how he could be restored to life. But how can one restore the life of another once it has been taken?

"How are you going to go about finding a Dragon?" Ramey asks me suddenly.

Yes, how am *I going to do that*?

"*Are* there any Dragons?" I reply. "There were when Mother was younger and commanded the Dragon brigade, but I thought they all perished in the war."

My sister nods. "That was my understanding, too."

I fiddle with the fringe growing off the undersides of my arms. It's longer now than before, and I don't think it is done growing. My skin is a deeper green, too. Olive in tone, but trending toward jade. All of us have different-colored skin — all with a greenish hue, but some are a deeper green, and some shade toward additional colors like mine. I wonder absently how long it will take for my transformation to end. I wonder if I will become fully Sylvan in appearance or always be a kind of hybrid.

"Why would that Aerkling tell you to bring him a Dragon if there wasn't a Dragon to be found?" Ramey says quietly. "What sense would it make to ask you to do something he knows you can't do?"

"Maybe he *thinks* I can do it, even though I can't. Maybe he's wrong about me."

"Or maybe he knows something we don't."

"Then maybe *he* should have gone after the Dragon himself instead of wasting his time on us. Maybe he should have left us alone."

Maybe, maybe, maybe, I think irritably. *Nothing but uncertainty to go on. I know so little.*

I am horrified by what this creature has done. I am furious with him for the pain he has caused us. One day there will come a reckoning, and I will be there to administer it. I wish I knew more about Tonklot — about whatever bizarre Aerkling magic he possesses and why he could do what he did. Why is it that he claims to know me? Why does he say that we have met before? Why does he insist I resisted him in some way, then and now? Perhaps the Seers will know

149

the answer.

But for now we must find a way to get Harrow the help he needs. When we set out once more, our path is circumspect. The healing center lies south of the city proper, so we circle west below the city and encounter no one. We do not cross through any residential districts and pass by only a couple of farms. Our efforts to travel unseen are successful, and we arrive just after nightfall.

We stop at the head of the lane leading up to the maze of conjoined buildings, and my sisters look at me questioningly.

"Let me go ahead to find help," I tell them. "I won't be long."

I know the center well; I have been treated here myself. I leave my sisters at the entrance and run to where new patients are admitted, shouting out for help and arranging for Harrow to be brought into emergency care immediately. All of which happens quickly and efficiently — and, ultimately, fruitlessly.

Callendra, the nurse who examines Harrow, takes me aside almost at once, holding one of my hands in hers. "I don't think we have the help he needs," she tells me.

"What do you mean?" I ask, stunned.

"This is a form of censure — a shutdown

150

of everything but essential functions. Harrow doesn't even know where he is. Whatever makes him Harrow is somewhere else entirely. He is not even aware of us."

"But there has to be something we can do," I say anxiously.

"Perhaps there is. The Seers have treated illness of this sort over the years, so I think they might be your best choice for a solution. If that fails, bring him back. But I think they will be able to help him in a way we cannot."

I give her a quick hug. "I trust you. I will do what you say. But can we get some help? We are all of us worn to the bone from transporting him back here."

Callendra summons aides, who lift Harrow and his stretcher. Then our newly formed caravan sets out for the distant home of the Seers.

I cannot help feeling a surge of hope. The sisters have done so much for me in the past, and they absolutely love Harrow. If there is a solution, they will find it.

We walk for what seems like forever, avoiding the busier streets and byways, keeping mostly to ourselves. Harrow has been wrapped in sheets and blankets so his face is not visible. People glance our way, but because we clearly escort an injured person, most of those we pass move out of the way.

When we finally reach the winding roadway and little path that leads up to the Seers' cottage, the door opens and Benith steps into view, her kind face reflecting both concern and dismay. "Bring Harrow up to us, Auris. My sisters and I have been waiting."

Our helpers carry Harrow inside, and Benith beckons us all into her tiny living room. The bearers lay Harrow on the floor at the room's center, then stand about looking uneasy, waiting to see what they should do next. Benith, always aware of the discomfort of others, summons Maven to bring a tray of biscuits. Once the treats have been handed out, Maven gives all four bearers a silver coin in thanks for their efforts, then shoos them outside again, urging them to keep what they know to themselves. She closes the door behind them as they disappear into the night.

Benith then gathers Char, Ramey, and me close. "You must stay calm and remain quiet. This is important. You must not speak while we examine Harrow. Can you manage this? If not, you should either wait outside or go home and wait there."

She is looking directly at Char, and the

youngest of us straightens. "Will you cause him pain? Will you make him cry out?"

Now Dreena is taking charge. "No pain, but he might cry out when we probe his memory of this event. Still, you must say and do nothing."

Char nods. "I won't. But I want to stay with my brother."

"Then you shall." Dreena shifts her hard gaze to Ramey and me. "All of you as well. Keep your promise."

We move to the couch, watching as the sisters kneel beside Harrow and run their hands over him. They appear to be exploring or maybe trying to sense something. They do not sing or hum, as they did when they probed my memories. There is only the murmur of their voices.

"Catatonic," whispers Benith. "The result of a deliberate, invasive intrusion."

"Extraction," Maven corrects. "He's been emptied out."

"Yes, I feel that, too," Benith agrees. "His memories are gone. All of them."

"We have known this to have happened before," Dreena declares, her hand firmly in place over Harrow's heart. "When was it?"

"Long ago, maybe twenty years or so. A man came to us — a man who called himself . . ."

153

Long pause, a shaking of heads. No one remembers.

"His partner had been emptied out much like this," Maven says. "Her name I remember. Meliore. She was all but dead, we were told. The man asked us to employ our special skill, but we did not know how to treat such a sickness. The way it was described to us suggested it involved some sort of predatory feeding. The woman was already lost."

"We could not help him," Benith continues. "So we sent him to the Dragons, who have been around so long they might have seen the like before."

"I wonder if he ever got his answers," Dreena said.

"We must assume nothing," Maven says tartly. "After coming to us that one time, he never returned."

"But now it seems that whatever did such wickedness is back," Dreena says.

"Poor Harrow," Benith laments.

The sisters then go quiet as they finish their examination. After a while, Benith looks over.

"His conscious mind has closed down, so we must go deeper. Into his subconscious, where some part of a memory of what happened to him today *might* still exist. Stay quiet now. Be patient."

Dreena begins to hum softly, and the other two soon join in — their voices blending, intertwining, in a soothing, searching song that causes silent tears to streak down my cheeks. I see my sisters crying, too. The Seers have laid their hands upon Harrow as they sing, and he is trembling. When he begins to jerk and thrash, Dreena quickly reaches over to hold him down. I feel my composure slipping away, and I am not sure I can stand to watch any more. But little Char's hands close around mine and Ramey's arm comes about my shoulder, and I am kept from breaking.

How long it goes on I will never know. It seems to take forever, but I know it ends faster than I realize. Harrow has begun crying out wordlessly by the end, and I have closed my eyes against the pain that causes. I must stay strong. I want Harrow well again, I want him back, and I must not break the Seers' concentration.

Finally, the Seers sit back and look at one another, then look over at us. I am quite sure they see our tear-streaked faces and know what we are feeling, but they say nothing. Benith rises and, without a word to us, goes off to make tea. Dreena and Maven converse quietly between themselves —

again, ignoring us, though now and again gesturing in our direction.

My sisters and I are not at all sure what's about to happen.

When the tea is made and served and we are all gathered about the couch, it is Maven who speaks first. "First off, Harrow is not dead. He is very much alive."

"But," Dreena interjects quickly, "he won't stay that way if we don't treat the source of the catatonia. As we said, we know this was done once before, long ago, to a young woman named Meliore."

"But you said she died!" I exclaim. "Will Harrow share her fate?"

"Not if we can help it," Benith says firmly.

"Indeed. What has been done to him is horrific and despicable!" Maven's ancient voice quavers with anger. "This is the work of a creature who lacks any semblance of empathy and conscience. He must be stopped before he does this again."

I cannot stay still a moment longer. "What has Tonklot done to Harrow?"

Maven gives me a look I cannot decipher, and then she whispers, "He has stolen Harrow's *inish*. He has taken his soul."

TEN

I stare at Maven. I stare at all three of them — these elderly Seers who must surely be wondering if I have lost my ability to speak. I replay Maven's words in my head as the silence between us lengthens.

He has stolen Harrow's inish.

I understand it in the abstract and had even feared something similar given Harrow's inert emptiness, but how is such a thing even possible?

"Stolen his *inish*?" I say in disbelief.

Maven nods. "All of it. And all his memories, too. He is merely a shadow of who he once was."

"But stolen his *soul*?"

"The soul, as you know, is essentially what his *inish* is," Maven confirms.

"But *inish* can come back," I argue. "If you use too much, you can drain yourself, but it will return. So won't Harrow's return with time?"

157

Benith shakes her head sadly. "Not when this Tonklot has taken it all."

Dreena elaborates. "Think of it like a plant. When you use too much *inish,* it is like cutting a plant back to the roots. It looks to be gone, but the roots are still there, underground, and from that the plant can regrow. But in Harrow's case . . ." She pauses. "They have taken it root and all. So there is nothing for it to grow back from."

"And how long can a body survive without its *inish?*" I ask, almost savagely.

It is Maven who answers. "As we've said, we have only ever seen the one case. But in that instance . . . a little over two weeks."

Her words gut me — worse so, because they fall so close to Tonklot's deadline. "All right. But . . . How can you steal someone's *inish*? Wouldn't that kill them? Wouldn't Harrow be dead instead of catatonic?"

"It is not so simple," Dreena answers, her voice surprisingly soft and almost comforting. "Almost no one can do what this Tonklot did. As we said, we have not seen even the like of it in twenty years. What he did to Harrow is an anomaly."

I don't care what she wants to call it. I only care that we can find a way to reverse it.

"Can we get his *inish* back?" I demand.

158

"Tonklot told me it could be restored, so what has he done with it? Where does he keep it?"

"We don't know, Auris. So perhaps you should tell us everything that happened, everything you remember," Maven says. "Then your sisters will do the same so we can compare notes."

So I begin recounting everything I remember, ending with Tonklot's final demand that I bring him a Dragon by the next full moon if I want Harrow back, and after I am finished Ramey and Char add their own memories. When we have finished, we wait a moment on the Seers, but they sit there in silence, until finally Benith says, "Well, whatever this Tonklot is, he is no Aerkling. We know the Aerklings, and none of them have this sort of power, or can change their faces in the way you described. What does that say to you, sisters?" she asks.

"That he has some sort of shapeshifting abilities," Maven responds.

"Like a Changeling?" I ask, startled. I have no desire to be anything like this Tonklot creature.

"In a way. But a shapeshifter can only shift their outward shape; it is a physical transformation. Whereas a Changeling can, if powerful enough, alter their very nature, becom-

159

ing another thing in both form and function."

I am not sure I completely understand the distinction, but it does not matter. Harrow does. Though again I am reminded of Tonklot's odd claim that we have met before, and again I wonder how that can be so. Still, he was very emphatic about it.

"Is there anything you can do to help heal Harrow?" I ask finally. "I'd rather deal with you than with Tonklot."

Dreena shakes her head sadly. "Nothing, at present. This is powerful magic at work."

"But one thing is certain," Benith interrupts hurriedly. "You must not take Tonklot's bargain. We may not know exactly why he wants this Dragon, but given that he possesses both shapeshifting and hypnotic abilities, his is a powerful magic. A Dragon in such hands could be deadly." Her admonition is forceful, even adamant.

"Even if giving Tonklot a Dragon is the only way to save Harrow?" I counter, fighting back tears.

"Oh, my poor girl," Dreena says. "But yes, even if."

Even knowing Tonklot as little as I do, I get the point. But if providing Tonklot with a Dragon restores Harrow to himself, isn't it worth the risk? Only, I suspect I know the answer to that as well — that the fate of one person is negligible against the fate of the entire world, should a creature as ruthless as Tonklot possess a magic that strong.

"Are there even Dragons out there?" I ask.

"Oh, there are Dragons, all right," Dreena growls.

"But few know of them," Benith adds hurriedly.

"If this Tonklot asked you to bring him a Dragon," Maven interrupts, "he must have some reason to want one, in addition to knowing they still exist. Did he explain that reason to you?"

"He explained nothing. He just told me I had until the next full moon to get him what he wanted. But I thought all the Dragons were killed in the Ghoul Wars."

"Killed?" Dreena says impatiently. "Some, yes. But not all. Some fled the battlefield for the lands north and have not been seen since."

"But you said you sent Meliore's husband to the Dragons, when he sought information on the creature that did this to his wife."

"That was before the wars, child, when Dragons lived among us," Maven says.

"But shouldn't I then talk to the Dragons, too?" I persist.

161

"And face the temptation of giving this Tonklot a Dragon to save Harrow?" Maven asks wisely.

"We will think on it," Benith announces, almost as if to cut off any further talk of Dragons. "We will keep Harrow with us and tend to him here. And we will continue to seek ways to heal the damage this hateful creature has caused. For now, you must go home and rest. It has been a long, hard day, and you have all suffered a terrible ordeal. Sleep tonight and come back to see us in the morning. Maybe we will have more answers then."

I turn to look through the windows and find to my surprise that it is pitch-black outside; the night has fallen hard about our city. I was so caught up in Harrow's plight that I had not realized the time, and I am suddenly very tired.

We are being dismissed, but I do not want to go. I do not want to leave Harrow. I cannot bear the idea that we can do nothing more for him. But it is clear also that the Seers want time to consider what has happened, and my sisters and I all need to take time to come to terms with our anger and grief. So I stand, too.

"Thank you for doing as much as you have," I tell them. "We will go now and return tomorrow to see if anything has changed."

With that, my sisters and I depart, walking through the nighttime down the lane leading from the cottage to the roadway and back toward the lights of the city. Viridian Deep is silent about us, wrapped in a vast, sprawling blanket of darkness with only a scattering of lights penetrating its fabric.

"They didn't do much," Char says finally, sounding both cross and disappointed. "Harrow's still gone."

"For now," Ramey points out sensibly. "After all, we just brought him to the Seers."

But Char won't be placated. "There must have been something more they could have done for him, but all they did was talk about Tonklot and Dragons. Maybe we need to speak to someone else. Maybe there's another solution. He's our brother, Ramey, and we can't just leave him . . . like . . ."

She breaks down in tears again, and Ramey and I close about her protectively and cradle her between us. "There, there, brave little sparrow," Ramey coos. "We will find a way to fix this."

"We will?" she hiccups.

"Yes. This isn't finished," I declare, giving her a squeeze. "We won't stop looking until we've found a way to get Harrow back again. I promise you that much. We won't ever give up."

But I am devastated by what has happened. I feel hollowed out, cored like a bit of ripe fruit and tossed aside to rot. Without Harrow, I do not think I can go on. I remember when he found me, near death in the wastelands — a recently escaped prisoner of the Goblins, a Human that he knew his mother would detest. Yet he took the risk and saved my life. He made every good thing that has happened since come to pass. The foundation of my future is that we will always be together. And now this . . . horror threatens it all, and I am at a loss for what to do next.

Ramey decides, suggesting we should find Ronden at the healing center and tell her what happened. So we do, even as late as it is, and find her awake. There is no easy way to break the news, so we simply tell her, watching her happiness dissolve as she is reduced to tears. Our own grief surfaces anew to join with hers, and we share it all over again in a mix both necessary and cathartic if we are to find a way through to a much-needed healing.

It doesn't arrive on this night, but a beginning is made. Ronden is being kept another two days, so she will rely on us to bring her further word. Ramey suggests we may know more on the morrow after we return to speak again to the Seers. Until then we should go home and try to sleep. Bidding Ronden good night with hugs and kisses, Ramey and Char and I depart for our homes, all of us grieving and all of us hoping that tomorrow will bring some form of relief.

We reach Ancrow's house, and I find that I cannot go back to my now empty house — not yet, feeling as I do. Nor can I abandon my sisters to the emptiness of their own home when both of their older siblings are gone. We need each other this night, so I suggest that I stay with them.

Char manages a smile. "You can sleep with me, Auris." Then she glances at Ramey. "That is . . . if Ramey doesn't mind."

Ramey shakes her head. "I can sleep fine by myself. You can have Auris. But she should know that you snore."

Char glowers. "I don't snore!" A pause. "I breathe loudly."

We go inside together, arms about each other, wash up, put on nightclothes (I borrow something that belongs to Ronden), and climb into bed. I am sure I will not sleep a wink as Char cuddles up close to me, but I am asleep before I know it. I remember Char telling me for what must be the hundredth time that she is so grateful I am her sister, that she loves me so much, and that she knows I will find a way to help Harrow because I love him, too — even if not quite as much as she does.

Then she goes to sleep, and I am quick to follow.

If Char snores, I do not notice.

I wake the following day to find Char already out of bed. I smell breakfast cooking and almost smile to myself. Self-sufficient, capable young girls, those two — though a quick glance at the sky outside the window shows a sun closer to noon than morning, so perhaps it is more lunch that they are cooking. I rise, stretch, and almost instantly a fresh gloom descends to crush my momentary good cheer. Harrow is gone, and — despite the Seers' assurances that they will search for a cure — I know that I need to do something as well. And my best way forward is to at least speak to the Dragons, see if they know more of what sort of creature Tonklot is, or why he seems to have encountered me before. I can decide what to do about Tonklot's demand for a Dragon later.

I need to see Harrow once more before I

166

leave, and maybe I can convince the Seers of my own need to speak to the Dragons. I will go to their cottage as soon as I can. I pull on my clothes — thinking I have to go home for fresh ones — then go down to breakfast. The atmosphere is tense and oppressive with grief, so as soon as I can I change clothes at my cottage and flee for the Seers.

"You look a bit flushed, young lady," Benith observes as she ushers me inside to join Maven, who emerges from the kitchen a moment later bearing a tray with tea service. "Would you like a cup to calm you?"

I wouldn't, but I accept anyway because it is an offer of hospitality and it would be rude to refuse. Sitting with the other two while Benith pours the tea, I blurt, "Like Meliore's husband, I believe I need to talk to the Dragons, to learn more of what this Tonklot is. You said last night that they are not all dead, so can we use the Scrye to find them? Couldn't you track them the way you do everything else?"

"We cannot track Dragons," Dreena snaps, almost as if I ought to know better. "Dragon magic is much more powerful than our own. If they do not wish to be found, even we cannot find them. But . . . Tonklot must have some reason to know they are still out there, if he asked you to fetch one."

"I wish I knew what he wanted the Dragon for," I reply. "What in the world does anyone do with a Dragon, even if it does show up on your doorstep?"

"I can't imagine he wants it for anything beneficial to either the world or the Dragon," Dreena declares, her face hard.

Benith rises to pour more tea into everyone's cup, and as she does she says, "Dreena is right. Even if we could do what Tonklot asked and somehow managed to restore Harrow's soul in doing so, we would likely be faced with another problem. A Dragon in the hands of a creature such as that would be . . . a problem."

"He's not going to get a Dragon," Dreena emphasizes, looking directly at me. "We've warned you of this. We have an obligation to the world to see that this never happens."

"I think we can be sure this Tonklot doesn't want the Dragon simply to ride," Maven elaborates. "He wants it for something much darker, and I think he will do whatever it takes to get it, no matter who gets hurt."

"But what harm would it be just to talk to a Dragon?" I argue. "It was what you told Meliore's husband to do, when he was in my position. So why is this not a thing I should do as well? What if the Dragons have a solution we have not thought of?" Even though I think we all know this is about more than just talk. It is hard to justify giving Tonklot what he wants, even to save Harrow. But I also know it is the only avenue I see open, and I can't pretend to ignore it.

"Mother rode a Dragon in the Ghoul Wars," I continue. "Are any of her fellow riders still alive? Would they know how to find the Dragons?"

"Just for talking?" Benith says severely.

Maven, tucked away between the other two, whispers, "There is always Riva Tisk."

And when both of her sisters instantly bridle up in protest, I know I have found what I am looking for.

ELEVEN

Minutes later I am sitting at Harrow's bedside, bending to look at him as I hold his hands in mine. He has been placed in a spare bedroom on the second floor of the sisters' cottage, layered in shadows behind curtained windows. Safe, they inform me, as if somehow his isolation protects him from the damage that he has suffered and the catatonic state into which he has been placed. I am alone with him, as I have asked to be. I search for any sign of life — any indication of even the smallest response to my touch — but I find nothing. He is there physically, but his mind and soul are missing. He is little more than the shell of the man I remember — the life partner whom I love more than anything in the world.

I want to cry, but no tears will come.

There may be a way to bring Harrow back that is not dependent on Tonklot's bargain, but none of us know what it is. Yet. And while I sense that I may have taken the first step in finding that way, I sense, too, that the journey required of me will be long and dangerous. I am likely to be gone from Harrow's side for days — and perhaps more — while I seek the answers I know are out there.

But time is precious, and I can feel it slipping away. I only have until the next full moon to find an answer to the problem.

So for these few moments, I sit with him and will him to be healed, letting him know I am there to offer comfort should he reveal even the smallest sign that the person he was is still there. My anger and dismay are ever present, but I know I cannot let them rule my life. I must separate myself from my darker emotions and focus my efforts on ensuring that I will not lose him forever. Tonklot does not seem likely to respond well if I fail to do what he wants in the time he has allotted me. He does not appear to be someone who cares about my affection for Harrow beyond knowing it will motivate me to do what he has demanded of me.

I cannot falter. I cannot turn back. I cannot fail.

Riva Tisk is the way forward.

I have heard of this woman before, from both Harrow and my sisters. She is another former Dragon rider like Ancrow — a member of a brigade that was instrumental in turning the tide of the Ghoul Wars. She might know a way to find the vanished Dragons — if she will agree to talk to me. At one time, she and my mother were the firmest of friends, but something went wrong and the relationship soured. No one seems to know the specifics of what caused this — though it happened sometime during the years of the Ghoul Wars, before Ancrow was taken prisoner by the Humans and returned from her captivity. I wonder if the two events are in some way connected.

But whether they are or not, it is all I have to work with and the first real chance I have to make something happen.

I am not at all certain how. I cannot give Tonklot a Dragon, even if I find one; the sisters have made this clear to me. So even if I could track the Dragons down and survive the encounter, I must not deliver one to Tonklot. I understand this. But I also realize that I may have no choice in the matter if I want to help Harrow. My dearest love, who will die should I fail.

I know precisely what is at stake. If Harrow's life should end, stolen away when his last few working bodily functions cease — as happened to Meliore — it would devastate his sisters. They can survive a lot, and have done so — Ronden, Ramey, and Char, those brave siblings who have already lost their mother and have not yet come to terms entirely with what that means. To lose their brother would be too much for them.

And it would certainly be too much for me, who will lose everything my sisters do and so much more.

"Harrow." I whisper his name, bending close again. "Do you hear me?"

No response.

"Can you squeeze my hand or blink your eyes or do anything to let me know you are in there?"

Nothing.

The knot in my chest that surfaced the moment I entered his room swells. Have I already lost him? Has he gone so far from me that there is no coming back? I cannot trust anything Tonklot told me. I can tell he would as soon lie as breathe if he thought it would benefit him to do so. There is no pity or sense of honor in that creature's heart.

I have been given approximately two weeks to solve this impossible dilemma. A day and a half are gone already, and I have done nothing worth mentioning, aside from bearing Harrow to a place of safety. But his recovery remains a mystery to all of us who love him. If even the Seers have no immediate solution, then my only hope does seem to lie with the Dragons — be it for information or . . . something else.

I place a hand on Harrow's brow and find it cool. No, not simply cool: cold. He is so cold. I can still find the throbbing of a pulse and feel a whisper of his breath on my face. I can still detect a faint heartbeat. And yet he is so like a corpse I am terrified.

I climb into bed with him, wrap my arms about his still form, and hold him close. I can feel the cold all through his unresponsive body. I pull him more tightly against me, willing my own warmth to infuse him, closing my eyes and pretending we are together in the way we once were. I will not let him go. I will not let him die. I will not allow it!

I whisper to him, almost soundlessly.

Come back to me, Harrow. Please.

My eyes blink open. Silence.

I look at Harrow's face to see if there is any sign of a response, but his expression remains fixed. I bury my face in the bedding that covers his still form, and I weep once more. I cry for a long time, sobs racking my body, but I do so quietly. If he can detect my presence, I do not want him to find me like this. I need for him to be strong, to stay untroubled as he sleeps. I will not add to his burden by allowing him to think I am faltering. I will not give him cause to worry about me.

With a final kiss on his lips, I slide from the bed and leave him. I go downstairs to the sisters and make my goodbyes. I hug each one in turn and thank them for doing what they have for Harrow. I tell them how much I love them and promise I will come back soon. I am lying when I speak these last words. I do not think I will be coming back for many days — or for at least whatever time I am allotted by Tonklot to produce a Dragon.

So I must leave my loved ones and my home and Viridian Deep behind. And I must do one thing more that tears at my heart: I must abandon my dearest love to fate and chance.

I have no choice. For now, we follow two separate paths. His will be one of rest and healing while mine will be one of discovery and action. He will remain here while I go in search of Riva Tisk.

As I return to the city, at first I think to go to Ronden and ask her what she knows, if anything, of her mother's falling-out with Riva Tisk. But I decide it is better to leave now than risk endangering another member of my family. Riva, as Ronden once told me, lives on the eastern edge of Viridian Deep, so reaching her will require an extensive hike. Time is seeping away, and I have done so little. This is my first real chance to change that. This is my opportunity to find a way to help Harrow.

So I return to the cottage I share with Harrow, stuff my gear in a backpack, strap on my fighting weapons, pick up my *inish* staff, and start for the door. But when I open it, there stands Ronden, as fully equipped and ready to leave as I am.

I stare in shock and disbelief.

She gives me a look. "I persuaded them to release me this morning. It took some doing, but here I am. Are you planning a trip without me?"

I don't know what to say. If I deny it, I have lied to my sister. If I confess, I have admitted my selfishness. But in the end, there is only one option. I can make all the excuses I want, but I owe it to Ronden to explain myself.

She steps closer before I can speak. "Let me guess. You think you have found a way to help my brother, and you have decided it is better not to risk any but yourself in the endeavor. Do I have that right?"

Chastened, I nod.

"How will you do this?"

"First, I need to talk to the Dragons."

She smiles, faintly. "Let me guess. You are going after Riva Tisk. You think she might have some idea of where the Dragons have gone."

She is too smart for her own good, is Ronden. I nod again, completely deflated.

She sighs and steps through the door, seizing my arm in an iron grip and dragging me over to the couch, where she forces me to sit. Still holding me in place, she lowers herself onto the space directly across from me. She is not gentle about any of this, but I do not resist because I know I deserve her censure.

She takes my hands in hers. "I love you, Auris — as a friend and as a sister — but I expect better of you than this. You should not be sneaking off on your own, as if my company does not matter. Do you think I love Harrow any less than you do? Do you think I would also not do anything I could to save him? And how many times during our training have I explained to you about the strength in numbers? You need my help . . . unless you intended this to be a suicide mission?"

"No! I . . . I'm not trying to be a martyr,

Ronden. And I was wrong not to tell you before leaving. I was still considering it when I went to the door. That's the truth. But I also could not bear it if I lost you — or Char or Ramey — along with Harrow. I was just trying to protect you."

"I would like to think that is so, but I'm not sure." She shakes her head, causing the tiny leaves in her emerald hair to shimmer. "I guessed your plan. I knew you would not be able to move away from the lure of a Dragon, so I sent Char and Ramey off and lay in wait."

"Ronden, I am so sorry," I say. "And it is not just about giving Tonklot a Dragon. The Seers do not know what sort of a creature Tonklot was, only that he is no Aerkling. But they thought the Dragons might have information."

"Understood — and apologies are not required," she replies, squeezing my arm. "You acted as I might once have — out of fear and anger, out of concern for one you desperately love, out of a misguided sense of a need for haste, and out of a worry that time is slipping away. But we have the time we need, and we should have a plan."

I shake my head. "We have only two weeks until Tonklot makes good on his threat, and I fear that I am woefully inadequate to the task. I am right on the edge of a cliff and very much in danger of falling off. I am holding myself together as best I can, but I'm not sure that is enough to see me through."

She squeezes my hands tightly. "You should have more faith in yourself, Auris. You are the girl who came here unwanted by everyone but Harrow and your sisters, and still overcame every obstacle you faced to make a home and a life with us. You stood with Ancrow against your father and his Human army and stopped them from destroying us. You are brave beyond words. Remember that."

She leans closer. "You have set yourself one difficult task after another, but since when have you not been equal to such challenges? What you need to remember is that it is not necessary that you accomplish them alone. There are those of us who want to help you."

She pauses. "That includes me, especially. Me. Your sister — your *older* sister — whom you know you can depend upon. Whom you *must* depend upon. As I said, I love Harrow every bit as much as you do. And I won't let you do this alone."

We consider each other for several long moments, our eyes locked, and then she smiles. "So here I am. What do you intend to do about it?"

We are still holding hands, she and I. Sisters, friends, and family — bound by blood, events, memories, and a deep affection. We have stood by each other through so much, and that demands loyalty and trust.

I squeeze her hands gently. "I intend to invite you to come with me. Will you?"

She leans forward and kisses me on the cheek. "I thought you would never ask."

TWELVE

We set out for the northeastern borders of Viridian Deep immediately. It is already approaching midafternoon, and even if nothing goes wrong, it will be getting onto sunset by the time we reach our destination. We could have easily waited for morning — and perhaps we should have, given the distance we have to travel and the uncertain welcome awaiting us on our arrival. But neither of us has any desire for delay. Delay is an extravagance we cannot afford. We look at each other as we leave my cottage and know at once that we are going. When I ask Ronden about the girls, she tells me she has already informed them we might both be gone for a few days and that both girls insisted they would be fine alone; they are sufficiently grown up that they can look after themselves.

I have no doubt they can. So I don't

hesitate to nod a quick response, and we are off.

The day began with bright sunshine and a blue sky, but now clouds have begun to gather in the west, and the temperature has dropped. The smell of rain is in the air, and my instincts tell me we are in for a storm later tonight. Both Ronden and I have packed rain-slicks and warm sweaters, so we are not unprepared for whatever the day chooses to bring. Also, should it prove necessary to continue on to a different destination than home at the end of our visit, we are ready to do so. Harrow's life is at stake, and we will do whatever it takes to save it.

We climb down from the tree lanes to ground level and head east. Ronden knows the way; she set out on this same journey once with her mother when she was still quite young. It was a quixotic visit — one Ancrow intended to complete, but then changed her mind near their destination and took Ronden home instead. But Ronden, being Ronden, did not forget the way. So now that a proper visit is required, I am quick to defer to my sister and let her take the lead.

We walk quickly, Ronden setting a steady pace, taking advantage of both the continued lack of rain and our shared sense of urgency. We greet those we recognize or who know us, but we do not linger. It takes us under an hour to reach the outskirts of the city and begin the trek through the forests and hill country beyond. The air is fresh and our journey pleasant, and I feel a renewed hope that our efforts will find help for Harrow.

Perhaps I will not find a Dragon — it does seem unlikely — but I might find something even better.

Something that will restore Harrow to who and what he was.

We do not talk at first, but simply settle for a quick march toward our destination. Riva Tisk lives in the deep forests of Cressidon. Ancient and untouched for centuries, it is a haven for all sorts of strange and exotic creatures, Ronden tells me. She does not describe or name more than a few, but she makes it a point to include Riva Tisk in their number. No one she knows — or has ever known — is more feral than Riva. She met Riva once, years ago, when she was still a little girl — before the Ghoul Wars, when Riva and Ancrow were still friends. Riva came to their house a few times and made a big impression on my sister. She was a huge, strong woman whose presence dominated every room she entered. Ronden remembers feeling cowed by her — but even then, as young as she was, she was her mother's daughter and had been taught never to show weakness. So she stood her ground in the presence of this giant female and spoke in a confident voice, and Riva had been impressed. She had told Ronden that she would do well to remember that, even if she was only a little girl, she should never be afraid to speak up when she had something to say.

I nod in understanding. "The Ghoul Wars were coming at that point in time, weren't they?"

"They were. After they ended, I did not see Riva Tisk again. She never came back to visit. I wondered what had happened to her and I asked my mother if she had been killed. Ancrow snorted and said something about how such a woman could never be killed, but also said she was as good as dead anyway and left it at that — in spite of my questions about what she meant both then and later. Whatever happened between them, it soured their friendship. I am sure of that much. And I am pretty certain nothing happened afterward to change this. But maybe we will find out for ourselves."

Maybe we will, I think. But maybe it's all

old news and forgotten history by now. Twenty-plus years is a long time to hold a grudge, whatever its nature.

We are still at least five miles from our destination when the storm overtakes us. The dimming light warns us what is coming, and we pick up the pace. But as the wind slams into our backs and the downpour increases, we recognize the futility in continuing.

We find a thick grove of conifers that provide us with some shelter under their shaggy boughs, and we crawl beneath. Already thunder is rolling across the valley and heavy rain is beginning to fall. The winds whip about with ferocious intent, but the heavy cluster of trees acts as a windbreak as well as a canopy, and so we are spared the worst. We sit with our backs against tree trunks, pressed up against each other for warmth, our sleeping blankets wrapped about us.

"Not exactly how I thought this would go," I confess, half jokingly.

Ronden sighs. "Maybe the storm will blow over. It's early yet."

We begin talking about other things — about our sessions on the practice field and how far Ronden thinks I have progressed, and how far I know I still have to go, and finally about the Seers and how good they have been trying to help us with Harrow. There is a subtle shift in our moods as we speak about him, and that brings up other issues.

"Auris, you must never leave me locked out again the way you did today," Ronden chides me. "Leaving me behind to find Riva on your own? I want your promise you won't do anything like that again. Do you understand why?"

I give her a long look, followed by a slow nod. "Yes. We're family, and we don't shut each other out."

"That's part of it. But it also suggests you don't trust me to make the right decision on my own, so therefore feel you should make it for me. If we are truly to be a family, we need to trust each other to make the right decisions for ourselves."

I reach for her hands and she lets me take them. "I do trust you, Ronden. I admit I lost my perspective because I was terrified about Harrow and felt I needed to act as quickly as possible to help him. Maybe I was wrong . . . All right, I *was* wrong. But I was afraid for you, too. I was thinking of what it would mean to lose you as well."

We stare at each other in the darkness; momentary flashes of lightning reveal the emotions reflected on our faces, letting each of us see something of the other's feelings. Then Ronden leans forward and embraces me.

"I love you, Auris. You are my sister, in every way that matters. We all feel that way — Ramey and Char as well. And as for Harrow, you mean more to him than you realize. Do you know anything about the women he was involved with before he met you?"

I am not sure I want to hear the answer, so I just stare at her.

Ronden smiles. "You don't know anything about them because there *weren't* any. His life revolved solely around our family and his duties as a Watcher, and as the years passed, he came to spend more time outside the city than he did inside. Admittedly, he took on the extra work in part because he loved it so much. Even as a boy, he was always off exploring, studying the forest and the land, learning about the creatures and plants that lived on it, visiting the other cities and villages, extending his knowledge of the world. Patrolling the wastelands never troubled him; he was confident in his skills and his understanding of Goblins and Humans alike. He was fearless."

She pauses, reflecting. "But he was intimidated by Mother. She exerted control over all of us, but especially over him. I could never understand why he didn't fight back, but he was compliant and obedient, and I always thought there was something missing in him because of it. Anyone else would have thrown off that sort of yoke a long time back — anyone as strong as Harrow, at least. But he accepted it, and it stunted him socially. His answer to that was to distance himself further. The more she tried to control him, the more he took off, removing himself from the family in slow degrees — both physically and emotionally.

"Meeting you changed him. It was like he found a part of himself that he had been missing without even knowing it. Before you arrived, I was his closest link to others, but that was mostly because I was his partner in his Watcher patrols. But he was starting to increasingly shut the rest of us out, and that hurt — particularly Char and Ramey, who had always worshipped him.

"And then . . ." She smiles faintly. "You arrived, and he brought you to Viridian Deep even though you looked just like a Human — which he had to know would both cause problems in the wider community and enrage Mother. It was all . . . distinctly out of character — or at least, out of character for the person he was becoming."

I don't know how to respond, and she sees it immediately.

"Don't misunderstand. I am not saying he made the wrong decision. On the contrary. It was just . . . an astonishing choice for him. He changed his life in a situation where he could have easily chosen not to, and it has been a revelation for all of us. He found someone to love — something I don't think he thought would ever happen. Because there is a kind of magic in loving someone, especially that deeply — although Char and Ramey and I love you just as much as he does, of course. We have a new sister, and because of you we have found again the brother that somehow strayed. Because of this and what happened to Mother, we now have a family that is bound by love and trust, and I would hate for anything to change that again."

She stops and waits for my response, but I am so tangled up in my emotions that I can barely speak. "I won't let that happen, I promise," I say as I reach out to embrace her. "And thank you so much for telling me this. Harrow seldom speaks of his past, but he does speak often of his family. I didn't realize how much he was keeping to himself before I arrived."

"I don't think he realizes what he did to us or what exactly happened to change things," she says, hugging me back. "But that's behind us now, and we should leave it there."

I can understand why she feels this way. What purpose would it serve to confront him with something he failed to recognize about himself before? The past is sometimes best left alone.

We sit quietly after that, staring out into the dark as the storm continues to run its course. The sun sets, and the dark skies grow darker still. But eventually the rains taper off, the clouds part, and a scattering of stars brightens the darkness.

With a nod to each other, we crawl out from under our conifer shelter and set out once more, proceeding at a steady pace, the world about us clearly revealed by a sliver of a moon that is growing bigger in the sky by the day. I find myself thinking about Harrow and his past. There was so much I didn't realize, even as close as we have become, even as much as we love each other. How much of my own life have I failed to reveal to him? I am not talking about the things I cannot recall; that is a mystery unique to me. But what of the rest of it, from my days in the prison with Tommy, Malik, JoJo, and Khoury? There may well be things I am keeping from him without even realizing it. When we are told to live in the moment, perhaps it is because that is where we know ourselves best.

Before long, we find ourselves standing on the rim of a deeply forested valley that stretches away in front of us for several miles in three directions. Below is Cressidon, home to the most exotic creatures inhabiting Viridian Deep — and to Riva Tisk as well. A thick layer of mist covers the valley from end to end, winding its way through the treetops and sinking below to the forest floor. There are night sounds emanating from the shadows — calls that echo and resonate to break the otherwise silent depths — and I see movement in the trees.

A single, clear path leads down.

I feel myself hesitate, my instincts suddenly on edge, a sharp feeling of foreboding jolting through me. Ronden does not sense it; I can tell by the way she surveys the path before us so calmly.

"Why would anyone choose to live here?" I mutter to myself.

But Ronden hears. She reaches over to give my arm a squeeze. "Once we meet

Riva, you will understand better. Let's go find her."

I don't want to go down there. I want to turn around and go back home. I want to get as far as possible from this dark, threatening place. But I also want to help Harrow, and the latter impulse wins. I smooth down the emerald fringe that runs along the undersides of my arms nervously, trying to rub away my dread, and then follow Ronden down the winding pathway until we eventually reach the forest floor. All around us birdcalls rise in the night air, some recognizable, most not. As we walk into the vast expanse of woods, the sole pathway twists and turns, and dark shapes pass through the trees to either side of and across our leaf- and needle-strewn landscape. But nothing approaches; everything is content to remain distant and obscure. All these strange blurred shapes probably have names, but neither Ronden nor I can identity or even accurately describe what we are seeing. The heavy mists twist and turn, giving what creatures lurk the look of wraiths or phantasms. We have entered a world where nothing is real save the pervasive sense of unseen risk that tracks us every step of the way.

I think even Ronden feels it now, for we

do not talk — not even in a whisper. Communication seems dangerous.

The things around us are not so constrained after our initial descent, and soon their chilling mewls, guttural grunts, and raspy cries surface — and it almost feels as if we are being tracked. We both carry our *inish* staffs, which should be sufficient protection, but still our uneasiness lingers.

Then something huge lumbers out of the dark to cross the path ahead — a creature that stands on two legs but is hunched so far over that its arms drag across the forest floor. Its crooked back is studded with spikes, and its body ripples with muscle beneath a hide of scales. Ronden and I freeze in our tracks, but the creature barely slows as it continues on its way, either not seeing or perhaps simply ignoring us.

We wait a few ragged heartbeats longer anyway, just to be sure it is not circling about to get behind us, before continuing on our way.

Only minutes later, the trail ends abruptly and we are faced with a wall of trees so dark and deep it looks to be impassable. Within this woodland fortress there are no movements and no sounds. Darkness and silence reign, and once again I feel a compelling urge to turn back.

We hesitate — both of us this time — staring into the shadows, trying to convince ourselves that it is safe to continue.

"I still don't understand why anyone would choose to live here," I say to Ronden as we ponder what lies ahead.

"Not very inviting," Ronden agrees.

"Not even a little." I study the wall of woods that lies ahead. It reminds me of prison.

Ronden clears her throat nervously. "Well, like it or not, that is where we have to go. Into these trees. These woods."

I sigh. Of course it is. "Then we'd better get going."

We push into the heavy undergrowth that clogs the spaces between the massive tree trunks, searching for a path. We find none. There is nothing to show us the way forward and, after a hundred feet of walking, I glance over my shoulder to find our way back has disappeared. It is impossible to know if we are moving in the right direction.

Then I hear the heavy breathing behind me. Something is tracking us. I glance back into a darkness that frames three pairs of gimlet eyes staring directly at me. I take a deep breath and release it slowly. No question about it. These creatures, whatever they might be, are deliberately following us. I nudge Ronden and motion to look behind me. She sees the eyes as well but does not react. I suppose she's used to this from being a Watcher, but I find it incredibly unnerving.

We proceed for several hundred more yards while I sneak repeated glances over my shoulder to monitor our pursuer. Once or twice, with the aid of the moonlight, I get a clearer look and discover that, first, the number of eyes has doubled and, second, their owners appear to be some sort of wolf — huge, rangy beasts padding along at a slow, silent pace, each of them looking as if it might be bigger than the others. After a while I notice they have fanned out far enough to suggest we are no longer being followed but herded.

I must be mistaken, I tell myself. But at the same time I know I am not.

So what are we being herded toward?

The wolves on the edges advance ahead of those in the center, to assume a formation that prevents us from moving anywhere but straight ahead. And so we have been made prisoners as surely as if we were shackled in chains. No harm is threatened, but no guarantee of safety is offered, either. We are to keep moving in the direction these creatures have chosen for us if we want to avoid a confrontation.

My inclination is to fight back — to turn and confront our self-appointed jailers — but I fight down that impulse. Nothing good can come of a reckless response at this point.

It all ends quickly enough. We push ahead — the wolves tracking us but never getting any closer — until we catch sight of a ramshackle building that slowly takes shape through the trees and mist. A worn, patchwork structure, it soon reveals itself to be an aging cottage. A solitary light burns from within, showing through gaps in shutters and cracks in seams. A second light emanates from a lantern hanging from a front-porch rafter. There is no sign of movement from within and no one in evidence without.

Ronden slows, not wanting to come too close without an invitation. She is unsure of how to approach the cottage, and so am I. But we will have to do something. The wolves have closed about us from behind — enough so that they stand only a short dozen feet away. Clearly they are in service to someone — Riva, perhaps? — and they have not herded us here by accident. They are crouched low and look ready to spring, so a wrong move at this point would be a big mistake.

"What should we do now?" I ask before I can think better of it, the words barely a whisper even to myself.

"You could try a greeting," comes a response from the darkness to one side.

My sister and I turn as one to look.

And there stands Riva Tisk.

197

THIRTEEN

It feels strange, but I know her immediately — even without having seen her before. She is the epitome of what I am expecting — and, as Ronden said, an undeniable presence. For one thing, she is huge. And while she should be somewhere close to Ancrow's age, she looks much younger. Part of this is because she is extremely fit. Her bare arms ripple with muscle. Beneath a sleeveless tunic and loose pants, her body radiates power. She is at least a foot taller than Ronden, and taller still than me. She doesn't loom over us like Malik would have, but she is looking down when our eyes meet. There is a sense of command in that gaze, and I can tell immediately that this woman was every bit Ancrow's equal.

Riva steps closer. The heavy fringe of auburn hair that trails from beneath her arms and grows tangled and wild from her head ripples as she moves. "What have we

198

here? Two little girls gone astray? Two waifs in search of shelter, come all the way here by accident? No, I don't think so."

Her voice is deep and husky — a man's voice at its core but softened by the way she rolls certain words. She speaks with authority, but not in a threatening way. Her tone is more like teasing. I marvel, too, at how dark her skin is — an almost onyx green, the sheen of it visible even in the moonlight.

She moves another few steps closer.

"*Pfft.* I know you," she says suddenly, pointing at Ronden. "But from where? How is it you look familiar?"

"It was a long time ago," Ronden answers, standing her ground. "I was maybe five years old."

"Ah! You're Ancrow's whelp. I *do* remember you. My, how you've grown. You could almost be another version of her. One can only hope a better version." She looks at me. "But you? You, I don't know."

"I am Ancrow's daughter, too," I say. "Ronden is my sister."

"Is that so? I hear your mother is dead," she says bluntly, dismissively. "Two years back now?"

"Yes. I was with her when she died."

A long pause ensues, but Riva's eyes never leave mine. "Did she die well? I would

199

expect that much from her, at least."

"She died saving my life and the lives of thousands of others." I pause. "I am aware she was not universally liked. I know she could be difficult, and I do not pretend to wholly understand her even now. But I am able to accept her for what she was — good *and* bad — and to forgive her for whatever harm she might have caused me and others. Finding her led me to a family I never knew existed. That is a part of the reason why I am here today. Ronden and I came here quite deliberately — as you have no doubt guessed."

Ronden steps forward. "If you don't intend to send us packing or feed us to your pet wolves, then maybe you could invite us in so we can explain."

Riva Tisk laughs — a big booming bellow. "Well, now. There are teeth behind those pretty mouths and determination behind those young faces."

She looks past us to the wolves and makes a guttural sound that sends them speeding away, back into the woods. They are gone in seconds. Then she turns her gaze back to us. "Do not mistake what you are seeing. Those wolves are wild; they are not pets. But they respect the strength that I possess. I speak their language and know their ways.

My *inish* allows this. I understand their voices and their ways. I am kindred to them. Dwell on that."

I can barely make myself come to terms with it. Harrow's *inish* allowed him a rough bond with creatures, such as the way he trained the ertl, but to fully speak a creature's language as if it were your own seems a stunning power. Yet I nod my understanding anyway. She studies me a moment, then turns away. "Come inside. If nothing else, perhaps your story will at least entertain me."

We follow her to her porch, climb the rickety steps, and wait as she opens the door and beckons us inside. What we find is such a contradiction that I stop just inside the entry and stare in disbelief. Despite the ragged appearance of both the exterior of the cottage and its occupant, the interior is immaculate. The room is filled with spotless furniture; the stone-and-wood floors are polished and uncluttered. The walls are hung with bright, colorful paintings and fabrics, and a fire burns in a huge old stone fireplace. The kitchen — which is just visible in the background to the left — is so clean and obviously well organized that I am envious.

On one wall at the back of the room hangs

201

a massive needle-point of a Dragon roosting on a cliff ledge, perched amid mountains and pine forests, the sky above dark and threatening. The artwork is so intricate it appears life-like, and I have to look twice to make certain it is only a piece of art and not a window onto the world outside.

Riva Tisk takes note of my expression and smiles. "I suppose you thought that a ragged woman like myself — a homesteader who splits logs and hauls timber and consorts with wolves — might not keep a tidy home."

I blush, nodding. "I should know better. How we appear on the outside is not always a reliable indication of who we are on the inside. I apologize."

She laughs and winks. "*Pfft.* It is a wise young woman who can admit to a mistake. No offense taken — not as yet. After we talk, I'll take your measure again — yours and your sister's both. For now, take a seat. You've obviously trekked here through at least part of that storm; you look more than a little ragged." She shakes her head. "Manners, manners. I'll find us glasses of ale."

She strides into the kitchen as Ronden and I sit next to each other on the couch. We are dirty enough that I worry about leaving a smear of wet earth on the leather covering, and glance at Ronden questioningly. My sister gives me a shrug. We have, after all, the shrug suggests, been invited to sit.

I await a reprimand, but Riva Tisk appears not to notice as she returns and hands us our glasses. Then she hoists hers in our direction and offers us a toast. "May we always remember to keep our friends close and our enemies closer still."

As we drink, I wonder which one she thinks we are.

She drains her glass and then sits in one of the chairs, leaning forward. The niceties are over. "What are you doing here?"

I don't hesitate or mince words. "We need your help. My life partner has been attacked by an unknown creature, who has stolen his *inish* and emptied him of everything he was, leaving him catatonic. The Seers told me that the Dragons might hold some answers as to what this creature is, and how Harrow could be restored."

I don't tell her the rest: that Tonklot asked me to bring him a Dragon in return for Harrow's life. Judging from the tapestry on her wall, she would not think too kindly of that.

Riva stares at me. "I've never heard of stealing one's *inish*. Can such a thing even be done?" But she holds up her hand as I start to open my mouth. "Doesn't matter. I can't help you. I don't involve myself with Dragons anymore. Your mother saw to that."

I realize I am treading on dangerous ground. I know nothing of her history with Ancrow, but it is clear I have to convince her that what brings me to her home has nothing to do with Ancrow, and everything to do with Harrow and me.

"Can I tell you a story?" I ask impulsively.

"I was hoping you would." Her smile is impulsive and instant. "I do like a good story. Is it about Dragons?"

"It is about me."

"Too bad. Well, then, keep it short and to the point."

I grit my teeth. "I spent a large part of my life — at least, much of the part I remember — in a Goblin prison in the Human world. When I managed to escape from that prison, it was Harrow who found me, saved me, and brought me to Viridian Deep. I didn't even know the place existed. All my life had been spent in the Human world. I believed myself Human." I hold up my arms and stroke my fringe. "Time has shown me otherwise, but Harrow somehow knew right from the start. He was the one who believed in me most. I love him more than I love my own life, and I do not exaggerate. I would do anything for him. I have to find a way to help him now, or I am lost."

"This is the reason you came here?" Riva interrupts. She gives me a long, hard look, then abruptly shrugs. "I don't know you. I was only around for Ronden."

"Let me explain. Will you listen?"

"I will listen for as long as I think it is worth my time, young woman. Not a moment more."

I nod. What else can I do?

I launch into the story of my escape from the Goblin prisons, the loss of my companions, and my lifesaving encounter with Harrow. I tell her of coming to Viridian Deep, of Ancrow's mysterious refusal to accept me as anything but Human, and of the complexities of our family. I mention, too, the desire of certain Humans to conquer the Fae, and how all these events culminated in the destruction of the army of Humans my father had brought to invade Viridian Deep. I tell her how my mother died to save us all. I speak of how Harrow and I became life partners and found happiness unlike anything I had ever expected, adding: "I refuse to lose this man I love from standing by and doing nothing. I would sooner die myself."

She sits in silence as I speak, but shows nothing of what she is feeling or thinking.

Her strong face remains expressionless, and I feel her support slipping away.

I continue anyway, providing a brief summary of the past two years — of changing physically into my current appearance, of the recent new attempts by the Goblins to seize me and return me to the Human world, and of my false belief I could stay safe from whatever or whoever is hunting me.

"Yesterday I went fishing with Harrow and my younger sisters. We were attacked once more — this time by Aerklings. The Aerkling leader mesmerized us, then sucked the *inish* out of Harrow — something the Seers say no Aerkling can do. Yet there is no better way to put it. He placed his mouth over Harrow's while holding him fast and inhaled his essence. Then he released me from my bondage and told me that if I wanted Harrow back, I . . ." *There is no point holding back now; if I want her support, I have to tell her the lot.* "I have to procure him a Dragon by the next full moon. I know nothing of Dragons or why he wants one or how he can possibly think I might be able to bring him one — and even if I could, I've been told in no uncertain terms that he should never receive one. But the Seers said the Dragons might also have answers as to who

206

and what this creature is, and if there is another way to restore Harrow, and they gave me your name, so I think that — somehow — you might know a way to help."

"The Seers?" Riva Tisk exclaims. "Are those old biddies still alive? And this soul-sucking creature must have reason to believe you can do what it asks; otherwise, it would have taken your *inish* as well as Harrow's. And the *inish* of your sisters." She pauses, eyes shifting away from me. "Do you not imagine so?"

I pause as I replay the moment of Harrow's fall once again, and a single tear leaks from my right eye. I brush it away quickly. "Riva, I don't know. I have no way to know. But I have to find a way to help Harrow. I don't think for a moment that presenting Tonklot with a Dragon is the answer. But if the Dragons have any knowledge of what might help . . ."

"If any creature did, it would be a Dragon," she confirms. "But . . ."

I sense again that I am losing her. I need to convince her to take me to the Dragons, if she does indeed know where they reside, yet how?

Then I have a sudden idea for how to make this happen. I take a deep breath. "Shouldn't we at least warn them — the

Dragons, I mean — that such a creature seeks to gain possession of one of their number? There may be a danger for them in this as well."

Riva Tisk makes a rude noise. "Well, I can tell you that no one wants a Dragon unless they covet the use of its power. Dragons are huge and unpredictable, and their ability to destroy is immense. It is clear this creature intends to cause trouble for someone — although the part about wanting *you* to bring it the Dragon makes little sense. *No one* can bring *anyone* a Dragon. Dragons do what they want. They will listen to their Fae riders, yes, but only if they are bonded."

She pauses, considering, and I remain silent — expectant, hopeful.

"I don't see how I can help you," she announces at last, rising. "You have to leave."

I stare at her in disbelief, and then I stand as well, indicating I am her equal in this business and not some supplicant. Ronden immediately stands with me. "I can't do that. I have nowhere else to go."

"What is it you expect me to do?"

"Are there still Dragons to be found?"

She gives me a hard look. "Perhaps."

"Can you tell me where?"

"No. I would be sending you to your death if I did so."

"But they do still exist." I make it a statement of fact. I am growing desperate, and I don't try to hide it. "You know where I can find them, don't you?"

She shakes her head reprovingly. "It doesn't matter if I do. They would tear you apart the moment they saw you! You are nothing but food to them — unless you can bond with them. And you cannot!"

I was losing patience by now. "Why not?"

Ronden reaches over and takes my arm, pulling me back from the inadvertently threatening step I have taken toward Riva. "Yes," she says, turning to the other woman. "Why not?"

Riva sighs impatiently. "Because no one can bond with a Dragon if they don't speak their language. I was born with the ability. So was your mother. But this is very rare. Others who seek the bond must learn it — and that study takes months, even years, to master."

"My *inish* enables me to understand any language," I reply. "So there shouldn't be any problem with my bonding, if that is what is required."

But I know as soon as the words leave my mouth that I am wrong. I can see it in Riva's eyes and in her expression. A Dragon bonding requires something more. "What is

209

it?" I ask as I see her hesitate.

"Your *inish* isn't enough. Dragon-speak resists *inish* translation. And the two weeks this Tonklot gave you is not nearly enough to learn what you need. Now go. We're done talking."

Stunned, I turn away and am walking toward the front door when Ronden seizes my arm and pulls me about. She is looking back at Riva as she asks, "What if we choose to take our chances and go to the Dragons anyway? Will you at least aid us? You can't expect us to turn back and give up on Harrow."

Riva stands there, arms crossed over her breasts, her powerful body locked in place. She is an immovable wall, her face like stone, and there is no hesitation in her reply. "No, I will not aid you. I will not be complicit in your deaths. And you will never find the Dragons. Go home. Do what you must to help Harrow but forget about the Dragons."

"At least tell us why you are being so difficult," Ronden presses. "Won't you at least tell us if you know of anything that might help?"

"We're not going to give up trying just because you send us away," I add. "So either way — whether you help us or not — you *will* be complicit in our deaths. Why not give us a chance to survive?"

Riva Tisk hesitates once more as we continue to stand there, then reluctantly motions us back. "Another few minutes — that is all I am going to give you. But it is my turn now to tell you a story. Go back inside and sit down."

We return to the couch. A flicker of new hope flares within me, even though I have no real reason to think that anything will change. Riva studies us for long moments after she joins us. Abruptly she rises, scoops up all three ale glasses, and refills them before returning. Then she sits looking at us in silence for long moments as she sips.

"You are not the only one who has lost someone dear to you," she says at last. "There was a young woman, back when I was teaching those who wished to be Dragon riders how to work with creatures disinclined to obey them. Her name was Favorist — an apt name for someone as young and beautiful as she was. It means as it sounds — 'fairest.' She was this and more. I saw the promise in her immediately."

She sighs as she looks away momentarily. "At the time, I was deeply in love with Ancrow. She, however, had no interest in me; she was wed to Carrowen, who was her one

211

great love. So I threw myself into teaching. Favorist was head and shoulders better than any of the other students, and quickly bonded with and mastered a Dragon.

"By the start of the Ghoul Wars, we were just beginning to ride our Dragons on scouting expeditions, keeping a close watch for Ghoul appearances as evidence of impending attacks on Viridian Deep. We were good at what we did. We kept ourselves well out of reach of Ghoul weapons — off the ground and in the air at all times. Before then, I had ridden in partnership with Ancrow, but now I was paired with Favorist. Her Dragon was newly trained but had never exhibited any evidence of bad behavior or disobedience. The two had bonded almost instantly, so I had no reason to be concerned."

She pauses here, taking a few deep breaths, and I can tell the story is conjuring memories she finds hard to confront. "At one point, Ancrow warned me that she had noticed signs of skittishness in Favorist's Dragon — certain behaviors that suggested it needed further training. But I had noticed nothing, so I did nothing. Or perhaps I was just angry at Ancrow for not returning my affections and so discounted her words.

"But then one day Favorist and I were

scouting near the Skyscrape and we caught sight of a band of Ghouls on the grasslands. We followed them for a bit, then Favorist guided her Dragon down for a closer look. She did not signal to ask for my permission, even though I was senior, but I trusted her to do what was needed on patrol, so she didn't have to ask. She flew close in, obviously seeing something that troubled her. When she got close enough, the Ghouls saw her and turned. One of them — whether deliberately or wholly by accident — reflected a splash of sunlight off a raised weapon or piece of armor directly into her Dragon's eyes. It startled the Dragon and caused her to twist and throw her rider. Favorist screamed all the way down. I told myself later that the fall alone should have killed her, but apparently it did not. She was struggling to rise when the Ghouls fell on her, tore her apart, and ate her while she was still alive. It happened so fast that there was nothing I could do to save her."

There are tears on this strong woman's face, and the pain in her expression makes me wince. I cannot imagine what this must have been like for her, how terrible it must have been to witness. Ronden and I sit unmoving, staring at her in horror.

"And that wasn't even the worst of it,"

she continues softly. "When I returned to tell Ancrow what had happened, she said she was sorry, but this should be a lesson. I should have listened to her, should have insisted on further training. If I was honest with myself, I would accept that Favorist's death was my fault. She said she hoped I had learned my lesson."

I want to reach out to Riva, but she sits too far away from me and her posture feels too defensive. "I knew my mother well enough, even in the few months I spent with her, to know how unfeeling she could be," I say instead. "But I am not sure I see what you . . ."

I stop speaking as she takes a deep breath and exhales sharply. "My story isn't finished. I did as Ancrow asked and accepted the blame she placed on my shoulders. I was given a new student, another young girl, this one named Trusen. She was big and strong like I was, and we took to each other at once. She lacked Favorist's skills but made up for it in work ethic and dedication. We were deeply engaged in the Ghoul Wars by then, and grief was an unwanted distraction. She was given Favorist's Dragon, even though I questioned the assignment. So I threw myself into teaching Trusen how to speak and understand the

Dragon language, and before long they had bonded. We were sleeping together by then, Trusen and I. All the other riders knew it, including Ancrow, but she never said a word to discourage it. She never made a comment or gave any sign of displeasure."

She smiles suddenly, and it catches me completely off guard. "I suppose I simply didn't believe she was capable of doing what she did."

I wait for more, but she only shakes her head dismissively.

"Those were heady days," she continues. "Fighting on Dragon-back all day, making love all night, living in the moment. I was happy for the first time. I should have known it was too good to be true. I should have been more careful or more aware or . . . more something. But I wasn't, and the same thing happened with Trusen as with Favorist. She was in the pens with her Dragon — the same Dragon — when without any warning at all it snatched her off her feet and bit her in half."

Another pause and a few more tears, but there is a hardness reflected on her face now as well. "I wanted to kill that Dragon on the spot, but I couldn't. I was grief-stricken and furious beyond reason, but killing a Dragon was forbidden — not to mention nearly impossible. Still, there was no excuse for what it had done — no reason for such a vicious, inexplicable act. I went to Ancrow and asked her to ban the Dragon from further service, but she said I should have kept better watch over what was happening in the pen. As with Favorist, the fault was mostly mine. I should have recognized the danger and acted sooner. I was so furious I said some things I shouldn't have."

Her laugh is bitter. "Instead of banning the Dragon, she dismissed me from my teaching position and reduced me to patrol work. We were in a war by then, and when you are engaged in a war, you have to put personal feelings aside. I didn't seem able to do that, so she decided she had to adjust my situation. Those were the words she used — *adjust my situation.* I could no longer be an instructor of fledgling Dragon riders. I could no longer serve under her in a fighting capacity. She diminished me in the eyes of the other riders. She embarrassed me. I stayed with her mostly because I was stubborn. I refused to quit. And when the war ended — after Carrowen was dead and she was taken and defiled — I came here to live instead, another monster living in a monstrous paradise, with the wolves my closest friends."

So typical of who my mother had become by the time I found her, I think — expecting exacting perfection from all around her, and woe to those who did not meet her standards. And though this was before Carrowen's death, it was clear those seeds had been in her all along and had only been nurtured and watered with his passing. It was likely what made her a successful commander. But it would be hell on relationships — of any nature. Then I find myself wondering: If Carrowen had not been taken from her early, how long would it have taken for that relationship, too, to sour?

"So now you see why I told you not to go looking for Dragons on your own?" She looks from one of us to the other. "They are extremely dangerous in the best of situations, and this would not be even close to a good one. Now pick up your gear and walk home while the weather still holds. Do not come here again, and do not go looking for Dragons on your own."

There is nothing more to be said. Ronden and I stand once again and thank her for listening to us and for trusting us with her story. I am bitter and disappointed; I understand Riva's reasoning, but I don't agree. I am determined Ronden and I will find the answers we need on our own — no matter what it takes.

My sister and I leave the house and trudge down the porch steps in gloomy silence. We have walked perhaps a dozen yards, neither of us speaking, when Riva Tisk calls out to us. "Asht conlughgh wranj ousten?"

We both turn, Ronden with confusion on her face and me with instant recognition.

"Pangjec stent!" I answer.

We all stand frozen in place for long moments, statues in the deep night. Ronden looks at me questioningly. "What did you say?"

I shake my head in disbelief as Riva Tisk comes down off the porch and walks over to us, her expression one of shock and disbelief. "Denksh ark asht nehet?" she asks.

The words are as familiar to me as my own speech. I know this language — which I assume to be Dragon speech. I have no idea how I know, but I do.

"Preshten," I reply.

Riva Tisk takes hold of my arms and holds me fast. "You understand the words?"

"Is it Dragon speech?" I ask quickly.

She nods. "Fae's magic! You have the gift, the same as your mother. I would not have believed it possible. You understood all of it?"

"I did. Every word."

218

"But you didn't know you could?"

"No. Why did you call to me like that? What made you try?"

She smiles for only the second time that night. "Something told me I should. Test her, it told me. See if maybe there is a chance."

She embraces me, hands gripping my shoulders, shifting her smile to Ronden momentarily and then back to me once more. "Since you can speak Dragon, I must reconsider. You deserve that much. Yes, I know where the Dragons reside. I have been there. I can tell you where to find them."

Suddenly, she shakes her head. "No, wait. That isn't enough. I must do more. You will need my help. I will take you there myself."

FOURTEEN

We go to bed that night elated. Riva Tisk
has a spare bedroom in her ramshackle cottage that we must share, and we are happy
to do so. But there is only one narrow bed,
so I immediately insist that Ronden take it.
She points out that she is the Watcher, not
I, and spends half her life sleeping on the
ground anyway, so it won't be any hardship
for her to spend a night on the floor. Besides, Riva has provided us with a second
set of bedding so she will be perfectly
comfortable. I do not argue the point.
Where Ronden is concerned, reason always
trumps emotion, and I can see her decision
is a firm one.

We lie awake for a long time after we are
wrapped in our blankets, whispering in the
dark about what lies ahead. We are very
lucky to be going on this journey — fortunate that Riva Tisk called to us in Dragon
speech at the last minute, when it seemed

our efforts had failed, and doubly fortunate that I inherited this gift from my mother. It is a mystery to me that I did inherit her ability with the Dragon language when I have no memory of ever hearing it before, but where else could it have come from? I wish I knew more about Ancrow's time as a rider, and I resolve to ask our hostess about it when I get the chance.

I want to learn more about my mother and Riva, too. There are untold stories there, waiting to be discovered, and I suspect they go well beyond what little I have been told so far. But I will have to be careful with how I go about it. There is clear anger and resentment in Riva Tisk over how she was treated by Ancrow, and these are the kinds of strong feelings that can be turned away from my mother and settled on me should I make a misstep. And I do not want to do anything that lessens my chance to save Harrow.

Besides, I am losing time. Already, almost two precious days have elapsed and I still have no solution for how to cure Harrow without risking the safety of the wider world by giving Tonklot his Dragon. I know I am doing the best that I can, but I am plagued by the knowledge that I am not doing it fast enough.

Still, perhaps the Seers are right, and the Dragons will have answers. If they know what Tonklot is, they might know how to reverse what he did. And even if not, and I do fulfill Tonklot's bargain — which the Seers have warned against — how can I reclaim Harrow's *inish* from Tonklot? I don't even understand how he can keep hold of such an insubstantial, ephemeral thing.

Unless, of course, he has been lying from the start, and Harrow's *inish* has already been destroyed just by the act of leaching it from his body. Perhaps Tonklot never intends to return what he offers in trade. It would clearly not be beyond him to attempt such a deception.

And what of his strange claim to know me, to have met me before? Was that a lie as well?

It is all impossible. On the one hand, I live with the harsh reality the Seers have so plainly revealed — that I cannot let this creature get his hands on a Dragon. Yet unless the Dragons themselves have the answer, what hope do I have of ever getting Harrow back to who he was?

When I broach the subject of what Tonklot wants with a Dragon to Ronden — something we have pondered endlessly

222

before — she is as clueless as I am. Trying to assume control over a beast you can barely connect with even when you can speak its language seems incredibly risky. What is to keep it from eating you on the spot? Does he plan to hypnotize it as he did us? What makes him think his mesmerism would work on so powerful a creature? More likely, it will be on him before he can think to stop it.

I suppose, in the end, I am hoping that I will find some answers to these questions just by making the journey. The Seers did seem to think the Dragons might know something — at least in Meliore's case. And confiding to the Dragons the nature of the danger that seeks them might persuade them to lend support.

Eventually, we drift off to sleep, trusting that the future will provide us with the insights and opportunities we require. We leave in the morning on our quest, and we will need rest if we are to be equal to the demands our journey is likely to require of us.

But when I wake, everything changes.

We have washed and dressed, repacked our gear, eaten breakfast, and gathered before the cottage to set out, excited and anticipatory, when Riva steps between Ronden and I. "We part ways here."

For a moment, I am not sure what she is saying. I stare at her as she waits for a response. "What do you mean?" Ronden asks quickly.

The other woman faces her. "I mean *you* are not going with us."

"Of course she is going!" I exclaim in dismay.

Ronden is less forceful, her voice calmer. "When did you decide this, Riva? And why?"

"I thought about how it would work if you both came with me, and it quickly became clear that it *wouldn't* work. In fact, it would be unacceptably dangerous. I told you before that Dragons are unpredictable if you do not have a way to bond with them. Auris and I can use Dragon speech; you cannot. So if they get the chance, they will tear you apart. I am not willing to risk that. And you shouldn't be, either."

"My sister and I . . ." I begin indignantly and am about to enter into a tirade on loyalty and family when Riva abruptly interrupts me.

"Auris, back away from your disappointment and just think about it. These creatures are majestic but mercurial. They are not so easily won over, and if they take a dislike to you, even knowing Dragon speech might not save you. I've watched more than one Dragon turn on a rider or attendant. These were people who spoke the language and had spent time with Dragons, and none of it was enough to save them. All of us were at risk all of the time. It was the price we paid for riding the beasts and using their power. Ronden stays behind."

"If we just keep her between us . . ." I begin.

"No! Either she remains here at my home or she returns to her own, but she is not coming with us." Riva takes a step closer. "I won't let another person in my care die because of a Dragon, Auris. I cannot live with that, and I won't. Either you and I go and Ronden stays, or no one goes. I won't settle for anything else."

She confronts me resolutely, but I stand my ground. I am her equal — and I might even be stronger using *inish*. I hate what she is suggesting, and I refuse to accept it.

But then Ronden says, "She's right, Auris. You two have to go without me. It isn't what we planned, but I doubt anything will go the way we think. I'll return to Viridian Deep and wait for you there. I can help keep an eye on Harrow and look out for the girls. The Seers will help me monitor your progress. Besides, we don't have a choice if you want to help Harrow. We both love him enough to make any sacrifice to save him — even this. Go with Riva. See what you can find out. And be careful."

She kisses my cheeks and hugs me, and I hug her back. I know how she must feel about being left behind, and I admire how she has chosen to deal with it. She is already walking away, back toward our home. I watch her go for long moments, then just before she disappears, I call to her.

"I will find a way! I promise."

Then she is gone into the shadows. I turn to Riva. Disappointment courses through me, but I shove it aside. "I'm ready."

She nods. "If I had a sister, I'd want her to be like Ronden. Let's make a promise. Whatever happens, we will try our very best not to disappoint her. I could not keep your mother safe from the dark things hunting her, but maybe I am being given a second chance — with you."

Maybe, I think. But promises are sometimes no more than good intentions, and good intentions can easily go astray.

We walk through the morning, heading northward. Riva chooses our path and sets a rather fast pace. I follow dutifully, keeping my thoughts to myself, concentrating on not slowing us down. I am used to hiking distances by now, but Riva's long strides eat up the ground much more quickly than my comparatively shorter ones and the effort is wearing on me. I am despondent as I think of Harrow, and I worry anew about time. I know how limited it is. If this journey proves a waste, it will be a crushing disappointment. Or worse. And when I look at things in that light, I immediately begin second-guessing myself.

So when we stop for a rest and some lunch, I decide to see if I can discover a little of what Riva might know that I don't — anything at all that might help me with what's coming.

"How much danger are you and I in once we find the Dragons?" I ask as we sip warm ale and eat cold sandwiches. "I mean, even without having to worry about Ronden, can we adequately protect ourselves with only *inish* and experience?"

"Pfft!" She makes what I am coming to see as a characteristic dismissive sound. "Our *inish* is of limited use against creatures the size of Dragons — and limited further by our lack of experience. Yours because you have none at all, and mine because it has been more than twenty years since I even

saw a Dragon, let alone attempted any form of contact."

"So how do we approach them once we find them? As strong and unafraid, or calm but determined? I just want to be prepared."

"Prepared?" She spits out the word as if it has a bad taste. "You can't begin to prepare yourself for what you will need once you are confronted by one of these beasts! You might as well ask me how to prepare for a nightmare become real."

She is silent a moment, then adds, her voice gone low and confidential, "You never want to appear weak. Dragons see weakness as an indicator of prey. Strong is good. Calm is better. Firm but steady, maybe. Your impact will be measured by the strength of will you present. And quite possibly by what they detect about your *inish.*" She pauses. "How strong *is* your *inish,* Auris?"

I shrug. "I am my mother's daughter, and she respected what she found in me."

"As angry as I was at Ancrow, I still admired her ability to assess strength and weakness. She was always able to manage it successfully. I resent how she treated me, but that doesn't diminish her skills. But back to your *inish.* How well have you learned to employ it? You already have command of Dragon speech, but what else have you used it for?"

"I stood with Ancrow against an invading Human army and used my *inish* to maintain illusions that tricked the army into doing what we wanted. I've also stood against as many as half a dozen Goblins at one time and driven them off. I have faced down Aerklings. Two years ago I broke into a Goblin prison and rescued Harrow, and when I was taken in the process, I used it again to get free."

She stares at me, clearly unimpressed. "Huh. Other than perhaps the illusions, the rest is likely to be of little help. I've already told you: Dragons are both powerful and intelligent, which is a dangerous combination. They like to think themselves rational, but like all apex predators that have nothing to fear, they can be impulsive. They do not always think and behave logically, or even with forethought — and what makes them so dangerous *is* their unpredictability. You need to be able to anticipate what they might do and then prepare for all possibilities."

She pauses, and there is an unexpected change in her expression. "Ancrow was once a Watcher. Her instincts were legendary — the best I've ever seen. There was nothing that woman couldn't do. She was so different then, at the start of the Ghoul Wars — such a reassuring presence. All that changed, of course, with Carrowen's death — or so I have heard."

Then she shakes her head, the memories dismissed. "Tell me, how do your instincts measure up to hers?"

I think to dissemble or perhaps downplay what I believe about my abilities to avoid looking arrogant but decide not to. "My instincts are as good as hers were, and better than Harrow's and Ronden's. Stronger than those of anyone I know."

Riva smirks. "Well, now. I've been warned. We shall see."

I shake my head slowly. "I hope I am judging myself honestly and not exaggerating. You ask a hard question. But I do not lay claim to anything that I am not sure is true."

She nods, the smirk fading to something that approaches approval. "You'll likely have a chance to prove it, one way or the other." Then she stands abruptly. "Time to get on. The wormhole we seek is just ahead."

We set out once more. In less than an hour we have reached the point she is looking for — a passageway into a field of giant boulders left from a long-ago landslide. Some of them are huge — each one thousands of pounds at least. We wind into this maze until we reach the biggest chunk of solitary rock I have ever seen. It has split in half, which allows for passage through — a good thing, for the way to either side is completely blocked by jumbled clusters of broken stone. We stand before it for long moments as Riva studies the passageway intently, then motions me back a few steps.

"Here is how the Dragons chose to leave Viridian Deep after the time of the Ghoul Wars. I was no longer a Dragon rider or an instructor, but I was still close to the Dragons. So when they decided to end their partnership with the Fae for good, they took a chance and came to me — to the one Fae they still knew would understand their predicament and who could be trusted to help resolve it. After all, I had already been effectively dismissed from regular service. I owed nothing by then to Ancrow."

She turns back to the split in the huge rock. "I knew of a way to help them move far away from Fae lands, and so I shared that knowledge with them."

She begins to sing, her voice deep and resonant. The song rises on the afternoon air, filling the silence. It sweeps and soars, and I am amazed at how captivated I am. Within only a few minutes, the entrance through the cleft boulder fills with a shim-

231

mer of light that wavers like water on the air. I am reminded of when Ronden and I used another wormhole to reach an imprisoned Harrow and how odd it was to watch her song reveal its entrance in the middle of a vast wetland. I stand now in a field of boulders in a different place entirely and listen to a voice that is very unlike Ronden's achieving a similar result.

Riva's song trails away once the wormhole is formed, and she beckons me forward as she moves toward its entrance — and toward a transparent light beyond which there appears to be little more than a dark nothingness.

"Stay close," she advises.

I do. "I didn't know this wormhole existed," I confess.

"Few do. And perhaps — save the Dragons — I am the only one left who does. I found it as a child, revealed it to the Dragons when they needed an escape, helped them to find their new home, and haven't been back to it since. It is very old. This stretch of rocky land has survived thousands of years with little change. This wormhole does not reveal itself easily, and the cleft in the boulder disguises its real purpose. This one was used for passage to the north by invaders either coming or going, when the Fae and the earth were still new."

"Yet you found it."

"There was a time when . . . it was important . . . when things were different and . . ."

She trails off and does not continue. I don't press her. She is working up to something. She will tell me when she is ready.

Then she surprises me. "When I fell from grace with your mother and the Ghoul Wars were winding down, the Dragons needed a place to go. I knew of this passage, and I had used it. It terminates in a mountain aerie, perfect for a Dragon Hold. I showed it to the Dragons and I took them through. I stole them away, for all practical purposes. Had your mother found out, she would have killed me."

The way she closes, the intensity of her words and the strength of her voice, suggests she has said all she cares to say. So I leave it there.

We walk on at a steady pace, and the air turns from warm to cold and then back again. The way ahead never brightens; the gloom is secretive and unrevealing. The walls of the wormhole seem fluid, appearing and fading, shimmering as if they might be nothing more than a trick of the light. I find myself wanting to touch them, but I know

233

that such an act would be a mistake. Wormholes are often fragile constructs, and you have to be careful when using them. The one in which Ancrow, Harrow, and I had stood against the invading Human army was incredibly strong. This one seems less so.

Our journey is completed in silence, and when we emerge it is nightfall. We stand in a forest at the foot of a vast stretch of mountains that I am guessing from their distinctive look are part of the Skyscrape. We turn long enough to watch the wormhole slowly vanish and the world about us return to what we knew. My vision sharpens to allow me a clearer view of our surroundings, and I listen to the night sounds rise up around me in a steady mix of croaks and humming.

Riva and I look at each other. "We go a little farther tonight and then we sleep. We'll finish our journey tomorrow, sometime in the afternoon. For that, we have to climb."

She points to the mountains and slowly raises her arm, her finger pointing toward a place high in the peaks. A long way up, I think. A climb like this will be dangerous.

"I'm ready," I say.

But ready for what? Ready to finish out the day, or to sleep, or to climb the Skyscrape, or to arrive in the midst of Dragons that will likely want to eat me? Which of these am I actually ready for?

I sigh soundlessly. The first, I guess. Probably the second.

One step at a time.

We begin our approach to the lower levels of the peaks. At first, our passage is easy. The pathways are clear and the landscape, while rock-strewn and uneven, is manageable enough. But quickly we enter a series of foothills, where the slopes are steep and occasionally rough. We hike to a trailhead I do not see until we are on top of it, but which my companion knows how to find even in darkness. Here we stop, our way forward uncertain in a night so muffled beneath a thickly layered cloud cover that it shuts away all but the faintest light from moon and stars.

Which is, in many ways, a relief. I do not need to see the moon creeping too swiftly toward full to remind me how few days I have left.

"We camp here," Riva announces abruptly.

We move to the relative shelter of a rocky overhang that juts from the mountainside as if designed for this very purpose. Unrolling our blankets, we wrap them about us for warmth. Our slickers serve as pillows as we back into our shelter and face out into the dark. The world about us has gone quiet save for calls of night birds and the flutter of bat wings and, from somewhere quite distant, the rippling of a stream.

"I used to do this with Ancrow," Riva Tisk says suddenly. "We'd hike and then camp somewhere close to the mountains and stay out two or three nights — just to escape our lives as Dragon riders for a short time. Hard to believe now."

I recognize my opening. "You must have been close once. Friends. Was it my mother who you were referring to when you said someone had hurt you badly once?"

She nods. "I've told you the story. You can judge for yourself."

"It must have hurt when she dismissed you from her service."

Riva laughs, and the sound is filled with bitterness. "*Hurt* is hardly the word for it. Honestly, what hurt most was when Trusen was killed. I was finally happy; I had finally found love and acceptance. With Trusen gone, all that was left for me was being a Dragon rider. And then Ancrow took that away as well. So I lost everything that gave my life meaning, due to an overly harsh reaction from a woman I had once admired."

I feel an impulsive need to reveal something in return. "Then you will understand how I felt when I learned she had given me up as a baby because I looked like a Human, and she couldn't tolerate how ashamed that made her." I remember even now the pain of learning about that rejection, and I find myself hurting all over again. "That was how I ended up back in the Human world and eventually inside a Goblin prison."

Riva looks appalled. "You didn't tell me this before."

I shrug. "I don't like to talk about it. But it feels like we are kindred spirits, you and me. We have both been cast away by the same woman. Both of us feel mistreated. Maybe we were, maybe not. I can't judge anymore. For me, it's all in the past; I let it go when she died. But that doesn't change the fact that the hurt she caused still lingers."

Riva reaches over and touches my arm lightly. "The hurt she caused us both will be there forever, Auris. I can hear it in our voices and see it on our faces. It will never disappear entirely. It will never wholly heal."

I hesitate before continuing. "Tell me something, Riva. The truth. Was my mother always like this? So harsh, so vindictive, so determined she would control everything? I don't know much about her from before two years ago, when I found her again. But so much of what I hear about the Ghoul Wars suggests she was not always so . . . unapproachable — so harsh and so cold."

Riva Tisk leans back into herself, and an unmistakable softness infuses her voice. "Your mother was once one of the kindest women I have ever known, and I loved her for that more than anything else. But she lost it all in the wars. The Ghoul Wars took so much away from all of us, but they took everything from your mother. Even before Trusen died and my service was diminished, we had been fighting for four hard years. She had lost friends and comrades and underlings — soldiers all, and many under her command, whose lives she felt were in her hands. She had turned bitter even before I was banished, even before Carrowen was killed in front of her and she was taken. I've heard it said that she lost whatever remained during her mainland imprisonment — though of course I was already living in the Cressidon by then."

She pauses. "When she gave you up — though she would have never admitted it — that may have been the worst. But she was not in the end anything of who she was in the beginning. By the end of the Ghoul Wars, she was transformed; we all were. If not for the Dragons . . ."

She breaks off quickly, shaking her head. "So maybe you understand better now?"

"The Ghoul Wars must have been terrible."

She snorts audibly. "Beyond belief. It was sheer butchery, all the time, in every place it was fought. The Ghouls kill because they don't know how to do much else, but it was those who urged them on — the Humans — that were most at fault. They were the puppet masters, pulling the strings. You cannot begin to picture what I saw, but I will never forget it. If not for the Dragons and their insistence on helping us . . ."

She trails off, shaking her head.

"Was my mother good with the Dragons? As good as everyone says?"

She surprises me with a smile. "Ancrow was better than anyone I ever knew. She might have been a Dragon herself, given her understanding of them. She had a sixth sense that told her when they were thinking of turning on her, and would use her *inish* to slap them down, make them obey. I don't know how she did it. Few ever managed to master a Dragon like she did. She became relentless in her need for control, and the Dragons always sensed this — and for the most part respected it. I learned from her,

239

but I was never her equal. I couldn't manage it. None of us could."

She shakes her head, looking inward. "There was one occasion — one I can't forget," she whispers. "Antrim, the dominant male, made a grab for your mother when she wasn't looking. I screamed a warning, but I needn't have bothered. Ancrow made a gesture without even glancing at Antrim, and whatever she did just flattened him. Took his legs out from under him — twenty thousand pounds of Dragon laid out like a rug. When he tried to rise, she put a hand on his snout and did something more — something that caused him to snarl but also to submit. That was the last time Antrim ever tested her. In time he became the Dragon she favored as a mount. He accepted her without argument. He warded her as he would have a child of his own. Unusual for a Dragon to be tamed to that extent, but he was."

"You don't know how she did it?"

Riva gives me a look. "No. And don't be thinking you can somehow do the same, just because you are your mother's daughter. You can't. No one can. No one since ever has. You watch yourself every moment you're within reach of those jaws, no matter which Dragon you're close to. Assume they will act out and try to kill you at some point."

"But we're not here to master them. We're just here to warn them — and to see if they know what Tonklot is, and if what he did can be reversed."

"Very reassuring. But they don't know this, do they? *Pfft!* You talk like a child. Be smart; be aware. Assume nothing, and you might keep all your limbs — and your life in the bargain." She shakes her head. "I knew this was a bad idea. I wanted to help you, but I don't know if that's possible."

We go silent for a long time — long enough that I wonder if she has drifted off. But when I look over, I catch the ambient light from the stars reflected in her eyes. She is staring off into the distance, her thoughts a mystery.

"I will be careful," I say. "I won't forget your warning."

She nods, saying nothing. But a moment later she sighs audibly. "I haven't seen a Dragon in years. I wonder if *I'm* up to it. I worry about you, but I suppose I should worry about myself as well. I'm no Ancrow. It was she who turned the tide of the war."

I meet her gaze as she looks over again. "I thought you just said it was the Dragons . . ."

241

"It was, but your *mother* made the difference. She wouldn't let us lose. She drove us all, but she drove herself harder. She hated the Ghouls, but she hated the Humans even more. When she took command of the Dragon brigade, everything changed. She was a force of nature. You've heard the expression? Well, she embodied it."

I think back. Yes, she was all that Riva Tisk claimed. But you couldn't trust her. She'd lied over and over — to me, to her other children, to everyone. She'd lied about how I was conceived, born, and abandoned. She'd lied about my father. She'd lied about my foster parents. She'd lied about everything, right up to the end. I came to understand her, and I told her I loved her. But I knew even then that I would never be able to forgive her.

"You seem every bit as strong as she was," I venture.

Riva's smile is bitter. "I was never able to be as ruthless as she was — not only to others, but also to myself. She went beyond anything I could manage, becoming cruel, harsh."

I remember how she treated me, with so much anger and disdain, while carefully hiding her reasons for those feelings. It took everything I had not to let it crush me, and more still to withstand her behavior long enough to discover the reasons behind it. But she's gone now, and she is remembered by most with admiration. Better that I remember her in that way, too.

"Perhaps Tonklot thinks he possesses the ability to control Dragons just as my mother once did," I muse, changing the subject, still trying to understand what Tonklot plans. "If I bring him a Dragon, perhaps he will mesmerize it and use it against us."

Riva Tisk snorts. "*Pfft.* One Dragon against a nation? Besides, no one but Ancrow could ever fully control a Dragon. I don't know if even this creature Tonklot could do it."

I hope she is right. If so, maybe I stand a chance of saving Harrow without endangering the world. But then I remember Tonklot's power and wonder again.

My eyes are growing heavy and I am beginning to drift off to sleep. But I fight it off for several seconds more.

Is Tonklot capable of fully controlling a Dragon?

I hold that question in my mind for maybe five seconds, and then I am asleep.

FIFTEEN

I wake to rain. It is still dark, but the spatter of droplets against the rock walls and the dampness in the air is unmistakable. I huddle deeper into my blanket as I realize I am freezing cold. The temperature has dropped significantly, and my immediate inclination is to stay wrapped up and not move from where I shelter. I peer out into the darkness but cannot make out much of anything. Clouds mask the sky and shut out the light of moon and stars. The dawn's arrival feels impossibly far off.

I glance over at Riva Tisk, who is still sleeping. I am close enough to her that I can make out her features, even in this pervasive gloom. She looks surprisingly vulnerable. It is a side of her that she has not revealed while awake, and I feel as if I am being given a peek into something she tries hard never to reveal. Riva prefers to present herself as the personification of strength and hardness, but that is missing now. I am seeing a woman who has suffered life's vicissitudes and harshness and weathered having youth and innocence and hope stripped away, reverting in sleep to what she was in an earlier time. The revelation is unexpected and at the same time oddly reassuring. It makes me wonder if she really was once not so different than I am now.

I watch her for a long time, studying her face, wondering if she is dreaming and if so what she is dreaming about.

Time passes. I have no idea what I am doing awake, but I am pretty sure I am not going back to sleep. I am too wound up, too edgy. Already my mind is busy with thoughts about the day ahead — of Dragons and what it will feel like to see one for the first time, and of how they will react to me. Dragons are mercurial, Riva says, and do not suffer fools. Yet somehow I must persuade one to help me, to listen. It is a daunting prospect, placing myself in such danger so willingly. But I must, for Harrow.

But not immediately. And not in darkness. Not until Riva wakes and we have climbed the mountain to where the Dragons are. For now, I do not have to face any of what lies ahead anywhere but in my imagination.

Which, in some ways, is even worse, as

245

my imagination seems more than ready to go off the rails.

So instead I think about Harrow — not that I have ever stopped thinking of him. My thoughts are always with him — even in the most unlikely of times, even when they should be focused on other matters, like now. Thinking of Harrow is an obvious distraction, but I indulge it anyway. I must undo what Tonklot has done. But how? I don't begin to know the answer. I only know . . . no, not even that much . . . I only *hope* that the Dragons have some sort of answer.

My instincts tell me that I am on the right path, and I have to trust my instincts because, as I am constantly reassuring myself, they are never wrong.

Still, I try to think it through. Tonklot wants a Dragon, and for some reason he believes that I can bring him one. But why does he think this? He knew I was a Fae; he knew I had use of strong *inish;* and he must have known I would dare anything — and risk *everything* — to get Harrow back. But how can he know this? We had never met before he and his Aerklings surrounded us and stole Harrow's *inish.* How can he know so much about me when we have never even spoken to each other?

Except, once again, he did claim to have met me before, though I have no memory of it. Could his knowledge of me have been from that time? Also, now that I think of our remembered encounter in more detail, he was able to penetrate my mind to a certain level before something stopped him and he was unable to proceed further. He had expected to find me more vulnerable and been enraged that I was not. It might have been the reason he ended up doing what he did to Harrow — an alternative method for getting what he wanted.

Which was what? A Dragon? Something more?

I have not thought of this latter bit since it happened, almost three days ago, but I know I am not wrong in seeing it as I do.

The wind blows a sharp gust of rain into my face, chill and damp as it strikes my skin. The sharpness knocks loose a realization.

In addition to his powers of hypnosis, Tonklot can read minds.

And somehow, some way — at some time — he has read at least a part of mine. Not all, apparently; something locked him out when he tried — perhaps my *inish,* perhaps my protective instincts. But his knowledge of Harrow and our bond has to have happened while I was mesmerized, my mind laid open to him. He could read my thoughts, then . . . but he must have been able to examine my memories, too. As he would have done to Harrow. Only in Harrow's case, he has stolen everything about him that mattered.

Oh Fates and Furies! I want to howl in rage and despair at what has been done to me. I want to tear his heart out.

Like the Seers, he has the gift of teasing out memories. But unlike those three kind old ladies, he uses it ruthlessly, plundering those memories — or stealing them entirely in Harrow's case. I opened up to the Seers willingly, but Tonklot took what he wanted — or at least what he could — in ruthless disregard for what it might do to me. Now I feel as if I have been violated physically, forcibly stripped of everything this evil creature chose to take from me.

I think of what he did to Harrow when he stole both his *inish* and his memories — how he inhaled it into himself, leaving the man I love nothing more than an empty shell.

And then I think of something that freezes me in my tracks. Tonklot claims to have met me in the past in some intimate way. If he can steal memories wholesale, could he be the one behind the huge void in my past?

The shock of this thought paralyzes me for long moments, but it is pointless. I need resolution, even if I do not yet know what that might look like. All I know is that I will save Harrow, and I will make Tonklot pay — for what he did to Harrow, and perhaps to me as well. Somehow, I will find a way.

When the sky begins to lighten — the sunrise still little more than a glimmer — Riva Tisk wakes. She gives me a questioning look, sees something in my expression, and makes her familiar sound with a harshness that is jolting.

"Pfft!"

Like an angry beast. Like a snake.

She sits up quickly, alert and ready. We eat breakfast in silence, repack our gear, pull on our warmest sweaters and coats, and set out on a day so misty and gloomy that it suggests the possibility of wraiths and spirits lurking behind its shifting curtains.

Our progress is steady for a while, our ascent of these lower slopes easy enough, the pathway clear. Boulders and slides slow us occasionally, and sometimes a rock wall or crevasse requires we go around. The air warms marginally, but the mist and gloom remain constant. I can see the sky only intermittently. There is a stillness to the mountains that is eerie, and only now and then does a stray sound surface. The wind increases the higher we go, and we tighten the stays on our hooded coats to keep out its chill. We exchange few words, and these mostly in service to our climb, as Riva advises on how and where to step.

We have been climbing for less than an hour when I feel something ratchet up my sense of danger, my instincts kicking in with a jolt that brings me to a complete stop. A quick look around reveals nothing. But then I notice Riva, several steps ahead of me, pointing skyward. I look and immediately shrink up inside. What soars above me is so huge it defies belief. It is serpentine and covered over from nose to tail in armor-like scales, its massive body suspended in the wind. Its stout legs are drawn up against its body, its wings spread wide like horizontal sails, and its wedge-shaped head is a mass of horns that shift from side to side like an array of spears as it surveys the earth below.

I freeze where I am — and not just because I am trying to remain unnoticed. It would be more accurate to say that I am trying to sink into the earth and disappear. What rides the wind above me is so terrifying, so impossibly imposing, that I am reduced to feeling as if I am nothing more than dust and fear. This is the promise of my death waiting to fall on me. It is implacable and inevitable, and I cannot hide from it. I have never been so frightened in my life. I want to turn around and flee. I want to shed all responsibility for everything I know I must do to help Harrow, because I know am bound to fail.

Just viewing a Dragon at a distance does this to me. What will it be like when I am face-to-face with one?

But the fear and the paralysis and the sense of helplessness pass with the beast's abrupt disappearance, and I straighten up from the protective crouch into which I have sunk.

I look at Riva in embarrassment. "I'm sorry."

She shrugs. "It affects everyone that way the first time. There is no way of preparing for how it feels to encounter such a monster. Next time you will be ready. Come."

We begin to walk again, and as we do I tell myself, over and over, that she is right. This will never happen to me again. I will not show fear or dismay the next time I encounter such a creature. I am stronger than that. I know myself, and I am not a coward. I will be better prepared.

But I wonder. Will I really be prepared, or

do I only tell this to myself to feel better about what has just happened? I think it is the former, but I worry it is the latter.

Our climb proceeds, and passage grows more difficult. The slopes steepen and the wind whips through the rocks and boulders, over the ridges and across the flats, and down passages and into my core as if with no other purpose than to hurt me. It is now bitter cold and there are snow flurries swirling on the wind and slapping into my skin. I squint against their sting. The skies above are clearing, and in the far distance I catch sight of the dark forms of other Dragons soaring and diving, dark forms sharp against the rising sunlight.

How am I going to confront such beings? How am I going to discover anything that will help Harrow?

How am I going to manage to stay alive?

We slog on until we reach some forested flats where we find a momentary windbreak within the twisted trunks and gnarled limbs. We pause, looking at each other.

"Dragons are not quite of this world," Riva says quietly. "They are present, but they do not belong. I think they must come from another time — possibly a time even before the Fae."

I nod, adding, "Mostly, they are just terrifying."

"No one sees them anymore. Even in the past, they were hard to find. They mostly kept to themselves. No one knows what it takes to satisfy a Dragon's hunger. No one knows where they come from or if they are the descendants of some other long-extinct species."

"Yet we can communicate with them," I remind her.

She laughs softly. "Communication does not necessarily mean we understand them. I think none of us who rode these beasts in the Ghoul Wars ever got to know them well. Even Ancrow, for all her other abilities, failed to uncover much."

She pauses. "Maybe it will be different for you. For all that you might think otherwise, you are an enigma even to yourself, Auris. I am not sure that will ever change."

We rest a few moments longer, then set off once more. We do not encounter another Dragon, although we see them off in the distance for the rest of our climb. Finally, we reach an opening in the rocks, and Riva leads us into a high, narrow passage that twists and winds with such persistence it is never possible to see more than a dozen yards ahead at a stretch. I would be more cautious than my guide in my approach, but she just strides ahead. Though apparently she knows the way when I do not, so maybe that is the sum of her confidence.

It takes a surprisingly long time to get all the way through this maze, and the walls tower over us at such heights that we are left in perpetual shadow. The sky is visible at intervals overhead, but mist and clouds obscure it for much of our path. We cannot see the sun, which is still too low in the sky to be visible over the walls. I think, for what must be the hundredth time, about what I should do once we reach our destination, and what I should be prepared for. All I do know is that I can't predict it. I have to remain fluid, be prepared to react to whatever happens. The situation is too uncertain for any other choice. My instincts will either save or doom me, and I have to trust that it will be the former and not the latter.

When we finally emerge from the passageway and can see what lies beyond, I stop in surprise. A broad green valley opens before us, surrounded by cliffs and spreading out for what must be at least two miles. Right away, I can feel the change in temperature, and take note of the steam that rises from cracks in the valley floor to mingle with trailers of mist that hang in the air like tattered rags. I can smell the sulfur and ash, and I realize I am looking into the crater of a live volcano that lies somewhere deep beneath the surface. Trees grow both towering and stunted to fill the valley, and their strong scents mingle with those of the volcano and . . .

I gasp, not quite able to believe what I can clearly see.

There are Dragons everywhere. Hundreds of them — large and small, flying and nesting. They are everywhere I look — some brightly colored, some barely visible, scattered all across the breadth and depth of the valley's broad expanse. This refuge is clearly their home and their safehold from the rest of the world. Some soar in great sweeping circles through the mists — not to feed or drink, because they never seem to descend, so perhaps only for the joy of it. Or perhaps, I correct myself as I see several pairs engage in sudden, unexpected aerial battles, fighting for dominance. Though, save for a few rendings of scales and skin, the combat seems more ritualized than deadly.

Other, less combative Dragons perch on rocky ledges and outcroppings as if surveying their home and their kin. Some are hatchlings or younger versions of their watchers. Many look as if they might still be too young to fly — fledglings still figuring out the rules of their new world. Others occupy massive nests and depressions where space allows for the birth and care of hatchlings, and I catch glimpses of small, ragged little heads rising up to seek food.

I continue to stare at the sweep and flow of this Dragon colony. How can a place such as this exist and not be known by the Fae? How can so many Dragons have gathered to make their home in such a huge refuge and still manage to stay so thoroughly secreted? Surely someone besides Riva must know they are here, yet it feels as if the Dragons are safe from the entire rest of the world.

How much distance did that wormhole cover, and how remote is this outpost? How far have they come since leaving their old haunts in Viridian Deep and their time of service to the Fae during the Ghoul Wars?

I stand there, staring in wonder. A world of Dragons — an entire civilization — right here in front of me. I take it all in, and the wonder of finding such a treasure makes me smile. For a moment, I am a little girl again, finding a magical world that is somehow now mine, and I laugh with such pleasure it causes Riva, standing to one side of me, to smile back.

"It is special," she whispers — lost, I suspect, in her own memories.

But already we have been seen. A few calls of warning echo across the valley, and I am again reminded of the danger facing us. Yet Riva Tisk stands firm. "Remember, do not show fear. Do not move or speak," she hisses at me.

So I don't. I stand firm and wait as a Dragon sweeps down to us — a slow, leisurely descent that gives it time to study us and me time to wish it would turn aside. I am still awed to the point of terror at the towering size of these creatures.

I wonder if this Dragon will land — a hundred feet of ledge lies between us and the edge of the cliff — but instead it wings past, head turning on its long flexible neck to better survey us with eyes as green as emeralds. There is no hint of emotion in that seemingly endless gaze. We might as well be pieces of rock for all the interest it shows in us.

Then the Dragon rises once more and gives several ear-piercing shrieks, each trailing off in a slightly different guttural croak. A moment later it is gone.

I glance over at Riva, and she nods back. "It calls the warren's Vinst — the leader — to come and decide what it wants to do with us. It notes our posture and resolve and says that we act as if we know this valley and must therefore have come here before. It warns of a need for caution. Their Vinst will come to judge us, and he is formidable."

Caution? Why would a Dragon need to be cautious toward minuscule beings like us?

But of course, Riva seems to have momentarily forgotten that I am able to understand what the cries mean. Worse, she mistakes their meaning. They do not suggest caution. They speak instead of something else entirely: recognition.

Of course they know Riva, as a former Dragon rider. But unless I am badly mistaken they know who I am, too.

Impossible.

Yet my certainty persists. Somehow, they know.

A huge black body slowly lifts away from the cliffs farther down to our right. It is there momentarily then gone again, rising high enough to disappear into layers of cloud. Just a glimpse — but I see it long enough to be able to recognize it. A Dragon the size of an airship, massive wings widespread.

It emerges anew from the concealing mists, swiftly closing the distance that separates us, and then the brume swallows it up once more.

I was terrified of this Dragon the first time I saw it earlier today, and I am no less terrified now. It is twice the size of any other and exudes a menace that is unmistakable even from a distance. It is all I can do not to break and run. And yet . . .

I know this Dragon.

I know he is the leader of the Dragons who occupy this valley.

I know he is the promise of my death.

And I know his name.

Antrim.

My mother's Dragon.

to break and run.

Snow He is the leader of the Dragons

SIXTEEN

Antrim surges anew out of the mists, coming for us aggressively, his posture and attitude clearly suggesting that he means to
tear us apart. I quail at the sight of him,
desperate to break and run, but Riva doesn't
move a muscle, and her resolve strengthens
mine. Nonetheless, I am certain that if we
stand firm, we will be crushed against the
cliffs when he lands. We stand a hundred
feet from the cliff edge, which offers plenty
of room to avoid harming us, but Antrim's
speed and power suggest this is not his
intention. So as Antrim passes into another
layer of mist, I summon my *inish* and
employ it.

Nothing seems to have happened; nothing
changes in a way that anyone would notice
— anyone but Riva and myself, that is. I
glimpse the shock on her face but trust she
will stand firm and say nothing.

Antrim comes barreling downward, flying

directly toward us. But at the last possible moment, he spreads his wings so that his speed diminishes sharply and he executes an effortless landing. Even so, once settled on our ledge, he towers over us at an apparent separation of no more than a dozen yards. He glowers as he studies us, his horn-encrusted face pitted and scarred, his baleful eyes a fiery green, his nostrils emitting thick clouds of steam as the sound of his breathing fills the silence.

We let him take our measure for as long as he wishes. After all, what choice do we have? Emerald eyes slowly shift back and forth between us before finally settling on me.

A grunt issues from his throat, and in Dragon speech he snarls and says, speaking to me directly, "Who are you?"

"My given name is Auris Afton Grieg," I tell him.

He responds with a harsh, guttural sound. "Ah, you speak our language. Well and good. But you have not answered my question. *Who are you?*"

I am at a momentary loss and just stand there, speechless.

Antrim hisses in disgust, and the stench is appalling. "Your *people,* girl! Who are your people?"

261

I gasp in relief. "I am Ancrow's daughter."

"I should have guessed it. There is immense power reflected in your *inish*. I can sense it. You are every bit her child in that." He leans forward with shocking quickness and sniffs me — or at least tries to. Which is when I drop the illusion I have employed and reveal that Riva and I are actually standing some yards back.

The Dragon's emerald eyes gleam, and he barks something that may be a laugh. "Clever, Ancrow's daughter. But I can smell her on you nonetheless." The Dragon pauses, then adds, "You are not only Fae; you are Human spawn, too. A hybrid."

"I am."

A long pause, as if he is coming to some decision. "Ancrow's daughter, even so. You are welcome. But your mother? I am told she is dead."

"Two years past. She died defending her people."

Antrim shows his considerable teeth. Is he smiling? I start counting teeth and then give up. "She was a Dragon rider who made us proud to serve with her," he declares. "She was the best rider I ever knew." A pause. "Have you come to discover if you might be her equal?"

I shake my head. "I could never hope to

be that. I come for a different reason entirely. I am hoping you can provide . . ."

"Why should we provide you with anything, child of Ancrow?" he interrupts. "Why shouldn't I kill you and be done with it? I could do so easily."

I hesitate. Then I take a deep breath and say, "You know the answer to that."

The Dragon's head dips in recognition. "I would dishonor Ancrow's memory of me."

"You can turn us away, if that is what you think you should do," I add quickly, taking a chance.

The Dragon snorts; belches. The stench is once again overpowering, but I do not flinch. "To what end? This conversation grows interesting." He shifts his gaze and finds Riva. His look darkens. "I know you, too, Fae woman. Why is that?"

"I am Riva Tisk," she answers.

The name awakens a memory and Antrim's rough features instantly tighten. "Yes, you served with Ancrow. You were a Dragon rider who issued a complaint against one of our people. But you were dismissed from service and outlawed for that." A long pause. Recognition, then assessment. "But you aided us, too! You helped us find the wormhole that brought us out of Viridian Deep at the end of the

Ghoul Wars and to this land!"

In a surprise move, Antrim straightens up suddenly and produces a deep bow to Riva. "To you, much is owed. Once upon a time, you gave up everything for us. You forsook your pledge of loyalty to Ancrow and guided us to this home. You showed us a way to regain our old lives."

"I only did what was called for. And I did not give up everything. Much of what I relinquished had already been taken."

Antrim breathes heavily and belches, and again I want to gag. But he makes no move to menace me, and I can tell from the tone of his voice that he is more curious than angry. "I sensed your *inish* was powerful, and that it is of a kind I have never seen before." He studies me carefully. "Dragons do not rely on *inish*. Dragons rely on other means to overcome their enemies."

"Are we enemies?"

"No. But I remain curious about what brings you here, where no Fae has been for over twenty years. And why this one" — he jerks his head at Riva — "felt it necessary to guide you to us, when she alone knows where we now reside."

I feel Riva stiffen beside me, and wonder if, in bringing me, she has violated some

264

oath to keep the Dragons' hiding place secret.

But in response, Riva merely raises her chin and says boldly, "Auris and I come to you because there is a threat to you and your people, Antrim, and we wish to give you warning."

"Threat? What threat?" Antrim's questions are flat and dismissive. "What could possibly threaten us? The Ghouls are destroyed. Viridian Deep is at peace. Goblins, then? Hah! Tasty snacks if they come anywhere near us. Tell me of this threat!"

I interrupt quickly. "I want your promise that no harm will be done to us while we are explaining. And that we will be allowed to leave after."

The Dragon gives what I think is a laugh but could also be something else. "Agreed. So explain this threat to me."

I do, keeping my recitation of the events leading up to our arrival brief. Too long, and I might lose Antrim's attention. I hit the high points — my mother's fondness for the Dragon brigade, her dedication to its members, and her pride in all that they did for the Fae people; my partnering with her adopted son and our love for each other; the appearance of Tonklot and how he stole Harrow's *inish;* and finally the task that I have been given if I want my life partner back again.

Antrim listens without interruption, then shakes his great head. When he speaks, his voice is full of dismissive contempt. "No one can *give* anyone a Dragon. What Dragons do, they only do willingly."

"I know this, and I certainly did not come here asking you to surrender to this creature. I just wanted to warn you that there is a powerful being out there who is intent on having a Dragon under his control. And to ask if you know anything of this creature — what he might be, and if there is a way to recover what he has stolen from my mate."

Antrim snorts. "These are creatures about which very little is known. There was once an abusive, destructive race of Fae called Barghasts. They possessed formidable powers of mind control and had some shape-shifting abilities that let them mimic and deceive their prey. They were vampiric by nature, but they fed on *inish* instead of blood. How they did this is something with which few now living are familiar, but it is said that any creature they devoured they could then absorb, extracting its sustenance and using it to enhance their own powers."

This is not something I have ever heard

266

mentioned before. "What else have you heard?"

He starts and then stops, suddenly lost in thought. "Barghasts are something of a mystery because nothing has been seen or heard of them for many years now. Yet in their day, the Barghasts killed too many of our people by feeding on the wounded and helpless. It is also said the Barghasts could absorb the particular magic of any creature they fed upon, so the more they devoured, the stronger they grew. Barghasts were predators, targeting not only other Fae but every known form of living creature. Because of this, they were despised and hunted. We thought we had hunted them to extinction, but each time they were deemed eradicated, they would resurface. It seems the same is happening again."

"So this Barghast wants a Dragon to . . . what, control one? *Become* one?" If they can indeed absorb the powers of their prey, this would make one who did so powerful beyond control.

Antrim growls. "As I said, no one can control a Dragon. And certainly not control *me.*"

Riva snorts at this, and I glance over at her in surprise.

But Antrim quickly regains my attention

when his eyes flash and he repeats, "*No one controls me!* Not now! Not anymore. Woe betide any Barghast who tries to feed off one of my kind. Barghasts may be powerful, but they are no match for a Dragon!"

"So you know of no way to restore Harrow's missing *inish* and memory, then?" I ask.

"I know of no way to restore your mate's missing *inish*. And I have never known of a Barghast to steal memories," Antrim says, then pauses, looking thoughtful. "Save perhaps . . ."

"Do you know of something?" I ask, eagerly.

"About twenty years back, a man's wife was taken from him in much the same way Harrow was taken from you . . ." The Dragon pauses, looking from me to Riva and back again, then spreads his wings. "But someone else should speak of this, someone who knows the story better than I do. Wait here for me."

I feel a sudden surge of hope as he lifts away without waiting to hear what response we might make and flies off into the mists.

We sit on the ledge with our backs against the cliff wall, staring out across the brume-shrouded bowl of the valley, waiting. Dragons fly here and there, going about their business, seeming to be either unknowing or uncaring that we are there at all. But we do not fool ourselves. These creatures are never unaware, and it would be a mistake to grow too comfortable with our situation. Antrim has promised we will not be harmed, and perhaps he means to keep that promise. But no other Dragon has promised anything, so we keep a wary eye on our surroundings.

A baby Dragon peeks out from its rocky shelter and stares at us. It is not a newborn, but not far removed. It shows both an obvious interest and commendable caution. It probably has never seen a Fae before and wonders what we are and what we are doing here. I find myself wondering the same thing. What exactly *are* we doing here? It is to our credit that we are still alive and waiting for what might be a lead, but it is equally possible that our journey has been wasted and there is no help to be found. But my instincts tell me I am on the right path, so I hold tight to that.

I am fixated on what my life without Harrow would be like. I would go on, of course. What other choice would there be? Viridian Deep is my home now, and where I belong. My heart and soul are firmly connected to this world and the Sylvan people, and I can never go back to the world of Humans — especially given my evolving appearance. I glance down at myself. My now greenish tresses are thick with tiny leaves. The silk that grows along my arms and legs brushes against my skin in soft caresses I have come to relish. The greenish color of my skin has continued to darken, if I am not mistaken, currently assuming an opalescent hue that I find attractive. My facial structure remains unchanged and the shape of my body does not alter save where exercise and training with Harrow and Ronden have hardened and slimmed and shaped me in a way that makes me proud.

I like that I am strong and capable and no longer dependent on anyone for my safety. My younger sisters look up to me. My older sister believes me her equal and sees me as her best friend.

But it is my relationship with Harrow that gives me my balance and my promise. Harrow, whom I love so much and who loves me back in equal measure. I cannot lose him. I will do anything to prevent it. I will give up my own life before I see him lose his. Whatever happens here in the Dragon realm — on this day or the next or any day after that — I will persevere. I will find a way. I will . . .

But my thoughts are interrupted by Antrim's abrupt reappearance. He wings out of the sky, his monstrous body descending as if materializing out of the clouds, settling ponderously on our ledge, head lowering in greeting.

"There is something you need to know," he says in a rough growl that reflects distaste and reluctance both.

I ignore the sense of caution his voice suggests I should exercise. Even without knowing of what he speaks, I feel a fresh rush of hope flood through me. But I wait for Antrim to explain further, not wanting to appear too desperate. I am still on shaky ground with this Dragon, whom I think I have captivated mostly through curiosity rather than caring.

We wait, but the Dragon says nothing more. "What is it?" Riva asks eventually.

The Dragon ignores her, looking at me instead. "You must speak to Gray Sanan. He may know of a way to help."

We wait for him to say something more, but he only glances back across the valley where a second Dragon can be spied winging his way through the mists to reach us. This Dragon's flight path is slower and less steady. His wings are ripped and tattered, and his legs are less securely tucked up against his body. His withered head is lowered as if a great weariness has overtaken him.

By the time he lands beside Antrim, I can see he is missing scales, so that patches of skin show through. His body is as ashen as his name, and his motions reveal that he is stiff and weak with age. Rheumy eyes regard us vacantly, and he has a momentary look of confusion. I am not entirely sure he even knows where he is.

"Sanan was Vinst before me," Antrim growls in quiet tones, looking again at us. "His infirmity required that leadership to pass to me." He looks to the other Dragon. "Tell the Fae what you told me."

The old Dragon nods once and shifts his gaze in our general direction. I wonder suddenly if he might be blind, but then how can he manage to fly, if so?

"This man," Gray Sanan begins, his voice soft and the words skipping and dragging as he speaks them so that I can barely understand him. "Several decades ago, he lost his mate. He was half Human, half Fae, but his mate was a Forest Sylvan. She had found him in the Human world, and they had fallen in love. She brought him back to live with her in Viridian Deep. After she fell victim to the Barghasts, he came here specifically to find us. He said he needed our help, as we might know something of this creature."

A long pause follows, as if he is gathering strength enough to continue. "The man possessed no ability to use our speech, but he found a rider who was willing to give him voice and address his wishes to us. So we agreed to listen, because the matter was of some interest to us. A Barghast had violated his mate. We had long fought the Barghasts — loathsome creatures that lived off the lives of others, stealing away their *inish* and leaving them as empty as the dead."

Tonklot, I think at once. *Described exactly.*

"We believed them all gone until this man and his companion came seeking us. I don't know how the man's mate encountered a Barghast. I don't know where they made their home in Viridian Deep. I don't know how long they lived here. All I know is that, while the man was away in the Human world, his mate was drained of her *inish.* The man went first to the Sylvan Seers, but they had no idea what sort of creature could have done this, so they sent him to us for advice.

"I told him what I knew of Barghasts, and how they steal the *inish* from a person and digest it slowly over time. No one knows if the victim's body dies once the *inish* has been fully digested, or if a body simply cannot survive for much time without *inish*. Whatever the case, death usually follows within a few weeks."

Which matches the timeline the Seers gave me and panics me all the more. If I miss my deadline, there may not be a Harrow to give the *inish* back to, even if I can somehow retrieve it.

"The man had no idea where the Barghast might be, or if there was any way to help his wife, so he came to us for both aid and information. He believed there was a chance she could be restored to him if he could find the Barghasts quickly enough. He was determined and persuasive, so we told him what we knew."

Gray Sanan pauses, his gaze wandering off to other times and places. I wait patiently. It is worth waiting for a chance to learn about another Barghast victim. There must be help for me somewhere in this story.

"When we explained the timeline, the man then confessed he was afraid his search had taken too long and that his mate was already beyond help. He worried there was already too much of her gone and not enough left to bring her back to who she was. Then he begged us to help him kill the creature that had violated her in this way."

The old Dragon sighs and looks away. "I said nothing, for what chance would a mere halfling have to kill a Barghast? Nor was it right to ask any of my Pride to risk their lives in such an effort. I told him where to find the creature but refused to aid him in his attempt, as his search for revenge was not the business of Dragons. As well, we were on the verge of falling into the middle of the Ghoul Wars. I do not know if he was able to find the creature, or confront it."

I nod, but I am chilled by his words. "Do you remember the Barghast's name?"

Gray Sanan shakes his scarred head. "I never knew it."

"Or the man's name?"

A frustrated snort. "It has been a long time." He pauses, reflecting. "But I think his mate's name was Meliore."

His voice shakes — perhaps with age, perhaps with sorrow. "He left shortly after we rejected his request for our help and he never came back. I regret to this day that I chose to send him away. I should have done something else. I should have acted with more compassion."

"But you can't remember the man's

name? You are sure?" I can feel myself growing desperate. "Can you remember anything about him?"

Sanan shakes his aged head, and the scales and skin along his neck shiver in response. "I do remember one thing. He was an incredibly skilled fighter — a master of hand-to-hand combat with any weapon you could name. He claimed there was no one who could stand against him."

I am gripped by a wild premonition — one too strong to ignore.

"This man?" I ask hesitantly. "Was his name Drifter?"

The old Dragon cocks his head in recognition. "Ahhh!" he hisses. "Yes, that was it. He called himself Drifter."

SEVENTEEN

I stand very still, trying to wrap my mind around what I have just been told. *Drifter!* My old teacher, recalled from my lost memories thanks to the Seers. And now, it seems, a halfling like myself, at least according to Sanan.

Is he the one who can help me save Harrow?

It is such a coincidence that I can hardly believe it. I always thought to go back and find him one day. Now I have a far more compelling reason to do so.

"I know this man," I whisper very quietly.

But not quietly enough. "You know him?" Riva demands. "How can you know him?"

"When I was thirteen, my father hired Drifter to train me in weapons usage and self-defense. I did not want this, but my father insisted. I did not understand why at the time, although I came to understand it later. I was living in the Human world as a

Human, though I was half Fae. I had not yet learned the truth about my Fae side or discovered the Fae world. But my father knew my true identity, and knew I might be discovered for who and what I was — a member of a race the Humans wanted to dominate and exploit. He knew, as well, that he had powerful enemies in the Ministry. He wanted me prepared for the day they discovered my Fae identity, in case he was not there to help. So I worked with Drifter for nearly two years, until I was just shy of my fifteenth birthday."

I pause, looking at Antrim. "You saw I was both Human and Fae when we met, though I look more Fae than Human now. But when I came to Viridian Deep after Harrow saved my life, I looked Human in every respect. Though once I promised myself to Harrow and made Viridian Deep my home, I began to change into a Fae. So really, everything that has given me back my true identity is because of Harrow."

I stop talking, not sure where to go from there.

"I have to find Drifter," I blurt out finally. "I have to discover what he knows about Barghasts and their ability to steal *inish.*"

Riva seizes my arm. "Do you even know

278

where he is now? Do you know how to find him?"

I shake my head. "I haven't seen him now in more than seven years. But I know that between seven and nine years ago, he was in the Human world, so perhaps that is where I need to begin."

"May I point out that you don't look very Human anymore, Auris? They will spot you at once if you go back."

Antrim and Gray Sanan say nothing, although they exchange glances. I know Riva is right, but I also know that I have no choice. I have to do whatever I can to save Harrow. I wonder momentarily if there isn't some way I could make myself look Human again. The Seers were so confident that I was a Changeling of some sort. Again, I find myself wondering if this could have played some part in how I looked Human earlier in my life, when I most needed to. Might it now be able to help me do so again?

"I know what going back into the Human world means. I have done it twice now, and both times it nearly cost me my life. But sometimes you do things you don't want to because you must. I need to return, because I cannot think of another way to bring Harrow back."

Riva shakes her head. "You really are like

your mother."

"To her great credit," Antrim adds in his gravel-encrusted voice. "Ancrow would dare anything."

"Then I must dare as much as she would." I turn to Antrim. "Thank you so much for what you've done. Ancrow was proud to call the Dragons her friends, and I hope you will allow me to do the same."

"Always, Auris." He uses my name for the first time. His scarred face crinkles like swamp water stirred.

"Farewell, Dragon Lord," I respond, turning to leave.

Teeth flash and lips curl. "Stand where you are, Fae girl. We are not yet quite finished with each other."

The rumble of his voice and edge to his words carry a certain force, and I find myself more than a little reluctant to find out what that means.

His great voice deepens. "I will tell you something you may not know. Before I was the Dragons' Vinst, I was something else of equal importance. I was your mother's partner. We fought together in the Ghoul Wars for four long years. I will always regret that I could do nothing to save her when she was captured by the Humans, and her mate killed. I failed her — and for that, I owe her a debt. I would ask you to allow me to settle it here. Were your mother still alive she would want me to help you, and I think I must honor her by doing so. You took a chance coming here. Now I want to take a chance by accompanying you."

I glance at Riva, who looks stunned — but not, I suspect, by the revelation. Looking back, it is clear she recognized Antrim from the start.

"I do not want you to put yourself at risk," I tell him. "This Barghast is too powerful — even for you."

The Dragon snorts. "Nonsense. Nothing is too powerful for me. Not anymore." He flashes his emerald eyes at Riva, and I recall her telling me how Ancrow had once laid him out like a rug. But clearly he feels himself beyond this now. "I sense something special in you, Auris — something more than simply being your mother's daughter. There is a fire in you, a brightness. Together we should be able to stand against anything. I will come with you."

"Your words honor me," I answer finally, "but I am not sure I deserve them."

"Nor am I. Not yet." The Dragon bends closer, and for a moment I picture myself being snapped in half. It takes a certain amount of effort for me to hold fast and not flinch, but I manage. I cannot afford to show fear.

"I will take you where you need to go," Antrim says, surprising me.

I take a deep breath. "I don't think . . ."

"Listen to me. You need to act swiftly if you are to save your mate. There is no faster way for you to reach the Human world and return than by Dragonback. A Dragon can fly you to your destination in half the time it would take you to reach it otherwise — and this doesn't begin to count the hours or days it will take you to find other means of transport should you refuse me. Do you understand?"

"I do." I hesitate again. "But still . . ."

"Are you afraid to fly with me?" Antrim asks bluntly.

There is only one answer to that question, and I give it quickly. "No."

"I wish to come, too," Riva interrupts. "I've come this far; now I want to see it through."

"Do you? Were you invited?" Antrim gives Riva a look I cannot decipher. Anger at her interference, or respect for her courage at making so bold a request? Either is possible.

"No. But I am asking anyway."

The Dragon nods, seemingly mollified. "If you promise to stand by Auris and protect her, I will allow it."

"I would welcome that chance," she says at once.

Antrim nods. "As you wish. It is settled."

I would suggest otherwise. To my way of thinking, nothing is settled. In the first place, I am not entirely comfortable with the idea of having Riva accompany me — in large part because it feels like she will be an unneeded distraction in the Human world. She is clearly a Fae and a large one to boot, whereas I am much smaller in stature and less readily identifiable. Hiding two of us is going to be a lot more challenging than hiding one. Still, she wants to come, and Antrim has accepted her offer, so I am hesitant to object when both seem so resolved.

But even if I let this go, there is a more serious problem. The truth is, Riva is right: I have no idea where to find Drifter. He has been missing from my life for more than seven years; he could be anywhere by now. There was never anything to guarantee he would stay in Harbor's End, where I once lived. The exact opposite always seemed more likely. So where are we to go to find him? How can this not be a complete waste of time and effort?

Unless . . . It suddenly strikes me that

while I might not know where he is, I am pretty certain I know someone who does. And someone I've been wanting to see one more time.

"I'll need to fly to Harbor's End," I tell Antrim. I glance at the sky. The light is dimming, lengthening, as sunset approaches. "Should we leave tomorrow at first light?"

Antrim growls softly at Gray Sanan, but the sounds are too soft for me to make out their meaning. Then the old Dragon turns and wishes me well. When I thank him, he flies off, unsteady as leaves in a wind as he goes.

"We could leave at first light," Antrim agrees, drawing my attention back, "but I think it imprudent to wait that long. Dragons flying into the Human world are generally advised to travel at night. It will be much safer for all of us if we leave now."

I see the wisdom in this. As does Riva, who nods immediately.

"If you think it best, I'm ready," I say. "Tell me what to do. I know Riva is comfortable riding Dragons, but I've had no experience or training, and I don't want to fall off."

"You won't," Antrim assures me with a recognizably derisive snort. "But maybe later you will wish you had."

■ ■ ■

In less than half an hour we are in the air, winging our way out of the mountain valley the Dragons call home and east across the jagged peaks of the Skyscrape toward the broad shimmering surface of Roughlin Wake. Our pathway requires that we use an aero-wormhole: a kind of cloud break that skims through heavily fogged-over snatches of sky at extra-quick speed, just as the earthbound wormholes do on ground — shortening our flight and getting us more quickly to where we wish to go. I had no idea such shortcuts existed in the broad expanses overhead, and I don't pretend even now to understand how this is possible or how you find such loopholes in flight. But they do exist, and I am more than happy to be using one on this occasion, because our flight is smooth and untroubled by winds, and Antrim's body sways slowly and easily as his great wings sweep the air. Riva and I are positioned well forward of those wings, astride the Dragon's neck, legs clamped tightly and gloved hands gripping leathery hide beneath scales that can be elevated at the juncture of neck and body. The girth of the Dragon's body is immense, but the scales help secure us and give me a welcome sense of ease.

It feels odd at first, but after a while I grow comfortable with it. The trick seems to be not to panic and lose your grip. Even so, Riva sits behind me and keeps one hand fastened tightly about my waist, holding me in place. The minutes pass, and then the cloud break ends and we are out over the Roughlin.

The sun has set while we were in the wormhole and it is almost fully dark now. I watch the mostly shadowed and heavily forested land unfurl beneath us under the light of the waxing moon, then that, too, sets and the darkness is more complete. At regular intervals, Riva asks if I am all right, and I assure her I am. We have found a calm and quiet night on which to fly, and my reservations have vanished. I look down at the waters below, and ahead to where the distant lights along the shores of the waste-lands — sporadic and dim — twinkle softly. It turns out that flying makes me feel euphoric — enough that I almost forget my fear over Harrow. But only almost.

We fly for what seems like hours, and then the lights of Harbor's End come into view.

"Can you find a place to land north of the city?" I call out to Antrim.

A nod of his head, and he swings slightly in that direction. I judge that we will be there in only minutes.

Until the airplanes fly into view — three of them coming in formation, Ministry jets with distinctive swept-back wings that immediately identify them. *Radar,* I think, remembering the Ministry technology that all such airplanes carry, and I am instantly gripped by fear. Nothing can avoid radar detection, and Antrim is a very large flying object indeed. We will be spotted and brought down in seconds.

Antrim instantly dives, dropping to a distance that puts us only a few hundred feet off the surface of the lake, but that isn't going to help. We can't hide while out in the open like this. Yet we continue to fly in a straight line. Why isn't Antrim searching for some sort of cover? Those jets are still high above us, but I know it makes no difference. No matter where we go, we will be discovered as long as we remain a moving target.

Yet we are not. The jets continue on their established flight path and in seconds are out of sight. I stare in disbelief. They must not have been paying attention. Perhaps they failed to turn on their radar or maybe they just didn't . . .

Riva bends close over my shoulder, her

lips inches from my ear. "Dragons have their own protections against Human detection," she says, her voice calm. "Human instruments cannot find a Dragon unless the Dragon wishes to be found."

Oh. As usual, I still have a lot to learn.

I look out over the city as we pass above it until we are far enough north that we are beyond even the residential sections, and then Antrim slows, taking his time as he searches for a place to land. Even if someone were looking, we would be hard to spot against a sky this dark. With no moon to reveal us, we seem safe, and I am already thinking ahead to the next part of my plan.

Antrim finds a grassy hill surrounded by forest and sets down so smoothly I can barely feel it when he lands. Riva and I scramble off, sliding down his wings to the ground, and right away I think I will never walk again. Because every muscle in both legs — all the way up to and including my backside — aches in a way I had never thought possible. Whether it was how wide I was forced to spread my legs, or the intensity of gripping Antrim's great girth the whole time to be certain I did not fall, I am paying the price.

I drop to my hands and knees and remain there for a moment, waiting for the pain to pass. Eventually, it does. When I try to rise, Riva is there to help me.

"Takes some getting used to," she teases, "but you did well. And the aching will end — eventually. You'll have to walk it off, though."

"I'm not sure I can walk at all," I protest as I take one step and then two. But of course I can; it's just a matter of plowing through the pain.

We speak one last time with Antrim, who promises to stay somewhere close by. When we return to the clearing, he says, he will come for us.

He wishes us good luck and flies off into the darkness. I don't like to see him go. I immediately feel more vulnerable.

"What now?" Riva asks, looking about in confusion.

"We walk," I tell her. "That way." I point southeast. Back into the residential neighborhoods that border the city proper. "A little over an hour's walk, if everything goes well."

She says nothing but tightens her cloak about her broad frame and pulls up her hood to hide her face. We have agreed that if we are accosted or encounter someone in our path, I will do the talking and Riva will stand back and hide herself as best she can.

289

I have some protections thanks to my *inish,* which I can use to disguise us for a short time. I will use it if it seems necessary, but I am hoping it will not. I don't want to drain my powers too fast if I require them for other things, like getting us back out of here in one piece.

Still, I find myself wondering suddenly if it is possible for me to use my Changeling powers to revert to my more Human appearance, which would certainly be safer under these conditions. It is nothing I have accessed before, so I have no idea how to go about it — or if those powers even exist — but maybe it is no different than employing my *inish*? I reach for that, trying to envision my former Human appearance, but feel a resistance inside me, a wall I cannot break through.

With a sigh, I abandon the effort. Perhaps it is just as well. My Human appearance feels alien to me now, a skin I no longer want to inhabit. My *inish* doesn't want to allow it and possibly will do something to forcibly stop it.

It is still dark, and there are few people about. And once we arrive at our destination, we might have to wait until the person I have come to find wakes. At least it will be easier to stay out of sight in the residential districts than in the city proper.

I find myself thinking back to the last time I was here, with Harrow, when I came to discover some truths about my past. Now here I am again, trying to learn something more. I try to put the discomfort I am feeling out of my mind, but it is not so easy. I almost died here the last time, when Allensby and his goons arrived. I have no wish to risk anyone from the Ministry discovering me now. Yet what am I supposed to do to avoid this when I am here to see the same person?

Because, to find Drifter, I must first locate my mother.

EIGHTEEN

Two years, it's been. Two years since I last saw her. At our last parting, I promised to return as soon as I could, but the logistics seemed harder the more I changed from Human to Fae. Plus, after years apart save one visit, we were virtually strangers. My adoptive mother still saw me as she had when I was a child. She has never really gotten to know me as a young woman.

How disappointing will it be for her to learn that I have all but abandoned my previous life — the life I had once enjoyed with my father and with her?

But there is no help for it. She is my best and possibly only link to finding Drifter. Harrow's life and our future hang in the balance, and I cannot allow either my mother's feelings or my own to interfere with that.

It takes Riva and I an hour and a half to make our way to my mother's neighborhood, where she had lived when last I came to find her. She was in hiding then, living under an assumed name, afraid of Allensby and the Ministry, worried that they were still hunting her, haunted by the possibility that her husband's execution and my disappearance had not been enough to satisfy them. When Harrow rescued us from Allensby and his soldiers, my mother and I had parted at the top of the street, her house engulfed in flames and most of our would-be captors dead inside. She had gone one street over to stay with a trusted neighbor. With Allensby now dead and the Ministry, I assume, moved on to other concerns, I have to hope she is still living with her friend. Or that, if she has moved, a few simple questions can uncover her new location.

It is another gamble, and perhaps a futile one. But neighbors tend to keep track of one another when they are friends, even if one moves away. And my mother is a homebody, happiest when things are settled and unchanged. Granted, she will have had two years to move, but I am betting that if she has, it will not have been far.

Yet when Riva and I reach our destination and stand at the head of that same street and I look down to where her former house had stood, I am shocked to find another house has taken its place. I stare for long minutes — long enough for Riva to take hold of my shoulder and squeeze gently.

"What are we doing?"

I shake my head. "Looking for something that is no longer there."

"Ah. What exactly would that be?"

"My mother's home."

"We've come to visit your mother?"

"No. Well, yes."

I explain quickly what I hope to discover. If we are lucky, my mother will know how to find Drifter. And if not, she will have some idea of where he might be. My parents were close to him while he trained me, and I cannot believe they would have lost touch entirely. Then I launch into a quick explanation of what happened when I was here before and how finding another house on the site is a surprise.

Riva shakes her head when I finish, gesturing at the new house. "Perhaps your mother lives there now. In the new house."

I have not considered this. How could I not? Staying with a friend — no matter how close you are — eventually becomes uncomfortable. And I know her to be a homebody, so why is it so hard to believe she would rebuild?

Dawn is close now, the scrim of light giving the eastern horizon a pale hint of brightness. We don't want to stand around out here for too long. I note, for the first time, a light on in the newly constructed home. If my mother is there, perhaps she is awake. Or perhaps whoever now lives there might know where she resides.

Because I have few choices in this matter and time is pressing, I tell Riva to wait where she is. She looks upset.

"I know you were not comfortable with me coming," she says bluntly. "That was clear enough. But I thought you might need someone at your back on this search. Shouldn't I stay with you?"

"I think this part will be easiest to do alone." I take hold of her hands. "It was generous of you to accompany me. I had no right to expect it and I admit I wasn't sure it was a good idea, but I think now it was. Still, for now, I need you to wait here. I won't be long."

She nods wordlessly, turns away, and walks to a bus shelter behind her where she slips inside, cloak and hood in place. I continue on across the street and down to the new house. It is dark enough that I cannot be easily seen once I am beyond the glow of the streetlights. There is no one around, so I am able to walk right up to the window and look inside. The house looks empty, but now I see another light deeper inside, in what appears to be a kitchen. I still do not see my mother, but a figure in a robe momentarily passes into and out of the light.

I scan the living room once more. Nothing there I recognize, nothing to confirm who lives here, but I don't think I can wait any longer. I have to take a chance. I walk to the door and give it three sharp raps. The porch light is off, so I am mostly in shadow. I have my hood pulled tightly around my head and face, and my leafy hair is tucked back out of sight. I am unwilling to let her see more than I need to before I have a chance to explain. I wait patiently for a response, and then the door opens and my mother is standing there, staring at me. She looks much older, much wearier, than I remember. But it is early and she may have been awake all night. I cannot make assumptions. I don't have the right.

"Auris?" she asks quietly.

"Hello, Mother," I reply, and step inside.

She embraces me at once, tears running down her cheeks and dampening mine as she presses her face against me. "I thought you would never come back. I thought I would never see you again." She pauses. "Funny. Now that you're here, I am already imagining how it will feel when you are gone again."

"Well, I am here now," I remind her. "Can we sit and talk a bit? Is this your new home? You made a good choice in deciding to rebuild. This is exactly where you belong."

Her head nods against me; her arms continue to hold me close. "I feel safe here now. I heard that Allensby was dead, and no one from the Ministry has bothered me since." She squeezes me closer, sighs. "Come in. Sit. I will make us some tea."

She goes off without waiting for a response and without bothering to look closely at me. Which I guess means she knows, but still I do not take off or even loosen my hood and cloak. The longer I can pretend I am the girl she remembers, the better.

I seat myself on this Human couch, surrounded by Human things, and feel entirely out of place.

My mother returns with the tea and sets the tray on the coffee table in front of the couch, then sits next to me and looks me directly in the face.

"I noticed it before, but . . . Will you let me see you now?"

297

I can't put it off any longer. I remove my hood and cloak and let her see me full-on. She looks so sad as she reaches out a hand to stroke my green leafy hair that I feel my eyes prickle with tears.

"For so many years," she says softly, "we tried to prevent this from happening — to stop your Fae side from showing — just to keep you safe. But now . . ." I see tears well in her eyes, and one slips out to fall unnoticed down her cheek. "You look beautiful, Auris. So beautiful. But it just makes me realize how far away from me you are, how much you can never be a part of my world again. And while I know it is natural for children to move on, to leave their parents, we had so few years together before the Ministry took you that I still feel cheated of all the lost time. And knowing how firmly you have moved on . . ." She grabs both of my hands in hers, her skin dark against my green. "I love you, Auris. Please, tell me you are happy."

How can I be happy, when the one I love most has been so brutally stolen from me? But this is not what she needs — or wants — to hear. So I muster the lie — which is only partly a lie anyway. "I am happy, Mother. I have found a land I love, and a family I love. I belong to Viridian Deep, in a way I never truly belonged here."

"So what brings you here? It must be more than just to see me. Looking as you do, the risk of being here remains too great."

"Yes, I know, Mother, but I need your help. I am looking for Drifter. You were friends for a long time — you and Father and he — so I am hoping you can tell me where he is."

She sighs. "I would prefer you not go back to him; he has already taken so much of you away. I still think of you in my heart as you were before he came into our lives, but I understand I cannot interfere with how you choose to live. Drifter resides far to the east, outside the residential districts, in Bonningham Woods. Go to the head of the street and follow it east to the old water tower, then take the path where it bends north. He lives out there on a run-down, unused farm — just a few buildings and some pasture, not much more. I see him now and again. He's much older. He isn't the same as you remember."

"Thank you, Mother," I say quietly. "And I need you to know that, despite this" — I gesture to myself — "despite how it must seem as if I have forsaken and abandoned all you have given me — I still love you."

She reaches for me then, and we embrace.

"I love you, too, Auris. I always will." She whispers the words as if she suspects she will never see me again. "Now go. Be safe. Be happy. That is all I can ask."

I embrace her once more, then rise and go out the door, heedless of the tears leaking down my cheeks.

I find Riva at the head of the street, still sitting in the bus shelter, still wrapped in her cloak and hooded like a vagrant. A few Humans have gathered to wait with her, but they stand apart, well outside the shelter, careful not to get too close. They look at her and see her as someone to be avoided, as someone so different from themselves that she makes them uncomfortable. They can't have caught more than a glimpse of her face, but she is big and wrapped up in her cloak and clearly not like they are. That's all it takes.

Perhaps that is all it has ever taken.

She catches sight of me, gets to her feet, and leaves the shelter. The Humans watch, wanting to be sure she isn't coming back before they move to occupy the bench she has abandoned. Even concealed by her clothing as she is, she is twice the size of most of them, an intimidating presence. I feel oddly sad for the mistaken impression, and almost decide to throw up a false image so that I appear as a small, winsome child coming to find its mother. But it seems wisest to preserve my *inish* for an emergency rather than spending it on an impulse.

And in any case, Riva and I are next to each other swiftly, and the moment has passed.

"Are you okay?" she asks, seeing the traces of tears still on my cheeks.

"I will be," I say.

Without the need for further explanation, Riva Tisk takes me in her arms and hugs me to her. I take the comfort for a moment, then wipe the tears away with the back of my hand and ease out of her arms. "I know how to find Drifter now. We should go."

I start walking east along the high street, leaving the past further behind than ever. For long moments we don't speak, and then I gather myself and say, "It is hard, saying goodbye to people forever. She's lost a husband and now a daughter. She's lost what she loved most in her life, and yet she goes on. I'm just scared that . . ."

Riva's hand rests comfortingly on my shoulder. "We will get your Harrow back for you, Auris, if at all possible."

I nod wordlessly, and we walk in silence

for a long time, heading east along a street that is paved and well tended by city workers. I think how familiar this looks and at the same time how alien. I miss the forest and the trails beneath my feet, and I think about how strange concrete feels when you have gotten used to earth.

The paved road ends and becomes a dirt road that disappears into a thick stand of trees. Off to our left stands the old water tower — a tall wooden barrel that has been out of use for years, a reminder of a past when life was simpler and less synthetic. Where once we used wooden barrels on stilts to catch rainwater, now we use steel containers — and groundwater is treated with chemicals to protect against the pollutants that we have infected it with. Drinking from streams is dangerous. Using untreated water is a hazard few are willing to risk. Humans have corrupted Nature so deeply. Is it any wonder I prefer to embrace my Fae side?

Forests loom beyond the tower like a wall. A sign announces that we are approaching Bonningham Woods. Here, not a hundred yards farther in, the road branches at a river. Following the directions my mother has given me, we take the north fork and walk on along a worn path. Soon, the woods give way to rolling fields. Farms dot the land-scape — homes and outbuildings, livestock and silos, pastures and fields. In the latter, farmers are hard at work plowing and clear-ing, planting and harvesting — some by hand and some using machines, all in service to the changing of the seasons and the requisite rotation of various crops. In the pastures, cows and sheep graze. The scene is tranquil and idyllic to look upon, even though the reality of farming is fre-quently demanding and harsh.

Like all life, I think. Like the whole of the world and everything that it has given birth to since the dawn of time.

It is about midmorning when we reach our destination, and I know it immediately. The farm buildings are very old; some are falling apart. There is no indication of any planting in the fields, and no sign of any livestock. Weeds grow everywhere, and pigeons have made a home in the rafters and on eaves. The house is in the best shape, but even so it needs painting, and its wooden slats and trim are sagging and broken. Once, it must have been a welcom-ing home, but now it just looks forlorn.

As we approach, we find that we have missed something. In the space behind the two-story house, backed up against a small stand of heavy woods and shadowed heavily by its overhanging boughs, is another building. This one might be a sort of barn or storage shed . . . or something else altogether. It is impossible to tell from the outside. But this one is much better kept, and its windows are securely shuttered and its doors padlocked.

"Cheerful," Riva observes, pulling a face. "Either run down to scrap or locked up so tight the sunlight can't get at it. Who lives here?"

"My old teacher," I reply. "Supposedly." I shake my head. "But maybe no one, from the look of things."

We stand where we are, taking it all in. I half hope someone will hail us or come out to offer greeting, and half hope I've made a mistake. I need to find Drifter, but I don't like the look and feel of this ramshackle farm, and I don't want to find him here. Now that I have recalled him, I remember him as a strong and confident man. But then, I remind myself, Riva's house was much the same from the outside, and she is one of the toughest people I have ever met.

Riva grows impatient. "Let's have a closer look."

We start forward, choosing the house first and finding no evidence that anyone has occupied it in months. We move from there to the barn and other outbuildings and find nothing different. There are no signs of habitation anywhere. I thought maybe there would be an animal or two in the barn, but the building is empty.

Finally, we survey the shuttered and locked structure. It seems to have no particular purpose — or at least not one suited to a farm. It looks more like a bunker. I am curious, but short of breaking in, I don't know what to do about it.

"Hello in there!" Riva shouts, startling me so much I jump.

We wait, but no one appears. All around us the forests and fields have gone quiet, and I am beginning to wonder if we haven't stumbled on something we would have been better off avoiding.

"Drifter?" I call out impulsively. "Are you in there? It's me, Auris!"

Nothing.

"I can break that lock," Riva announces, giving me a look that suggests she wants to.

"So can I," I answer. "But is that a good idea?"

She shrugs. "It is if we want to find out whether anyone lives here. We're wasting our time otherwise. Come on."

We walk over to the door and she reaches

for the lock, apparently intent on wrenching it off its hinges, but I quickly reach out to stop her. "No need for that."

I use my *inish* to reach inside the mechanism, and the lock opens on its own.

Riva grins. "You have to teach me how to do that. I can use *inish,* but not as cleverly as you do."

I smile, pleased with the compliment. But when I hesitate to follow up, she snatches off the lock and pulls the door wide. I get just a quick glimpse of what lies within: a room filled with weapons and equipment of all sorts, with everything neatly hung or shelved in an orderly fashion.

If I had any doubts about this being Drifter's place, they are gone now.

Then, just as my instincts give warning, a voice behind me says, "Hello, Auris. Would you like to come inside?"

NINETEEN

I turn around slowly to face the speaker.
The voice could only belong to Drifter, but
the man who stands before me appears to
be someone else entirely and in no way that
man who taught me everything I know
about self-defense. This man seems barely
able to defend himself, let alone anyone
else. He is long and lean, bordering on
gaunt. He stands stoop-shouldered, looking
both worn down and used up. His beard
hides the larger part of his features, and the
tangled mess of his hair — brown, shot
through with gray — hangs to his shoulders.
His big hands fist loosely at his sides, his
fingers gnarled and scarred from hard use.
He cannot be much more than forty by my
recollection — which, admittedly, is limited,
since I had forgotten about him entirely
until the Seers retrieved my memory of him.
But still.

"Is this how you usually enter someone's

house these days?" Drifter asks, a faint spark of humor in his tone. "Or are you just practicing for a career in breaking and entering?"

"We weren't sure if anyone was home," I reply, blushing in spite of myself. "No one answered our shouts or came out to greet us."

He nods but says nothing, and I continue to stare at him, trying to make sense of what I am seeing.

"Not the way you remember me, am I, Auris?" he says finally. "Well, you've changed a bit, too. Gotten a bit green and leafy. Finally embraced your Forest Sylvan side?"

"I have."

He glances then at Riva. "And I see your companion is Fae, too."

I nod. "This is Riva."

A quick grin. "Well, she looks like she might be useful. So, what *are* you doing here, Auris?"

"I could ask you the same. This isn't where you used to live, is it? Out here, in the back of beyond?"

"Nope. I lived in the city when you knew me. But after your father and mother were taken and you came to me for help, I found myself in the middle of something I didn't understand and didn't much want to be involved in. Then, when you disappeared, I took some steps to cover my tracks and moved away — out here, as you put it."

He knows something about me that I don't! He knows what happened to me after I fled my parents' home, the day the Ministry came for my family. I stare at him with a slow smile spreading over my face.

"What did I say?" he asks suddenly. "All at once, you look happy about something."

"I am. Can we sit and talk?"

Drifter runs his hand through his long hair and shrugs. "Since you have already opened my door, why don't you come all the way in? We don't want anyone stumbling into a scraggly hermit and two green-skinned women, do we?"

The room we enter takes up most of the building — wide and broad, with a ceiling that is easily twenty feet high. I spy a kitchen alcove at the back left that reveals a small dining table, cabinets, a refrigerator, and a cooktop. To the right there is a closed door that I am guessing leads to a bedroom. The room in which we stand seems more in keeping with the Drifter I remember. There are weapons everywhere I look, and training equipment is spread across the floor from wall to wall. Thick wrestling mats have been placed end-to-end at the center of the floor to form an arena for combat. Robes and towels hang from racks to one side, and a broad sink sits next to them. I note the meticulous organization of the weapons. Ancient blades, bows and arrows, spears, knives, throwing stars, and a few things I have never seen before can be found on one side of the room. Automatic weapons, both single shot and repeating, along with hand-guns of every imaginable sort, sit off to the other.

"Looks as if maybe you are expecting an invasion," Riva ventures. "You could outfit a brigade with all this."

"My collection," Drifter admits. "I don't train others anymore. I train by myself — just enough to be prepared in case there is need. The Ministry charges me with imagi-nary crimes — crimes against the state, as they so eloquently phrase it. Disruption of the law, the creation of rogue militias, you name it. It all amounts to a continuous litany of spurious charges. But their claims are so far-fetched I doubt anything could ever be proven or that anyone besides them even cares at this point. They just like the idea of calling me a criminal. They just want to keep me running."

He makes light of something that sounds

very serious, and shows no particular concern about it. But I wonder how much this harassment has changed his life.

"Are you not in trouble because of all this?" I press.

He smiles. "Less than usual. Certainly less than I was when I hid you from Allensby and his goons. Come sit with me, now. We'll talk a bit."

He leads us over to the small kitchen table and gestures to the four chairs. "Take a seat. I'll pour us a beer."

We sit while he pours and then he returns to join us, handing out the glasses. "Where should we begin?" he asks me once we are all settled. "We have a lot of ground to cover. How did you find me?"

"My mother told me."

"Yes, Margrete." He shakes his head. "We've remained friends. Well, acquaintances, at least. She's never been very happy with me; she can't forgive me for not keeping you safe. I made it a point to keep in touch anyway after your father was killed. I don't see her so much these days, but she knows how to find me. How is she?"

"Well enough. But she still seems so sad."

"Yes. She never got over Dennis being taken away and then having you disappear. What happened to you anyway?"

I'm not sure, of course. I am hoping *he* can tell me. He's right about the two of us having a lot to catch up on. There is so much we need to talk about that I don't know where to start — so I just jump in.

"I escaped when the Ministry took my parents away. Slipped out the back door and got away. Your training helped make that possible. But I lost my memory — of what happened after my escape from the Federation, of most of my childhood. Of everything but ending up in a Goblin prison just before I turned fifteen. I have started to recover a few snatches of memory over the past two years, thanks to the Fae Seers, but only a few. Though of course, everything after the Goblin prison I remember perfectly."

"Shock, maybe?" he suggests. "Or drugs? I know your father gave you quite a few early on, when he was trying to suppress your Fae side. Oh, don't look so surprised, Auris; he told me all about it. He thought I ought to know if I was to train you. He thought I should understand the danger. He wasn't wrong. He was the one who told you to find me if the Ministry came for him and Margrete. I promised to provide you with shelter and keep you safe. So you came, and I took you in and hid you. You were with me for maybe three weeks. I was looking for a place to live outside the city — somewhere you could grow up in relative safety — but when I came back one day, you were gone. I tried to find you, but you had vanished. All I could discover was that you were seen leaving in the company of someone — I never could discover who — and you never came back. You don't remember *any* of it?"

I shake my head. "Nothing at all. I ended up in a Goblin prison out in the wastelands with no memory of anything from before my imprisonment. I was there for almost five years before I escaped with a few of my friends. All of them were killed — all but me. And one other, but I only found out he was alive a few weeks ago. After my escape, I wandered in the wastelands for two weeks before a Sylvan Watcher found me. He took me into Viridian Deep. He was the first to tell me that I was Fae — even though I looked entirely Human then. But I live with the Fae now and am partnered with my rescuer, so things have changed."

Drifter cocks an eyebrow. "I know how Viridian Deep can make you feel. I was there once, on and off, some years back. I, too, lived with someone I loved, though we stayed far from others during my stay. But that can wait for another time. Tell me the rest of your story."

I badly want to know his. All I know is he sought the Dragons to restore his Fae wife after a Barghast stole her *inish*. It is why I have come to find him. But I have to be patient.

So I continue, telling him of Harrow and my sisters. Admittedly, I crave every chance I am given to tell anyone who will listen what it was like to find my real family and to fall in love. I am embarrassed by my willingness to tell it so many times over, but at the same time I seem unable to stop myself. I notice the look of fascination on Drifter's face as he listens, and I catch glimpses of a similar expression on Riva's.

At one point, as I am talking about how Harrow and I survived the Ministry's invasion of Viridian Deep and our subsequent partnering — something I don't even need to go into but somehow just do — I break down completely, tears streaming down my face.

"I know all about Ancrow," Drifter says quietly, shifting subjects as I struggle to compose myself. "I never met her, but her story is legendary. She was respected by everyone I knew."

I want to laugh. My mother, a complex and difficult woman, who fought so hard to

314

see me gone, who constantly lied to me to conceal my past, then gave up her life to save me and everyone else in Viridian Deep. The familiar emotions to which this memory is inexorably attached surface in a rush, and I tamp them down again firmly.

"You said you went to Viridian Deep before you taught me." I manage to find the words to broach the subject amid the jumbled mix of emotions I am struggling to control. "But you never told me anything about that."

"It wasn't necessary at the time. Maybe now it is."

I nod. "I already know at least part of the story. I know that you loved a Fae woman, Meliore, and that she was taken by a Barghast."

His eyes narrow. "And who told you this?"

"A Dragon. His name is Gray Sanan."

"You spoke with Sanan?" Drifter asks with a smile. "You are full of surprises. But then you always were. Always defying expectations." He sighs, running his fingers through the tangled locks of his long hair. "Gray Sanan; it seems like it happened in another lifetime."

I lean closer, wait for his eyes to meet mine. "This is why Riva and I are here," I tell him. "This is why we've come to find you. Harrow, too, has fallen victim to a Barghast. And I need your help to set it right."

Drifter's smile fades, and I see a flash of unforgotten pain in his eyes. His is the fate I am trying so hard to avoid. "Better tell me the rest," he says gently.

"There is another Barghast . . ." I hesitate, unsure of how to put it to him. "Or perhaps it was the same Barghast who harmed Meliore. Who knows? His name is Tonklot, and he has made himself the leader of a band of Aerklings living in the Skyscrape Mountains. When I was on a fishing trip with Harrow and my two younger sisters, the Barghast and his Aerklings surrounded us. We didn't understand what he could do, so he was able to use his powers to mesmerize us so we wouldn't fight back. Then he stole Harrow's *inish*."

I pause. "You know that word? *Inish?*"

Drifter nods. "*Soul,* in the Fae language. Yes, I know it."

"Tonklot stole Harrow's *inish* by sucking it out through his mouth. It was terrible to watch — and made worse because I could do nothing to stop it. Once Harrow was reduced to little more than an empty shell, the Barghast told me that if I wanted him back, I had to bring him a Dragon by the next full moon. Then he and his followers

316

disappeared, leaving my sisters, Harrow, and me behind."

"Your Barghast sounds like my own. I never knew his name, but the description is the same. A feeder, a predator, a scavenger of the helpless? Surely the same. I find it a strange coincidence, otherwise."

"This is the same Barghast," I decide aloud. "It has to be."

Drifter looks grim. "Let me finish your story, then. You asked the Seers and they sent you to speak to the Dragons, much as they did with me. Ancrow was a Dragon rider, so you used your relationship as her daughter to gain an audience. I am not sure where Riva comes in."

"I was a Dragon rider, too," Riva says. "I rode with Ancrow in the Ghoul Wars."

"Which would have helped you immensely. Dragons respect their riders. You seem like someone I would do well to respect, even without knowing more. So you spoke with Gray Sanan — presumably, you both know Dragon speech — and this is how you learned about me and my connection to the Barghasts. Am I right?"

I nod, then push on. "Tonklot ordered me to bring him a Dragon by the next full moon if I wanted Harrow's soul restored. But you were in Viridian Deep years before

317

with Meliore. Sanan told me that the Barghast stole her *inish,* too, and that you had sought Sanan's help too late to save her. So instead you asked for aid in pursuing the Barghast, but this was just before the time of the Ghoul Wars, and Sanan had other obligations. He wasn't sure if you had ever managed to find and kill the creature in the wake of Meliore's death. Did you? What do you know of these creatures? You are the only person I know who has ever encountered a Barghast."

Drifter's smile is brief. "I was very much in love with Meliore — enough so that I was persuaded to go back with her to Viridian Deep after we met. Very much the same as it was with you and Harrow. My own life meant nothing to me without Meliore. Once her *inish* was taken, I thought maybe there was a chance I could get it back."

He pauses. "This all happened before I met you or your father. Your father I knew from when I was under contract with the Ministry security forces to help with their training. Your father and I became close friends, and eventually he told me your story. I knew of his situation at the Ministry and I feared for him even then — and for you and your mother later. This was why I agreed to teach you the arts of self-defense and weapons mastery when he asked me. But my relationship with Meliore happened earlier, well before I met any of you."

He takes a deep breath, breathes it out slowly. "I knew Meliore because she crossed out of Viridian Deep and came into my world on some sojourn of a personal nature; I no longer remember what it was. We encountered each other by chance and were attracted to each other immediately. We fell in love quickly, and she asked me to return with her. I did so, unafraid and trusting. I knew of the Fae; I knew of their history. Meliore lived alone, so I moved in with her. We had a good life. We lived apart from other Fae because I was effectively Human, but we were enough for each other. She was a healer; I worked in weapons construction. We were very happy. But while I was away on a visit to the Human world, Meliore encountered a Barghast and was taken. I came back to find her much as you found your Harrow — gone, but still alive. The Seers, when I sought their help, did not know what sort of a creature could have done this, but they did inform me that the Dragons might be willing to give me some advice."

"Sanan told me that you were half Fae, like me. Is that true?"

He looks almost startled. "They knew that? I never told them. But yes, I am Fae-blooded like you, Auris. I was born to a Fae father and a Human mother, and I was told so early on. So the Fae world was known to me, even though I had never been there."

I am shocked to hear this. "But you don't look anything like I do — like one of the Fae," I blurt out. "You look entirely Human!"

He shrugs. "Blood is fickle, and genes are quixotic. Your father told me that. I am what you see. I have always looked this way — never as one of the Fae."

He shakes his head. "So much history lost. Most of it forever." His smile is dark. "Even now, I wonder at the capriciousness of our lives. Anyway, I went to the Dragons and persuaded them to hear me out. Gray Sanan was Dragon Lord then. He said I was too late to save Meliore, but he told me how to find the Barghast — though he refused to accompany me on my quest. I knew I could not get Meliore back, yet my pride and anger clouded my good judgment. Sanan warned me that the Barghasts were dark and treacherous and vampiric. If I were to look the Barghast directly in the eyes, I would be lost. I promised I would be careful and call for help if it was needed, but I was not careful enough. I was not sufficiently prepared for what I found when I tracked him to his lair."

Drifter shakes his head. "Barghasts have an unusual passion for collecting live creatures and transforming them into lifeless decorations. I had seen what was done with Meliore, emptied of life, and I thought I was prepared. But it was much worse than I imagined. Dozens of husks were pinned to the walls, suspended from the ceilings, and positioned in grotesque representations of what they were like in life. I caught the creature enough off guard that I managed to slash at its legs and wound it, but still it fled from me and escaped."

I think back to Tonklot's limp, and suddenly have no doubt that the two Barghasts — his and mine — are the same creature.

"But there is still hope for Harrow, isn't there?" I ask.

Drifter nods. "The Barghast would not have told you to bring him a Dragon in exchange for Harrow if it were impossible for your partner to be restored. He must know you will demand that Harrow's *inish* be returned before giving up the Dragon, so I think there is still a chance to save him."

I feel relief wash through me, but an instant later I wonder if Drifter is missing something. Perhaps it was Tonklot's intention all along to trick me into thinking Harrow could be saved, and when he has me close again he will steal my *inish* as well, along with the Dragon. I shudder at the idea; I cannot manage to dismiss it.

I start to voice my fears, unable to help myself, but Drifter immediately interrupts.

"Think about what he has done, Auris. Why offer to give Harrow back to you? If his goal is steal your *inish,* why wait? Why not take it when he had the chance — when he had you mesmerized and in his power and had already taken Harrow's? Why not drain all of you at once — you, Harrow, *and* your sisters? It makes no sense, so there has to be something more, something he wants. He really must need that Dragon, and somehow he thinks you are the one who can give it to him. Perhaps he has reason to believe this. After all, you managed to persuade Sanan to speak to you."

I am grateful for his attempts to reassure me, if unwilling to embrace them fully. But I think back to how Tonklot had tried to penetrate my defenses, and then been turned aside. He had even muttered something about an obstruction — and indicated he had encountered it before.

That he had encountered *me* before.

"You've seen a Barghast," I find myself saying. "Did you ever see what it looked like? I mean, *really* looked like? When I saw mine, it looked mostly like another Aerkling. But it must have looked different to you. These creatures apparently can shapeshift."

"Shapeshift? Yes, probably so. When I saw it that last time, it was mostly serpentine in appearance — as if it was an overgrown lizard or a swamp creature of some sort. It had a crooked, rigid backbone, and scales covered its body. There were parts of it that looked Dragon-like and parts that looked reptilian. It was upright, but its movements and body shape suggested it would be just as comfortable on four feet as on two. It seemed flexible, as if . . ." He trails off.

"As if it was capable of changing shape," I finish.

So, no way to be absolutely certain if it was the same Barghast or not — but given the injuries Drifter described giving it, it does seem likely, even with the shapeshifting added in.

I let the matter drop for now and go back to what we were talking about. "After the Barghast fled, did you go after it?"

"I searched for it." He looks momentarily lost, then simply angry. "But within days I knew I wasn't going to find it, so I eventually decided to go home again — though not before I had destroyed its lair and all its trophies. My failure haunts me to this day, but I still think I made the right choice. I had lost Meliore, no matter what happened with the Barghast, and losing her was all that really mattered. I returned to Harbor's End and began working with the Ministry forces, which is where I met your father. You know the rest."

I place a hand on his arm. "I am so sorry for what happened to you. I am so sorry for Meliore. I haven't lost what you did — not yet at least — but I can imagine it, and that alone is enough to break me. But I know this much — I am going after Tonklot, and I am going to get back Harrow's *inish.*"

Drifter nods. "Brave talk, Auris."

"Desperate is more like it, but I have to try. At least I know how to find Tonklot on the next full moon."

He shakes his head slowly. "Auris, this creature will be intent on destroying you when you do meet up with him again, and I think you already know you will not have a Dragon to bargain with."

"But I do have a Dragon," I say. I tell him of Antrim, the new Vinst, who is waiting in the woods north of the city. "Don't get me wrong; I never seriously considered making that trade. The Seers have warned me that would be a huge mistake. But just what I *am* to do, I still don't know."

He looks at me gravely. "Auris, I don't know how much I can help you. As you can see, my encounter with the Barghast was a disaster and there is nothing I can teach you there. But I would still like to come with you."

I stare at him wordlessly for long moments, repeating his words back in my head. He is offering his help — help I know I desperately need. But doesn't he put his life in danger by doing so? Can I agree to let him do that?

He takes a deep breath. "Understand, I am making this offer because I want to help you, but I am also making it because I want to atone for my failure to do more for Meliore. I failed her, and I do not want to have to live with failing you, too. Helping you will allow something positive to come out of this whole Barghast nightmare — and perhaps help me get my revenge as well."

He gazes at me for a moment longer, and still I cannot speak. How many lives will this mission cost me? The more I take, the more I risk. "Please," he insists, "let me help. I have a stake in this as well. I failed once when it mattered. I do not intend to fail again."

I find it almost funny that he is asking me to allow him to help, as if the student is now the master.

I glance at Riva. "I think he means it," she says. "Perhaps you should listen to him. I think it possible that my own help — while of considerable value — might not be enough."

I smile at her small attempt at humor. "Maybe we should go find ourselves a Dragon and fly home."

Of course, this is easier said than done. It is not even noon yet, and none of us wants to risk flying a Dragon over Harbor's End in the full light of day. Plus, there is the small matter of our exhaustion to contend with. The last sleep either Riva or I had was the night before we reached the Dragons, and that was out in open country on the ground. I've been awake for nearly thirty hours straight and am feeling an intense weariness — though one subsumed by my desperate need to save Harrow. Already, it feels as if I have somehow failed him. He has no one else who can save him, and I still feel rudderless, without a concrete plan. And the clock is ticking.

But sleep is key if I am to remain focused, and we cannot leave until nightfall anyway, so Drifter provides blankets and a place to sleep, and wakes us near sunset. After we have eaten, he begins to pack provisions and weapons, offering Riva and I our pick of the latter. Riva is ecstatic. She quickly chooses a deadly looking crossbow and bolts, which she straps across her back, and I select a brace of finely wrought throwing knives. We would take more, but we have to be realistic. For one thing, walking about laden with blades and automatic weapons is likely to draw attention we don't need. For another, you can only use one weapon at a time anyway, and we already have what we brought with us for protection.

Once supplied, we set out, all three of us hooded and cloaked. Drifter is not green and leafy, but he is still wanted by the Ministry and does not think it a good idea to let anyone see his face. We are hunted creatures, so caution and concealment will serve us best. We walk through the last of the waning daylight, passing into sunset and then twilight. We reach the northeastern outskirts of Harbor's End quickly enough, and — staying where traffic and habitation is light — pass on west toward where we left Antrim.

I wonder how the Dragon will be able to see us when it is this dark, but I decide starlight is probably sufficient. The skies are partly cloudy, but the stars are out in the gaps, and the lights of the city reflect off the low-hanging screen to provide a pale glow that falls over everything for miles. There is a silence to the night I find welcome but also disturbing. Shouldn't there be night birds? Shouldn't there be the sounds of engines and tires and nighttime industry rising up from the streets and buildings of Harbor's End?

But the rhythms of the city are yet another thing that have vanished in the haze of my missing memories, so perhaps this is not unusual — a fiction I manage to maintain until we are perhaps a mile south of where Antrim is supposed to be waiting. And then I see the first indications of a fresh glow ahead — one caused by neither the city lights nor the stars.

Right away I know something is wrong.

We push ahead more quickly, my concerns growing by the moment — enhanced when I see the circular beams of man-made spotlights. I begin to hear shouts and cries and the clanking of armored vehicles. The sounds are distinctive and deeply troubling. None of this should be happening out here in the middle of nowhere, in the darkness of nighttime.

"What is that?" Riva asks finally, unable to stay silent any longer.

"I don't know," I answer as I look over at Drifter.

For a moment, he doesn't answer. But his superior experience takes over as he continues to listen, and he shakes his head in warning.

"A confrontation of some sort," he says. The expression on his face is unreadable. "Not something we want anything to do with, if we can avoid it."

But already I know that we are not going to be given a choice.

TWENTY

We stand where we are for long minutes —
Drifter, Riva, and I — staring off at the
northern horizon as spotlights flare and
sweep across the sky and forest canopy. We
can barely see what is happening, but I
suspect we already know.

And I am very afraid of what it means.

Finally, Riva says, "We have to get closer."

We move ahead once more, with Drifter
leading the way as our most experienced
scout and fighter. Dread coils in my stomach. Something has happened to Antrim. I
don't know what, but it can't be anything
good. I shouldn't have left him alone. I
should have sent him back to his Dragon
homeland.

Our progress takes us across open grasslands and through patches of woods at
regular intervals. Ahead, the landscape rises
in forested hills and heavy stands of conifers
that continue to mask the source of the

spotlights yet show clearly that they have formed a partial barrier about a large section of woods — one that stretches back toward the mountains for close to two miles. We move cautiously, not wanting to draw attention until we are sure about what we are doing.

The surrounding darkness creates a somber atmosphere, and the glow from ahead does nothing to alter this. We are venturing into an unknown situation, save that whatever is happening likely involves Antrim. I thought the Dragon would be safe this far out, but perhaps I was mistaken. We walk steadily, but with a caution for sounds that would betray us. I wish I had the power of foresight so that I could know what lies ahead.

It takes us awhile to reach our destination, and our approach still tells us nothing about what is happening. The spotlights continue to play across the sky, their beams stabbing holes through the darkness. But now I can tell there are also other lights flooding the landscape, and that these are pointed into the trees as well. All about, the heavy clanking and grinding of wheels and treads, and the humming of machinery, continues. Fresh equipment has been brought forward from Harbor's End and is moving into position.

Then we climb a wooded rise and all of our questions about what is taking place are answered.

Below us, the land falls away in a gentle grassy slope toward a broad stretch of open meadow filled with lights and vehicles, artillery and barriers — and men. The men are all armed Ministry soldiers. Both men and fighting equipment confront a stand of heavy forest as if they have trapped something inside. I know what that something is. Or, rather, who: Antrim. I can sense his presence.

My worst fears have been realized.

How they managed to find Antrim I cannot begin to guess, but he is in serious trouble. As big and strong as he is — as able and experienced as I imagine him to be — he cannot escape this. Huge cannons and vehicles bristling with weapons are everywhere I look. Even though the lights fail to reveal the Dragon, they will do so easily if he tries to break out. If he takes flight, the spotlights sweeping overhead will illuminate him against the night sky and the cannons will bring him down.

Dragon scales offer substantial protection, but how well will they withstand the impact of heavy shells and automatic weapons fire?

We have to do something to help him. *I* have to do something.

I am really afraid now, but I know it is up to me.

I am the one who possesses a powerful *inish*. I am the one endowed with magic that might be able to spring him from his trap. But it will require considerable risk and effort.

I turn to Drifter. "Can you tell who commands those Ministry soldiers?"

He scans the scene below and finally points. "Do you see the vehicle that sits behind that barricade of cannons, the one with the emblem of a clenched fist on its door? Look at the group of men standing beside it. The one who holds a communicator but no weapon — the one the others are listening to — he is in command."

I find the man he describes and start sketching out a plan in my head. First, we need a distraction. "Can we do something to draw everyone's attention to this commander and away from Antrim?"

Drifter and Riva exchange a quick look. "Auris?" Drifter says. "That commander, as you called him? He's not military. He's a civilian. No uniform and no weapons, yet he commands anyway. I don't know why. It's very odd."

Allensby, I think at once. But Allensby is dead.

Something tugs at me. A warning. I cannot decide why, but it is strong enough that I don't dismiss it out of hand, even if I can't identify it. I know myself well, and I know how my instincts work. They are alerting me, and ignoring them would be a mistake.

"Can you just do it?" I press. "I need to get into those woods."

Drifter reaches into his pack and pulls out an odd metal cylinder in which a timer has been inserted. "Here. This will blow the wheels right off those cannons and trucks. Set the timer to ten seconds, pull the pin on the other end to release the trigger, and immediately throw the explosive." He fetches out a few more and hands three of them to Riva. "You take these; just pull out the tab. Same thing with all of them. I'll do the other three. That should confuse everyone long enough for Auris to reach Antrim." He looks at me. "That is what you're going to do, isn't it?"

I nod. "I have to, if he's to know we're here."

Drifter's eyes are hard as he looks into mine. "Be careful, Auris. The Ministry likely wants you more than it wants that Dragon."

I know it's true. That's how it's always

been — though I still don't know why. But what the Ministry wants and what it is going to get are two very different things. We don't have the power to disarm this entire army or to silence their weapons, but we can cause enough disruption that Antrim might have a chance of escaping.

"I need time to circle around to the east of the Ministry line and into the woods. Then, once you create those distractions, I'll get past their cordon, find Antrim and bring him here, and we can all fly out together."

"Are you out of your mind?" Riva demands. "How can they not see something that big when it tries to fly?"

"Because she will disable their lights," Drifter says, correctly guessing what I have in mind. "It's a big risk, though — and will require a huge amount of *inish,* Auris. Can you really use up so much of it without going down yourself? How many lights are there?"

"Too many." I shrug off my worries. "But I can get most of them. And I have to try something. Wish me luck."

Though part of me also wonders if I could not use my *inish* to render Antrim invisible once I reach him. Then he could remain undetected long enough to make an escape.

But I don't know if he would agree to let me do that. Nor am I sure my magic is strong enough to make it happen. Or if, indeed, my magic will work on a Dragon, which is itself a magical being.

I slip off my backpack and hand it to Riva. She shakes her head doubtfully and takes it. "If the risk is too great, come back. We can find another way."

We can't, of course. And I do not plan to come back. She knows this, but she is trying to be encouraging. I walk up to her and give her a hug. "Thank you for coming this far," I whisper into her chest — as high up as I can reach.

"Just be careful, youngling. This journey is not done yet."

I glance at Drifter — he has never been a hugger — but he comes over and embraces me as well. "Remember your lessons," he says.

For a moment, I am frozen in place, astonished. He has never touched me before other than in combat work. He has never shown this sort of affection and commitment, and I am momentarily at a loss.

And then I am off in a rush, a dark figure crouched low as I scamper along just below the crest of the hill, hidden by the night and my *inish,* which I quickly summon to produce some concealment.

I wish I wasn't so scared.

I wish Harrow was here with me.

But that is the whole point of this mad undertaking, to make sure that the next time he will be.

I clutch that thought to me like a precious jewel as I run.

At first everything is easy.

I creep downhill, diagonally toward the far end of the Ministry line, being careful not to expose myself to any of the lights below. Though I am under an illusory concealment by now, my *inish* engaged, I am still a presence and my shadow might betray me. But no one is looking my way, and I give no cause for anyone to do so. The lights continue to play across the sky overhead — vast circles of illumination that will expose anything that ventures within their range. The soldiers stand about, looking mostly bored as they man their vehicles and cannons, waiting for the lights to reveal something.

Down the hillside I go with steady, silent movements, then across the backside to the eastern edge. Once there, I crouch down.

Waiting. Waiting.

Anticipation is surely another form of

torture. It goes on and on, and nothing happens. What are Riva and Drifter waiting for? Surely they know I am in place by now. Do they think I am capable of staying hidden for an infinite . . .

Just then, the world explodes.

Though I was expecting a diversion, the reality catches me by surprise. Explosions erupt close to where the army commander is standing. Earth and plants fountain upward, and a transport vehicle flies apart, pieces showering down erratically.

The camp erupts into chaos, and I am on my feet and running an instant later, down along the eastern edge of the lines, trying to stick to the darkness against the thin screen of trees that borders the hills beyond, moving as fast as I can to reach the heavy woods ahead. I am wearing dark clothes and I am cloaked in my *inish* concealment, praying to the Fates of the Fae and whatever gods might be watching over me that this is enough. For a moment, I suspect it is not. The explosions have ceased and heads are starting to turn.

I stop where I am, crouching down close to the earth.

But then a second attack commences, new explosions farther down the line drawing everyone's attention. In an instant I am up and running once more, and the heavy woods are directly ahead. No one is looking. All eyes are directed down the Ministry lines west, to where the explosions occurred. Large numbers of soldiers are on their knees or prostrate the ground.

I cross through the front lines, streaking toward the edge of the woods, only yards away now. No one has given warning; I remain unseen. I do not hesitate; I barely glance at the men and machines I am racing to get past. I am afraid that even that small exposure risks drawing their attention, but I tell myself just to keep moving. To remember what's at stake.

And then I am plunging into the forest, surrounded by the old-growth trunks and limbs, engulfed in the darkness. I have made it. I am safe.

For now.

I come to a stop and look about cautiously. I listen to the silence, realizing I now face a different sort of problem. Dragons are not house pets. Dragons are instinctual creatures and will often act without thinking — as they did with both Trusen and Favorist. A Dragon's jaws can open and close in the blink of an eye. I must be very careful not to blunder into those jaws. I must make sure Antrim hears me coming and knows who I am.

So I begin moving again, slowly and cautiously, speaking Antrim's name as I go. I hope he will be listening. I hope he will know who I am before he reacts. I hope this hasn't all been for nothing. I ease my way deeper in, thanks to the Ministry floodlights filtering through the trees. From outside my haven, I hear the shouts and cries of the Ministry soldiers and wonder what they are doing now. I hope my companions are safely hidden and have not been caught.

Hope — such a fragile thing, and all I seem to have these days.

"Antrim. Antrim. Are you there?" I whisper. "It's Auris."

Over and over, I repeat the words. I am deep into the woods and should have found him by now. A Dragon isn't a chipmunk. A Dragon is huge. How hard can it be to find one?

I hear something moving — something big — but I can't tell which direction the sound is coming from. I slow, pause.

"Antrim. Are you . . ."

"I'm right here."

The familiar gravelly voice is so close it feels as if he is speaking right in my ear, and I jump three feet into the air. "Where?" I blurt out in a frantic hiss. "Where are you?"

"Hush, Fae girl! The woods have ears. Look left."

I do, and there he is. Or at least his head is, poking slowly out from between the huge trunks, his baleful eyes a pair of burning green embers, his enormous snout within six feet of me. Somehow he has slipped through the trees to this spot and settled in to wait. Wait for what, though? For the Ministry to grow bored and leave? For Riva and me to come back? What does he think is going to happen with an entire army camped just beyond the trees?

"How did they find you?" I ask.

A low growl that speaks of discomfort. "I left the woods. Just for an hour or so."

Can a Dragon look sheepish? I think Antrim has managed it.

"Why would you do that? Leave when I told you to stay?"

"I had good reason." A long pause follows. "I got hungry."

He left the safety of this forest because he was *hungry*? I can hardly believe it.

"I ate a cow in its pasture," he explains, his voice barely audible. "Then I ate another. A farmer came outside to chase me off." He snorts derisively. "I should have eaten him, too." A pause. "I could stand to eat another cow, for that matter."

341

There is no point in continuing this discussion. The Dragon and I will always have different worldviews. "Well, it was a mistake! Now you've given yourself away, and there are soldiers and weapons all around you. We have to get away from here. Right now. There is an entire army out there that intends to take you prisoner. Or maybe just try to kill you."

A disinterested grunt. "Let them try. I still have plenty of room in my belly." The irritation in his voice is apparent.

"You aren't paying attention. This is an entire *army*! Do you think nothing can hurt you? Are you really that strong? Because there are cannons waiting out there. *Huge* cannons!"

Now I am irritated, too, but I can't afford it. "Never mind. We can talk about it later. What we have to do now is get away from here. I think I can help."

"Men lack the means and the courage to harm Dragons! I don't need help."

I wonder suddenly if he is right. After all, he is a Dragon and I know almost nothing about what Dragons can and can't survive. But I also know it is a chance neither of us can afford to take.

I exhale sharply. "Well, you're getting some help anyway, like it or not. Can you crawl closer to the edge of this forest? Toward the army soldiers? Can you manage to fit yourself through all these trees?"

Whatever he says to that is unintelligible, but he sounds irritated. I let it pass. "Once we get close enough to their vehicles, I can try to disable their lights. Then you can take flight without being seen and escape their weapons. Riva and I found Drifter. Fly to the hilltop behind the army lines, directly south. Both are there, waiting for us."

Antrim stares at me blankly for long moments. "You want me to leave now?"

Why is this so hard for him to understand? "I think that would be best."

He huffs in my face, and I have to fight hard not to gag. I will never think of Dragons in the same way again if I get us out of this.

"Climb on my back."

I hesitate, but it might be easier to stay with him if we are physically connected. I am already thinking ahead to what I need to do once we reach the forest's edge and those lights are within striking distance. I have to extinguish all the lights as quickly as I can and hope the darkness and the resulting night blindness it causes the Ministry soldiers give us the cover we need to flee.

I will need to exert a huge amount of *inish* to make this happen — much more than what was required two years ago to create the illusions my mother required to trap my father's soldiers and eliminate them — because this time I am altering a physical object.

I don't know for certain if I can manage it, but it is all we have to work with.

With the aid of a nearby tree, I climb up on Antrim's back, gripping his scales to keep from being knocked off or falling, and he begins to snake his way forward on his belly, squirming between the trees and through the darkness. It is slow going, for there are few avenues available for something his size. I stay quiet as he proceeds, pressed against his back and hanging on as best I can, hoping the racket from the machines and soldiers drowns out any noise we are making.

Before long we are close enough to the forest's edge for me to believe Antrim can break cover and take flight, so what we need now is less illumination and a few more distractions. And I am hoping I can provide both.

From my lofty position on Antrim's back, I can see the spotlights up and down the Ministry lines, as well as the army, still in place but roiling in confusion from Drifter and Riva's attack. Smoke rises from ruined vehicles and craters left by the explosives, and soldiers stand about uncertainly as they await orders from their officers. Unfortunately for Antrim and me, they are positioned between us and the bluff where Drifter and Riva wait.

Off to one side, I can see a heated argument taking place between the civilian commander and his attendant army officers. For the moment at least, no one seems to have decided what to do. But I suspect it won't be long before they come to a decision, and I would be surprised if it didn't involve shelling the woods.

I take a deep breath. I have to act now.

Summoning my *inish,* I form it into a corrosive package that will either short-circuit or overload all the spotlights, causing them to explode or go dark, depending on their construction. And I have to take them all out at once, which means a blanket attack against everything that illuminates the darkness. But such an effort will not be easy. It will drain away most or all of my strength and leave me weakened and vulnerable. Still, I don't hesitate. The risks don't matter.

I tighten my grip on Antrim. "Get ready."

He grunts, and I feel the muscles of his huge body bunch.

When the impact of my *inish* explodes across the Ministry lines, it seems as if thousands of lights blow apart in a matter of seconds. Tracker lights, headlights, flares, and handhelds — all erupt and die, plunging the camp into darkness. Ministry soldiers drop to the ground, many of them covering their heads — all of them certain they are under attack.

I shout to Antrim, and he bursts from cover onto a darkened field already engulfed in chaos. The Dragon's huge wings immediately spread, and he begins to lift off. The rippling surge of his body as he takes flight is ferocious, and right away I feel myself slipping from his back. I clutch desperately at his scales to hold myself in place, but my hold is precarious and I feel my grip slip further. My strength is hugely diminished by the employment of such massive amounts of *inish*.

I tighten my grip. I squeeze those scales so hard pain ratchets up my arms and leaves me fighting to keep from screaming.

It doesn't matter. I cannot hold on.

But I have to. I must!

I fail.

And tumble away.

My last memory is of Antrim rising into the sky above me, unaware of what's happened, still believing he is flying both of us to safety.

TWENTY-ONE

When I wake again, I am surprised to discover that I have suffered no obvious damage. I must not have been as far off the ground as I thought or something must have broken my fall. Or maybe I am just the luckiest young woman in the world. Then I remember that as I fell — right in those final seconds — I made a last desperate effort to save myself and called up the last, faltering shreds of my *inish* to break my fall. Apparently, my effort was a success.

Except that now I am pinned to the ground by more hands than I can count, with Ministry soldiers all around me. I wish I had my staff in hand, but I left it behind when I chose to make the journey with Riva to the Dragons, afraid it would suggest an unwarranted aggression, so all I have are my blades. When I try to access my *inish,* it appears to have burned out completely. But for how long, I cannot be sure.

I am so woozy and light-headed at this point that I find it hard even to breathe. I know where I am, but not what might have happened after I blacked out. What was it that drew them to me? Maybe the fact that someone saw me falling off Antrim's back? Or maybe the fact that I landed near someone? It doesn't matter, really. What matters is that I am back in the hands of the Ministry, and there is no help for me now.

And this means Harrow is doomed as well.

Lights blaze all around me — though whether through repairs or replacements I couldn't say. The illumination reveals that at least a dozen soldiers are leaning over me and more are coming to join them. They talk among themselves, and a multiplicity of familiar words wash over me.

Who is she?

Where did she come from?

Was she really riding that Dragon?

How could she manage that?

If I were in better command of my senses, I might try making an escape. I have not yet been bound or gagged or restrained in any way that would stop me. Hands are pinning my wrists and arms and legs, but my *inish* alone could scatter them like tiny birds in a wind. If my head was a little clearer and my *inish* would return, that is. As things stand, that well is temporarily dry, and hands alone are more than sufficient to keep me from going anywhere.

I tighten my resolve.

Just a few minutes more.

Even one minute.

Then I can test my *inish* again . . .

Too late. A bevy of new faces appear, their owners shoving aside the onlookers to join the men who hold me down. I don't know any of them, but I do recognize the civilian commander from the clothes he wears. He seems surprisingly young to be in charge — not much older than I am — but still he has a worn and tired face. What might have once been delicate, finely honed features have been twisted into something that reveals both distrust and dissolution. Hard eyes and a cruel mouth suggest an unpleasant nature.

He kneels and bends close. "Well, well. What have we here? A Fae child? No, that is unkind. You are no child. A treacherous rat with a penchant for disruption? That would be more accurate, I think. Do you agree?"

I stare at him blankly, giving nothing away. In return, he slaps me hard across my face. "Answer me when I ask a question, girl!"

I can feel the heat and sting of that blow, but I hold my expression in place and do not respond.

He straightens. "I see. Well, there will be plenty of time to question you later. That should prove interesting — though I don't imagine it will be very pleasant for you. Bind her. Everywhere from the waist up. Leave her legs free so she can walk."

He stands, steps back, and watches as his attendants push aside those holding me and fasten restraints about my arms, my wrists, and even my fingers, pinning them against my body so I cannot move them at all. Then they place tape across my mouth and a blindfold over my eyes, but I can still smell and hear. And, more important, my instincts tell me what surrounds me. I lie still, obedient, because there is no other choice that makes any sense. Not yet anyway. My *inish* is still gone, and for once I am exactly as helpless as I look.

I am hauled to my feet, where I stand straight and unmoving, waiting.

"Put her in the ATV and take her back to the Ministry compound." It is the young commander speaking again. "Take her to the holding cells and keep her there until I call for her. Do not release her restraints. Do not even loosen them. Chain her to the wall — body and ankles. Then leave her. But place a guard on her. I want two men right outside her cell door at all times. No exceptions!"

The impact of his words hits like a hammer blow, yet I catch a glimpse of something unexpected. He is afraid of me . . . but why? Also, my instincts tell me he fears not what I will do now, but what I might do if I were allowed to escape. He is not going to let that happen under any circumstances. Whatever he has in mind for me, he intends to see it through.

I consider the unpleasant possibilities — physical torture, or experiments meant to change who and what I am. Am I to share Malik's fate? The commander's youth and civilian status imply that he might be Malik's creator — and the man who has been after me all along. So does he know who I am or not? Could he believe me just a random Fae, and might that give me a chance to escape? But there is nothing I can do about it now, so I try to remain calm. I will get through what lies ahead. I am strong and capable enough to do so. I am my mother's daughter.

I feel him approach once more. I can hear his breathing as he leans in.

"Welcome to Harbor's End, Auris," he hisses.

And for the first time, I am afraid.

■ ■ ■ ■

I am driven back through Harbor's End in a circuitous route, with many starts and stops and constant turns. I can hear enough to suspect where I am being taken — to some sort of Ministry headquarters. Once again, I don't need my sight to discover what's around me. My instincts serve me well enough, and what they find is not reassuring.

I sit on a bench with guards on either side of me and across from me on a bench opposite. The ATV is a large metal box — a carrier, not a fighting vehicle. The clank and rattle of chains hanging from racks and hooks and the smells of blood and fear tell me that lots of unpleasant things have happened in this box.

The journey is made in silence save for once, when a voice across the way says, "She doesn't look all that dangerous. She's just a girl."

A pause, then a laugh. "Would you like me to put her on your lap, see what happens?" another voice responds.

"Are you crazy? *He* might find out."

"*Him?* He probably plans much worse for her."

353

"Leave her for him to mess with, then. I don't want any part of it."

"Admit it — you're afraid of her."

Silence.

"Come on, admit it."

After that, there is silence, which is just as well. I've heard all I need to. I am not in a good place. The only solution is to find a way to escape the Ministry compound before the young man who might be Malik's creator can start doing whatever it is he has in mind. I am strong but not invulnerable. Eventually, I will break. And then I will tell him — or do for him — whatever he wants. I can pretend otherwise, but that would be a mistake. I have to meet this head-on and find a way to prepare myself for what is coming.

Perhaps my *inish* can help, when it returns. *If* it returns. I try to access it again, but it does not respond.

I hope I can find another way to be strong.

Eventually, we rumble to a stop. I hear the rear doors to the ATV open, and I am lifted out of the box and set on my feet. The guards force-march me across a paved walk, then up steps and into a building. Because it is still nighttime, the building is very quiet. Our footsteps echo loudly as my guards walk me along several hallways and then through a heavy door with hinges that squeal as it swings open. We descend a long set of stairs and arrive in a place of total silence. Another door is unlocked and opened, and I am moved inside. The air is rank with unpleasant smells and cool against my face. Hands direct me to yet another bench, where I am seated with my back against a cold stone wall. I hear the clank of chains being shifted as cuffs are fitted about my ankles and a heavy length is fastened about my waist.

Then the hands release me, the footsteps recede, and the door closes.

I am alone.

I am helpless.

Time passes as I sit there trying to come to terms with my situation. My *inish* is still missing, and I still feel weak and disoriented. I am in the hands of the Ministry, and if my captors have their way I will never leave. Or if I do, I am likely to leave as a profoundly different person than I am now. I cannot forget the moment when the young commander spoke my name or the cruel look on his face as he struck me. It could be how he treats all his prisoners, but I don't think so. This rage feels more personal, and I am as certain as I can be, knowing so little about him, that he hates me —

and that his hatred runs deep.

After a while, I lie down on the wooden bench and try to sleep, but my thoughts won't let me. Every second I am stuck in here means one less second that I can help Harrow. And my physical discomfort doesn't help, either. The chains are heavy and obstructive, and with my arms and hands strapped to my sides, lying on my back is the only way I can find any comfort. I still can't see and my mouth is still taped over — the latter less important at this point than the former — but both are unfamiliar and distressing restrictions. Everything that has been done to me feels like a deliberate punishment — although I cannot assume that it isn't mostly to make certain I cannot use my *inish*.

Which would mean they know something of what I can do.

I calm myself with an effort and wonder if Antrim reached Drifter and Riva and carried them to safety. I tell myself that, by providing him with the protective cover of darkness, I prevented his death and saved my friends. So at least I helped someone. Though Harrow . . .

I feel myself starting to break down. Unbidden waves of fear, dismay, and helplessness wash through me, threatening to overwhelm my resolve. The enormity of the danger I am facing and the fact that, as long as the Ministry has me, I cannot save Harrow, are too much for me. I am a twenty-two-year-old woman, and while I have survived much, I have never felt so vulnerable as I do now. How long before they come for me? How long can I endure what they will do to me then? And how am I supposed to extricate myself from this mess and save Harrow?

Harrow.

In my mind I speak his name over and over as I sob quietly. Four days have passed since Tonklot gave me my deadline, and the first of the two weeks allotted is already half gone. I cannot afford to remain imprisoned like this. I cannot be kept trapped and helpless. I cannot fail Harrow.

I have to do something.

I fall asleep wondering what that something is.

I am woken when the door to my cell creaks open and footsteps approach. Hands seize me and haul me to my feet. The hands are not gentle or considerate.

A blunt metal object is pushed against my temple. "If you move one muscle while I am preparing you, my companion will blow your brains out. So stand very still."

I freeze. Hands roughly remove the ties and tape from my arms and wrists and fingers. My arms have gone numb from being so immobilized, and pain rips through them when I try to move. Next, I am stripped of my clothes and left naked. Finally, my hands are cuffed in metal bracelets that are fastened together in front of me. The blindfold is left in place, but the tape is removed. I stand shivering with the chill air on my bare skin, feeling humiliated and enraged and violated.

The gun is moved away and hands seize my arms from either side.

"Walk," the same voice orders. "No talking. Not one word."

I am force-marched out of my cell and down a long hallway to a room where the dampness on my feet and in the air tells me I am in a shower. The hands position me, release me, then move away.

"Stand where you are."

Water sprays me from head to toe, cold and biting. I gasp audibly behind the binding that covers my mouth, and I shiver hard when the spray momentarily stops and the rough hands return, covering my body with soap. When I am deemed sufficiently clean, they towel me dry. Then hands seize me anew, and I am marched back to my cell. Once returned, I am dressed in fresh clothing that feels rough and stiff against my skin — pants and a shirt, but nothing else.

I am reseated on the bench, and my body and limbs are resecured by the chains. Abruptly, my blindfold is removed, and I am left staring at two women who regard me as if I am nothing better than filth.

"Listen carefully," one says, her face and eyes hard-set. "One wrong movement from you and you'll be blind again — and maybe for good, this time."

"Nod if you understand," says the other.

I nod, but I notice they are careful not to get too close to me. They stand back as they deliver their commands, and do not attempt to come within reach even though my hands are still chained before me.

The women stare at me a few moments longer, then turn and leave the cell. The door is closed and locked, and I am left alone again with my thoughts. I have more than a few, and all of them are dark. I give them space for a time, then push them aside and begin to consider how I might make an escape.

The possibilities are depressingly small, and all of them require that I get free of the chains and recover the use of my voice. I can feel my strength returning but there is still no sign of my *inish,* which is troubling. I realize that with my voice silenced and my arms and hands secured I cannot summon it, but I would be somewhat reassured if I could feel its presence.

I am more troubled by the fact that the Ministry seems to have learned from its previous errors. Allensby believed my magic was contained in my *inish* staff, but I did not bring my staff on this mission, and yet still they bind me. So somehow, they now know that the magic comes from within me, meaning that — even when my *inish* does come back — it will be harder to reach it. I will need to be doubly clever to outwit them this time.

But there is one bright spot in all of this. It may be that the Ministry and its young commander still do not know that only *one* of the two is needed. All I need is momentary freedom for either my hands *or* my voice — and, of course, my *inish* back. But I think that moment will come, and I will have my chance.

And if it fails to appear on its own, I will find a way to create it.

Time passes, and no one comes. An entire day passes — for though I have no windows in my cell that would enable me to see the sun's journey, my instincts tell me anyway. It is nightfall before anyone comes to bring me food and drink — two new women, replacements for the first two but stamped by the same mold. One puts a gun to my head as the other pulls the tape off my mouth, and I take in a huge gulp of air for the first time since my captivity began.

If only I had my *inish* . . . But alas, it is still gone.

Then the one holding the weapon stands to one side with the barrel placed against my head while the other feeds and waters me like an animal. I am thirsty and hungry, so I eat and drink as much as I can to make up for what I have been denied. There is nothing to be gained by being stubborn. I need my strength.

When they are finished with that, my mouth is retaped and a bucket is produced so that I can relieve myself. They pull down my pants and hold me fast, positioned over the bucket so I can make use of it. I force myself to endure their stares and snickers and comments before they wipe me and pull up my pants and sit me back down on the bench.

Then they leave me alone once more.

I begin to wonder what it is I am doing

here. The young commander knows who I am, so why isn't he already using me for whatever nefarious purposes he wanted me for in the first place? I have to escape this place as quickly as possible. I am unwilling to accept that my captivity will end without my *inish* returning. I speak softly to Harrow in my mind, assuring him I am surviving, that I am stronger than those that imprison me, that I am just waiting for my chance to break free. And when it arrives, I am coming back to him and we will be together again.

I ask him to be patient. I tell him to be brave. I beg him for understanding and love in spite of all that has happened.

I find a kind of grace from doing this, and — almost — I feel him with me.

TWENTY-TWO

My captivity continues through the remainder of the day with no discernible changes. My *inish* remains unresponsive, and I have only a little more than nine days until Tonklot's deadline comes due.

I have to get out of here.

I have to get back to Viridian Deep and Harrow.

The following morning they come for me again, but with different intentions. I realize it the moment the cell door opens and four soldiers enter. They stand me up, remove my hand shackles but chain my feet with a two-foot length, retape my mouth, and literally drag me from the room — two of them manhandling me while the other two follow — perhaps to provide backup if dragging me proves too tiring. I find humor in all of it because if I don't do something to alleviate the overwhelming fear that fills me, my courage will give way. This is what I have been waiting for, but at the same time it is what I have been dreading. I want out; I don't want to end up dead.

If my *inish* had returned, I could use this chance to escape. But it is still elusive.

Down the hallways of the cellblock we journey, my efforts to find footing and walk on my own deliberately sabotaged by sudden yanks every time I get close to achieving it. These men do not look at me and do not speak. They are simply intent on making me as miserable as possible until we get to wherever we are going. What happens then is anyone's guess, but I imagine things will not improve.

Once or twice I think to say something — perhaps ask them to slow down or let me walk on my own or give me a chance to catch my breath — but each time I pull back. No one is going to respond to anything I ask for. No one wants me here or likes me or thinks I deserve anything short of rough treatment. To them, I am an alien creature. I am pretty sure the young commander with the hard eyes has advised them that, as long as I arrive in one piece, he doesn't much care how brutally they treat me.

We seem to take forever to get to where we are going, but eventually we pass through a set of securely locked double doors where a fifth soldier stands guard and enters a code on a switch plate. The doors open to us, and the soldiers yank me off my feet once more and drag me into an anteroom not much bigger than a bread box and shove me into a chair. A man sitting at a desk beside yet another door picks up a communications device and speaks into it so quietly I cannot make out what he is saying.

Someone answers. Then we wait.

We wait a long time. Another form of intimidation, I think. Another ploy. They would do better to just cut to the chase rather than wasting time fooling around with my emotions. If they want something out of me that I am not already prepared to give them, they will have to resort to torture anyway. Even then, I am ready to refuse them for as long as I can manage it.

Or so I tell myself.

Finally the door opens and the young commander walks out.

"Good morning," he greets me, his voice pleasant enough, but his face expressionless. He gestures to the guards. "Bring her inside. Sit her down in front of my desk."

I am hauled back up and dragged through the door and across the floor of a much larger room. There, a metal chair that sits

365

before a stunning teak desk that is polished to such a bright sheen I imagine I might be able to see my face mirrored in its surface. The desktop holds nothing but a pitcher of water and four glasses.

The young commander goes behind his desk and stands there, studying me. Then he walks around the desk and rips the tape off my mouth. The pain is intense, but I don't acknowledge it. "Will you agree to speak with me in a civil manner?" he asks me. "Or do I have to bind you first to assure you won't try to attack me? Answer, please."

I shake my head. My *inish* still lies dormant within me. What sort of attack could I possibly mount? "I'll listen."

He makes a dismissive gesture to the guards. "Seat her. Then wait outside until we are finished. I don't think there will be any problem."

The guards go out and close the door behind them and the young commander and I are left alone. If ever there was a chance to make an escape, this is it. If only I had my *inish,* I think longingly. But perhaps, if I am patient, my powers will resurface and my opportunity will come again. I just have to make sure I am compliant enough to allow that to happen, while still not giving them any of whatever they want from me.

"My name is Winton," he tells me. "And you, as we both know, are Auris Afton Grieg."

"What is it you want from me?"

"Much. But first we have to talk."

I study him carefully. He seems older now than when he made me his prisoner in the woods. He appeared then to be about my age. Now he looks to be somewhere in his mid- to late thirties. His face remains young, but his dark hair is shot through with gray streaks and worry lines runnel the skin along his temples and under his eyes. He seems fit, his physique lean and whiplike, and the tops of his hands, which are visible to me as he rests them on top of his desk, are smooth and strong. He appears calm, but his knowing eyes give him away. He is a predator, waiting for his prey to break and run.

I intend to disappoint him.

"I want to ask you some questions," he announces. "If you answer them in a satisfactory manner, your conditions will improve. If you refuse to answer or if you lie to me, they will become worse. Are we clear?"

I nod.

367

He pours water from the pitcher into one of the glasses, which he then hands to me. "Drink this. You will feel better."

I take the glass, study it a moment, and sip from it. Water, clear and cool and fresh. I drink deeply.

"You are a Human/Fae hybrid," he continues, "yet when last you were in Ministry custody, you looked all Human. Now you look mostly Fae. How?"

"I am honestly not sure, but it all started once I settled in Viridian Deep. The change was gradual at first, but it has been progressing. I expect to be fully Fae before the end of the year."

"So the change was not a deliberate act?"

"No, it happened naturally. Maybe because of my heritage, maybe because the climate agreed with me. I don't know."

I am telling him more than I should, but I've revealed nothing important, nothing that can help him. Or so I hope.

"Are you happy in your new home?"

"Yes."

"No thoughts of coming back to the Human world? No regrets about leaving it behind?"

"No."

"How did you learn to fly that Dragon?"

I pause. Now we're probably getting to

what he wants. "I was allowed to fly him. No one taught me anything."

"Oh, come now. No one just gets on a Dragon and flies it. Even I know that much."

"And yet I did."

"You have a special relationship with Dragons?"

I almost say yes, but just manage to avoid it. I do, however, wonder how to avoid going further with this line of questioning. "My family and my friends helped me," I say, sidestepping the question. "Because I am Fae now. Because Viridian Deep is where I belong."

"Is someone special waiting for you back there?"

"Yes." This time, I don't seem able to stop myself.

He just smiles. "And you would like to be with him, wouldn't you?"

My throat clenches. How does he know about Harrow? I hesitate, trying to avoid telling him the truth, but somehow I can't seem to help myself. "Yes."

"Were you in the prisons once?"

"Yes."

"But you escaped?

"Yes."

"With friends, perhaps?"

"Yes."

"When you escaped from the prison, what happened to your friends?"

"They were killed."

"All of them?"

I almost gasp aloud as I realize the truth. He isn't talking about Harrow. He likely doesn't even know about Harrow. He's talking about Malik! I must be careful with my answers. My throat feels dry, so I take another long drink of water. "No," I reply. "Khoury survived."

"Yet she was killed in the prisons after being recaptured. You were there. You saw her die, didn't you?" He smiles — a little like a cat with a mouse — but I don't seem to care anymore. I am pleased that he feels he is smarter than me. Complacency leads to errors.

"There is someone else I am interested in. Another friend, perhaps? Another who escaped with you? Do you remember?"

"Yes."

The word is out of my mouth before I can stop myself. I feel a sudden rush of confusion. Why did I tell him this?

"Do you remember his name?"

"Yes." No, don't! But I do.

"Was his name Malik?"

"Yes." Now I can't stop.

"Is Malik still alive?"

I struggle to deny it, but I fail miserably. "Yes."

I realize suddenly what is happening. The water he offered me — the water I have been drinking willingly — was treated with something that makes me want to answer this man's questions truthfully, to give him all the information he seeks. I try to stop myself from speaking, but it is of no use. Because a euphoric part of me wants to give Winton these answers, wants to cooperate.

Besides, what harm can it cause, since I am telling him things he clearly already knows?

"Do you know where Malik is?"

"No."

"Or who he is with?"

"No."

"Or who he was with last?"

"The Goblins."

"Is he taking his medication?"

"He was when I last saw him."

He leans back in his chair, smiling. "Very good, Auris. See how easy that was? Now let's try something else. Drink some more water. It will make talking easier."

Without much conscious thought, I find myself drinking.

"Now tell me about your *inish* powers —

371

what they can do and how they work." Winton's voice is soft and comforting. Encouraging. I smile in response — and then am instantly horrified.

No, this is not right. I have to stop this now. I cannot do this, I cannot tell him anything that would jeopardize my one chance to get free, to get back to Harrow . . .

Rage propels me into action. Without warning, I lurch to my feet and strike out, sending the glasses and pitcher flying. Then, feigning unconsciousness, I slide to the floor, pretending to hyperventilate. For the first time, I feel a distant flutter from my *in-ish,* deep within me, as if it wants to help in my deception, and a fierce joy stabs through me. If my *inish* is beginning to return, I may yet have a chance.

Winton springs out from behind his desk and rushes over to me, yelling for his guards. He kneels down and slaps my face, then shakes me for good measure.

"Auris! Stop this! You're all right . . . Guards! Auris, look at me! Stop shaking and everything will settle down. Look at me!"

I allow my eyes to flutter open and I stare into his. I see something there that is unexpectedly familiar, but I cannot decide what it is. "What . . . what happened?" I gasp.

The guards arrive. Hands reach down and drag me to my feet. I allow my head to loll and my words to slur. "Don't . . . let me . . . fall . . ."

One of the guards slaps me hard across the face, and I use the blow as an excuse to curl into a tight ball.

The guards are having none of it. They reach down to pull me up, slapping me again for good measure.

"Stop it!" Winton shouts. "The more you damage her, the longer I'll have to wait before I can start working on her. Now hold her up so I can talk to her."

I am reseated in the iron chair. I hang my head as if defeated, to avoid showing the anger in my eyes.

"What are you going to do to me?" I ask, trying to make myself sound broken, pathetic, when really I am brimming with rage.

"What do you think?" Winton says, taking hold of my chin and lifting my head so I am looking at him. "You've met Malik, haven't you? I don't need another killing machine. But what I do need is for you to be willing and compliant. I need to know what you know. So heal well, little Auris. I want your body strong before I start working on it."

I feel myself go cold all over. So he plans to leash me as he leashed Malik, dependent on his medicines for the chance to live without agonizing pain. But to what ends? What does he want from me?

It is nothing I am going to find out today. He looks at the guards. "Put her back in her cell. Give her food and water, then chain her up again. But no more hitting. You are forbidden to strike her for any reason without my permission."

The guards lift me to my feet, then Winton calls out, "And have a nurse sent in to check her over."

I am hauled away marginally less roughly than before. I refuse to look at my guards or anything else as I think about what has just happened. Through the doorways and down the hallways we go, and I feel the effects of the drug beginning to fade. I am furious that I let myself be duped so easily. I should have known. I should have suspected. I was looking for the wrong things today — expecting pain and threats and harsh treatment. Instead, I was duped by their absence.

I am so stupid!

I am placed back in my cell, given food and water as ordered. My feet are unchained but my wrists are reshackled in front of me, and my mouth is taped shut once more. When the guards have gone, I sit and wait for the nurse. She appears more quickly than I expect, and she brings a roll of fresh bedding, which she deposits at the end of my bench before she begins to examine me. She barely looks at me as she concludes her work and tells me that nothing is broken. I could have told her that much before she walked into my cell, but I keep silent and wait for her to leave.

Once she is gone, I reflect on the day's events.

Winton was more clever than I gave him credit for, but even so I managed to deny him what he wanted most — information about my *inish*. As for his questions about Malik, they make it plain that my old friend has gone missing, and they want him back. But it is the fate that looks to be in store for me that scares me most. Whatever happens, I must not allow Winton to get me anywhere near his labs.

Tomorrow, I promise myself, things will be different. I will be ready. He thinks he knows me well enough to manipulate me, and I will use that against him. For one thing, I am experiencing familiar stirrings deep inside that tell me my *inish* is starting to return. Only the faintest flickers, but perhaps by tomorrow it will be strong enough to employ, even if just enough to escape.

Then my thoughts shift once again to what I saw in Winton's eyes as he stood over me, trying to tell me I was all right. What was it that I recognized? It was there; I just can't quite manage to identify it.

I breathe in deeply and exhale. Six days have passed since Tonklot stole Harrow's *inish* and issued his demands. Eight remain until the next full moon — and I am still no closer to a solution. I have to find a way to get free.

Harrow needs me, and I cannot fail him.

I cannot fail myself.

I awkwardly unroll the bedding with my chained hands and spread it over the planks of the bench. As I do so, I notice a barely visible slip of paper wedged into a small tear in one of the seams. I reach over to work it free and unfold it. A message is scrawled on it.

Courage. Get to the roof. D.

Drifter!

In spite of all that has happened, I smile.

I am not alone after all.

TWENTY-THREE

I sleep poorly that night, dozing in fits and starts, feeling haunted. My dreams are filled with things waiting in the shadows, movements at the corners of my eyes, teeth and claws never seen but clearly grinding in the darkness. When I wake for the final time, I am neither rested nor refreshed.

But I do wake angry.

I wake determined.

Winton will not get the better of me, will not get me into his lab and turn me into a puppet forever under his control. Because my *inish* has returned. Not fully, not with all its power, but it is there. A shallow pool, but one I can hopefully draw on to do what is needed.

In addition, there is my newfound belief that I have gained a step or two on Winton by letting him think me so badly shaken that I suffered a seizure and collapsed in his presence. He will think that a decided weakness — and one I can take advantage of.

Because I have realized at last why I experienced a sense of recognition when I looked into his eyes. What I saw reflected there and failed to comprehend I understand now. It came to me at some point in the middle of my troubling sleep — unbidden, shocking, and revealing. I know him now in a way I did not know him before, and this provides me with a weapon I had not realized existed. It gives me power over him as well.

Though there is still the matter of escape. Where is Drifter at this point? Up on the building's roof, as the secret message cryptically advised? Are Antrim and Riva there, too? Unknown, all of it, but it is enough to realize that all of them are near, and will be looking for a way to reach me.

So I have some assurance that I can find a way to break free of Winton and the Ministry and return to Viridian Deep.

But for now I must wait, and waiting is difficult. I am ready to act, and yet I cannot. All I can do is endure while a slow roiling anger builds inside of me.

When they come for me, I have been awake for hours. I sit calmly as a new set of four guards unlocks and enters my cell. I don't even bother to look up at them as they haul me to my feet.

Instead, abruptly, I attack them. My hands are still chained, so I know this attack will fail, but it is not my intention to get free. Not yet anyway. My intention is to distract them. I slam into the guard closest, barrel into another, and break for the open cell door. But the other two are on me at once, bearing me to the floor and pinning me fast. The first two join in, and then they are all beating me, slapping and punching me, unable or perhaps unwilling to control their fury. Their blows hurt, but I am prepared for that. I bear them with stoic certainty in what I have planned, then go limp.

I am gambling here, but my instincts say it is a risk worth taking. With my face and body stinging from the blows, I am given a final kick and then seized and dragged from the cell and down the hallway. I stay limp and unmoving, wanting to cultivate a sense of both weakness and submission when I reach Winton's office. I want him to see me like this: a helpless, beaten prisoner. Yesterday he tricked me. Today I will do the same to him.

We pass back along the same corridors and through the same doors, and then I am seated anew in the metal chair before Winton's polished teak desk, the pitcher of drug-treated water and the four glasses replaced with fresh ones. And the man who controls my fate is rising from his desk to take in my unexpected appearance.

"What happened to her? What have you done?" he barks at the guards. "I told you I needed her healthy!"

Yes, this is working as I thought it would. He is seeing me as the victim. And he does not see what I am doing, as his attention is fixed on his guards.

"She tried to escape," one ventures.

"Did she?" Winton's voice is soft and dangerous. "One girl tried to escape, and it took all four of you to bring her down?" I do not look at him but I can hear the mix of disbelief and sarcasm in his voice. "What a terrible blow it must have been to find yourselves almost overwhelmed by a girl in chains. We must look into finding better ways to see you properly trained. Get out!"

The soldiers depart. Winton waits for the door to close, then comes around to help straighten me in my seat, ripping the tape off my mouth as he does so. "Well, that wasn't what I intended, but I promise you will get better treatment from here on. Water?"

Without asking, he pours water from the pitcher into a glass and hands it to me. I

380

reach for it with my shackled hands before lifting it to my lips and trying to drink. But I make it seem as if, between the manacles and the beating, I cannot swallow and spit the water out, choking and gasping.

"All right, here, give me that." He takes the glass from my hands and sets it in front of me on the desk. "You can drink it later. Take a moment to recover, and then we can talk."

Generous of him. I keep my head hanging and my eyes averted. He walks back behind his desk and sits down.

"I must warn you, Auris, your situation is precarious. Yes, I want you healthy so I can work on you, but I'm willing to delay that in favor of getting the answers I want. Do you understand?"

I nod slowly. *I understand, all right.*

"I need to ask you questions, and I want you to give me honest answers. Refusing to answer or lying would be foolish, so let's begin."

Yes, let's.

"You said yesterday that you've had contact with Malik but do not know where he is presently. Is that correct? Or can you guess at where he might have gone?"

I shake my head.

"Did he say anything about where he has

been these two weeks?"

I shake my head again.

"Do you think you could find him for us if we sent you back?"

With how many of your Ministry soldiers for companionship? But I don't answer.

"Let's try something else. How did you manage to ride that Dragon? Are you bonded with it in some way? Do you have the power to make it do whatever you wish? Does it respond to words or actions that you provide? Because clearly it was following your directions."

I take a deep breath, straighten myself on my increasingly uncomfortable chair, and look him straight in the eyes. "I know who you are."

He pauses — caught off guard — but he recovers quickly. "Do you really? Who am I, then?"

"You're related to Allensby. A son or a brother, but kindred of some sort. You worked with him in the labs on his experiments with Fae subjects. After all, it was you who made Malik what he is."

He puffs up a little at the mention of Malik. "Of course I made him. He was my ultimate project. I planned to remake him to show my father the extent of my talent. I was determined to prove my capability as a geneticist. Sadly, my father died while the project was still in its infancy, but I know he would have been proud of me, had he lived. I know I earned my place as an Allensby. And Malik belongs to me; I want him back."

I feel a moment of shock, realizing what he has admitted. This vile creature is Allensby's son, which makes him my half brother.

"How do you know about this?" he presses.

"Your eyes. I remember them from when I was taken prisoner two years ago. It was Allensby who questioned me then, and you have the same eyes. Malik mentioned them, too."

I pause, wait a beat, then ask, "Why do you hate me so much? Because you do, don't you? I can see it in the way you look at me. I can hear it in your voice."

"You're mistaken," he says shortly, but my instincts tell me he lies.

"This is about your father's death, isn't it?" I press. "You blame the Fae for what happened to him."

Any attempt at pretense falls away. "Blame the Fae? I blame *you*! You trapped him in a tunnel or a cave or whatever and killed him."

I shake my head. "I didn't kill him. I was

383

there, and I saw him die, but it wasn't someone else who killed him. He killed himself."

His composure slips another notch. "Don't lie to me!"

"I'm not. Your father was invading my country with every intent of enslaving or killing my people. It was not an assassination or an execution or anything that wasn't entirely his doing. He brought what happened on himself. He caused his own death."

For a moment I think he is going to attack me. His face is red with fury. "No more lies, Auris! He died because the Fae wanted him to die."

"It was my mother who wanted him dead," I return. "Believe me, she had better reason than I."

He is on his feet, seething. "I should take you to my lab today, start your treatment. You've seen Malik; you know what I did to him. The level of pain I gave him to make him behave — pain only I can control. And I do control it. But I may not be so nice to you. Maybe I'll make you suffer a bit more each time, in recompense for what you did to my father . . . ."

I stand up to face him, no longer looking quite so submissive, meeting his fury directly. "Really? Can you live with knowing you are torturing your own sister?"

"Why do you . . ." An ashen look twists his features. "What are you talking about?"

His disbelief is apparent. I guessed correctly about how much his father has told him. Young Winton doesn't know nearly as much as he thinks.

"Listen to me, little boy! Your father violated my mother when she was his prisoner. He was *experimenting* on her, and he used her to create a half-breed child — *me*! And that makes you my brother, Winton. So whatever you do to me, you will be doing to your own sister!"

His face is purple with anger, and the rage in his eyes would burn me to cinders if it could touch me. But I am beyond anything he can do; he just doesn't realize it yet.

"You claim to be my sister, you little tramp? You are a cowardly, stupid *freak* who is simply trying to save her life. It won't work. My father would never allow a . . ."

He searches for the words he wants to say and cannot find them. I give him a moment, then smile. "Allow what? A *freak* to be his daughter? Is that what you are trying to say? Funny, I think the same about him. I never thought I would have a *freak* for a father."

He shakes his head in denial. "Lies won't

save you. I don't need anything more from you."

He starts to call for his guards, but I stop him with a shout. "Wait!"

The force of my words stops him.

"Want to see a magic trick?" I ask.

His confusion is evident. I slowly bring my hands out from below the desktop and hold them out. The iron cuffs at the ends of the connecting chain are no longer fastened to my wrists; instead, the chain hangs across my palms.

He stands frozen in place as I set the chain gently on his desktop. It clanks and scrapes as the links settle down against the polished surface. He stares at it, mesmerized. When he looks up again, I meet his gaze and hold it fast.

"If you speak one word or try to bring help, I will use the same magic that freed me to set you on fire. I can do it easily. Nod if you understand me."

He looks undecided, but when I show him a flicker of blue flame burning at the end of my index finger — an illusion, but a persuasive one, a clear indication that my threat is not idle — he nods quickly.

What I have done to escape my chains might seem like magic to him, but it is due mostly to a dogged persistence. The *inish* I spent blowing out all the Ministry lights in my attempt to save Antrim . . . Well, it was the largest working I had ever done, covering a circle that had to have been more than a quarter of a mile in circumference. It was a vast expenditure of power — and one that cost me everything. I had drained my reserves; I had expended all my strength. It has taken me days to gain even a flicker of it back. But Winton is not aware of my limits. For all he knows, I have a deep well to draw from, not a spluttering pool that fought me back.

I had to work diligently with what *inish* I could summon once I found Drifter's note last night. And even then, it took considerable effort to focus it with enough intensity and precision to significantly weaken my chains before the guards arrived. The final severing was accomplished during my pretense at escape.

I give Winton a smile. The beating I received from his guards was well worth it seeing the look on his face now.

"What are you going to do to me?" he asks, his eyes on my hands and the tiny blue flame.

"Nothing. I get to leave. You get to stay."

He shakes his head. He senses I mean what I am saying, and a bit of his former confidence surfaces. "You'll never get out of this building, *Auris Afton Grieg.*" He speaks my name with a sneer. "Not looking like that. If you ever were Human, you aren't now. *And* you're wearing prison clothes. You'll be recaptured at once. How about another solution, a better solution, one that involves you surrendering Malik to me in exchange for your freedom?"

"I don't think Malik would agree to that."

"I don't expect you to ask his permission. Just tell me where to find him. I can take it from there."

I want to laugh out loud. He still thinks he has the upper hand. He still thinks I need his help in order to escape. On top of that, he's lying. He has no intention of letting me go. He wants something more from me than finding Malik; otherwise, why would he have sent Malik and the Goblins after me? He just hasn't told me what it is yet.

"Thanks for the offer," I say, smiling. "But no."

"You'll need my help, Auris, if you want to have any chance at all!"

There is a hint of desperation to the way he says it, which I find encouraging. A good thing, too. Because for all my bravado, I have no idea what I am going to do next. I have no plan for getting out of this room, let alone out of the building, save following the words in Drifter's note: *Get to the roof.*

And still only the smallest pool of *inish* to draw from.

"What is it you want from me, Winton?" I ask him suddenly. "Because it isn't just Malik, is it?"

He scowls. "I want you dead."

I laugh aloud this time. "Stop being so pathetic. If you wanted me dead, you would have killed me when you had the chance. And you've already said it yourself: You want me in your lab, to make me your puppet like Malik. But why?"

"I don't have to tell you anything!"

I lash out with my *inish* and knock him backward into his desk chair with enough force to slam both against the wall. His gasp is audible, but I pin him fast as he struggles to rise.

"Our positions are reversed, *brother.* Now it's my turn to choose what I want from you. And maybe I'm the one who wants *you* dead!"

I reach into my paltry pool of *inish* and twist my hand to silence his voice, and he starts to gag as his throat seizes up. "Having trouble breathing yet?" I turn my hand slightly and his gagging increases. "Still getting air? That won't do." Another twist. He

389

is clearly choking now, his face turning purple. "Maybe I should just put you out of your misery?"

He waves his hands frantically, finally deciding I am not fooling around. Or maybe he is indicating that he cannot breathe at all. I really don't much care at this point. But I release my choke hold and let him gulp in huge mouthfuls of air.

"Better?" I ask. "We can do that again . . ."

"You . . . didn't have to . . ." He shakes his head. "Witch! I want you . . . to show me a way into . . . Viridian Deep!"

"Oh, please!" I exclaim in disgust. "What is wrong with you people? You and your father and your . . . I don't know — all of you! Why is it so important for you to invade Viridian Deep? What do you think you would gain even if you could go there? Which, by the way, you can't."

"Everything!" he screams at me.

The scream is loud enough that there is an instant commotion from outside. I drag Winton's chair back into place and plop him down in it, then scurry around to my chair. "Dr. Allensby?" a voice asks questioningly, as the door opens a crack. "Is everything all right?"

My hands are back in my lap, cupping my chains out of view, but a blue flame flickers at the end of my index finger where Winton can see it. I give him a knowing look. "Careful."

"Stop interrupting!" he shouts. "Just leave us!"

The door closes at once. Winton squirms in his chair, still pinned in place.

"You were saying?" I urge him on.

He glares at me. "Let me make it simple for you. We want access to what you and your people are keeping from us. Your lands, your magic, your knowledge — all of it! It belongs to us as much as it does to you, as denizens of this land, and we deserve it! My father knew what the Fae were hiding, and the Fae killed him and destroyed his army. I intend to do what he couldn't, and you are going to help me!"

I don't know what to say to this. I don't know where to begin. Winton is as deluded as his father — obsessed with this false belief that what we have and what we are as Fae is accessible to Humans. It never occurred to him — as it obviously hasn't to Winton, either — that this isn't something that can be given or even shared. It is a crucial part of our *inish* — our Fae *inish* — and Humans cannot access it.

But it is too late to explain all this now, even if I cared to try, so I shake my head.

"You are mistaken, Winton, if you think that our magic is something you can use. You cannot. You have to give up on this foolish hope once and for all. If you don't, it will kill you."

I stand up, tossing the chains on his desktop. "I'm leaving. Be grateful. But know this. If you come after the Fae or Malik again, I will be back for you."

I reach out with a sharp surge of *inish* and render him unconscious. "You are as repulsive as your father," I mutter.

I take the chains off the desk and strap him in place in his chair, then I walk over to the door and pause to consider what waits on the other side.

Once again, I think of my supposed Changeling powers. If I could regain my Human form now, I might actually have a chance. I reach into my shrinking pool of *inish* and try once again to summon that magic, but again only find a resistance within me.

So, the hard way, then, I think, as I summon my faltering *inish* to defend myself. I have the chance to escape, but everyone in the building will try to prevent it. I will have to be quick. I will have to be sure.

I only hope I have enough *inish* to do it.

I fling open the door and step out. Five

392

guards loiter about talking and joking. I put three of them down before they can blink. The other two bring out their weapons, but I have already blocked the muzzles. The weapons explode in their hands as they pull the triggers, metal shards fragmenting their fingers and dropping them to their knees in pain. Then I flee the room.

Get to the roof.

I'm on my way.

TWENTY-FOUR

I burst out into the hallway and run as fast as I can in search of a stairway leading up to the roof. I use my *inish* to cloak myself, but in these brightly lit surroundings I cast a sharp shadow — and my powers are still not at full force — so any attempt at disguise is only partially successful. Still, when no shouts of pursuit follow, I think this will be easier than I expected. But as I round a corner, still searching for an escape route, I run smack into a gathering of Ministry workers on their way to a meeting or a lunch or who knows what. I barrel into them so hard that I knock two of them off their feet. I immediately lose control over my *inish* and the concealment it is providing me. Everyone gets a good look at me — with my green skin, leafy hair, and prison garb — and that is all it takes. Screams and shouts rise up, and chaos ensues. I see my chances of escape slip away.

Guards begin to appear as doors burst open and the hallway fills. I would hide if I could, but there is no hiding for someone who looks like me caught in the midst of so many that look entirely different. I attempt to invoke a fresh concealment, but don't have the time and concentration I need to summon it. Instead, I break for freedom, pushing through the tangle of bodies, fighting off the hands seeking to grasp me, and charging ahead, heedless of everything but the need to stay on my feet. I am battered from every side, but no one is able to stop me.

With my head turned the wrong way as I flee the crowd, I run into what feels like a brick wall and am knocked off my feet.

Hands reach down and pull me to standing. I am face-to-face with the woman I have blindly charged into. *Riva?* I think, looking up, but it isn't. While she is Riva's size, she is clearly a Human. She gives me a stern look. "Are you the one they're all after?"

I nod. Why deny the obvious?

"Well, you're leafy but you don't look dangerous." She shrugs. "Better keep running. Go on now — quick!"

She steps aside, and instantly I am racing away once more. But my strength is ebbing as my *inish* starts to splutter out.

Then strong hands seize me, whip me about, and hold me fast. I can't see my captor's face, but I recognize the uniform he wears from the sleeves visible on the arms crossing my chest. Ministry issue. Just great.

I fight to free myself, but I am held fast.

"It's all over!" A deep voice penetrates the chaotic din and brings everyone to an uncertain standstill. "I have the interloper. She's safely in hand. Everyone please return to your duties. Go on now! Excitement's over."

A slow dispersal begins as my captor bends close. "Are you all right?"

Drifter!

I manage a small nod. "Just get me out of here."

"Patience." His hands release me, and I see he is wearing a full Ministry commander's uniform. A quick smile reassures me. "Walk beside me. And try to look defeated."

Together we head down the hallway in the direction I was already running — away from the remnants of the mob — and I feel a bit of my old confidence return. We pass more than a few guards. All salute him, but Drifter ignores them pointedly. More than once I falter, but he is quick to take my arm and hold me steady as we continue. I realize suddenly that I am completely exhausted, my *inish* stores again hovering on empty. Whatever energy I put into making my escape seems to have diminished my *inish* to almost nothing.

"You look like you've been beaten," he observes at one point.

"My own fault. I needed a diversion. I'll tell you about it later."

We walk on in silence, and within two minutes reach a door marked STAIRS. Drifter opens it and steers me through, and we begin to climb. The effort seems endless, and I feel myself fading more quickly. Drifter slides one arm around my back and under my opposite arm to help hold me up. Good thing. I am all tapped out. A decidedly worrying turn of events, but at least I am free again.

About halfway up the first flight, the door above us opens and two officers walk down, talking to each other. As they pass, they salute Drifter, then one of them slows.

"Excuse me, Commander, but you must be new here," he says.

Drifter smiles. "Just helping out Central Command."

"Taking that creature back with you?"

397

"She's to be questioned."

"I was told all Fae were handed over to Dr. Allensby — and those orders came from Central Command."

"That's where I am taking her. Move on, Lieutenant."

"But Allensby's office is down, not up."

Drifter's brows draw together in a heavy scowl. "What is your name, Lieutenant?"

But the other man has already brought out his sidearm. "What is *your* name, Commander? I think you should . . ."

I watch as his face suddenly loses all expression and his body spins and falls. I catch a glimpse of the throwing star buried in his neck, though I saw nothing of its delivery. Drifter is so fast that the lieutenant is killed instantly. The other officer freezes in place.

"Weapons down," Drifter orders, his own sidearm drawn and pointing. "On the steps. Quickly."

The man does as ordered. Drifter takes two steps down to reach him and, with a single blow, renders him unconscious. Then he kicks the weapons down the stairs, where they clatter away into the shadows. Coming back up, he tightens his grip on me once more. "Keep moving. We don't have much farther to go."

But we end up having to climb two more flights of stairs to reach the roof, and by then I am clinging to him like a limpet. From below, the commotion of earlier has died away and there is only silence. I can only assume that the two officers lie quiet and undisturbed on the stairs. It seems no one has come to find them, and there is still no pursuit.

"Is Riva here?" I ask. "Antrim?"

"Let's hope."

"I can't afford to be caught again," I whisper.

"You won't get caught," Drifter assures me. "Stop thinking about it."

But I can't, of course. It is all I can think about — all that matters to me. I have to get away. I have to get back to Harrow. I have to . . .

I collapse, crumpling to the floor. Drifter catches me as I go down and lowers me carefully onto the stairs. "Auris?"

"I can't go on," I tell him.

He regards me patiently and then reaches into his breast pocket. "Here, swallow this."

The pill is unidentifiable. "What is it?"

"A regenerative. It will give you the energy you need."

"Is it safe?"

"It's effective. And taking just one won't

hurt you. Just do as I say if you want to get out of here before they find us."

I hesitate . . . but what else am I going to do? I need to keep going. I pop the pill into my mouth and swallow it dry. In less than a minute, I feel a rush of fresh energy sweeping through me. With Drifter's help, I stand up and climb the rest of the way to the rooftop door.

"Wow," I mutter, amazed.

"It won't last long. Then you'll have to sleep. But it will get you to somewhere you can do that. Come on."

He opens the rooftop door and we step out into a gray daylight, filled with low clouds and a thin, dispirited drizzle. The roof is flat, with large appliance housings scattered here and there in clusters. Some of them are huge, capable of containing ventilators and oxygen recovery systems, but some are mysterious shapes that suggest nothing in particular. Off to one side, aerial weapons sit empty, their barrels pointed skyward.

Riva Tisk is already coming toward us. Without a word she embraces me and then lifts me into her arms. She's so strong she makes it seem effortless. "You had us worried."

I feel like a child being held like this, but I

400

give her a smile. "I had myself worried."

She carries me over to the low wall of a machine housing and sets me down with my back against the wall. "For someone so small, you certainly know how to cause a lot of trouble. We knew you would have been taken here if you were still alive — or Drifter knew anyway — but we didn't know where exactly. He was forced to go inside to find out. You found his note?"

I nod. "It gave me hope when I needed it."

She smiles. "He lost patience with waiting early this morning and went back in to bring you out himself." She examines my face. "How badly hurt are you?"

I shake my head. "Not so bad. Can we go now?"

"*Pfft.* You really are your mother's daughter."

"Where's Antrim?" I ask.

She smiles. "Close."

She walks over to where Drifter stands, and they speak quietly for a few moments. I hear snatches of their conversation, but not the whole of it. They speak of my condition and then of the danger of flying in daylight and the even worse danger of trying to wait until nightfall. It seems that, in my absence, Riva has taken charge. I am secretly pleased.

After they have reached some sort of agreement, Riva comes back over to kneel beside me.

"Is the pill helping?"

"I can travel, if that's what you're asking."

"I don't have the luxury of asking. I just want some reassurance. We have to get off this roof. Flying in daylight is dangerous, but we don't have a choice. The plan is to go somewhere nearby to hide out, then fly back to Viridian Deep after nightfall."

I nod. "I can manage that."

In the next instant, an alarm sounds from deep inside the Ministry building — a long, sharp wailing that clearly signals my absence has been noticed.

Riva is on her feet at once. She reaches down and lifts me back into her arms. I start to object, but she overrides me quickly. "No arguments. It's faster this way."

She rushes over to one wall of the building, carrying me as if I were weightless. I feel foolish being hauled about like this, but I keep my thoughts to myself and consider how lucky I am to be able to feel as safe as I do. She sets me down again as Drifter joins us, handing me over to him as she leans over the wall edge and gives a shrill whistle. As if by magic, a monstrous dark shape ascends from between buildings, long neck twisting, huge teeth baring. How Antrim managed to fit between buildings and still spread his giant wings defies reason, but this is no time for questions. Drifter leaps aboard the Dragon and Riva hands me up to him. Then, with a lurching spring, she boards as well, scrambling forward to assume the lead position.

"Fly south," I hear Riva call out in Dragon speech to Antrim. "Find us somewhere we can hide. Quickly!"

There is no verbal response, but Antrim pumps his giant wings and arches higher still. Below us, the city of Harbor's End falls away, the buildings and streets and people diminishing in size until we reach the concealment of the low-hanging clouds and everything below disappears completely. Has anyone seen us go? Impossible to tell, but we rise so quickly I have to think it will have been only a glimpse at best. With luck, no one has seen us at all. But luck has been a bit of a stranger thus far, so I take nothing for granted.

I sit in front of Drifter, who has his arms about me, holding me in place. I am much stronger by now, more assured about my ability to keep my seat. But the wind buffets us in wild gusts, and for all his size and weight Antrim is knocked about more than a little. His sudden lurches and drops give me good reason to be grateful for Drifter's steady grip about my waist. Ahead of me, Riva is bent low over the Dragon's neck, speaking to him as she strokes the soft skin that lies hidden beneath his scaly hide, urging or guiding or both, I cannot tell. But we stay concealed within the clouds, and for a time there is no indication of any pursuit.

Until an airship surfaces ahead of us, and I realize that the roar I had mistaken for the wind is actually a pair of engines jutting out of its tail section. Antrim dives at once, losing us again in the clouds. But the wind is starting to break apart our cover, and it is clear we will soon be out in the open and visible to all.

"We have to land now!" Drifter shouts forward, and I see Riva glance back and nod.

Even though the Dragon cannot be tracked by radar, we will be visible to the naked eye soon, so our position will not remain a secret for long. Plus, the Ministry likely has additional technology to track us, and I am afraid we are still too far from the Fae border to expect any protection from its wards. We are on our own until nightfall, and we have to find cover quickly.

Antrim continues to descend, and suddenly the ground appears less than two hundred yards below us. We are directly over a swamp, and there is no apparent place for us to land. Cliffs ring this marshy expanse on three sides, while to the west a narrow stretch of rocks and scrub form a barrier against the waters of Roughlin Wake, which is clearly visible through a fragmented swirl of heavy mist. I glance about anxiously, but I can find no signs of other airships. But they will be on us quickly enough. Overhead, engines signal their approach.

"Tighten down!" Riva calls back to us in warning.

We swoop downward toward the eastern cliffs, flying directly for their ominous walls. We are coming in way too fast. We are flying toward this jagged barrier at breakneck speed, and Antrim acts as if he doesn't see it. I want to scream something at him in warning but my throat locks up, and I see Riva urging him on as if she's got a death wish. I close my eyes, hoping I am wrong, praying that one or the other of them recognizes the danger.

But not seeing proves even worse, so I quickly have to look anew, and by then we are right on top of the cliff face. Abruptly, Antrim's huge wings widen and flatten out against the rushing wind and we brake sharply in midair, slowing so quickly I am almost thrown from the Dragon's back. If not for Drifter holding me in place, I am sure I would be flying through the air to my death. But his efforts succeed, and as we finally come to a stop, we are inside a low, wide alcove partially concealed by brush and grasses where its opening cuts into the side of the cliff just far enough to offer a Dragon and three passengers shelter and concealment.

Breathing hard — which is difficult when your heart is in your throat — we slide down Antrim's wing and stand waiting for our insides to unknot and our pulse rates to slow. I am reminded anew of when Riva and I stood on that cliff awaiting our initial encounter with Antrim, and how the Dragon appeared to be on the verge of crushing us but was able to stop instantly. This experience feels similar, and I experience the same momentary shock at finding myself still alive.

When we are recovered, we take a few moments to look around. Directly outside, to a height of less than a hundred feet, a mix of swirling mist and gases rises from the swamp, obscuring our vision — but more critically, hiding the entrance to our enclosure. Higher still, the low cloud cover through which we descended veils the sky completely.

Of the Ministry and its airships there is no sign.

We move back inside the overhang, finding a non-Dragon-occupied space in which to sit and wait out the daylight. Antrim is curled into a ball and already fast asleep. The rest of us follow suit, but with mixed results. My companions are quicker to sleep than I am. I rise and move silently to the forefront of the cave opening, peering out at the broad expanse of the marsh and beyond to the choppy waters of Roughlin Wake.

It can't be much more than midday, so hours remain before we can leave. Nightfall will provide us with the cover we need to make our return to Viridian Deep, but even after all this, I am still no closer to any answers. After all I have been through and learned, I still don't know how to save Harrow.

A surge of desperation washes through me, and I am momentarily overwhelmed. Almost half of the time allotted to me by Tonklot has passed. Seven days have gone, and I have seven days left. The full moon is rapidly approaching, and there is nothing I can do to slow its arrival.

"Can't sleep?"

Drifter's unexpected voice causes me to jump as he seats himself beside me.

I shake my head. "You?"

"I haven't slept well in years. Too on edge, I suppose. Want to talk for a bit?"

"About what?"

"You said you would tell me what you learned while you were imprisoned. I'd like to hear. At least, it will help pass the time."

As reluctant as I am to speak of it, I agree. Drifter listens intently and does not interrupt. Off to one side, Antrim's snoring tells me we are unlikely to disturb him. Not so Riva, who wakes and wanders over to join us.

My tale begins with my first interaction with Winton and ends with his desire to turn me, like Malik, into his puppet, so he can use me to find a way into Viridian Deep.

"Also," I add, "he hates me. He is convinced I am responsible for the death of his father, so I can't imagine he will ever treat me kindly — not even knowing I am his sister. Even if we can dispatch the Barghast and restore Harrow, Winton will just keep coming for me, because he has nothing to do with any of the rest. He's just a stupid little boy with daddy issues, who never got a chance to prove himself to his father in life, and now is determined to carry on his father's last, fruitless quest as a way of, what? Honoring him? Finding validation at last?"

"Perhaps after what you did to him today, he might think twice," Riva says quietly.

But Drifter shakes his head. "No. He and his father are both cut from the same cloth — intelligent, gifted scientists emotionally crippled by their inability to see the Fae as anything but a threat. I learned that when I was working back in Ministry security. Winton, like his father, will keep coming until he is stopped."

"Thank you for the reassurance," I deadpan.

Drifter smiles. "It's always better to be honest about your enemies, even if you cannot always be so about your friends. Winton is dangerous. You should have killed him when you had the chance."

I stare at him. "I don't think I could have managed that — even as much as I hate him for what he did to Malik and still wants to do to me." I shake my head. "Besides, he is my brother, and I am not yet come to that."

Drifter smiles. "I don't suppose you are. And you shouldn't ever be. Still, someone will have to do it, sooner or later."

I shake my head. I have no interest in any

further interactions with Winton. "I just want to get Harrow back."

Though, as I have also realized, it is Winton who is indirectly responsible for everything that has happened to me. If Winton had not sent Malik to fetch me, Malik would not have led me into the Aerkling territory to free me, meaning the Aerklings would never have captured me and brought me to their Winglish, where Tonklot spotted me.

"You'll get him back," Riva says. "And we'll help you do it."

But Drifter shakes his head in disagreement. "Auris doesn't need us. Only herself."

I stare at him, speechless.

"Auris," he says softly, leaning close, "I've been thinking about this a lot. I think you already possess all the skills necessary to overcome this creature. You remember what I once told you about self-protection, that you are always going to be your own best defense? It was the sum of what I was teaching you all along. You were an able and highly talented student — an accomplished young woman made even stronger because you were also smart and intuitive."

I blush. This is high praise indeed. But I think he is wrong. "I don't expect I can ever claim . . ."

His hand clamps down on my shoulder, silencing me.

"I am telling you the truth. You are ten times better now than you were when I last saw you. Not only have you retained your combat skills — which you have honed since — but you also possess the infinite power of your *inish.* Remember, I know something of *inish* from my time among the Fae and from my father's Fae blood, and while I am far from an expert, I have never seen an *inish* like yours. Mine was never so strong."

"You told me you were hybrid. Did you always know your history?"

"I was told I was a halfling early on, but I never looked it. I always looked Human. Nor did my *inish* ever become as evident as yours has. I was always mostly reliant on my combat and weapons skills. And once Meliore was gone, I dismissed my Fae side entirely. I went back to Harbor's End and returned to being just another Human. Viridian Deep became a thing of the past — a memory of a better time, but I did not crave a return to it. I was content to be Human again and nothing more. Hybrids are unusual, rare. They are often regarded as alien — parts of two species and not really either one. I did not want that identity. You, on the other hand, seem as if you were born

411

to be Fae — physically and mentally."

"The Seers have said much the same," I confess. "They think it is because I am a Changeling, but I've never been able to access a Changeling's powers. I can't take another form; I have tried. I can't even revert to my own Human form again, to protect me while I am here in the Human world. And I have tried that as well. Twice."

Drifter shrugs. "Maybe there are different ways to be a Changeling. Maybe it's less about looks than it is about powers. Or maybe you simply weren't able to access your Human form because there is no part of you that truly wants to be Human anymore."

He may have a point with that one. The more I see of the Human world, the more disenchanted I become with it. So maybe my resistance there is less about the magic than about me. But still . . .

"Still," Drifter echoes, "here is what I see about your *inish,* Auris. I see a young woman with almost uncannily accurate intuition, who always seems to figure out the best way to solve any problem set her. So what if *that* is your magic — the ability to solve any problem, get out of any situation you get yourself into? You said yourself that the Barghast wanted something from you — something it tried to dig out of you on at least one occasion that you can remember. It does not need a shapeshifting magic; that it already has. But what creature would not kill to get its hands on that level of intuition?"

This seems crazy to me. I have not solved every problem I've been presented with, have I? But Drifter is already continuing.

"I am no longer the teacher and you the student. I am not even your equal. You are better than I am. You have progressed to a point where *you* are the master. If you want Harrow back, you will find a way — or maybe your *inish* will."

"But we can still help," Riva quickly interjects. "You are not saying we should let her go alone, are you?"

Drifter nods slowly. "I am saying she needs to look inside herself for the answers she seeks. If she does, I believe she will succeed."

His admonition is reassuring, but troubling, too. For him to say I am more accomplished than he is seems a misjudgment of the worst sort. I am still too young and inexperienced. "I don't know if I am up to it."

He leans over and hugs me to him. "You are one of the best and bravest people I have ever known, and I have missed you. It is a relief to find you still alive, and still as skillful and capable as ever. I am confident that both will serve you well."

He then draws back and looks at me sadly. "But I have been thinking, Auris, and I don't know that I can stand going back to Viridian Deep. Too many memories. Too much pain. My time in Viridian Deep is over. My place now is here, in my own world, where I see needs that require tending. I believe I can better help you by staying behind. Forgive me."

Then he rises and looks down at me. "When this is over — when you are done with the Barghast — come back to me. Come tell me everything that happened, if you can. Will you promise?"

I don't know exactly why, but I give him a nod of agreement. Without waiting for anything further, he turns away and walks from the cave and is gone. Riva and I stare after him silently.

"Well, that was unexpected," Riva says finally.

I'm still reeling under everything he told me. "Do you believe any of that?" I ask her. "What he said?"

"Don't know. He certainly expects a lot of you, doesn't he?" A long pause. "But he *thinks* a lot of you, too."

"He expects too much," I whisper in reply.

She gives me a look and then a bitter smile. "*Pfft.* I don't think so. It just seems that way at the moment."

Then she, too, rises and wanders off again, presumably to sleep, and I am left alone with a mix of confused feelings about what I have just heard.

But the effort to concentrate on it is beyond me by now, the stimulant Drifter gave me is wearing off, and in minutes I am asleep.

TWENTY-FIVE

I wake sometime around midnight to find Riva by my side, shaking my shoulder. "Time to go."

I have slept deeply, and it takes me a few long minutes to shrug off the lethargy and rise. The cave is dark, but I can make out Antrim as he stirs near its back, his huge scaly body working its way forward toward the entrance. Riva is shrugging on her gear and peering out at the darkness. The skies are black; there is no light visible from the moon or stars. Apparently, the cloud cover is thick enough to hide the heavens utterly. It will be good flying for a Dragon and two passengers seeking to escape detection.

Drifter is gone. I have to accept that he is not coming back.

I wonder if the Ministry still searches for me. But of course it does. Winton would not have given up so easily. There will be patrols and radar emplacements. And there will be aircraft ready for instant deployment if we are detected.

I take hold of Riva's shoulder to gain her attention. "How do we avoid being caught out once we are airborne?"

"Antrim knows about Human detection machines. As we told you before, Dragons are not detectable by technology. And if we fly south along the edges of the marsh into the wastelands and cross over from there to Viridian, we will not be seen. On a brighter night eyes might spy us, but not tonight."

I nod, thinking her right — or hoping so, at least. Riva scrambles up Antrim's extended wing, fitting herself into the juncture at his neck and shoulders. "Are you coming?"

Do I have a choice?

I follow her up, positioning myself just behind her, my body pressed against hers, my hands gripping the heavy leather belt she has rucked up about her muscular midsection. I dig in my fingers to secure a firm hold. "Ready."

She leans forward to whisper to Antrim, who moves across the cavern floor to the cave entrance. He edges outside to clear the opening, his body sinking into the tidal waters until they are up to his belly. Then he spreads his wings to catch the wind currents blowing in off the Roughlin, gathers himself, and jumps. Two quick flaps of those great appendages, and we are airborne. Soaring skyward, Antrim banks and levels off not fifty feet above the surface of the marsh, and angles south toward the northern edge of the wastelands. We fly low and swift, and our passage is little more than a silent shadow. I look for evidence of pursuit, but although I search long and hard, I find nothing. We pass into the wastelands, surrounded by darkness and clouds and mist, and nothing intrudes.

Within an hour, we are flying west across Roughlin Wake and its choppy black waters — a Dragon and two riders alone beneath an empty sky. I hug myself against Riva's broad back, closing my eyes. Wind whips at me in wild, chilling gusts, and its cold seeps into my bones. I shiver in spite of myself and know it is from more than the cold.

The night drags on, and my weariness grows more pronounced. I find myself drifting in the quieter moments of our flight, sleep prodding at my consciousness. I blink and shift to fight it off, but it lingers. Ahead of me, Riva sits firm and steady as she holds her position astride Antrim's neck, now and then leaning forward to say something to him, her words lost in the rush of the wind.

Overhead, the clouds part and the moon and stars come into view. But the night continues to pass, with no signs of a lightening in the eastern sky.

How long has this flight been? How much longer until I am home safe?

I am still trying to think of a way to save Harrow — to overcome the Barghast's ability to bend people to his will and make them his puppets. I remember what he did to me when he stole Harrow's *inish.* I remember how terrible it felt to be so helpless. I remember how ashamed I felt afterward at how easily my will had been overcome.

I have power to spare at my command — or will again soon — but how to use it?

And then I recall Drifter's words. Drifter thinks I can manage this, that I have a unique magic that will get me through. He believes me capable of doing what he could not do all those years ago. He believes I will find a way. I wish I could believe it as strongly as he does, but the harsh truth is that I cannot. Everything he told me sounded wildly improbable, and therefore unbelievable, and I feel the tightening grip of hopelessness and the inevitable failure it will bring.

My despair deepens as we fly, and my

exhaustion is suddenly overwhelming.

My eyes close, and I sleep.

When I wake, it is with a stab of fear. In spite of the danger of doing so — in spite of the fact that I promised myself I would not — I have fallen asleep astride Antrim's broad neck, still pressed up against Riva Tisk, my hands still somehow maintaining their grip on the other woman's belt. I spy land ahead in the faint glow of the rising sun — the rugged eastern shores of Viridian Deep, behind which lie the ragged peaks of the Skyscrape Mountains and the receding darkness. Home at last. I exhale sharply, and a wave of relief suffuses me at the sight. I am still exhausted and aching from everything I have been though over the past eight days, and my *inish* is once again gone. How much longer will I have to wait for its return? But I am able to push aside the discomfort its absence creates and embrace what expectations my arrival back home provides. Perhaps it will come back faster in Viridian Deep. But it must, mustn't it? I only have a scant six days in which to save Harrow.

The remainder of my journey passes quickly, and I push aside my thoughts of desperation and worry in favor of enjoying the spectacular views of the countryside over which we fly. It is so good to see it all once more, so unexpectedly reassuring. It is almost as if I am being promised a way forward — as if I am being assured that everything is going to work out.

Almost.

Less than an hour later, we are on the ground, landing in a field east of the city. I slide down from Antrim's back along the length of his lowered wing, but no sooner do I reach the ground than my legs threaten to give way. Only through sheer force of will do I manage to stay upright as I watch Riva whispering to Antrim and the Dragon saying something back. Then she is on the ground beside me, pulling me back.

"Antrim has brought us within walking distance of the city proper," she says quietly. "Maybe three or four miles of walking and we are there. He chooses to leave us here because he is unwilling to fly closer. Too many people, too many chances of being seen. Most believe the Dragons dead and gone, and he thinks it safer for his people if that belief is maintained, with Dragons far away and out of sight."

She pauses. "But he wants to speak with you."

I move forward to stand close to Antrim's

huge muzzle as he bends down close. "Home again, Fae girl. Have you your wits and *inish* about you yet?"

I smile. "Not all the way. But soon."

"When do you wish me back?" His voice is rough and edgy, but the commitment is clearly there.

"I didn't think you were coming back. I didn't think you would want anything more to do with this business."

"I want the Barghast dead just as much as you do. Such creatures are a scourge to all of us — and they are as much a threat to my Dragon pride as they are to your family. It thinks itself my equal. It thinks it can take control of me as it has done with other creatures. No, I need to come with you — if only to ensure that you will have sufficient time in which to overcome him."

I understand his meaning. If he flies us to the Winglish and back again, we don't have to travel afoot. It will save an awful lot of time. One in, all in, it appears.

"You are brave and kind to offer," I answer. "I would leave now, but I need time to let my *inish* replenish itself. Give me three days, and I'll be waiting for you here at dawn. I'll need you to fly me right into the Aerkling Winglish."

"Well and good. Once I have this Barghast

before me, I will offer myself as his Dragon — then give him perhaps five seconds to think about what that means before I devour him."

Antrim sounds gleeful, but I have to stop this thinking here and now while I still can. "No, Antrim, you cannot speak with the Barghast. You cannot engage with him at all. It is you the Barghast wants, and I will not chance that he might find a way to ensnare you. I will deal with Tonklot myself."

The Dragon hisses at me with such ferocity that he nearly knocks me off my feet, snarling and spitting with rage. "I will not be told what I can or cannot do! The terms of my service are my own business."

I straighten with some effort. "But Tonklot desires to take control of you, Antrim. He wants you for a reason, to compel you to do something . . ."

Antrim's roars reverberate through the very ground on which I stand, cutting me short. "What that creature wants matters not a whit to me! No one commands a Dragon, Auris. Not even you."

Abruptly, he spreads his massive wings and lifts away in a whirlwind of wind and dust, rising in a great swooping circle that leaves me struggling to shelter my eyes as he flies off into the sunrise.

I watch him go, wondering what I have done. Riva walks over to stand beside me. "I think that could have been handled better."

"Probably."

"Tell me, do you have any idea at all about how you are going to overcome the Barghast? About how you are going to take him prisoner, haul him back here, and force him to restore Harrow's *inish*?"

I sigh. "Not really."

She nods. "So have you considered that maybe Antrim is right, that maybe he can overcome the Barghast?"

"But what if he can't? You didn't feel what that creature could do, Riva. And if Antrim can handle him, why are the Seers so afraid of letting a Dragon anywhere near Tonklot? They must have seen something that we are not privy to."

"Perhaps," she concedes. "Let's just hope we come up with a better plan in the next three days. Now let's start walking so we can reach the city before we lose this day as well."

And without waiting for an answer, she hikes away and leaves me to follow as best I can.

■ ■ ■

We walk at a steady pace for a couple of hours and reach the city shortly after mid-day. We say little to each other during our journey, although I am pretty sure we are both thinking the same thing. I am convinced that Riva intends to come with me to confront the Barghast, and — as with Antrim — I am trying to decide how to prevent this. I am also convinced that Ronden will insist on coming too.

I cannot keep risking their lives. The burden for saving Harrow has been placed directly on me by the Barghast, and if anything happens to any of them, it will be my fault for including them. Ronden, at least, has a vested interest in her brother, but the other two are doing this for me. It all feels wrong, but I cannot think of a way to stop it from happening.

When we reach the city proper, Riva suggests we need to find Ronden first. I was thinking that I should go to Harrow instead, but she points out that we told Ronden we would find her as soon as we returned and we should keep that promise. I can't think of a reason to do anything else, so I agree. Harrow has waited this long; he can wait a bit longer. Besides, Harrow is under the care of the Seers, so when I go to him, I will need to spend some time with them, too. I will need to ask them for help once more, although I haven't been able to settle yet on exactly what sort of help to ask for. What I need is a way to defeat the Barghast and take him alive, but the sisters, although proficient at recapturing memories, are not able to conjure solutions out of thin air.

Still, I have to try something.

I think again of Drifter's words — that perhaps being a Changeling is not about looks — and again dismiss them.

Instead, I steer Riva through the city streets and the throngs of people. At her size and with her clear presence, she draws attention, but she seems not to notice. I smile, glad for once not to be the one everyone is sneaking glances at. My transformation from Human to Fae is continuing, but I am close enough to being fully Fae now that I no longer show much evidence of my Human side.

We climb the tree lane steps closest to Ronden's. An old familiar dread surfaces, of something bad happening in my absence — that mix of fear and guilt that I cannot manage to banish. I know its origins. I have lost everything in my life before, and now that I am being given a second chance — a wonderful, magical do-over — I cannot bear the thought that I might lose this, too.

But I tamp down my intrusive, unwelcome worries and think only of reuniting with my family. So much has happened in the last two weeks that it feels as if I've been gone for months, and I smile with a mix of relief and expectation as Ancrow's former home appears ahead. Beyond, the cottage I now share with Harrow is clearly visible in the day's warm sunlight.

I slow and turn to Riva. "Are you ready?"

She blinks. "Are you?"

A valid question — and one I have no answer to.

We walk to the front door and I knock. There is a pause, and then the door opens and Ronden is standing there. She startles, then smiles broadly and lunges to embrace us both — which startles Riva in return.

"I should be furious with you for leaving me behind," she announces through hugs and tears, "but I am so happy to see you I don't want to bother wasting time on that."

"We'll tell you everything," I promise. "For now, it is just good to be home. Is . . . Is all well here?"

She takes a deep breath and exhales. "Well . . ."

"Harrow?" I ask at once, the blood draining from my face.

She shakes her head. "Still in the care of the sisters. No, this is something else. You might as well come in and see."

She steps aside and allows us to enter. We walk into the living room and I stop in my tracks.

It seems that I now have the answer to at least one of Winton's questions.

TWENTY-SIX

"Hello, Auris," Malik says.

It is beyond surreal to see this giant faceless figure sitting on a couch in my family's living room, but stranger still to see him gently bouncing Char on one knee and Ramey on the other. Though all encased in metal and composite, he occupies his seat as if perfectly at ease, comfortable with the two smiling, laughing girls who are entranced by his attention.

I have encountered more than a few odd sights in my lifetime, and I imagine I will encounter others, but I doubt that anything will be able to top this.

"Hello, Malik," I reply, conscious of Riva's hands on the blades she wears strapped to her sides. "Are you moving in with my family?"

"Yes, yes, yes!" Char shouts immediately. "Do it, Malik! Come live with us."

I hear Malik chuckle, the sound reverberating from within his helmet. "Can't do that, Char. I'm just here for a visit."

"It doesn't have to be just a visit," Ramey declares in her no-nonsense voice. "Isn't that right, Auris?"

Char seems to suddenly realize I am there, and before I can reply to Ramey, she leaps off Malik's leg and rushes over to embrace me. "You're back!" she exclaims, then her face dims. "Did you find anything to make Harrow better?"

I hug her to me and ruffle her shaggy green hair. "Maybe. Be patient, and I'll tell you. But . . ."

I look questioningly at Ronden and raise my eyebrows.

"Malik appeared several nights ago. He arrived very late, because he didn't want our neighbors to see him and be frightened — though of course he had to reveal himself to me. He came here to find you, but since you were gone, he convinced me he wasn't here to kidnap anyone or cause trouble, so I invited him in. We had a long talk about the past and some other things, but he can tell you about that himself — if he can ever rid himself of those two leeches clinging to his knees. They seem to have found a new source of amusement, and I can't pry them off him."

Any hesitation I might have experienced on finding him here disappears when I learn that Ronden feels safe. I know Malik's gentle side from when we were prisoners of the Goblins, and in spite of his size and his formidable look, that gentleness remains.

"Maybe you should tell us what happened after I left you with Riva," Ronden suggests. "I think we all need to hear about it — Malik included. He might have a few things to add to what you already know."

After introducing Riva to Malik and the younger girls, we all sit down so I can tell my story. I begin with what transpired during the search for the Dragons and our subsequent discovery of what kind of creature Tonklot is, and our search for my old teacher Drifter. With Riva adding bits and pieces to my story, I recount how we were carried by Antrim to the Human world and Harbor's End. There we located Drifter with the help of my adoptive mother. Ramey and Char both interrupt, begging me to tell them more about what it was like to fly on a Dragon and did they breathe fire and so on until finally Ronden shushes them with an admonition to save all that for later and let me finish my story.

I do so quickly, touching only lightly on the details of how Drifter joined us, how I was captured and encountered Winton and discovered his desire to make me like Malik — I see Malik flinch at this — and my subsequent escape and return and Drifter's departure. I conclude with Antrim's promise to return, and our walk back to the city to find Malik waiting.

Ronden wastes no time. "The Dragons had no answers about Harrow, did they?"

I shake my head. "Though Antrim will take me to the Winglish to face Tonklot."

"So what will you do now?"

All eyes fix on me, and I want to be somewhere else. "I'm still trying to figure that out. Antrim has offered to be the Dragon I give to the Barghast, as he is convinced there is no way Tonklot can control him. But I am not so sure. I am hoping I can find another option."

"You will, once you think about it some more," Char declares.

I am less certain. "I know more than I did," I say, "but I don't have a clear path forward yet. I don't know the whole answer."

This is a generous assessment of my plan to help Harrow, but I cannot make myself suggest otherwise when I see how she looks at me.

"You'll think of something," she announces, glancing about to find confirmation in the faces of the others. And when there is not much to be found, she frowns. "Ramey, say something!"

Her sister shrugs. "Auris has always found a way in the past. She will this time, too."

She says it with such conviction that I am left shattered — and stunned by the similarity to Drifter's words. Is this how they see me, as the person who can never lose? But they have to believe this, of course. If they think me vulnerable, then what chance do they have? I have not given up; I will never give up. But I also have not found the solution she is expecting me to find.

"You are lucky to even be alive after all you've gone through," Ronden says quietly. "I can't imagine what it must have been like to be back in the hands of the Ministry yet again. This Winton, your half brother — how could he treat you like he did? What sort of monster *is* he?"

"The same kind as his father," Malik says.

"He was the one who changed you?" Char asks abruptly.

Malik nods. "He was — though I never knew his name until now."

I turn to my friend. "He asked me where you were. He clearly wants you back."

"No surprise. He lost an important experiment that he thinks belongs to him. He thinks he is not yet done with me. But he is."

The way he says this is troubling, and I stare at him. "What do you mean?"

Ronden stands. "This seems like a good time to let Malik tell Auris why he has come. Riva, why don't you and the girls come with me — perhaps for a treat at the sugar fruit stand — so we can give old friends a chance to speak alone."

The girls are on their feet at once, ready to go, but Riva hesitates, giving Malik a long look. "Auris, I know Malik was once your friend" — and there is a decided emphasis on the word *once* — "but I don't like leaving you alone."

I smile. "I know. And thank you for that. But I am safe with Malik, and I'd feel better having you with my sisters."

She nods, gives Malik a hard look, and turns away. The women all troop out of the cottage, closing the door behind them. I wait a moment, then move to sit beside Malik. "Tell me what's wrong."

"I was just thinking how nice it would be to have a guard dog like Riva," he says instead. "She's loyal."

"We met a week ago," I say. "We have become friends, but still her protectiveness

434

is surprising. She didn't even want me near her, at first."

Malik chuckles from within his metal skin. "You were always full of surprises, Auris, right from the first day we met. You had this unshakable confidence in knowing what it would take to survive, and I think Tommy relied on you more than you relied on him. You reassured him when he doubted himself, and you were always there for him. I admired that. I tried to be there for Tommy, too — for all of them — but you were better at it. Now look at you: the only one of us who truly escaped from the Goblins. That's really something."

I don't miss how he says this. "What do you mean, truly escaped?"

"I can't go on like this, Auris." He says it as if he was describing a headache or a sore arm. "You know the hold Winton has over me — and how he handed that leash over to Chorech, the leader of the Goblin pack, when he wanted me to collect you. Well, Chorech decided I had led them into an Aerkling trap the night we were ambushed and you and your sister were taken. He was right, of course; I wanted to help you get free. He had no proof, but it didn't matter. He decided to punish me by destroying my medicine, saying that if I wanted to live I could go back to my master like the nasty little dog I was. We fought, and I overpowered him. I managed to save most of what he would have destroyed, but Winton had never given him that much to begin with. I have enough to get me through a week — maybe a shade more — if I take it every three or four days instead of every other day. But even that" — he shakes his great head — "it's not enough, Auris. The more I try to stretch it, the worse the pain starts out when the meds wear off. I can't keep living like this."

I hear him sigh. "Winton might have lied about a lot, but not about that. It seems that unless I have that medicine every other day, I pay a worse and worse price. So I have chosen my path forward. I found Winton's tracker and removed it, laid low until the Goblins dispersed, then came searching for you instead. I hoped to catch you outside of the city, but when you never appeared I decided to risk a visit to your home. There was no one there, so I went to your sisters' house. Ronden let me explain and then told me I could wait for you here until you returned."

"Maybe your body will adjust to the lower dosage, or maybe you can wean yourself off it," I suggest.

"And maybe cows will fly, too. Even without wings."

"Don't joke."

A shift in his posture signals his discomfort. "I know myself well enough to know when something is wrong. Winton told me what would happen without the medication, and he was right, Auris. My life has become untenable, so I've come to you for help."

As if I had any help to give. I cannot even manage to find a way to fix Harrow. "What can I do?"

"Come back with me to Harbor's End and get the formula for the medication from Winton. That way, I gain control of my own life again. But I need a way to persuade him. Your *inish* can do that. I need you."

I feel a surge of panic. Why is everyone so convinced that my *inish* will provide the perfect solution? First Drifter, then Ramey, and now Malik. And they are all wrong.

To begin with, I have no *inish* right now. And even if I did, Malik is asking me to abandon Harrow and go with him. And this I cannot do — though the guilt I feel at having to deny him is immense. I do not want to fail him as I did Khoury and the others, even given what it is likely to cost me. But Harrow has to come first.

I try to explain. "Malik, I burned myself

437

out rescuing Antrim and then again getting myself out of Ministry clutches. But even once I get my *inish* back — *if* I get it back, having treated it so recklessly — I have an obligation to Harrow. I need to . . .."

"I understand that Harrow comes first," Malik interrupts. "And I will help you."

I'm not sure I hear him correctly. "You will? But . . . isn't your deadline even tighter than his?"

"Maybe . . . but maybe not. I can endure a lot if I know there is a chance for me to recover. Besides, it will be my repayment to you for helping me. I never intended that you should abandon your lover, Auris."

"But you . . . your condition . . ."

"My condition has not left me helpless," Malik points out. "I took a dose yesterday, and I won't take another until the day we leave; I can manage two days of agony, trust me."

The flat acceptance in his voice nearly undoes me, and I feel my anger at Winton surge anew. But Malik has already continued.

"I may even be able to help against the Barghast. My armor and my faceplate might well protect me against his enchantments. He cannot see my eyes, and I can turn off my hearing, too. I can capture him and render him helpless, so you can bring him back here to restore Harrow. Then you can take me to Harbor's End to find Winton."

I don't have to think about it; I'm going to accept his offer. The opportunity it provides will not allow me to do otherwise. But I worry for Malik's condition, despite his claims, and the timing is an issue. Two urgent clocks, counting down, and I must decide which is the more pressing. I have six days left to save Harrow, but if we do that first, we may run out of time to get Malik back to Harbor's End in time. Can I risk Malik descending so far into agony that there is no coming back from it in the time it takes me to save Harrow? But if I go with Malik first, there is not enough time to save Harrow. It is an impossible choice.

And to add further uncertainty, there is a third clock to consider — the one ticking inside me as I wait for my *inish* to replenish itself. How long will it take this time for my *inish* to return? I am gambling hard on the fact that being back in Viridian Deep — in the Sylvan homeland — will somehow renew it faster. But what damage have I done by burning it out of me a second time in making my escape? If it takes longer than a couple of days — assuming it will come back at all — then Harrow and Malik are likely *both* doomed.

But Malik has made up his mind. He stands and faces me. "I know that Tonklot now leads the Aerkling Winglish. I know how to get there. I will show you. And I can fly a Dragon, even if I have not done so before now. Together we can find a way to overcome this Barghast."

He turns toward the door and reaches it in three quick strides.

"Malik . . . ."

He turns back, shaking his head. "There is nothing more to say, Auris. The matter is decided."

"I know. I just want to thank you. I want you to know how much this means to me."

He gives a small nod. "I know. But it means no more than what you will do for me in return."

"Wait!" My call to him is sharp to bring him about. "There is one other possibility of finding you the help you need. The Seer sisters are powerful — healers with extraordinary power. They once offered me their services on your behalf. So why not accept that offer? Why not go to see them and determine if there is anything they can do?"

He stares at me. "They offered?"

"I told them what had happened to you. They were appalled. They said if you came

440

back, they would try to help you heal."

He shakes his head. "No one can help me become what I was. They can only do what the medicines stolen from me would do — provide relief from the pain I will face should my treatment be terminated."

"And if they could do so permanently? Why don't the two of us go to them? I have faith —"

"You may have faith," he interrupts quickly, "but I have none. Don't you see? No matter how good their intentions, whatever they do, however they do it, I will just be reliving what I already have lived too much of — efforts to change me from what I am. It will still be just another effort to remake my body and my mind — another reworking of old Malik to make new Malik. I don't want any more of that. I don't want anything more done to me. I only want the medicine."

"Just talk to them," I beg him.

He is quiet for a long time, and then he nods. "All right. I will go to them. I will talk to them. I will decide then. Thank you, Auris. I know you mean well. But you cannot know what it is like to be me."

He goes out into the daylight, the sun flashing off his metal skin as he disappears into the trees, ignoring the startled looks of passersby. And then he is gone.

I eat dinner with my sisters and Riva that night, gathered around the dining table in their home, recalling the moment when I first sat down to eat with Ancrow and her family shortly after my arrival in Viridian Deep. Char prepares the dinner — a succulent fish poached with vegetables and rice and fresh bread; her cooking skills are still better than those of the rest of her sisters. Then, at the urging of both younger girls, I describe what it feels like to ride Antrim and to be so far above the world that you seem to be entirely free of its hold. I manage to put aside the memories of weariness — and of aches and pains from having to maintain my seat astride a saddle of scales and muscle — and focus on the sweeping and soaring and the feeling of the wind all about me. Now and then Riva adds a word or two, and after I have finished, she provides a few chilling reminders of how dangerous the Dragons are and how careful a rider must be. My new friend avoids the graphic details in deference to how young Char still is and concentrates on the extent of the training that the riders are required to undergo.

The evening passes comfortably, and no

one asks me further about how I will proceed. Tomorrow I will go see Harrow and ask the Seers if they have any way of helping me resist the Barghast. It may be that Drifter is right and that somehow my *inish* will enable me to prevail — if indeed my *inish* returns — but the specifics continue to elude me. I will have only a single chance to overcome this creature before he overpowers me and I am rendered as helpless as I was on the fatal fishing trip that first took Harrow from me.

When dinner is finished, I sit with Riva and Ronden in the living room sipping glasses of ice ale and speaking quietly about Winton and what it is like to have found yet another relative I did not know, only to discover that he hates me and blames me for what happened to his father. A relative I will shortly have to face again, in an effort to help Malik.

"Whatever happens, Auris, he will continue to hunt for you," Ronden says at one point — a realization I have already arrived at. "Malik is right; he is every bit as driven to see the Fae subjugated as his father was. The Ministry will use every ally at their disposal to hunt for you until you are caught."

"As I have been telling her," Riva adds.

I say nothing to this, but it is even more reason to accompany Malik back to Harbor's End after we restore Harrow — to end the threat from Winton forever. But none of my sisters know about this part of the plan, so I just nod and smile and change the subject.

I ask about the city and its people. I ask about the girls, who by now are almost finished with clearing the table and cleaning the dishes. I speak at length of my memories of Drifter and my latest encounter with him after all these years, and how much he has done for me both times. And how sorry I am that seeing Viridian Deep again felt too much for him.

I am growing sleepy, so with Riva in tow (I don't question that she will want to stay close), I say good night and retire to my cottage. I have barely finished showing my companion the guest bedroom before I have fallen into bed and a deep, dreamless sleep.

TWENTY-SEVEN

Come morning, I feel decidedly better —
rested and refreshed, and hungry enough to
eat a large breakfast — and relieved to find
my *inish* stirring again inside me, although
still but a seedling. I am also anxious to see
Harrow. Has he changed at all in the days I
have been away? I cannot help but think of
what both the Seers and Sanan said, about
how a Fae will eventually die without their
inish. But a part of me also fears facing what
can only be his inevitable decline, so I spend
the morning organizing the supplies, weapons, and equipment we will need when we
depart for the Aerkling Winglish and the
home of the Barghast. I try to think of
everything that might serve to help but end
up discarding most of it. Our arrival must
be quick and our actions quicker still. There
won't be time or opportunity for anything
else.

In the afternoon, I go alone to visit with

Harrow. The sisters are there to greet me, each in her characteristic way.

"So wonderful to have you back, Auris," Benith says, embracing me fully. "It will do Harrow so much good to have you here, even if he doesn't understand entirely who you are."

"Please understand. He will not be able to say anything or even to take your hand." Maven's aged voice drops to a cautionary whisper. "It will be up to you to hold his hand and let him know you are there. He will take heart, hearing your voice. But say nothing about how he appears to you."

I feel a spike of fear, and my earlier worries come flooding back. How badly has he deteriorated? How much has my search for answers cost him?

Dreena's acerbic, judgmental words cut right to the chase. "It took you long enough to decide to come here. You've been home since yesterday, I am told. Harrow is your life partner and your soulmate. He should be your priority."

I explain about Malik, hoping to find out that he has done what he promised and come to the Sisters for help. He has not. I am severely disappointed but keep it to myself. Perhaps he will come to them later. Perhaps the matter is not yet settled. I move

446

on, detailing the struggle I am having with my *inish* and my continued lack of a plan to deal with Tonklot — though I carefully leave out any mention of Antrim's final offer. When things have settled a bit with Dreena, the sisters guide me to the bedchamber into which Harrow has been placed.

I am leveled by the sight of him. Harrow lies empty of expression and even — seemingly — of life. The bedsheets have been pulled up to his neck, so that only his head is visible. But still he has visibly shrunken, withered. Unlike in the Human world, no tubes or implements are attached to him. Wires do not run from his extremities, monitors do not beep, and neither charts nor trays of instruments are anywhere in sight. Instead, he lies alone, almost untouched — but in many ways, that makes it worse. A single bag of a blue liquid feeds into an incision in his arm, and a series of odd-shaped, colored stones have been placed on the bed around him.

Benith lingers to explain their purpose.

"We feed him restorative sustenance from the drip line, although this is meant to maintain rather than restore. The stones — which are called Revealers — monitor his vital signs and enable us to detect if there are any further disruptions to his body. Thus far, there have been none. But he is sinking, Auris — and if you cannot find a way to get his *inish* back soon, we are going to lose him. I don't tell you this to frighten you, but I do want you to understand. He needs to have his *inish* restored so he can begin to recover."

I nod numbly, and she slips from the room.

I sit on the bed with Harrow, letting him sense my weight and feel my presence. Without disturbing the stones, I take his hand in mine and lean close. I fight the urge to cry, holding back my sobs. He does not need to hear my despair. I wait a long time before saying anything, wanting him to become aware of me, to sense that I am here and maybe take comfort from it. It has been almost two weeks since I have come to him. For all I know, he may think me dead. I have to let him know I am alive and ready to help.

Even if I don't yet know how I will do this.

"I'm here, Harrow," I say finally. "I've come back. I've found out more about the creature that did this to you. I have met a Dragon and found my old teacher. But through all of it, I have been so afraid for you. The sisters say you are doing well, though, and I know we will find a way to bring you back. So when I leave you this

448

time, it will be because I am bringing your *inish* back again. Ronden and the younglings are well, and the sisters care for you as if you were their own child. If anything were to happen to you while in their care, I think they would die of heartbreak, so please stay well."

I pause to wipe away tears and steady my voice.

"If anything happened to you, it would break my heart, too. I cannot imagine life without you. I love you so very much. I must do for you what you did for me when we first met in the wastelands. It is my turn to give life back to you, so we can spend the rest of our lives together. You cannot d . . ."

I trail off, unable to say the word.

"Harrow, I am afraid of what might happen to me, but I am more afraid of failing you. We have gone through so much to be together that I cannot . . . cannot . . ."

I break down then, crying, feeling a wave of such desolation sweep through me that I almost run from the room in response. But I force myself to stay, holding his hand and squeezing it gently, memories of him sweeping through me in harsh reminder of what I have lost. But I refuse to accept it. I will get Harrow back. I swear it on everything I hold sacred.

I stay awhile longer. I don't know what else to say (I would probably just repeat myself) before I finally get to my feet, kiss him on both cheeks, and say goodbye. On returning to the living area, I find the sisters have prepared tea. They invite me to stay for a bit more, and I cannot find any reason to refuse. Black currant, for strength of body and steadiness of mind, Benith announces as she pours. I receive my cup gratefully and sip the steaming liquid as I fight to keep my composure. It is not easy. Harrow looks . . . so drained, so empty, so bereft of everything that once defined him.

The sisters ask what has transpired, and I give them a brief account of my journey — again, leaving out Antrim's final offer. Then, "What can I do to help him?" I beg.

"What you've been told, of course," Dreena snaps. "Restore his *inish*. Make him whole again."

"I know that!" I snap back. "But I cannot even think how to do it. I must take the Barghast alive so that I can make him restore what he stole. But if I cannot get close enough to do that . . ."

"Auris, stop it!" There is real anger in Dreena's eyes. "You can do whatever you set your mind to. That is who you are and always have been — a young woman that

450

no one and nothing can stop. It is your entire history, young lady. Do not sully it with talk of failure!"

Benith holds up both hands in a placating gesture. "Now, now, sister, no more harsh words. Auris knows what she needs to do and what that requires of her. What she asks is if we have any help to give her."

I am on the verge of tears again and furious about it, but I manage a small nod. "Any thoughts, ideas, or insights?"

Maven, silent until now, clears her throat. "The answer lies somewhere within your heritage as a member of the Fae nation. That heritage is strong enough that it has transformed you entirely from Human to Fae. You are now a Forest Sylvan, and your *inish* is one of the most powerful I have ever seen."

"This creature — this Barghast, as you say he is — possesses one solitary, terrible ability to cause harm," Benith says. "Yet you possess dozens of abilities to do good. The balance is in your favor. You just have to decide how best to invoke the power you possess to fulfill the need you have."

"Think over all we have told you about yourself and your history," Maven adds, her ancient face wrinkling with unexpected warmth. "But do as Dreena advises and be

451

strong. Without strength of mind and body, you set yourself up for failure. So go into this with no doubts, no hesitation, and no thoughts that do not end with your success. It is easy for me to say this, but it is possible for you to embrace it as well."

"You are your mother's child," Dreena says suddenly. "You are Ancrow's daughter — and you are not only the best of her, you are her better. I know this sounds odd, but think of all you have accomplished in the two years you have been here. You and Ronden saved Harrow. You and your mother saved this whole city. This time, you have a sister, a friend, and apparently a Dragon willing to carry you. How can you possibly fail?"

Easily enough, I think — sister, friend, and Dragon notwithstanding.

Then I remember I have Malik, too. Malik, with an uncertain future ahead of him, will nevertheless stand with me against the Barghast in exchange for a chance at freedom. Four allies to accompany me in my quest, and I seem able to do nothing but dwell on the ways I could fail.

I get to my feet and set my teacup aside. "You are right — all of you. I should not be wallowing in self-pity and thoughts of failure. I should be thinking through possibilities and deciding which of these I can best put to use. Please forgive me for asking you to solve my problem for me. That you care for Harrow is more than enough. Keep him safe and well, and I will do my part."

I go out the door in a rush, the sounds of the sisters wishing me well trailing behind me as I go.

The following day is a more pleasant one in several ways. First and most important, I wake with confidence that my *inish* will soon fully return. It is already growing steadily, though still not at full strength. I wonder if I should exercise it, test its limits, but I am also afraid of trying anything too soon and draining myself again. I think it sufficient for the moment that I know it is there and that it again seems a force to be reckoned with.

As well, I wake fully aware that in two days I will travel to the lair of the Aerklings and confront Tonklot for possession of Harrow's soul. So today and tomorrow are perhaps my last opportunities to consider what lies ahead. I am not overwhelmed, surprisingly. I am feeling strong enough to carry on, even without knowing just how I am going to do it.

I leave my cottage shortly after dawn and

walk through the city, as much to feel my home beneath my feet as to clear my head. I walk for perhaps an hour, taking in all the familiar sights and sounds, exchanging greetings with other Fae, and breathing in the scents of food and drink. I am cheerful and confident, though I don't know why. I should be worried and nervous and wholly terrified of what lies ahead, but somehow I keep it bottled deep inside.

Eventually, having walked all the way to the western edge of the city, I turn back again, intent on returning to my cottage. But then I change directions and move toward the Gardens of Life and Promise Falls. The day is sunny and bright, and the warmth makes me drowsy — exactly the sort of distraction I don't need. Fighting off an encroaching lethargy, I walk down to the lake and its falls, searching for a place to sit. I find a bench far to one end and two tiers up. The view is partially obscured, but that is what I need. I don't want to be recognized or approached while I think through what lies ahead.

I stay where I am for entirely too long, pondering everything that lies ahead and reasoning through the ways I can make events unfold in my favor. I arrive at few useful conclusions, but I do consider every possibility. The first two hours pass quickly, but the next begins to drag. The day and my surroundings are pleasant enough, but my progress in concocting a working plan remains nonexistent. I seem to be going over the same ground endlessly, and always arriving at the same dead ends. I still have no good solution for overcoming Tonklot; not one fresh, original, or even marginally clever idea. I weigh the chances of each possible solution to my problem carefully, but the odds never seem quite in my favor.

Lunchtime passes, but I eat nothing. I have no interest in food.

I go then to see Harrow and stay with him for several hours — mostly just sitting there, but sometimes offering encouraging words when it feels like the silence has gone on too long.

After, I go down to question the Sylvan sisters about Malik. To my surprise, he has come to them. To my disappointment, he has departed without accepting any of their advice.

"He is deeply wounded, Auris," Benith says, her voice quiet and steady. "He has no interest in the cures that might help him. He has no desire to be further invaded, even though it might help him. He wants peace and quiet and solace. For that, he chooses not help but separateness and whatever the medicines he takes can provide him. He is at the end of a short rope, and his patience for all things possible is pretty much gone. You have to accept his decision."

I do accept it. But only for now. I will not give up. When this is over and done with and Tonklot is no more, I will pursue his healing beyond what Winton's medicines can provide.

So the day passes, and I am still no closer to a solution for how to save Harrow — though it quickly becomes clear that it may well involve sacrificing my own life for his. I cannot allow the Barghast to mesmerize me a second time; I cannot allow him to gain control over me. But by the same token, I cannot let him keep Harrow's *inish,* either.

And what of Malik? Worn, stripped of his medicines, on the very edge of madness through pain — can he really help?

I am unsure. It might be true that his armor protects him from the Barghast, but he has clearly never tested it. He wants to help; he wants to save Harrow because, in doing so, he might be saving both himself and me. But does this cloud his thinking?

Which begs the question: How ready am I to risk watching him fail?

The answer is disturbing, because I am

456

more ready than I should be.

The second day unfolds much like the first, with my *inish* growing stronger within me. I visit Harrow, speak with Seers, and spend hours contemplating my options. In the late afternoon, I climb to the tree lanes and walk on until my cottage comes into view. I find Ronden sitting on the bench outside, watching my approach. Her face is concerned as she pats the bench beside her. "Sit."

I do, wondering what's up. "How are you doing, Auris?" she asks.

"If you are wondering if I made any progress on figuring out how to save Harrow, the answer is no."

"Well, Ramey and Char have offered to take you to dinner and help you work out a solution. Riva will remain behind with me at the house."

"Ramey and Char?" I repeat doubtfully.

"I know they seem unlikely problem solvers — and perhaps the offer was more to make you feel better than to actually solve anything — but I cannot count how many times those two have actually aided both Harrow and me with other problems. None so serious as yours, but sometimes inspiration comes from unexpected quarters."

I can't deny this. Besides, dinner with my

457

young sisters *will* help take my mind off my own worries if I give it half a chance.

So after a quick shower and a change of clothes, off I go to meet up with the redoubtable Char and the unflappable Ramey. They come to the door before I even get a chance to knock, walk out to greet me, then link arms with me and lead me away. Char chatters on while Ramey walks in silence as we journey down the length of the second-level tree lane to the restaurant they have chosen. To my surprise, it is one with which I am intimately acquainted. It is here that I dined with Ancrow on the fateful night she revealed our true relationship and the discovery of my past began.

Even more surprising, our server leads us to the very same table at which Ancrow and I sat that night. I tell this in mild surprise to my companions.

"Oh, we know," Ramey says with calm acknowledgment. "We made a point of finding out."

"Mother would never have told us," Char adds.

"But servers will tell you anything for a few credits," Ramey adds.

I remind myself never to underestimate these two.

We sit and visit for a bit, enjoying glasses

of sweet fruit drinks (them) and ice ale (me). We chatter about mundane matters, and I find myself drawn into discussions about what the girls have been doing while I have been stuck in the Human world. They have visited Harrow every day while still carrying out housecleaning and schooling duties as assigned by Ronden. Frequently, they have gone hiking in the surrounding woods. Char is learning to become a tracker and Ramey has begun to recognize and put names to trees and plants.

The biggest shock comes when Char announces rather blithely that Ramey has a boyfriend. She calls him a "special boy," but her meaning is clear enough.

"I think they've kissed, too," she adds with a sly look.

I glance at Ramey, who shrugs. "Maybe," she says.

The feeling that spears through me is one of joy and sorrow combined. Joy for Ramey, and a fervent hope that she will find a love like I share with Harrow; and a sharp sorrow as I realize once again how much I stand to lose should I fail. Wouldn't Ramey be better off never falling in love if it meant she never experienced this level of pain?

But I tamp these feelings down as drinks are consumed, salads are served, and dinner is produced with some small amount of fanfare. We are eating vegetarian this night — a luscious onion tart accompanied by stewed mushrooms and a fresh salad. I realize I have eaten nothing since breakfast, and despite my fears and anxieties, I find I am starving. Conversation dies out as we clean our plates and move on to tea and sweets.

During the entirety of our meal, not a single world has been spoken about finding help for Harrow, but that changes now.

"What will you do after you leave tomorrow?" Ramey asks me.

I explain as best I can. I will go with Ronden, Riva, and Malik to meet Antrim, and from there we will fly to the Aerkling Winglish and confront the Barghast. Somehow, the four of us will evade the Barghast's minions, subdue Tonklot, and transport him back here to restore Harrow's *inish.*

They wait for me to finish, then give each other a knowing look. "So you have a plan," Ramey says slowly, "but not a very good one."

"A plan," Char adds, "that seems to lack any real details."

Can't put anything past these two. "I'm afraid so."

"What you need to figure out," Ramey continues, "is how exactly you can get close enough to Tonklot to overpower him without being mesmerized, as we all were when Harrow's *inish* was stolen. Am I right?"

I nod.

"Can't you use your own *inish* to knock him down and then jump on him?" Char asks, completely serious. "Your *inish* is stronger than his, isn't it? All you need to do is find a way to keep him from getting close enough to hypnotize you like he did before."

I wonder if she might be right. What is to stop me from doing exactly this?

Just about everything, I think.

"He can't do much if he is unconscious," she adds, trying to be helpful. "Make him that way."

"What about Malik?" Ramey asks.

I explain what he told me, but she shakes her head reprovingly. "He can't know if his armor will protect him against something like a Barghast. We don't even know what can protect you. Have you thought about it carefully, Auris?"

I think I have thought about it every which way, but I can't be sure I have examined every last possibility, for there may be some I can simply not envision. But thus far, if I am honest with myself, either there isn't any sure way or I am missing something.

We talk about it for a long time, working through all the possibilities and scenarios we can conjure. But at the end, I still don't have an answer.

"I still think the solution lies in using your *inish* in a way you haven't considered," Ramey eventually declares.

"What if you use it to shut down your hearing and your sight so the Barghast can't affect you?" Char asks suddenly.

"Then I would be deaf and blind," I point out.

"Maybe you could just rush him before he could get away from you," she suggests.

I don't bother answering this; I just shake my head. Attacking such a creature with handicaps like these would be reckless.

"Didn't one of the Seers tell you that you were a Changeling?" Ramey asks suddenly. "Maybe that is something you can use."

But my Changeling side — if it even exists — has never surfaced. I have tried time and again to see if I could switch identities or forms, and have failed to be able to do so. But then I again recall Drifter's words, that maybe my own variety of this magic is something other than I suspect. Still . . .

"How are we even sure I have Changeling powers?" I ask.

"Because the Seers said you did, and the

Seers are never wrong," Ramey declares.

"The Seers said I might have them, not that I did," I correct her, but she seems stubbornly adamant.

"No, the powers are there. It's just that you either haven't figured out how to use them or you haven't understood what they are."

"And maybe you need to find a way to use those abilities — whatever they are — differently," Char jumps in. "Maybe you just haven't looked at it in the right way."

"Suggestions are welcome," I reply with a smile.

Neither of my sisters seems to have any. But even when we move on to other possibilities for overcoming the Barghast, the thought lingers. Benith said I might be a Changeling, and she must have had some reason for thinking that. Yet if nothing has revealed itself by now, does that mean she was wrong? And if not — if Ramey is correct — how would being a Changeling help me in this situation?

We eventually talk ourselves out and decide it is time to go home and to bed. The girls are quick to assure me that they know I will find a solution to my problem even if we haven't done so tonight and reassure me that they believe in me. This makes me want to cry, and I suddenly love them even more than I already do — which I hadn't thought possible.

Riva is already asleep when I return to the cottage, and I creep into my bedroom and slip into bed. Lying in the dark, I consider everything that we said during the evening, weighing the options, measuring the chances, giving careful consideration to what I might do on the morrow.

But I keep coming back to the word *Changeling.* Something about it keeps nudging at me.

Finally, my eyes grow heavy and my thoughts sluggish, and I fall asleep, still hoping I might stumble over a possibility I haven't yet considered.

It is deep in the night when the banging comes at the front door, loud and insistent. It is impossible to ignore, and as I am already half awake with lingering thoughts of what the new day holds, I am on my feet immediately, charging to the front room to answer.

Ronden stands before me in the middle of a rain squall, her face a mix of rage and frustration.

"The Seers were attacked about an hour ago in their home by Aerklings under the command of Tonklot. The Aerklings distracted them long enough for the Barghast to snatch up Harrow and steal him away. It couldn't be helped; it was all too quick and unexpected. After all, who tries to steal anything from the sisters? Those Aerklings who tried it tonight are probably wondering what they were thinking. Anyway, the Barghast has Harrow now. He left you this."

I take the note from her shaking clenched hand. It reads: *I know you have the Dragon, and I am done with waiting. Bring him to me tomorrow, or Harrow dies.*

And I feel my world drop away into the darkness.

TWENTY-EIGHT

I do not sleep for the rest of the night, listening to the blanketing silence of the city and feeling the chill in the air. I have no way to get word to Antrim, so I can only wait until dawn, when we are to meet, thankful beyond words that today was the day we had already planned to reunite. Had I asked for four days for my *inish* to recover instead of three . . .

I shudder, and then feel a surge of anger.

If Tonklot had only waited one more day, he would have had what he wanted without risking Harrow in his diminished condition. Now the stakes feel so much higher. Harrow is back in his possession, but who knows what seizing him like this has done to weaken him further. And knowing that he so easily outwitted three of the most farsighted, powerful women I will likely ever know is not reassuring.

Of course, once I heard what had hap-

466

pened, I set out immediately for the sisters'
home, with Ronden, Riva, Ramey, and Char
beside me. And it is almost odd how disturbing I find Harrow's absence when I get
there. He had barely been a presence at all
when I visited earlier, but seeing the bed
without him in it feels like a violation. And
the Seers . . . They are full of apologies, and
their failure to protect Harrow adequately is
a blight that shows in their expressions and
makes me feel even worse.

Back in my cottage, I wait until I see hints
of light to the east, then rise. There is no
more time for preparation, no more time
for anything but getting out to meet with
Antrim. I dress, then buckle on my weapons
belt, sheath my various razor-sharp knives
and throwing stars, pick up my *inish* staff,
and exit the bedroom.

Riva is already sitting at my small dining
table with fruit, bread, and cheese laid out.
She has scrambled some eggs, and boiled
water for black currant tea. Her smile on
seeing me is a wonder.

"There you are, looking every bit as ready
and able as I wish I were." She laughs.
"Ready to cut some flesh and drink some
blood?"

I nod. "Though I hope it will not come to
that."

"As do I. Do you think the Barghast will have harmed Harrow?"

I shake my head. "Not yet; not if he wants Antrim. This is just his way of making certain we come to him. But I intend to give him something else to think about."

"You have a plan?" she asks, not quite able to keep the disbelief from her voice.

I shrug. "A suggestion of one."

I do not dissemble. As Ronden had surmised, last night's conversation provided me with fresh fodder for thinking. I fell asleep with the germ of something in mind, and I refined it somewhat in the dark, sleepless hours of the morning, but it all depends on a magic I am still not even sure I possess.

We are mostly quiet as we consume the remainder of our breakfast. I think about Ronden and hope that perhaps she has slept in and will not appear. I feel guilty for thinking this but justify it by telling myself I don't want her risking her life.

A foolish, doomed hope. As soon as Riva and I finish eating and emerge from my cottage, I find my sister sitting on the bench outside the door, packed, armed, and dressed to travel.

"Good morning," Ronden says rising. "A fine day for Dragon riding." A meaningful pause. "You weren't planning to leave without me, were you?"

"Never crossed my mind," I deadpan.

"Do you think Antrim will accept me?" she asks.

Riva grunts, shrugs, then mutters, "Apparently he won't have much say in the matter." Then, astonishingly, she hugs Ronden tight and claps her soundly on the back. "Glad you chose to join us. It never did feel right leaving you behind the last time." She holds my sister out from her, arms stretched as she gives her a look. "I thought you would be here, even if Auris tried to tell you no. She didn't, did she?"

A scant minute later Malik joins us, looking as calm and collected as a giant armored monster can. "I've taken my next dose," he announces. "Are we ready to fly?"

"You spoke with the sisters?"

A long silence. "I listened to them, and I will consider their offer. But not just now."

Not what I wanted to hear, but certainly what I expected. I have to be grateful he did this much.

I give him a warm smile. "I know better than to spit into the wind when I can be certain it will come back to slap me in the face," I say. "So let's go cause some trouble!"

"Pfft!" Riva makes her familiar dismissive sound, drawing it out a bit. "You better at least cause a little, or we are all in trouble."

She leads the way along the length of the deserted tree lane to the stairs leading down, our footsteps silent and our breath clouding in the chill morning air. The day promises to be fair and the skies clear; the stars are still bright to the west, but I pay scant attention. I am already thinking ahead to what awaits us at the Aerkling Winglish. There are few Fae out at this hour, and those we do see we pass in committed silence — as if this is how dawn meetings should be conducted. Around us, birds sing out in mournful calls that echo through the silence. A great leather-winged creature flies past on its way to its nest, its night hunting a success judging from the dead creature that hangs from its beak.

I try not to think of it as an unfavorable omen and fail. In truth, nothing feels quite right.

But my resolve is buttressed by the strength of my commitment to Harrow and my companions. This is to be a trial by fire, so I am required to walk through the flames and not turn aside. I cannot let the memory of what Tonklot did to me in our first encounter weaken my resolve. I cannot let

470

fear or doubt erode my courage. I am Ancrow's daughter, and that alone should give me the courage I need.

We descend to the avenues below, and still the city sleeps. A few early-morning workers walk the darkness — street cleaners, garbage collectors, shop owners, and one or two passersby whose purposes and destinations are unknown. As before, no one gives us any kind of greeting, though Malik attracts a good bit of attention. Lights appear in shop windows and on porch fronts as we pass, and down the road a hauler pulled by bulls with great curling horns rumbles into view.

We pass out of the city heading east, watching the buildings and the tree lanes and the lights and all evidence of Fae existence disappear behind us.

As we walk, Riva starts to whistle. She is actually rather good at it, and the tune is unexpectedly cheerful. If it wasn't for the crossbow and shafts and huge broadsword she wears strapped across her back — not to mention the knives hanging at her waist and stuffed into her belt and boots, and daggers hidden up her sleeves — one might almost think she is off for a day of fun and relaxation.

I wish I could feel that calm. But then I

wasn't a Dragon rider in the Ghoul Wars, and I haven't been embedded in the Sylvan life long enough to reach a place of such equanimity. In spite of all I have been through in the past two years, I am still striving to feel like I belong.

I consider my ongoing evolution from Human to Fae. Knowing I am changing helps me feel more as one with the Fae culture, and I have been reassured repeatedly by my new family and friends that I indeed belong, but I still have my doubts. I am almost there, I tell myself — almost all Fae and no longer some sort of halfling. My skin is a uniform pine color now, from head to foot. The silky fringes that grow along the undersides of my arms and the backs of my legs are a deep emerald. My once dark hair has become thicker and greener, and sports tiny leaves woven all through it. Only the rough shape of my features remains the same.

I have embraced my Sylvan heritage, and I want my appearance to reflect this.

When we reach our appointed destination, Antrim is waiting, seated on his haunches. "Ready to fly, are we?" he growls.

"Do any of you know where this creature can be found?" Ronden demands, looking from one of us to another.

"I know," Malik declares. "Or at least, I

know where they were."

"That will have to do," I say, determined not to hesitate longer.

Antrim lowers his wing and we scramble aboard, Riva sitting farthest up to act as pilot, with me directly behind, then Ronden, and Malik occupying the rear. I explain to my sister and Malik how the heavy, flexible Dragon scales will help hold them in place and how to gain a solid grip on them when they are uplifted. We are quickly settled and swiftly rise into the early-morning sky.

It doesn't take long for the sunrise to surface, and its light is blinding. As the sun brightens, it reveals a cloudless expanse of sky that stretches from horizon to horizon and promises an absolutely beautiful day. I wish I could feel better about it, but the persistent awareness that it could be my last drains away any peace it might bring me.

We soar toward the Skyscrape Mountains at a steady pace, on winds that are calm but buoyant, the air warming quickly as the sun climbs. The earlier chill vanishes, and the freedom of being high above everything almost makes me smile. We experience very little wind and no heavy cloud cover. The flight is smooth and untroubled, and I start to feel better in spite of myself.

But soon enough my thoughts turn to what will happen when we reach the Winglish. I know what I want to happen, if not exactly how to make it come about. I want Antrim to stay safely away from the Winglish and the Aerklings while the rest of us confront the Barghast. If we are successful, Antrim can return to fly us out. If not, he will leave us to our fate. Of course, I have no guarantee that he will do anything that I have asked of him, but I have done what I could to protect him, and now I have to worry about the rest of us.

I think I am ready. I have reason to believe I will be able to do what is needed, but hopes are frail tools and plans seldom go as intended. I have to be prepared to change mine on the fly, even without knowing how I would do so. I must remember not to panic and not to lose control of my emotions.

Though this is Harrow I go to save, and it is hard to divorce myself from my panic over how high the stakes are.

We fly for two hours, then Antrim sets down beside a forested lake to drink and rest. The three of us climb down his wing to stretch our cramped muscles, then drink from a nearby stream where the water runs fresh and take food from our packs to snack on. Neither Ronden nor I is very hungry, but Riva eats as if she hasn't been fed in weeks. I watch her, amazed that she can manage to devour so much, given what's coming.

She sees me looking at her. "What?"

"You eat like a starving wolf. I can barely keep anything down."

She laughs. "Fighting a war teaches you to eat when you can and not worry about what might happen later."

"I could use a little of that mindset just now."

Ronden stirs uneasily, her attention shifting to me. "Don't you think you should tell us a little about what to expect once we are face-to-face with this creature? What is it you intend to do, exactly?"

"We won't catch him by surprise," Riva adds. "You realize that, don't you? He knows you must come today if you want to save Harrow, and his Aerkling followers will be patrolling the skies surrounding his lair. They will see us miles off."

I nod. "I want them to see us coming. I particularly want Tonklot to see Antrim. I am supposed to be bringing him a Dragon; it will help convince him of my good intentions, if he thinks I am doing as ordered."

"Fair enough. But what about the rest of

us?" Ronden presses.

"You have to keep the Aerklings at bay while I overpower the Barghast."

"Which you know you can do?"

"Which I *hope* I can do."

"That doesn't sound very reassuring. Can't you tell us more?"

I shake my head. "It's still too unformed. But . . ."

"*Pfft.* You're not sure what you're going to do, are you?" Riva challenges.

"I'll figure it out."

"What about Malik's offer to help?" Ronden asks. "All that size and strength and armor ought to count for something."

It should. But Malik is dying, and I've already decided that this puts the effectiveness of his help in serious doubt. Besides, I can't afford to depend on anyone else — even my two stalwart companions. The Barghast is my problem. If my friends can give me the support I have asked for, then I will have my chance.

"I don't think you're ready," Riva declares. "You certainly don't sound ready."

I don't care what I sound like. I climb to my feet. "I feel ready enough. Let's go find out."

Our flight resumes, the sun climbing toward noon. We can see the Skyscrape

476

Mountains by now, and I feel the first twinges of fear in my belly. I am not panicked, I tell myself. I am just feeling the uncertainty anyone in my situation would feel. I must remember to stay calm and steady. I must not lose faith in myself. It doesn't matter what Ronden thinks about my readiness, or Riva, or even Malik. They simply need to concentrate on their own objectives and leave me to mine. If Harrow were here with us now, he would agree.

Harrow . . . I allow my anger to surface anew, furious all over again on thinking about what has been done to him. I will see him healed, and I will make the Barghast regret doing something so wretched and unforgivable. Tonklot believes me defeated already, so unable to stand against him that I will submit to his every demand. Well, let him think what he will. I have his measure, and I will destroy him.

We near our destination, and for the first time I see the winged shapes circling ahead. These are Aerkling sentries, and we have been spotted. For just a moment, I wonder if there is any chance they will challenge us — but that would run counter to what the Barghast commanded. What matters is the Dragon. At all costs, the Dragon. They will leave us alone so that we can bring Tonklot his prize.

Once again, I wonder what the Barghast plans to do with Antrim once he has him. How does he plan to subdue such a formidable creature? Does he even begin to understand how impossible it will be for him to make use of a Dragon that is not prepared to submit willingly? Tonklot is talented and his power to mesmerize is formidable, but Dragons are a force unto themselves, so how does he think he can control something that primal? I imagine that the fact that Dragons have powers of speech and reasoning makes them vulnerable, but a creature that can rip you apart in an unguarded instant does not seem a good candidate for mind control.

And yet yesterday I might have said the same of the Seers, and look how easily he managed to confound them.

Still, I can't help thinking there is something more to all this — something I have either missed or don't know about. But what can it be?

Be careful, Auris. Don't let yourself be fooled.

We swoop through skies suddenly abandoned by the patrolling Aerklings to come within sight of the Winglish and its inhabitants. Riva leans forward and speaks with

Antrim, and the Dragon wheels left to a ledge no more than a hundred yards away from the stone bridge on which a crowd of Aerklings have gathered to watch our arrival. As we descend, I search for Tonklot, but I do not see him. I look for young Orphren and do not see her, either. Has something happened to her? I tighten my resolve to set things right.

We land smoothly, Antrim setting down with barely a bump, occupying most of the ledge with his bulk. One wing extends and my companions and I slide down, taking a closer look at the cluster of Aerklings looking back. Women and children, mostly. A narrow trail connects us, with sheer cliffs above and below its length. We will be very vulnerable crossing it, but we have no choice. I wonder suddenly at the wisdom of what we are doing.

"When Tonklot comes to meet me, I want you to fly somewhere safe," I say to Antrim. "I promise to call you if we are overmatched. I'm not foolish or vain enough to think I must do this alone, no matter the cost, but I am afraid for you. I worry the Barghast knows something I do not. Please."

Antrim dips his head slightly. "Say what you will, it remains my choice to make. I will wait for Tonklot to appear and then decide if I should depart. We are not the same, Auris. We must respond to this creature in the way each of us feels we should. Go where you will. Do what you must. I hope your courage and your magic will sustain you. I will do the same and hope the same for myself. But remember that I must act when I see what is needed."

I glance at Riva and Ronden and walk out onto the ledge. I look for Malik, but he has already slipped off on his own. There is no reason for me to wait now. I start forward along the ledge, with Ronden and Riva following.

This high up, the air is cold and the winds gust. We follow our narrow path with cautious steps and slow our pace as the shelter of the cliffs diminishes and the wind picks up. It takes longer than I thought it would to make our passage. I keep my eyes fixed on the crowd of Aerklings gathered ahead, searching for Tonklot and any signs of treachery. I do not expect anything of that sort this early; why would I have been brought here if it were only for the purpose of killing me outright? It might be the Barghast's intention to kill me later, but not until he has what he wants. He will let us cross first and then reveal what he has been planning.

Thoughts of Harrow surface, and I force them away. No distractions. No intrusions. I must stay focused, alert for Tonklot's manipulations.

We are almost across — almost to the Winglish and its people — when the crowd of mostly old men, women, and children begins to back away toward the shelter of the cliffs. As they do so, Aerkling warriors crowd forward to take their places, forming a solid line to greet us.

There is still no sign of Tonklot. I make a quick search of those gathered and do not find him anywhere. I do, however, catch sight of Orphren's young face in the watching crowd. Without thinking, I give her a quick smile. She smiles back, but she looks terrified. I hesitate, trying to decide what to do about my situation. Then I call out, "Bring me the one called Harrow! Bring him to me now!"

It is a vain and desperate demand, but I need to know if he is even still alive.

But none among those gathered moves to respond. All stand quietly in place, just looking at me.

Then those Aerkling soldiers gathered on the ledge part at their centermost point, and Tonklot appears, his strange eyes fixing on me. I instantly shift my gaze so that I am

481

looking slightly away from him. He does not speak as we step from the pathway onto the ledge, my companions to either side of me, their hands already on their weapons.

"Time's up, Tonklot. I've brought you your Dragon."

The familiar syrupy voice responds. "You brought it, and yet now you leave it safely tucked away on a distant ledge."

"Just long enough to make certain you intend to keep your word." *As if,* I think.

"Caution is always well advised. You must understand why I took the liberty of collecting your partner as well. I had to make certain you would come."

"And in doing so, you risked his life yet again. Bring him out so that I know he is well."

A shrug. "It seems that neither cares to put much trust in the other. You refuse to move your Dragon, so why should I give you time with Harrow? Call over your Dragon, so we can put an end to this business. I will bring you your partner once I get a closer look at my Dragon."

I shake my head. "As you said, neither of us trusts the other. So I must ask that you not only produce but also heal my partner before the Dragon crosses to us. Prove the worth of your bargain, Tonklot."

"And you will not concede we do both at the same time?"

"No."

"Then we have a problem, don't we?"

I realize suddenly what I have done. I have placed myself in an impossible situation where neither the Barghast nor I can force the other to do anything. How does this end when we are locked into such a stalemate?

"You can't force me to give you the Dragon," I insist.

"Perhaps not," he replies with a shrug. "But I am not the one whose time is running out. How many days does Harrow have left before his life drains away? We are still two days from the full moon, but I set that deadline for a reason, for after that there is nothing even I can do to save him; there is only so long a body can live without its soul. So will you just let him die, Auris? Because until I receive the Dragon, Harrow's essence stays with me. Are you that determined to keep me from what I will have soon enough anyway?"

I say nothing, but then I feel Riva shift beside me.

"Auris," she says, "look behind me. I hope you have a plan for *this*."

I turn and find the bridge we just crossed now filled with Aerkling warriors. We are surrounded with nowhere to turn.

Tonklot sighs. "I thought you were smarter than this, but now I know you are nothing more than a foolish little girl. You will call your Dragon over voluntarily, or I will force you to do so. Look at me. You will see that I am trying to make this easy for you."

But I keep my eyes firmly averted while I consider what to do next. Any sort of battle with the numbers arrayed against us can only end in disaster. So what to do?

I stall for time. "Why would you want a Dragon? What do you plan to do with it?"

He does not answer right away, and then he laughs. "I don't want just *one* Dragon. I want them *all.*"

I stare at him in shock. "All?"

"Once I have this one Dragon — their Vinst — I can have every Dragon under my control; you will see."

"But why? To do what?"

"Anything he wants," Ronden declares, the anger in her voice unmistakable.

"Exactly! Dragons are a force of nature — a weapon nothing can withstand when properly directed." The Barghast makes an expansive gesture. "With an army of Dragons at my command, anything is possible!"

There is a long pause as my companions and I let that sink in. It is such a wild, impossible claim. "You're talking nonsense. Dragons can't be made to fight for you like soldiers, and there is no way you can mesmerize them all. How can you even communicate with them if you don't speak their language?"

His beaked face twists. "And who are you to say I can't? As for mesmerizing that many Dragons, I won't have to. I have my ways to make them obey me."

"This is ridiculous!" I blurt out, my confidence slipping and my patience exhausted. "And even if you could, what will you do? Attack all of Viridian Deep? Conquer the entire country? Is that your plan?"

The soft voice drops to a whisper. "Why stop there? Other lands — much bigger lands — await."

Here is an entirely new level of madness. I recognize his intentions immediately and realize how insane this creature is. He doesn't want to control just the Fae of Viridian Deep; he wants to control the inhabitants of the Human world, too.

"You can't take over the Human world with a pack of Dragons," I spit. "It won't work!"

"Ah, but I think it will. Call your Dragon over and let's ask him. Go on. Call him back. Now."

I take a moment to assess my options and realize I am in a hopeless situation. I can't let Tonklot get near Antrim, and yet I can't keep them apart, either.

I am suddenly filled with desperation. I underestimated him and misjudged everything. I need to stall. "How did you know I could bring you a Dragon?" I demand.

"Such a blind, foolish little Fae child. You've never known anything! You haven't even suspected. I know *everything* about you."

The enthusiasm in his voice suggests he believes this, and likely has reason to do so.

"You say we have met before," I tell him, "but I have no memory of that moment."

The Barghast actually laughs — a hideous rattle of throat and heaving of shoulders. "Of course you don't, because *I* possess that memory — along with countless others that once belonged to you."

I feel myself go cold. Harsh realization floods me with panic. Tonklot and I have met before. Somewhere, sometime. We met, and he used his powers and he stole my memories. I always knew they were missing for a reason, and now it is confirmed. My memories were stolen. By Tonklot.

His voice turns strident and cold with disdain. "I first met you when you were hiding from the Ministry — a child of rebels and under the care and protection of the man they call Drifter. And you may have guessed by now that I encountered this Human in the very distant past. I stole his Fae partner and fed on her. He came looking to retrieve her *inish*, but he was too late. So he attacked me and made me what I am — broken, crippled. And he destroyed my home. So when I found that he was hiding you from the Ministry, I saw a chance to repay him by taking away something that mattered to him. I waited until he went out, and then I convinced you to let me in — both to Drifter's house and to your mind."

The feeling of familiarity I experienced at the fishing hole when he was attempting to subvert my mind and strip me of my thoughts — that odd certainty that I had experienced this somewhere before — comes back to me now. Along with the memory that I was somehow protected from his efforts, that he could not reach into me as far and as deep as he wished.

I could defy him!

And somehow, I did.

I dare not look at Riva or Ronden or anyone else. I dare not allow myself to be distracted. I must stay composed. I must not give way now or I am lost.

"So you stole every memory I had, everything from my past."

"Everything I could. You had powers even then that prevented me from taking it all. Your Fae side surfaced and your *inish* came to your protection. What a shock that was! But just discovering what you could do was enough. You were hiding a delightful little secret, one that I was determined to have. You didn't realize how valuable you were — so much more so than you realized. The power you hold is unique. And I wanted it."

"But you could not take it, could you?" I fire back. "You could not purge me of my *inish* then, and you cannot do so now."

"I was able to do enough." The Barghast brushes my attack aside. "I was able to steal your memories, just as I stole Harrow's. And I was able to discover your hidden abilities — things even you did not know about yourself. Things you still do not know. Your Changeling powers. Your ability to solve any problem presented to you."

So he, too, thinks I am a Changeling — and supposedly one who can solve any problem. So why can't I solve the problem of him?

"Yes, you resisted me, and I could not penetrate your *inish* to do more. But I knew I could break you down eventually, if I kept you. So I found a deserted house, locked you up. Kept trying to break you. And I would have done so. But somehow you slipped away from me while I slept, and I lost you for a time. You remember none of this, do you?"

His laughter is a squawk. "As I realized two weeks ago, when I dipped back into your mind, it seems that you managed to break your chains and pick the lock on the room I had you imprisoned in while I slept, then stumbled into the hands of Goblins, who put you into their prison system. They had no idea of your value and locked you away like some bit of trash, so it was not only the Ministry who lost track of you. But I never forgot you. I was always looking. Imagine my surprise when you appeared with your sister at the Winglish, looking fully Fae!"

"What is he talking about?" Riva demands.

I ignore her. All of my attention is focused on the Barghast.

"I knew you the moment I saw you, and I realized I had another chance to acquire your abilities. When I absorb someone's *inish,* I gain control over whatever powers they possess, and I wanted yours. I still do."

"Why? You already have a shapeshifting ability."

489

"Ah, but what you have is not just a shapeshifting ability. It is much more . . ." Then he stops short, and his expression suddenly goes sly. "But if you do not know this for yourself, then why should I tell you?"

My best hope, I know, is to keep him talking to distract him from all that I don't know about myself. "So why take Harrow's *inish* and offer it back to me in exchange for a Dragon?"

"If you want an answer to that question, you will agree to make the exchange I suggested. Harrow for the Dragon. Now. Do what I ask, and I will provide an answer to your question. Give me the Dragon."

"I will give you nothing!" I spit at him.

"And risk your mate's death? I think not. Call the Dragon."

But I won't. I can't. I take my staff and hold it upright before me like a shield. Ronden does the same with hers. Riva Tisk pulls the crossbow where it is strapped to her back and shifts the quiver of bolts to where she can reach them easily.

We have been given no choice. We will fight. We will likely die, but we will do so with the knowledge that we have not given the Barghast what it most desires. I try not to think about Harrow's fate. There is nothing more I can do for him.

But Tonklot is not finished with me. He holds up his hands in a commanding gesture. "Wait! All this talking is pointless. A little more persuasion is required." He takes a step back. "Let's settle this here and now. You need to change your mind, Auris. Here is someone who can help you better understand how wrongheaded you are being."

He turns to the soldiers standing at his back and makes a sharp, birdlike call. The call reverberates with surprising power against the silence of the mountains. Ronden, Riva, and I look about but see nothing. The Aerklings shift uneasily on the pathways and stone platform. The Barghast does not move at all.

Then a cluster of Aerkling soldiers shoulder their way through the crowd bearing Harrow on their shoulders like a worn rug, limp and ragged.

I have to fight not to run to him. I have to steady myself as my worst fears surface, and I see how far gone he is.

"Hold him up so she can view him!" Tonklot orders, and Harrow is lowered to his feet and held in place by Aerkling arms. His head hangs down and his body is so limp I cannot tell if he is alive or not.

Tonklot stares over at me. "Call the

Dragon or I will have these Aerklings haul him aloft and drop him from such a height that he will break apart before you."

I feel broken, defeated. I cannot let this happen, no matter what I have promised myself and others. I have to find a way to defeat this monster, but I cannot do it without bringing Antrim into the mix. I have to risk it.

"Auris!" Ronden's voice is edged with a clear warning.

I shake my head in response. *No.*

Then I call for Antrim — a deep booming howl, enhanced by my *inish.*

And Antrim leaps from his ledge.

TWENTY-NINE

Even as Antrim rushes toward us, the Barghast begins howling out such terrible sounds I clap my hands over my ears protectively. He shrieks as if gone mad, filling the air with cries that grip and twist and consume me. The cries rise, build in power, and then fall into the sweeping rush of high-mountain winds and finally empty silence.

But I don't miss the way Antrim responds to them — as if he, too, has gone completely mad, writhing and twisting and roaring.

The Dragon's massive dark form seems to engulf the entire sky — his huge wingspan and thick reptilian body absorbing all of it as he draws closer. He rises above the rock formations on which the Aerklings, my companions, and I all stand, then plummets toward the close end of the ledge on which stands the mass of Aerkling soldiers, blocking our escape and holding us fast. With a flurry of beating wings and ripping claws, he lands right in their midst on the trail-head and they have nowhere to run. His fury beyond description, he shows the Aerklings no mercy, wings sweeping most of them off the trail and into the void while his huge clawed feet grind the remainder to pieces. There is blood and savaged flesh everywhere. There are howls and shrieks of despair.

His butchery is savage. I watch it happen, horrified.

Antrim thunders in a voice I do not recognize — and I realize almost immediately that it is in response to the sounds the Barghast has made. Bodies fall and wailings rise. In seconds all of those who occupied the trail moments earlier lie dead. My hopes for exercising any control over the situation are shattered. My ability to understand why this has happened is futile. This savagery accomplishes nothing.

I must put a stop to it immediately.

"Antrim!" I scream. "Look at me!"

He ignores me. Instead he rumbles and growls, responding to an inner fury or predatory urge, and begins to ingest the remains of the fallen Aerklings.

"Antrim!" I cry out a second time, horrified.

The Dragon looks up, his huge maw

bloody and snarling. "Have I not done what was needed? Am I not come to you in time?"

I take a step toward him, risking a confrontation that I know I should not. I am challenging his power, and I see a wink of doubt reflected in his eyes.

"Do not approach me!" he growls.

But I know I must ignore him, and I do. "You and I were allies only an hour ago. We were comrades — you and me, Riva and Ronden — come here to face the Barghast and destroy it. Why do you attack the Aerklings?"

"I am protecting you!" he roars in angry response. "Do you not realize how they threaten you? Can you not hear their cries of rage? They would tear you to bits if they could reach you. I knew I should have stayed with you in the first place! You must let me do as I think best! You must let me be what I am!"

"Show respect, Fae girl!" Tonklot cries out suddenly. Somehow he has managed to make his shrieks and howls seem to come from the Aerklings rather than himself. Somehow he has made them seem much more dangerous than they are. The strength and tenor of his voice reveals it. "He answers to the demands of his blood and calls upon memories given him by his ancestors! He needs not explain himself to you — or to anyone else. He is a supreme being. He is a Dragon Lord!"

Antrim snarls, spit and rank breath flying everywhere. His words are directed now to one and all. "No one controls a Dragon Lord!"

And all too quickly I sense a shift in the balance of things. In some way, whether he realizes it or not, Antrim is responding as our enemy wishes.

"Antrim!" I shout at him once more. "Think of what you are saying. Think of how you sound! The Barghast is trying to use you, twisting your words and feelings to try to make you do things you would otherwise never do."

Tonklot approaches Antrim almost as if he seeks to be a supplicant. "Let her be, Dragon Lord. Let her find her own way. I know you are doing what you should. Do not do anything less." Turning to me. "He is afraid of nothing, girl. Show him some respect! Extend him the honor he deserves. Who are you to challenge a creature of such size and might? Who are you to question his judgment?"

It is as if he is Antrim's friend and supporter and I am something less. I am in it now, up to my neck. I shake my head firmly.

"Do not be fooled, Antrim! The Barghast is the black shadow of all that threatens Fae and Dragons alike. He is a creature of no honor and has no right to consideration. He has taken Harrow. He has allowed hundreds of Aerklings to die beneath your feet and wings. Reject him! Reject anything he has said or done to you!"

Tonklot raises his arms in a placating gesture. "Do not listen to her! Listen to your heart! I am your . . ."

Antrim's abrupt howls silence Tonklot, who stops where he is. "No more words! I can make up my own mind about what to do and what not to do."

"I honor you for your wisdom and your power!" the Barghast declares, ignoring him. "No one should ever tell a Dragon what to do. I am not an enemy. Auris mistakes me for something I am not. She sees me as liars have tried to make me seem, but no Dragon could ever be fooled by such trickery." He drops to one knee. "May I say one thing more? One thing, and then I will be silent?"

"No!" I scream. "Don't let him!"

But Antrim ignores me, and instead eyes the Barghast boldly. Their eyes meet. I want to tell the Dragon to look away. But my voice fails me, and suddenly I feel the power of Tonklot's magic close about me.

"Do not speak further, girl."

And I don't. I can't. My voice is suddenly gone.

"Speak what you will, creature," the Dragon orders.

Slowly Tonklot rises to stand before Antrim. But now, he is no more than fifteen feet away, and he no longer looks uncowed. "Pshshshsh, coseten venerren spohhhhh."

The words are in Dragon speech, but I do not recognize nor make sense of them. They fill the air with strange power, and instantly I see a change in Antrim. He looks enraptured. He looks captivated — consumed by knowledge to which I have no access. I want to do something to stop what is happening, but I have no idea how to manage it.

Tonklot advances closer to the stunned Antrim. Now when he speaks, his words are clear to me. "I knew her as a child. I was her friend and her guide once. I know of you, great Dragon child. As a pup, as a little one, as something much less than you are now. But I have not forgotten your promise, your skills and bravery, even in those early days."

I am bewildered. What is happening? What is he talking about? What is he trying to do? Or already done, I amend, given the look in

Antrim's eyes.

"Besshinettru," Tonklot whispers, and Antrim's eyes blink slowly.

The worst has happened. The one thing I wanted to prevent at all costs has come to pass. For all intents and purposes, the Dragon has been taken.

The Barghast steps forward — steps right up to where the Dragon's maw looms over him. He begins to speak, his voice so soft I can hear nothing of what he says. The great head lowers and the Barghast places one hand on the creature's huge nose. More words and hand movements follow.

It is done, I realize. Antrim is fully mesmerized.

Tonklot turns to me, black robes widening as he spreads his arms triumphantly. "The Dragon thought himself immune to my magic, but all it took was knowing the key to gaining control over him. I just had to get close enough to him to let him hear my voice. I read his memories quickly enough, and I stole from him what I needed. I made his history mine. A simple enough skill for me. I now know his weakness. His mother's voice and words captivate and bind him; they imbue him with a precious taste of a past he has never forgotten. Hearing that voice again — hearing her words spoken anew — captivates him as nothing else can. And you made it all possible. All I needed was for you to bring him close enough to let me make him mine."

He mocks me. I am enraged. I turn to Antrim once more. "Dragon Lord, listen to me!"

But Antrim doesn't hear. He is too far gone, too deeply under the Barghast's spell, too subverted and twisted by Tonklot's words and motions — by his insidious ability to mesmerize.

"We better do something about *this* right now!" Riva Tisk says over my shoulder. "Is there nothing you can do to bring him back?"

If there is, I don't know what it is.

The ranks of Aerkling soldiers are tightening further, and both Ronden and Riva draw their weapons and prepare to make a stand. But there are too many. Our chance of saving our lives is quickly slipping away.

"Look to me, Fae girl. Listen closely." Tonklot is speaking again. "You wondered how I could gain control of a Dragon. You thought me deluded. But watch what happens next. Watch closely. It is the height of my magic and the foundation of my unmatchable ability to control everything!"

His hand rests on Antrim's nose, and he

holds it in place for almost an entire minute. His minions have ceased trying to approach me, watching their leader instead, waiting to see what fresh magic he will unveil. His head is lowered as if he is deep in thought. His hand on the Dragon's maw is rubbing slowly, soothingly against his victim's skin — almost as if he seeks to rub something out. Antrim jerks once, twice, then a few times more, each response followed by a long pause. The Barghast never slows his efforts, never changes his position. Hands moving, voice whispering, he brings Antrim into a willing and subservient crouch. Then the rubbing and the whispers stop, and all of those gathered on the edges of the mountain wait to see what will happen next.

Quite suddenly, Tonklot disengages from his prey, his hand sliding free as he slowly moves several long steps away, his head lowering, his face hiding in the folds of his hooded cloak. His body seems to shiver beneath the fabric, and then suddenly . . .

He literally explodes, his body expanding and altering shape. In mere seconds Tonklot becomes . . . something else. I watch aghast as he grows to a monstrous size, his clothes ripping apart, his skin thickening and toughening as his body becomes decidedly reptilian. Power radiates from him — a swell of magic surging out as he summons and engages a new form of power. I detect it flowing from him but still cannot begin to imagine what my enemy is doing.

And then I discover the truth for myself as the Barghast transforms entirely. His physical presence alters in both size and shape, and he becomes something different.

He becomes a Dragon.

Worse, Tonklot becomes an even larger, more terrible version of Antrim, towering over the fallen Dragon Lord — a Dragon of even greater size and power, an enemy more terrifying than anything I could have imagined. Tonklot lifts his terrible, horn-encrusted head and roars in fury.

Then he opens his huge jaws and reaches down to fit them almost gently about a complacent Antrim's vulnerable neck and bites off his head.

I scream — I cannot help myself. But it is too late to help. Antrim collapses in a heap, killed instantly. Blood flows copiously, and Antrim is gone, dead almost before he realized what was happening, a victim of exactly what I had feared the most.

I am horrified almost to the point of collapse. To watch the powerful Dragon become mesmerized, enthralled, weakened to the point of docile acceptance, and then dispatched with barely a whimper leaves me feeling helpless. I was so sure I could manage to find a way to control the Barghast — especially with such powerful allies standing with me. But to watch the most powerful of my companions — a creature that it seemed no one and nothing could subdue — be destroyed so casually leaves me wondering if I have any possibility at all of surviving whatever is coming next.

I feel Ronden and Riva move up beside me, weapons in hand, but I realize how little they will be able to do to change things. I motion them back. Neither moves a step.

The Barghast Dragon is coming for me when a new voice rings out. "Stand, creature! If you would fight with someone, start with me!"

Through the Aerkling ranks strides Malik, the iron giant, all flashing metal and sleekness. I don't know where he has been or what he has been doing since we parted, but his purpose seems clear enough. He will face the Barghast himself, and he will do so without my help. I know this because, as he passes me, I try to grab his arm in an attempt to hold him back, but he brushes me aside.

"Let me be, Auris," he growls. "This monster is my enemy, too."

And he goes straight for Tonklot.

"Leave the cliffs, Barghast," he orders, "and do not ever come back. What you did to Antrim was cowardly. For you to threaten this girl as well is too much."

That Malik is incredibly brave cannot be questioned, but he is dwarfed by Antrim, and Tonklot's Dragon is of another magnitude altogether. But then I wonder what sort of weapons he hides within his armor. Still, I don't want this. I don't want another friend dying for me.

"Malik, no!" I call once more. "Let this be! Give me another chance first. This is my fight . . ."

Except I am not going to be given a chance. That ship has sailed. Tonklot roars in fury and snatches at Malik. His great jaws yawn wide and snap closed like a steel trap — and miss. Malik has already moved to one side and opened his hands to reveal weapons embedded in his arms that emit burst after burst of fiery charges into the Dragon. Tonklot staggers backward as smoke and ash rise in clouds from his damaged scales, some of which are sent soaring skyward on the mountain winds. His tail thrashes in response, and a dozen new Aerklings are swept away to fall screaming from the cliff, bodies smashed and broken.

Malik advances, but Tonklot lunges back at him with such force that he breaks through the weapons fire and bears Malik to the ground. Giant claws rip and tear, and massive feet pummel my would-be protector. Even so, Malik remains whole. Nothing breaks through the armor. The iron giant is back on his legs and counterattacking so quickly I barely see how it happens. One minute Tonklot has Malik pinned to the ground and the next his challenger has rolled beneath him and is striking from behind.

Riva and Ronden are pressed up behind me, weapons still held at the ready, but all three of us are mesmerized by the battle taking place before us. Tonklot shifts his position, swinging all the way about, and now he has Malik trapped between what remains of the Aerklings still clustered on the trail and the cliff edge.

In scant seconds, the space in which Malik can maneuver shrinks to almost nothing.

"We have to do something!" Riva screams suddenly. "He's trapped!"

And abruptly she charges into the battle, flinging Ronden and me aside. She rips out her massive sword from where it hangs from her belt, the blade flashing in the midday sun, polished and gleaming. She is so quick that she is away before Ronden and I can even think to act. She goes straight for Tonklot's massive foreleg and hacks off two massive claws and part of a footpad. The Dragon screams in fury and pain and goes for her.

Yet she stands her ground. "No more! You shall not . . . ."

A blow from the damaged leg sends her flying away into a wall of rocks, weapons torn from her hands, the great sword broken, her face a mask of pain and disbelief. When she lands against the cliff wall, she lies so still it appears as if the rock has claimed her.

I start for her, but Ronden pulls me back. "No! We stay together, Auris! Whatever happens now, happens to us both!"

With Riva out of the picture, Tonklot and Malik have resumed their battle. Malik has broken past the Dragon and is out in the open again. The Dragon is bleeding badly from his damaged foreleg and a dozen other places, but he shows no inclination to stop fighting. The two combatants shift and turn to find an opening, but both are more cautious now, more aware of the danger the other poses.

Suddenly the Barghast finds an opening, feinting twice and then coming at Malik with the quickness of a snake. Malik's weapons are not enough this time, and Tonklot bears the armored warrior to the ground. Jaws part, then the Dragon's teeth close around Malik. I can hear the sounds of metal crunching, and I can see my friend thrashing in agony.

But then he is free again, leaping up again, finding the strength from a source I cannot imagine. He dives for the Dragon's throat, blades extended. Tonklot jerks backward, avoiding the blades, his roar so immense it feels as if the rocks of the mountain are breaking apart. Malik tries for him again and again, but the Dragon makes contact first, slamming his attacker against the stone battlefield with such force that his armor splits in several places and blood spills out.

This time, he does not rise.

It is over, I think. It has to be. Malik is too badly injured; likely he is mortally wounded.

Tonklot leans slowly downward to where Malik lies, bloodied and unmoving. He intends to put an end to things, I realize, and this time he has the armored man at his mercy.

But a flash of metal whisks past me, and Riva Tisk is there once more. Her blade might be broken, but almost two feet of sharp metal edging remains affixed to the handle. With a final feint, Riva slides past the Dragon's weakened defenses and attempts to drive the whole of the blade into its exposed breast.

But Tonklot just smashes her down again, leaving her broken and silent. With an enormous show of strength, huge body shaking off whatever pain and damage it suffered, he rises and turns to face me.

"Now, foolish little girl," he snarls, "what shall I do with you?"

THIRTY

I offer no answer to the question. I only know that it is now my turn to face this monster. Save for Ronden, my allies are all down, and none of them will be rising. Riva and Malik lie motionless on the ledge, and Antrim's huge body lies beheaded at the cliff edge.

For what feels like an endless length of time, I stand there wordlessly, trying to come to terms with what has happened. It was all so quick, and at the same time seemingly eternal. What am I to do?

Impulsively, I start to approach my fallen friends. I know all too well what I am going to find, but I go anyway because the pain is too great to ignore. I should have kept them all away — Riva, Malik, and Antrim; I know this. I should have refused their help. I should never have brought them to this hellish place. If I had made the better choices, this monstrous tragedy might have been averted. Only Ronden and I remain, and what chance do my sister and I have to change things now? What must we endure to bring about the end we all so desperately sought? I should never have believed that we stood even a small chance of surviving an encounter as deadly as this one.

I must go to them now, one last time.

But once again Ronden stops me, seizing my arm and yanking me back. "No, Auris. There is no time for it. Not now. We must stand and fight!"

"It might be best if you simply accept me, as all of my other followers have done," Tonklot calls out sharply.

He begins to transform once more, diminishing in size, his Dragon body changing back to what it was when we first engaged — smaller, but equally threatening. Yet his eyes are no longer his own but the Dragon's, somehow preserved. The marks of battle are still visible through his tattered clothing, but none of them look as serious as they did when he was a Dragon. I blink in surprise. By changing shapes, he appears to have healed.

A bevy of moans and gasps issue from the Aerklings. I look again for Orphren, find her, and look away. No time for this, either.

"Do you see how much stronger I am than

you will ever be?"

Tonklot's voice is a poisonous whisper in my ears. He stands facing me, his arms folded, his dangerous gaze fixed on me, and I force myself to look away. His voice is always so compelling, though, and I struggle to keep from looking. As much as I want — as I *need* — to go to Riva and Malik, I know better than to try to do so now.

"Stop looking so anguished," he chides. "Your companions are dead because they were foolish. Not one could be persuaded to give way. Do you want to share their fate?"

I wonder if he knows how he sounds. I hate him so. I want to make him pay for what he has done. For in the end, he is the cause of all this tragedy. He is responsible for all the harm caused and all the hurt inflicted. He has brought about everything that has happened by luring all of us to this cataclysmic standoff.

I turn to face him, and I can tell from the shift in his features that he notes the mix of hatred and destruction reflected in my eyes.

"I would throw myself into a pit of poisonous vipers before I spent a single moment with you."

He is unfazed. "Your protests are pointless, Auris. You should understand that by

511

now. I am capable of so much more than you think. Yes, I can mesmerize other creatures and steal their lives. Yes, I can take command of a body and its *inish* and make them my own. But I can also compel anyone or anything that breathes to do whatever I wish. I can make anyone my own personal automaton. You have seen what happened to your friends. You have seen what I can do. What purpose will it serve if you force me to do the same to you — to dominate you, overpower you, and make you another creature subject to my will?"

I am not giving way this time. "Perhaps, this once, you are doomed to disappointment."

His laughter is taunting. "You still don't understand, do you? You are alone now, save for your sister. You have no allies besides her, and she is powerless before me. You have no options."

"I have one. I can fight you, and I intend to. Right up to my own end."

I am speaking nonsense and the Barghast knows it, but it makes me feel better to defy him. The last thing I will do is give in to his demands. I will die before I become his creature.

"Submit to me," he orders. "Acknowledge me as your master. Do it now!"

He loosens the remnants of his ruined robes where they cling to his body and lets them fall open so that his hands and arms are laid bare. I recognize the motion. He will come at me now, advancing on me in the same way he did at the fishing ponds. But I will not give in. There must be a way to defeat this creature. There must be a way he can be overcome that I have not yet recognized.

"Reconsider, Fae girl," he calls to me, his voice booming across the emptiness. "Think of the precious gift you carry that might be lost if you resist me."

Precious gift? My sanity? My freedom? I have no idea what he means and no interest in listening to his threats. How is it he always knows how to get into my head? How is it he always seems to be one step ahead of me? That he has read my mind and stolen my memories — as he does with all his victims — is no secret. But how is it that he knows things I didn't even know about myself?

Think!

He held me prisoner as a young teen long enough to wipe my brain clean, back when I knew so little of the truth about myself. I was ignorant of my skills, my history, and my Fae potential, save for what I had learned during my time with Drifter. He did not have me close again until he stole Harrow's *inish* and memories. And even then, his attempts to read my mind were limited by my own defenses — by defenses that, at the time, I didn't know I had.

Somehow, those defenses acted instinctively to turn away the Barghast's attempts to steal my *inish*. How did they manage to do this? Did they come unbidden to my defense, as I think they must have, or did I somehow trigger them?

Did my body know? My subconscious? My formidable instincts?

Did any of those medications given to me by my foster father during my childhood impact who and what I grew up to be?

I want to scream my frustration, but I hold it deep inside. *Think! Think!*

Then I remember suddenly something Benith once said to me when I first came to Viridian Deep, back when I was first struggling with my identity and could not fathom why my *inish* was so unpredictable.

In the Fae culture, a Changeling is one who can assume a different look or identity at will. And even though you have not showed these powers as yet, I still think it is possible.

But was I really a Changeling? If so, why was I unable to access any real understanding of what it was I could do? Was it that complicated, that impossible to come to terms with? If I am a Changeling, what is it that I can do?

In the next moment, Char's questions during our last night at dinner, when referring to the Barghast, recall themselves.

Can't you use your own inish *to knock him down and then jump on him? Your* inish *is stronger than his, isn't it?*

My memory closes tightly about these words. *Yes,* I had wondered in an almost musing fashion, *why couldn't I?*

All along, I have assumed that my Changeling powers had to do with how I looked — with my appearance, with my physical persona. But what if I am wrong? What if I can actually adapt myself not only to look but to *be* something else? What if my understanding of Dragon speech had nothing to do with my mother or my heritage, but only came about because of who and what I am? What if I am able to generate from an instinctive sense of need exactly what I want? What if my *inish* can make it real?

Possibilities only, perhaps. Yet I sense they might be more. There is within me a deep-seated recognition of something that has always been there. I sense a truth to all of it.

My eyes settle on the Barghast. *Killer of my friends, what if I can do it now, to you?*

"Think carefully, Fae girl," he calls to me — not with any genuine concern for my welfare but with a harshness that sends a clear warning.

He is two dozen yards away when he suddenly stops. Caution, self-protection, and hesitation are all evident in his posture. He sees something in my eyes. He has that ability. But I have it, too. My vaunted instincts that are always right — I have had them all along.

Boldly, I fix my eyes on his and keep my gaze steady. I see flickers of something working in his Dragon's eyes, still unchanged. I do not react outwardly, but inside I am suddenly a mess. Doubts crowd to the forefront. He was right about me not realizing the extent of his powers. He is far more dangerous, far more formidable, than I believed. He overcame Antrim, with all his strength and conditioning, with his enormous physical presence and the iron-hard scales warding him. Antrim, with his hatred of Barghasts and his determination never to be subdued by any creature of any nature. In the end Tonklot owned him.

516

Will he not do the same to me now?

What makes me think he will not? What makes me believe I can prevent it?

Then I realize all at once that he is working on my confidence, trying to break down my resistance.

And I am enraged.

I start forward with slow, steady steps. I carry no weapons; I leave them sheathed and belted. I straighten myself in an effort to project confidence, even though inside I am a roiling mess. If I have guessed wrong about the Barghast's vulnerability, I am going to end up a burnt piece of toast.

But if I am right . . .

Which I have to be . . .

I keep walking, taking my time, closing the distance between us. There is no backing down now, no rethinking. This confrontation is all that is left to me.

We are less than ten yards away from each other, our eyes locked, when I feel the attack. It comes with the weight of a stone wall, and I feel as if I have been slammed backward. I gasp audibly and draw upon my *inish* to defend myself. I tighten down my defenses and keep going, pushing past and through the wall he has thrown up to stop me. I seek a way past it, a way inside his body, his brain, his everything. *Inish*

517

engaged, I seek to do to him what he would do to me.

And then, abruptly, I am inside him. My Changeling self fully engages, and Tonklot has no time to defend himself. I barely give it a thought as I strike out — no longer a young Fae woman but a mirror image of what he is. I take on a Barghast persona — a mirror of this creature I hate so much. I reach out to seize his abilities, his thinking, everything he is. I penetrate right into his darkest corners, shove aside his still-confused defenses, and with relentless savagery I *inhabit* his mind.

To engage with such a creature is beyond loathsome. The webs of dark thoughts and memories his mind harbors are so abhorrent I recoil just from brushing up against them. But I do not let my revulsion stop me. I will not allow myself to become unmoored by memories of what he did to Harrow, Malik, Riva, Antrim, and so many others whose names I will never know. And yet I am aware that engaging the Changeling magic requires a certain amount of actual changeover. I can feel the evil that inhabits the Barghast creeping through me like a sickness, and I shudder. I feel myself being wrapped about by its coils, sense the vast, wicked darkness of its willingness to embrace me. I feel myself slowly adapting to its landscapes, to their touch and feel.

The Barghast senses what is happening, but it mistakes it for a reflection of my weakness and allows it to happen.

A mistake, I think at once, and push on. I am well beyond anything this creature can do to stop me.

Step by step, I draw closer, able to feel now the suffocating heat of his eagerness to take hold of me. I note a change in the modulation and tenor of his voice. Then there is a shift in his attitude, and I detect the first hints of fear. I sense his raw urgency to disengage. Tonklot's mind contorts through a series of strange motions intended to subvert my efforts — twists and turns of thought that suggest he is threatening me — but I lock myself down harder and ignore them.

In an instinctual sweep that involves a slow and careful search of all the various corners of this monster's mind, I access his memories as he once did mine. It is a disgusting prowl through fields of dark intentions and deliberate hurts — down corridors containing the detritus of the lives of other, less fortunate creatures. There are thousands of memories in the Barghast's ancient mind. But I will not stop until I find the core of him and destroy it.

Dimly, I sense the Barghast reacting to my invasion — a sudden flurry of efforts to evict me, to stamp me out. Tonklot is aware now of the danger he is in. But I am deep inside him, too deep to be dislodged easily. I brush aside his efforts, finding pleasure in the shock my invasion is generating.

Then I sense the Aerklings stirring and detect a handful starting to hurry toward me. So the motions were not just threats. The Barghast has summoned help.

Ronden, however, is equal to the challenge. Stepping between me and my attackers, she brings down the foremost of those who threaten me with sharp gestures of her hands, leaving the recipients sprawled motionless and frozen. I can sense my sister using her *inish* to shield my back as she awaits further attacks, but the Aerklings are backing away again. Perhaps they realize that their powerful leader is not as powerful as he claims. Or perhaps whatever ties bound them to him are breaking.

I burrow deeper into his mind — into the darkness of his being. I sift and sort through memories I am afraid I will never be able to forget. I access all that he has stolen from the creatures he mesmerized. I witness their suffering and their demise; I endure the pain they experienced. I do nothing to hold on to any of it; they mean nothing to me and feel like acquisitions that will only serve to diminish my sanity. I search only for the personal memories that matter — for Harrow's memories and mine. And when I find them, it is easy enough to release them from their placement in the Barghast, where they do not belong. I find it almost comforting to store them back inside my own being — in the case of Harrow's memories, waiting to be returned to their appropriate place of residence. It is a long strenuous effort, but I persevere.

The Barghast increases his struggles to dispatch me, employing every loathsome destructive invention and assault he has ever used. His efforts verge on frantic, and I gain a measure of strength from knowing this. When his efforts turn so dark I am made sick to my core, I begin to strangle him. He fights as hard as he can, but it isn't nearly enough. He is reduced to a shadow of what he was — his strength stolen, his power lost. I have leached away so much of his *inish,* by either stealing or destroying it, that he is now but a shadow of his former self.

Eventually, his efforts lessen, and his consciousness diminishes.

Soon I am able to do what is needed with

barely any resistance. He goes still beneath my hands as I hold him fast.

He is mine.

I take the time I need to gather up the balance of my memories and Harrow's. I do not sort or examine them; that must wait for another time. I collect everything that offers even a trace of Harrow or myself and discard the rest. In other, better circumstances, I might think about harvesting all these memories and returning them to their rightful owners. But the catalogs are too vast and their sources too uncertain in almost every instance. I can only do so much and still remain sane. I can only venture so far inside this darkness.

So I take what is Harrow's and what is mine, and I exit the blackness of this lost creature for the brightness I know will be waiting without.

It takes me long moments to recover, but when I feel sufficiently in control of myself once more, I stand over my fallen enemy. How pitiful he looks. I hold within me the memories I need to heal Harrow and myself. I sense bits and pieces of both as I make a quick search of what I have gathered, and know I am going to be able to replace all of the missing memories of my empty past once I have finished what still needs to be done.

I take a deep breath, reliving momentarily all that has happened in the last hour. I watch it all unfold in my mind, broken and jagged, memories good and bad that I will live with forever. I feel no elation or satisfaction to have survived. Instead I feel sadness and resignation. The cost of my life has been too great, the loss of my friends too large a price to pay. I am left with what that means, and I have no idea how long it will take me to come to terms with it. But I will have to find a way to do so, no matter what it takes out of me or how empty it might leave me.

I turn to face the massed Aerklings, hundreds of whom now cluster about me. None makes a threatening move or attempts any sort of advance. They look on in awe and shock at their fallen leader as the realization of how they have been deceived slowly surfaces. But by now Ronden is beside me, and the look on her face is enough to make them think twice about acting on their feelings. We face them squarely, weapons in hand — several dead Aerklings at our feet — and the threat we pose is obvious. Some of those we confront bear expressions of anger and regret. There are some, I am sure, who want their fallen leader back.

But the expressions of most are calm and relieved, marked by a keen awareness that things will now be different.

Harrow lies off to one side, abandoned by those who thought to use him in an effort to make me the Barghast's willing supplicant. Fresh rage fills me.

"Bring me my partner!" I cry out suddenly, giving no thought whatsoever to a quieter approach. "Now, damn you! Carry him to me!" My patience is all used up.

A few Aerklings rush to do what I have demanded, lifting Harrow into their arms and carrying him over to me. No one interferes with their efforts. Even those who are still in thrall to the Barghast are quick to step aside. No one cares to challenge me now.

A slender figure bursts from their midst and rushes over, causing me to startle. Orphren throws her arms around me. I am happy to see her, pleased she has come to no harm. Neither of us speaks, but we continue to hold on to each other for long moments.

"I knew you would come back," she whispers.

It feels good to embrace her, to feel her pressing close against me. Just this little moment does much to restore me.

"Are you all right?" I reply.

She nods into my shoulder, her small face pressed against me. "Grandfather would be so pleased."

I disengage from her gently. Harrow has been laid on the ledge beside me, and I look down to see what can be done. Much, I can tell. He is thinner, weaker, and more debilitated than ever. His eyes are closed and his body is limp.

Ronden shakes her head. "He's barely breathing, Auris."

Orphren raises her head for a look. "Can you make him better?"

I give her a slow nod. "I can try."

She continues to cling to me, her wings fluttering in a clear indication that some part of her wants to escape what she sees.

"He looks so pale!"

"But inside he is very strong. We must try to heal him so that he can be the way he was."

I bend down to feel his pulse, and then I kiss him. He breathes — barely — but he remains inert. I will have to act quickly if I am to save him. After giving Tonklot a quick glance to be sure he is still unconscious, I try to decide how to do what is needed to make Harrow well again. Restore his memories and his *inish,* I know. But how? What

525

do I need to do to place them back where they belong, back inside the man who owns them?

I remember watching as his memories were stolen, so I now wonder if there is a chance I can restore them in the same way they were taken. But I have to try something.

I summon my *inish* and let it build, feeling it rise within me until I am filled by its presence. I bend down to my love and sort through the memories I stole back from Tonklot, sifting out all those that belong to Harrow, making sure I am giving him only those that were his to begin with, keeping my own carefully held back.

I use my fingers to open Harrow's mouth, take a deep breath, place my lips upon his, and — with my *inish* to back my efforts — I breathe deeply into my beloved's mouth, exhaling back into his body everything that is rightfully his.

It is easier than I hoped to send it all home again. I can feel his memories and *inish* react to my efforts as if they were tiny butterflies, fluttering joyfully as they rush back into their owner's body. It is an instant response — as if they seek restoration and are happy to find it through me. I have little to do but to hold the kiss as everything that was taken finds its own way home. It requires some time, yet is accompanied by a profound relief. All those memories, going back where they belong. All those memories, going home.

There is a mix of sadness and happiness both when I am finished and the last tiny memory has been restored. Not willing to let go all at once, I continue the kiss — remembering others that we shared, living anew the feeling of a union I have always wanted and adored. It restores my love, but in a way I cannot explain it also restores the rest of me. It reaffirms that our union is so strong and complete that we cannot ever find the same satisfaction and fulfillment in separateness that we experience when we are joined.

When the restoration is as complete as I can manage, and all Harrow's memories and his *inish* are back inside him, I break the kiss and lift away. Still he sleeps, but there is a peacefulness in his expression that was absent before. I breathe in with deep satisfaction and real hope. I think Harrow is better. I think he is restored.

Now I need to go to Riva and Malik. I have put it off too long already. I know what I will find, but I need to make sure. And I need to say goodbye.

I reach Riva first. It is sad to see her like she is now. She lies where she was left by Tonklot, her body crushed and her eyes open and staring. I look down at her and wonder how I could have come this far without her. I bend close to kiss her cheeks. "Rest well, brave rider, my good friend. You were the truest warrior of all."

I remain with her for several long minutes, then I rise and go to Malik. His massive iron shell is cracked and dented, despite its previous look of invulnerability. Even so, I catch sight of a small movement from within. I kneel and lean down to him. "Thank you, Malik," I whisper.

He moves once more, whispers to me. "Was . . . it enough?"

I want to cry. "It was. More than enough. We are all well."

"Then . . . it was worth it. Now . . . you be worth something that . . . matters . . . in the years waiting for you."

I am crying. I do so silently. "I will try. Every day. Every time I think of you."

A small movement of his head. His voice is unexpectedly strong. "We were . . . always friends. Remember . . . me."

And he is gone, too.

I am tempted to look beneath his mask to see for myself what was done to him, but it

528

feels invasive and wrong, so I just squeeze his hand, rise once more, and move away.

I return to Harrow, kneeling beside him once more, bending down so I can study his face. He seems less tense, almost relaxed. For the most part I cannot be certain about what is happening, but I am encouraged. There are indications of life returning in the greening of his brow and cheeks, in the steadying of his breathing, in the settling of his limbs. But what is happening inside him? Is he healing in the right way? Once or twice, Harrow jerks violently, and each time I wait to see if he will settle. Each time, he does.

Ronden kneels at my side, saying nothing as she watches, the look on her face hard and certain. For long moments she remains silent, and then she glances over as the Barghast stirs for the first time, and she whispers, "If he makes a single wrong move, I will make sure it is the last one he ever makes."

Then she is gone again, and Orphren is back, her arms closing about my shoulders in a gesture of support. "He looks better," she whispers in my ear.

And indeed, I think, he does. The pallor that was marking his face earlier is mostly gone, and his features are returning to what they were. There are fresh signs of life — of awareness and vitality — once more, and I feel another surge of hope. But even so he just lies there, breathing in, exhaling out, and with no other signs of movement. In desperation, I pull his head closer to mine and bury his face against my breast, willing him back, begging him to come awake, praying for him to show me he is well.

Long moments pass, and nothing happens.

Orphren gasps suddenly. "His hand moved."

I loosen my grip on Harrow and look down at him. His eyes blink open, then fix on me.

"Hello, Auris," he whispers. He gives me a faint smile. "What happened?"

I am crying. "You got hurt, but now you are better."

He nods. "I think maybe I am. I feel it. Have I mentioned lately how much I love you?"

As I bend to kiss him, my eyes full of sudden tears, my attention is completely diverted from Tonklot. So I catch only a glimpse of what happens next. But to one side and behind me, the now fully conscious and deeply enraged Barghast scrambles to his feet, a hidden blade drawn from his clothing.

Even as I begin to turn, he is already almost on top of me, and I have no time to act. I see a flash of metal reflect in the sunlight, a burst of brightness that warns me of my danger, and I throw myself over Harrow protectively.

Then another flash of metal intercepts the first — this one larger and more striking as it flashes past my shoulder. A clang of metal on metal rings out, and gasps rise up from the Aerklings. The second blade flashes again, passing just over my head as it sweeps through the air and connects with a sound I know all too well — metal cutting into flesh — followed by silence.

Still holding Harrow to me protectively, I swing around to determine what has happened. I have my answer immediately. Tonklot's body lies three feet away from me, motionless and bloodied. His severed head lies a bit farther off.

Ronden strides past me, sword in hand. Without giving me a glance, she walks over to the Barghast's head and looks down on it. With the toe of her boot, she tips it over so that the lifeless eyes are staring back at her.

"I told you what would happen," she says.

Then she kicks the head so hard that it flies all the way off the cliff wall and disappears.

THIRTY-ONE

Of course it doesn't end here, but it is a new start.

I bid farewell to Orphren and her companions, promising to return one day soon. I arrange for the burial of Malik and Riva in the mountains. The rest of us — Ronden, myself, and now, of course, Harrow — are flown by a unit of Aerklings safely back to Viridian Deep. Freed of the stultifying presence of Tonklot, most are by now ready to accept us as friends in the way Orphren's grandfather did, and any lingering animosity is stilled.

By nightfall of that same day, we are home again.

I will never be certain exactly how much of what I think I remember actually happened. It isn't that my memory isn't capable of calling to mind the events that took place. It is mostly my inability to fathom how such strange and bewildering uses of my *inish* and my Changeling abilities made all of it possible. My Changeling heritage supported my transformation from Fae to Barghast, but how was I able to do this and stay sane? How was I able to avoid the infection that had so clearly poisoned Tonklot's thinking and yet retain my own steady adherence to what I believed? My *inish* kept me strong and stable, but how was I able to pull out all of those memories stolen from Harrow and myself? How was I able to separate them out from all those other terrible memories and safely restore them to us, to my love and me?

I thought on it constantly afterward at first and many more times since, and yet so much of it remains muddled and confusing. But you heal yourself and become whole again with time's passage, and it was so with me. My effort allowed me to discover the truth about my Changeling abilities. It brought my one true love back to me. It provided me with the memories of my youth I had believed lost or forgotten, and it restored whole sections of my life that had been missing for years.

I didn't try to absorb it all at once. When memory begins to recount the specifics of any event, it does so at its own pace. Mine was no different. One thing would occur, and that thing would lead to another or perhaps another few. Sometimes it was disjointed and confusing, and I would have to wait for something more before it was entirely clear. I was absorbed in the effort, but I did not work hard at trying to piece it together.

Still, I recalled my adoptive parents taking me camping, because they thought it was important I be exposed to more than my father's endless talk of science and work and my mother's cooking skills. And how they homeschooled me, keeping me mostly to myself and away from other people because my mother was constantly afraid my Fae side would reveal itself — as it sometimes did when the drugs wore off. I remembered the drugs and injections and other ways my father worked to keep me from changing — to keep me looking Human and not Fae. I came to understand, finally, what my father risked to keep me safe. And I suddenly knew how deeply my parents cared for me. Everything they did, and all the sacrifices they made, were for me.

Sometimes the memories have made me cry — not because they are sad, though they sometimes are, but more from the sheer relief of having them back. Of having a part of *myself* back.

Yet more important than the recovery of my lost or stolen memories has been the retrieval of Harrow's. While I had assiduously recovered everything of his I could find in Tonklot's mind, I couldn't be sure how complete my collection was or how thorough my restoration. So we talked constantly for weeks about incidents and events I thought he should easily remember and questioned him about bits and pieces of my own memories of our time together. I had worried that perhaps my restoration of what had been stolen was somehow faulty. But for the most part he seemed to see himself as whole again, and my efforts successful.

That alone still feels like a very big miracle.

I wanted Harrow and me to resume our lives as a couple immediately, but Harrow remained weak from being thirteen days without his *inish,* so I put him back in the healing center in the care of their nurses but do not ever leave him alone for long. To the extent that we can, we resume our walks through the gardens and parks of the city. We return to dining in the open-air restaurants suspended in the limbs of the huge old trees. We spend time with our sisters, all of whom are immensely overjoyed to have him back.

Mostly, however, Harrow must rest, give himself time to recover, and I must abide. It is hard to wait on something you want so much, and I frequently wander off on sojourns of my own — with or without Ronden — to visit with the Seers. And to reassure myself that everything that is happening with my partner is normal and not an aberration.

And then there is Drifter. I gave him my promise I would return if I could, to relate everything that happened once he left us, and I feel an obligation now to do so. Also, at some point, I must find a way to deal with Winton. I know with Malik gone it doesn't matter as it once did, as the primary reason for confronting Winton was to get Malik a supply of the medication that kept him pain-free. But my half brother still wants to use me for his purposes, and he will come after me again — especially since I escaped him once. Men like that don't take defeat easily.

So eventually, leaving Harrow in the care of Ronden and the younger girls, I go off to find Drifter and see if I can tie up some loose threads in Harbor's End. But before doing so, I travel to the Dragon safehold in the Skyscrape. I need to tell them about Antrim. I have taken their leader to his death, and it does not feel right to just leave his fate hanging.

In doing this, I permit myself a single indulgence. I have promised myself I will not use my Changeling powers again for a time — though how long a time, I am not sure. But the exercise of engaging my Changeling nature still feels risky. I do not have a firm grip on how much this will impact me or the ways in which it will do so, and I don't want to rush the process of learning about my new abilities and unwittingly make a dangerous mistake.

But I think I can do it just this once more, to simplify these two journeys I must make. And perhaps doing so will enable me to learn a little more about what I can expect if I choose to do so again in the future.

I have told no one about what I can now do with my Changeling powers. I have sworn Ronden to secrecy. I don't want to visit this new reality on Ramey and Char, and I won't tell Harrow until he is fully recovered. I don't yet want to reveal it even to the Seers — though I will in time.

So I leave the city and travel afoot for most of a day before making the change.

To my shock, I am able to do so easily. I

envision what I want to be, and almost on its own my body makes the adjustment and creates me anew. I let it happen, but I also pay close attention to how it makes me feel. While it feels definitely foreign and strange, it causes no pain or discomfort, and no sense of having made a wrong turn.

It allows me to believe that I can safely engage my Changeling nature when I find the need. But it also raises a question I have not considered before. It causes me to wonder how easily such immense power can prove corrupting. While I am pleased that it saved me from the Barghast earlier and allows me to take the form of a Dragon now, I am not at all sure it would be a good idea to rely on its use in any but the most desperate of situations. Yes, it provided me with a path to victory in a life-threatening situation. But how tempting would it be to use it in a way that could prove seductive and permanently damaging? How easy would it be to employ it too casually or too hastily? Isn't it enough to rely on my *inish,* over which I have much greater control, and leave my Changeling powers sleeping?

Besides, how many more adventures do I intend to engage in? None, I hope. So isn't it better to start setting aside reliance on the use of Fae magic now, while I have the chance and time to do so?

How many more friends and companions do I want to risk?

Just thinking about the losses I have already suffered makes me want to cry. One by one, my companions have been taken from me. I have a family still, but I have no wish to ever again place any of them in danger.

For now, though, I set aside my misgivings and fly to the Dragon safehold. Still in my Dragon form, I land and wait for a greeting. It doesn't take long. A bevy of younger Dragons descend to question me, and I tell them I am here to speak to Gray Sanan. When the aging Dragon appears, I tell him and the others of the fate of Antrim and the Barghast. I tell them that Antrim came when he was needed, provided the help he could, and died in the same cause for which we all fought.

Then I reveal that I am not who I seem and transform back to myself. The Dragons are startled, and a few are angry with my willingness to assume a form I do not own. Until I explain the importance of understanding both what this power means and how it needs to be used. I tell them the Dragons should be the first to know of its existence and assure them it will never be used to harm or humiliate Dragon pride. Gray Sanan accepts the explanation on behalf of his fellows and asks only that I promise to use it wisely where Dragons are concerned. All seem satisfied when I do agree.

I then offer my apologies and regrets over the loss of Antrim, but my words are dismissed as unnecessary. In the minds of Dragons, it seems, no apologies are required when the death of a Dragon comes honorably. I am welcomed for my efforts to bring this news and promised that I will always be considered a friend.

Reverting once more to my Dragon form, I depart by nightfall and fly over the mountains and across the Roughlin to Harbor's End, using the cloud tunnels to speed my passage. I am surprised I can make use of these quick passages, but it makes my journey easy and swift. Low rain clouds provide cover once the tunnels are behind me, and I pass unnoticed into the wilderness north of the city, landing close to Drifter's home. After assuring myself I have arrived safely and unnoticed, I set out through a stretch of woods that lies not a mile from Drifter's isolated homestead, doing my best to avoid any chance encounters along the way.

I briefly consider making a detour to see my adoptive mother but decide against it. I can't cause her more pain, knowing only too well now how a life of losses can eat at your soul.

Riva. Malik. Antrim.

I have more ghosts of my own now, too.

There are no lights visible anywhere as I approach Drifter's farm. There is no sign of life at all, save for a fox that scoots away into the woods as I close in on the darkened buildings.

I don't think anyone will be occupying the house, but I have to make sure. I slip my way through the shadows until the door is only a few feet away. There I pause, considering the wisdom of attempting an unwanted entry.

Finally, I lose patience and just go up to the door of the ramshackle old home and knock. The door swings open on its own, but there is no one waiting. I walk inside and look about. Everything looks undisturbed; nothing appears to have changed since I was here last. Dust coats the floors, walls, and window glass. The siding and roof have deteriorated further. Drifter wasn't living here then, and it doesn't look as if he is living here now.

Instead I seek out the building in back — the training and weapons center that Drifter actually occupies when in residence. Again, I find it locked. Again I knock, but there is no response. Using *inish,* I break in. There is no sign of life here, either — though when I walk through the training area and scan the walls, there are vast numbers of empty spaces where weapons had hung or been shelved when I was here last.

I search the other rooms, but it is clear no one is about, and that no one has been here for a while. Bedding is stripped away and closets and drawers are emptied. I find nothing to tell me what has happened to Drifter.

I walk back out into the main room and stand looking about, wondering what to do next. "Where are you?" I ask the walls in frustration.

"Right behind you, Auris," a familiar voice replies.

I wheel about with the speed of a surprised cat and find Drifter standing there looking at me. Although I recognize him immediately, I find him changed — more heavily bearded and shaggy-haired, rangier and gimlet-eyed. He is an unnerving presence at best. My insides manage to settle . . . . but slowly.

"I've been in hiding," he offers, giving me a wry smile. "Have you come back to tell me everything that happened once you finished with the Barghast?"

I give him a brief nod. "Can we sit down while I do so?"

We move over to the small dining table and sit. I notice he is limping visibly. "Are you hurt?"

He shrugs as if it is nothing. "Tell me about the Barghast. What's become of him?"

"He's dead. Ronden killed him. Riva and Antrim are dead, too. And an old friend named Malik. They gave up their lives to save me."

I give him a short recitation of that final battle. When I finish my tale, he clears his throat. "Sorry about Riva. I liked that woman. Sorry, too, about the Dragon and your friend. But no one could have seen exactly what was coming. I thank you, Auris. You bring fresh peace to my life — as well, I hope, as to your own."

He pauses. "But we are not quite done, you and I."

I give him a look. "We aren't?"

"One more thing needs attending to, and I would like for you to see what it is. I would like you to see it finished. You don't need to do anything; you will not be at risk. I just

544

want you to watch. Yet it is important that you be there. Will you agree to come?"

He leads me from his homestead and back into the surrounding woods, moving south. He picks his way carefully, advising me to step exactly where he steps, taking his time, choosing his path.

We are deep in the woods when he finally halts. He reaches down through leaves and earth and uncovers a wooden trapdoor buried beneath a waterproof shield. When he lifts the door, he uncovers a ladder leading down into the darkness below. We descend into a cellar where Drifter lights torches that reveal a sizable room filled with engines, mechanical switches, and chamber boxes. There are also tools, weapons, and supplies shelved, pegged, and otherwise fastened to the wooden walls. It is a workshop of some sort, clearly, but I have no idea what it is meant to do.

Without explaining it, he walks over to a long wooden bench and picks up a series of ten or twelve small boxes, which he places in a sack he then slings over his shoulder.

"Igniters," he says. "I've been working on the project since you and I parted. It's time to put a stop to all these ill-considered attempts to subjugate the Fae people. It is time to show our friend Winton the exit."

I find myself smiling; how well Drifter knows me. I want Winton gone, but I never wanted to be the one who did it; he is my half brother, after all. But if Drifter is willing to take this on, then perhaps I will have the satisfaction of real peace for the rest of my life.

I give him a silent nod, and we leave the basement hideaway and exit into the night.

We return to his training center and go back inside. When I ask him how long this will take, he tells me it will be done by midday on the morrow. He jokes about it in vague terms, but I am able to gather that he wants in some way to disable the Ministry's operations against the Fae and perhaps cause some major disruption to those who serve as agents for Winton's destructive passions. There is to be an Assembly meeting tomorrow, where Winton will be addressing the Ministry on the subject of the Fae. So what better way than to stop him before he can speak? Drifter does not reveal his plans, but I can draw some conclusions from the words he speaks and the anger his voice reveals.

I sleep that night in his spare bedroom, and wake before dawn when I hear him moving about. I am growing increasingly concerned over what he intends, but on the other hand I am not at all sure I want to know any more than I already do. He is not talking at all about what he intends, and there is little question that this is a very deliberate choice.

We leave while it is still dark, heading for the city. Drifter pushes ahead at a pace that leaves me trotting to keep up with him. He may look ragged and he may be limping, but he is intent on his mysterious purpose. We enter the city at sunrise and progress to a storage center close enough to the Ministry buildings that I can see them all clearly; the Assembly, in fact, is directly in front of us, though still some distance off. We stay hidden as we work our way up to a higher floor, and then Drifter turns to me.

"I want you to wait here while I do what is needed. Stay hidden. Keep watch. I'll send up a flare when it is time for you to leave."

"And then?"

He smiles. "Go home. Go back to Harrow. You and I will be finished, and Winton will have something to think about besides the Fae."

I shake my head. Without knowing anything, I say, "I should go with you."

He smiles through his ragged beard and

leans in to hug me. "No, Auris. This is on me. I wanted you to see what I intend, and now you can. But remain here. Don't try to follow me."

He says it in a way that makes it clear I am not being given a choice. I am not invited to participate further. Whatever Drifter intends, I am not to be part of it.

"Promise me you will do as I ask," he adds when he sees me hesitate.

The insistence present in his words cuts like glass. Whatever it is he goes to do, he will do alone.

A final hug, a mischievous wink, and he is gone.

I wait in place with one eye fixed on the Assembly buildings and one ear teased for the sound of my teacher's return. Time passes. One hour, two. I wonder more than once what I am waiting for.

The answer comes near midday. Explosions tear through the silence — one, two, three, four, and I lose count. They begin with such shocking suddenness that at first all I can do is press myself against the stone walls and close my eyes, picturing what I will see when I look out again. I have already heard enough to guess.

And I am not wrong.

The entire Ministry Assembly Hall and the three adjoining buildings that provide offices for the service workers and staff have been blown to rubble. I watch them fall, coming apart wall by wall, roof by roof, stanchion by stanchion. Roofs collapse, walls are breached, and ruins are all that is left. When the explosions end, everything that was once either Assembly or part thereof is destroyed. Clouds of smoke and ash rise from what remains. Fires burn where fires can. Screams and moans are audible even as far away as I am. How many have died? How many are gone who were nothing more than servants to the higher powers, or custodians, or even simply visitors? No way for me to know. The Assembly was in session, so all the ministers in attendance are likely dead. It was a workday, so all the regular Ministry employees are likely gone as well.

So this was not just about stopping Winton from addressing the Assembly, but sending a clear message to the Ministry as a whole. And I suddenly understand why Drifter decided to keep his intentions secret. He could have told me his plans; I couldn't have stopped him. But he said nothing at all of what he intended. He must have wanted to shoulder all the guilt for his act himself and leave me blameless.

My half brother Winton — along with the entire Assembly he was addressing — is gone.

And Drifter himself?

He would have needed to be very close to be certain the igniters all worked in sequence. So he is gone, too.

He made me a witness to his passing. He made me a reliable chronicler of the Ministry's destruction. He wanted me to know he had done something for the Fae that would have lasting results, and he wanted to be sure someone he could trust knew the truth. It was how he wanted to leave this life. It was the ending he was searching for that I was asked to witness.

I linger long enough to watch the rescue vehicles assemble and the emergency techs begin their search for survivors, then I turn away. I walk back down the stairs to ground level and go out through the entry doors and back through the city. There is nothing more for me to see here. Nothing more for me to do.

I am bitter and I am chilled deep. Enough of this. It is time to go home. Maybe this time I can remain there in peace.

I return to Viridian Deep and give myself

over to spending time with Harrow and the girls, forgetting everything else. No longer do the Goblins come for me in the dark of night. No longer do I live in fear of further attempts to drag me back to the prisons or the Ministry compound and those misguided scientists who would experiment on me as they see fit. Only now and then do images of the destruction of the Ministry Assembly recall themselves. Only vaguely, after a time, do I even remember my half brother's face.

Drifter's visage, as I saw it there at the end, will never leave me.

Harrow heals as we all hoped he would, returning to the man he was, regaining his Watcher skills, and reconnecting with his unique *inish* instincts. My sisters continue to fuss over him for a time, but eventually he is well enough that the entire incident fades from our conversations and our thoughts.

Months pass, then two things of consequence happen.

The first is that I lose the last of my Human traits, finally becoming the person I have been evolving into over the past few years.

The other thing is less immediately apparent to others — though I recognize it instantly, because there is no way I could miss it. And while walking with Harrow on one beautiful day down to the Gardens of Life and Promise Falls, I decide to tell him. Really, I am getting to a point where I can no longer put it off. I am reminded of a similar day two years earlier, when he brought me here to become his life partner. It was one of the best days of my life, and I want to repeat it at least once more.

When we are standing together at the foot of the pathway just across from the shimmering waters of Promise Falls, I turn and kiss him. I do not back away as the kiss goes on. I hold it in place for long moments.

The old, familiar Harrow looks at me with those amazing eyes I can't help but fall into every single time. "I love you back, Auris. Just as much, if not more." He pauses. "But is this kiss for something?"

"You know me too well."

He looks bemused. "Please. Not another unexpected journey."

"No. I'm not going anywhere. You either."

"What, then?"

"I want to give you a present."

"You have already given me everything I could ever ask for."

I find myself smiling. "Not this. This is new."

552

"Enough teasing. What is this special gift?"

I take a deep breath. "A child."

His eyes brighten. "I would love to have a child."

My smile widens. "I was hoping you would say that, because I can't exactly give it back now."

"You never said anything about adopting a child . . ."

"Not adopting, Harrow!" He is so dense sometimes. "The child is *inside* me. He will be out to greet you in person in about six or seven months."

Harrow stares. "He?"

"It's a boy."

"You know this?"

"Of course I know." I reach for his hand and place it over my stomach. "There. What does *your inish* tell you?"

The look on his face is priceless.

ABOUT THE AUTHOR

Terry Brooks has thrilled readers for decades with his powers of imagination and storytelling. He is the author of more than forty books, most of which have been *New York Times* bestsellers. He lives with his wife, Judine, in the Pacific Northwest.

terrybrooks.net
Facebook.com/authorterrybooks
Twitter: @TerryBrooks
Instagram: @officialterrybrooks